Lord's Curse

Kitsune-Ken, Book II

Brandy Ackerley

Inked Fox Press

Calgary, Alberta

This is a work of fiction. All the characters and events portrayed in this novel are products of the authors imagination. Any similarities to anyone living or dead are accidental.

Edited by Kai Kiriyama

Cover created by Starla Huchton

©2020 by Brandy Ackerley

All rights reserved. This book or any portion within may not be reproduced, or used in any manner whatsoever, without the express permission of the publisher.

ISBN: 978-1-9995165-5-0

Thanks for this book go out to my husband, without

whom I would have never finished this,

and my friend, Stephanie. Thank you for willingly reading

my first edits and helping me shape a better story.

LORD'S CURSE
KITSUNE-KEN, BOOK TWO
BRANDY ACKERLEY

Chapter 1

*D*eckard knew that healing people wasn't easy. It took skill, patience, and knowledge to mend bones, close wounds, and stop disease. His innate abilities helped, of course, but he refused to rely on their power. Mainly because he had always wished that he didn't have it at all. Blessed were rare and prized; they could heal anything short of true death. Unfortunately, due to their rarity, they were treated much in the same way a rare animal was; they lived fine lives in gilded cages. A beautiful contraption, so long as you didn't think too hard about the fact that it was still a cage.

He had never been kept that way. Instead, his mother had taught him to use his ability sparingly, gently encouraging the body to mend itself faster while he healed with more conventional means rather than let his secret out. He was the youngest healer in Hidan, but he had studied hard, trained for years to learn the trade and gain the trust of the community. He had built himself a normal life.

All that work and effort… wasted.

Dark thoughts fouled his mood, and the weather seemed to follow suit, bringing winds that chilled him to the bone. He shivered, pulling his jacket snugly around him. Deckard turned the corner with relief as he saw the warm glow of the Lucky Koi Inn. The chill of spring hadn't been replaced by summer's warmth yet and wouldn't be for another month or more. The cold had gotten to him more than he liked lately, a condition he hoped the fire burning in the Koi's huge stone fireplace would be able to solve.

He studiously ignored the fact that the cold he'd been feeling had nothing to do with the weather.

He jogged to the heavy door and opened it, slipping inside.

The lamps were lit in the center of the room, the area most densely filled, leaving dark, lonely spots against the walls where young lovers could pretend they had privacy. The stone fireplace sat against the far wall, beside the door that led into the kitchen. The fireplace was a two way, open to both rooms and through it, the scent of old fish stew and new bread with melting butter wafted into the main room.

As the door closed behind him, every eye turned his way. Their eyes judged him warily; the same as they would Tieni simply for being one of the Corvidae. He waited to be recognized and his heart skipped in an unhealthy way when he realized that while they knew him, they weren't sure if he was a friend or a stranger anymore.

Deckard had been living in Hidan since he was eleven. He'd fought hard to be accepted, to be welcome in their places. It had taken years and becoming a healer to do it. The idea of working his way back to that acceptance among them seemed insurmountable.

He would have left were it not for seeing Tieni in the far corner, near the kitchen, strumming her lute. Her hair and face were dark, but her clothes were bright, garish when compared to the rest of the townsfolk. She saw him and smiled. That smile still made him feel giddy. She quietly played another measure and then shook her curly hair out, thanking everyone. Even from the door, he could hear, faintly, the sound of her thick hair beads clicking. She gestured towards the bar with the instrument and quickly began tugging a thin string through its bridge. She bit her lower lip as the cord stretched.

Deckard walked over to the bar focusing on Tieni's strong hands rather than the stares of people he'd thought of as friends. As he neared the bar, Kenneth caught his eye, an expression of pity on his face.

"They'll get over it soon enough, Deckard," he said, cleaning a glass. "It's only been a week, after all." His expression was friendly, and Deckard relaxed seeing it. At least one person didn't think he had suddenly changed just because they'd found out he was a blessed.

Kenneth had been the bartender here since Deckard had moved here, but he thought the man was wrong in this case. Nothing had been right since the stranger, Richard, had come to town. With the way things were going, he didn't think they'd get any better when he finally left again.

Richard had been searching for a ship lost at sea decades before. While in Hidan, four men had nearly succeeded in murdering him. It had been Kuzunoha, his own ex-girlfriend, who had saved the stranger's life by bringing Richard to Deckard. Once healed, Richard had convinced her to go treasure hunting with him. Deckard had thought that neither of them would be his trouble again. Until the stranger had returned to town a week later with Kuzunoha nearly dead in his arms.

During their adventure, she'd gotten herself infected with a mold that had been turning her insides to jelly. His heart had been caught in his throat, choking him as he'd felt her heartbeat stutter and stop. He shivered remembering the feeling of her dying in his arms. He'd been lucky that the healing itself hadn't killed her. He hadn't considered the consequences before he'd made use of his power, forcing the mold and sickness out through her pores.

Everyone thought he'd brought her back from the dead.

He hadn't, of course. There were limits to his power and death was one of them. Kuzunoha had been on the brink, unconscious with a heart stuttering to a stop, but it was close enough for his power to restart it as the sickness was forced out of her body. Everyone had seen him do it, his body practically glowing with the magic released.

Of course, he didn't regret saving Kuzunoha's life. He just hoped that people would come to their senses soon; that saving her wouldn't end up costing him the life he'd built here.

"I hope so. Could you have a couple of drinks and some stew brought over to my table?"

Kenneth nodded.

"The usual drinks for you and the cro– and Tieni?"

Kenneth was a good man, but he still referred to Tieni as a crow. Strangers were always treated with a mix of suspicion and attraction, and that held double for the traveling folk known as the Corvidae. Fortunately, Tieni could sing and play the lute more than passably well. Since she'd left her family, they let her play in the inns, walk around Hidan and outwardly, people welcomed her like they would have any other traveling bard. So long as she didn't steal their men, their children, their coin, or caused any trouble. Of course, his relationship with her was seen as proof of the other three and some people were becoming vocal about it.

Kenneth's eyes flicked to Deckard's left, noting someone walking up to the bar and gave Deckard a nod.

Deckard glanced behind him to see who was coming and smiled, recognizing Carol, the smith's youngest daughter. She was younger than him, wearing her bright hair bound into a matron's hair clip. Her wool dress was undyed, other than a single tiny handprint in bright blue. She carried her young son in her arms.

He knew her from around town, but the first time he'd spent time with her was when he'd helped deliver her son a few months back. What had she named the boy again? Calvin? He hoped the child hadn't taken ill. It was all too easy for cold to get into the lungs when they were that young.

"Good eve, Master Healer," Carol said, pausing when her voice caught. She could be terribly nervous at times. He tried to smile warmly, even as he stepped back towards the bar.

"Good eve to you, Carol. How is Calvin doing?"

She'd come in much closer than she usually preferred to. Her expression was intense; wide unblinking eyes and the rest of her face set as if rigor mortis were about to set in. Before he could worry about what might be wrong, she thrust a thick set of blankets at him. The baby burbled happily inside, smiling as if he recognized Deckard, at least enough to know that he was a friend.

"I didn't ask before; I didn't know to ask... can you bless my baby? I want him to grow up strong and handsome and skilled with bow and fishing rod..."

Deckard held up his hands and moved away.

"Carol... I helped you deliver him. I'm the same guy I was then."

Her eyes filled with tears of relief and she pulled Calvin towards her chest, hugging him.

"You blessed him when he was born? Thank you!"

That was not what he'd been trying to say. He tried again. "Carol, I didn't... I can't…"

She looked confused and then her expression turned stricken and she squeezed Calvin to her chest protectively. The babe squeaked and then burbled at his mother in annoyance.

"You don't approve of my son?"

"Calvin is fine-"

"Is it me you don't approve of?"

Calvin had started to whimper now, not sure why his mother and friend were arguing. In any other situation, he would have taken Calvin from her, playing with him to make him smile again. He wouldn't do it with Carol acting so erratically.

He had to stop this before it got out of hand. Tieni stepped in front of him and gestured at Carol's baby.

"The blessed doesn't feel worthy of your thanks but he knows that you will be a perfect mother to the little one."

Carol pulled Calvin closer to her breasts as if worried Tieni might try to reach out and grab him. She looked up to Deckard for confirmation. She smiled after he nodded and glanced back at her baby as she walked away.

"Thank you," he whispered.

He was normally better with words, but the idea that he could do what Carol had asked was ludicrous. He was just a man. One with a God-given gift that could heal nearly any sickness, but a man, nonetheless. Who would have come up with the idea that he could grant wishes and make people's lives easier? Everyone's eyes were still on him.

Tieni pretended not to notice.

"You need to learn how to escape from people like that."

At her words, every eye turned to glare at her. More than a few of those included him in their wrathful stare. Kenneth growled loudly behind them.

"Hey! No one messes with one of Hidan's healers. Blessed or not, he's safe in my establishment. Go back to your drinks."

There was a pregnant pause before everyone returned to their food and talk. Deckard let out a breath.

"Thank you."

Kenneth picked up another glass, filling it.

"My momma nearly died of the flu; didn't because you helped her. Whether you healed her or blessed her, I got nothing to say either way. You got the job done and that's what matters. Now, go take a seat." He slid their drinks towards them.

Tieni smiled at Kenneth and grabbed the ale he'd pushed towards her with one hand while he grabbed the light-colored wine. Tieni led the way to one of the dark tables, near enough to the fire that Deckard started to sweat. He put his drink on the table and pulled his jacket off, tossing it on the back of his chair before sitting down. This close to the fire, it should be thoroughly heated by the time they wanted to go back home.

"Thank you Tieni. I'm sorry you had to see… that."

"I hadn't expected anything else. I mean, I waltzed in and took the best-looking guy in town from them. They were never going to like me," she said, pretending as if he'd meant the glares she'd received, rather than his embarrassment. She continued, "I will say that I'm surprised to get it from the menfolk too. Normally it's only women that are the vindictive ones, fearing I'll steal their husbands and sons."

He wanted to argue, but even if it hadn't been true before, with his status as a blessed known, he would certainly be Hidan's most eligible bachelor. Some were treating his newfound status as if he were a gift of the heavens, but even the ones that distrusted him were willing to thrust their daughters at him. Elder Zeisolf had begged him to consider his twelve-year-old granddaughter for a betrothal since she wouldn't be able to legally marry for another five years.

"They don't seem to understand that if I was going to marry someone here, I would have done it already." His tone had venom to it.

Tieni took a drink from her mug and licked the ale froth from her upper lip.

"No one wanted you to marry her, but they still would have preferred her to me."

It was a nice assumption, but he wouldn't have bet on it holding water. Most people in town wanted nothing to do with Kuzunoha. They tolerated her, would accept her spending her family's money in their establishments, but that was as far as it went. Even her beauty and her family's wealth hadn't been enough to entice more than one or two to offer, unsuccessfully, for her hand. He admitted that after he'd broken it off between them, that realization had cheered him, petty as it was.

"I'd hoped they would start accepting you as one of them." He told her.

She scoffed. "Deckard, some of these people still refer to you as the 'new boy'."

The new boy… while he preferred wine, with the way this conversation was going, he wished he'd ordered something harder.

"What are they saying about Kuzunoha?" He asked.

"What you would expect; you healed her for old times' sake, that you still love her and are using me," she snorted. "I don't mind admitting that I had wondered. Now that she's been with us for a week, I see those rumors are just that. Speaking of, how long before she can go home?"

Deckard frowned, looking to his drink again.

"The sickness that nearly killed her is gone. Unfortunately, it did a lot of damage before I pushed it out. Her body is weak and thin, her blood flows sluggish and her muscles could take weeks to fully repair themselves. And don't get me started on that leg injury."

"You could heal her faster, couldn't you?"

He resented the question. First, he didn't want to rely on his power that way, had trained hard for years so he wouldn't have to. He also didn't want to set the precedence that he would. Healing was difficult enough the way he used it, bolstering all his patients to heal a little faster than they would have naturally. He didn't even know if he could use it the way she suggested, and he wasn't going to put any energy into finding out.

"I don't want her in my home any more than you do, but I won't turn her out until she's well."

He was also concerned that she wouldn't stay at her sister's, meaning that she'd be staying with Richard. In addition to the Koi being less than optimal for someone convalescing, he also didn't think that sharing a room with that man would result in the rest she needed.

Tieni nodded and hesitantly put her hand on his. "My father's letter arrived. He's wondering when I'll rejoin the caravan."

Deckard sipped his wine again and leaned back. The Corvidae didn't settle often. They might for a season, maybe two, but if they stayed longer, they tended to stay forever. Tieni had been here since the festival of light, a full season already.

"What did you tell him?"

"I'll wait until he gets here and see how things are if I haven't decided before then." She shrugged. "He should arrive by late summer."

"That wasn't what I asked." He moved a hand to hers and wrapped it around her fingers.

She looked away. "I can't stay forever, Deckard. I like you. But if you're asking if I'd ever give it up and stay in one place…" she shook her head. "I can't answer that yet."

He kept his hand on hers, but she turned hers so that he could caress her wrist. She knew how much it soothed him.

"Would you consider leaving Hidan?" she asked.

The idea nearly gave him hives. Travel was dangerous; his father had died on the road and his mother had never been the same. Inside the walls, there was safety… but even more than that, Hidan was home now. His heart was pounding. Could he leave town, leave everything that he knew for her?

Brandy Ackerley

"Can I think about it?"

He saw a shadow move out of the corner of his eye and turned to
see Kenneth's wife bringing out their dinners. Tieni leaned over the
table and kissed him over the bowls of thick stew and fresh-baked bread.

"Of course."

Chapter 2

*R*ichard watched Isashi walk ahead of him. Her hips didn't tilt or sway the way a normal woman would. Instead, she walked more like a man did, every movement working towards a single goal of getting her economically to where she needed to be. He tilted his head, trying to figure out how she did it. Women had hips, and while Isashi was thinner and willowier than a human, her body was still an hourglass, just a taller thinner one. Her hips should have moved side to side. They didn't.

Isashi cleared her throat and he looked up at her. She looked annoyed.

"Can you pay attention, please? We're out here for you."

He smiled at her. He'd been caught out, but at least this time he had an excuse.

"I was paying attention."

"To the area around me. Not to my a... not to me."

She was right about why they were out here, but there wasn't much to pay attention to outside of Hidan. He'd seen much of it before, while they'd run through it just a few days earlier. Tall grasses warred with weeds and flowers, with the beginnings of an actual forest, rather than swamp, popping up. There were bushes here and there and a few larger trees, but everything was a very similar green and brown, like a watercolor painting with only two or three colors in it.

He supposed he should be on the lookout for monsters, but he was certain that the goblinoids wouldn't be coming back for quite a while. He wasn't a hunter, but he knew that the creatures wouldn't be back until they forgot that the humans had slaughtered their oversized friend. Their fear should last a few months, at least, if they were anything like the fish mongrels they'd had to deal with in Jiza.

"Despite what you think about me, I wasn't looking at your ass," he told Isashi. "Or at least, I wasn't checking you out."

"Oh?"

He shook his head and jogged up beside her.

"You don't walk like other women I've known. Your hips don't sway, and you walk economically. I was trying to figure out why."

"I don't walk right?" She was blushing and wouldn't meet his eyes.

"You walk fine. I was trying to figure out if you walk like you do because of your race."

Isashi looked particularly striking, in his opinion, if not hers. Eleden grew bark-like flesh that seemed closer to silver than any trunk he'd ever seen. They kept their hair color, which made her bright red shade that much more striking.

Eleden were nearly immortal, regular people changed by something unknown during puberty. She was the first he'd ever met.

Some people didn't consider them human, not in the same way they were, but from what Richard had seen of Isashi, they still were… they just had a different perspective after living longer than anyone they'd grown up with.

Isashi slowed, and her nose wrinkled. She'd enjoyed the light flirting but now she seemed annoyed again. "Why would my being an Eleden change the way I walk?"

Richard shrugged. "I don't know, but you don't walk like, say Kuzunoha or Himiko do."

Isashi snorted. "I should hope not. I wasn't given lessons on how to walk like a frivolous noble."

"Almost every woman's hips sway side to side, not just nobles. Even women who have grown up only among men, in my experience. Yours don't."

She closed her eyes and rubbed her brow with her right hand. "How does this matter?"

"It doesn't. Not to our purpose here. It was just something I noticed."

Isashi rolled her eyes. "We're only ten or so minutes away from the site. Get your head in the game."

He shrugged and continued to walk beside her. The tips of her ears were as red as her cheeks, which meant that both stood out starkly against the pale silver-grey of her skin. Even against her cherry bright hair, the lighter pink stood out like a bent nail among a row of straight ones. Also, despite her words, she started walking as if she should be swinging her hips. It was too much and worse than noticeable. He smiled and looked ahead. There wasn't any good way to recover from mentioning it, he supposed.

Moments later, he paused and lifted his hand to cover his nose. The scent of a rotting corpse was impossible to mistake; cloying and sickeningly sweet, it hung in the air, a palpable presence beside them. They had to be closer than she'd said. Unless…

"What did you do with the creature?"

"As our usual M.O., we buried it, no less than four feet deep."

With any other creature, it probably would have been the right decision. Unfortunately, these monsters didn't come from this world. They came from one more vibrant, green, and alive than the human world. That strangeness meant that everything here thrived on their remains.

He rushed forward to find the creature laying on the ground a few feet away from the patch of dirt its body had been consigned to.

The remains had been ripped from the ground by some sort of canine, a wolf or coyote perhaps. What was left looked like it had been bitten and shaken more than a few times while being unearthed. The growth suggested years buried, not days. It was surrounded by a black puddle of decay, a thin moat of sickness and filth. Around that was a circle of the greenest grass Richard had ever seen. Roots and vines were reaching from the empty grave towards the corpse as if they'd been torn from its flesh as it had been dragged out of the hole.

In a tree to the right, Richard caught sight of two birds, black as the puddle, watching him. When he pulled his knives, they flew off. If he saw them again, he'd take them down. Anything that had eaten of this corpse had too much fey in it for his liking.

"Do the animals here always dig up the graves of the dead?" he asked.

Sometimes animals were intelligent enough to avoid the monsters in the same way they were smart enough to avoid humans hunting for them. Unfortunately, scavengers tended toward stupidity. Some, like the vultures in his homeland, would dig up and consume anything that had a scent, including shit and garbage. These scavengers were half monsters themselves by the end, dangerous to everything around them.

"Not usually," Isashi said. She was crouched over a small divot in the grass. "They wouldn't be the problem, even if they had. This track looks like it may have been a wolf. These plants though. I've never seen their like."

Richard took a closer look and felt a shiver start in the back of his throat. He hadn't recognized them at first.

The plants surrounding the puddle had long full leaves, a thick grass closer to something you might see in a jungle or a ruin, than a swamp this close to civilization. Their shade was the most telling feature, a green darker and more alive than anything else around them. He didn't need to wait for night to know that there would be tiny flickers of radiant neon that would make the whole area glow with an unholy ambiance.

"Don't touch the plants." He told Isashi as she started to stretch towards them. "They release a drug into the air that makes you open to suggestion, makes even the most unreasonable ones seem reasonable."

She looked at him and stood before backing away. She took a deeper breath once she was standing beside him.

"So, how do we deal with them? Will burning work, or would that release the drug?"

Richard wanted to raze them, destroy them and the creature until they and their ilk couldn't haunt his dreams anymore. Unfortunately, it wouldn't be able to make a dent against the glimmering network that he knew was already infecting the ground beneath them; burning alone wouldn't free the area of its taint.

"Burning is good, but it leaves a network of veins behind, spider-silk thin and glittery. Even sliced up and burned, it can remain dormant for years before It starts growing again. After burning the plants above ground, the area needs to be plowed and sown with shavings of cold iron. I suggest checking it multiple times over the next five years, burning and sowing with more shavings every time a new plant grows in the area. If you're lucky, you'll get it all in a single run; it can take three to four repeats to get everything though."

"We can do that," Isashi said. "If we burn it now, will it be fine until we can get back with the iron shavings?"

He bit his lip. "I'm not sure. I'm not a hunter..."

Isashi looked at him. "I understand."

She didn't, of course. He wouldn't have expected her to. He'd lived a life full of danger, excitement... some of it he remembered fondly. Most of it, he wanted to forget, wanted to deny that it had ever happened.

Life never gave you what you wanted. It gave you what would hurt you most.

He gave himself a mental headshake. What she would understand was that he didn't know the answer and that would be enough. He had never been the type to sit around asking the universe why things weren't fair. He wasn't going to start now.

"Here, we can start with this." He pulled out the tiny bar of cold iron that he'd procured to use as a weapon against the creatures right after he'd escaped. It looked darker than regular iron, closer to a dark slate grey than the silver-black of most weapons and was more brittle due to the frigid temperatures it had been kept at while being processed. "You should be able to find out more by sending a message to Corvine on the other side of the Great Bowl. People who live near the forests there should be able to answer your questions."

"The other side of...." Isashi muttered though she didn't question him further. It was understandable. Corvine was on the other side of the continent. She'd probably never known someone who had come from that far away.

"I'll send them a message when we get back. In the meantime, we burn it and mark the area. I'll do what I can with the bar you have and my knife."

It only took them a few minutes to have the creature doused with some lamp oil and a torch to start it merrily burning. They watched to make sure it was destroyed before Richard spoke again.

"The creatures usually leave a doorway behind. If there is one, we'll want to destroy it as well."

Isashi nodded, looking at the small pile of shavings she'd managed to carve out of the small block. "Call me if you find anything. You aren't a hunter; taking care of this is my job."

He nearly snorted out loud but nodded. It was a lie, of course, one of the few impulses to do so that he indulged in. If he found a gate there would be nothing that could stop him from burning it to the ground, reveling in the hungry flames.

When the fey sent their minions into this world, there were two types of gates they could use. The first was a temporary gate. It would force a gate into existence that would disappear within days of being created. Those caused no true damage or destruction to the world.

The permanent gates were much more of a problem. They would begin infecting the land around them, making it look more like the vibrant land on the other side. Animals and plants would start changing, the primal magic of the place making them grow and go mad.

Both kinds tended to look like doorways, ornately carved trees twining together, though he'd seen a few carved of stone to look like tentacles coming out of the ocean floor. Either way, they were highly identifiable. He didn't see anything that looked like one, but he kept looking.

If there was a gate he would have to flee immediately once it was gone, promise or no. She'd tracked him here once. Only the fact that she should have lost it once he'd left with Kuzunoha had kept him here this long. With any luck, they would still be following the false trail he'd laid for them.

Well, not the only reason.

Kuzunoha was the other one. She wanted a relationship and Richard found himself loathe to deny her anything. That made him wary, but once bitten, twice shy, he supposed. He tried to put her from his mind. They were still out in the woods, after all. No matter how safe it looked. Disappointed, even if he had disliked the consequences of finding a gate, he turned and walked back to Isashi. She had finished sprinkling the iron dust onto the burned-out spot and was turning the dirt carefully with her shovel.

"Did you find one?" Isashi asked.

"Nothing, and no more of the animals either. I think he used a temporary gate. It means that they won't bother coming back, hopefully."

"Good. Help me work these into the ground and we'll go. I'll have the blacksmith make me a few pounds more and come back later this week with the rest of the hunters to do it once more."

He unpacked his shovel with an eagerness that he didn't feel and got ready to begin mixing the soil with her.

Chapter 3

*I*sashi knocked on Himiko's door, feeling the same trepidation she always did. Once she was inside the house, everything was fine, but standing outside reminded her of the times Himiko's father had reminded her that she wasn't human enough to consort with his daughter. Fortunately, Miya opened the door quickly, her too-pretty voice grating on Isashi's nerves.

"Good afternoon. How may I…" She paled as she realized who it was at the door. Swearing, she ran for the stairs, yelling a hasty, 'She's in her office' while she ran.

Isashi stepped in and took off her shoes. The servants were supposed to announce the guests and keep them at the door. Originally it had been done to allow Hayate, Himiko's father, to vet her guests; to decide if they were worthy. Once, before Isashi had found out just how unworthy he thought of her, she had gotten angry, stomping past the servants to see Himiko. Since then, the maids had started running, to stop such an event from happening again.

She tugged on the slipshoes that Himiko had made for her to wear during her visits and took to the stairs. Normally, she liked the speed that Miya used when trying to make it to Himiko's room before she did. Today, she wished she'd just asked the girl to get Himiko for her. She had too much on her mind and none of it seemed to make sense.

As she crested the top of the stairs, she saw Miya glance nervously at her. Her eyes flicked between the open office door and Isashi and back again. She looked about ready to start sweating.

"Mistress Himiko," Miya said, making her decision. There was iron under her tone, though her body language suggested she was ready to bolt. "Your hunter friend is here to see you."

She stepped out of the way, bowing, just as Isashi got close enough to stride in.

The room hadn't changed much since Himiko had taken over her father's office.

Hayate's desk was nestled against the wall, directly across from the door. It was large and dark, with drawers on either side of the too-big seat that Himiko still used. A second smaller desk sat against the wall near Hayate's. The rest of the room had bookshelves, filled with business accounts. Behind the bookshelves on the right was a small space filled with two benches, varnished the same shade as the desk and the chair.

Himiko smiled and closed up the old book that she had been reading. She may have never settled into the too-big furniture, but at least she looked happy with the work.

Himiko's smile dropped and she was wrapping her arms around Isashi before she could even open her mouth.

"What happened?" Himiko demanded.

Isashi didn't want to say, didn't want to move or breathe. It was so nice having Himiko's arms around her. She wouldn't have been bold enough to ask for a hug. It was just like Himiko to know without her even saying a word.

"Hana's family were waiting for me at my house when I got back into town."

Himiko pulled away, leaving Isashi feeling colder than she had been. She let herself be pulled over to the benches. The two benches, like the desk, were impersonal and cold. Even the table was richly plain and utilitarian. They weren't Himiko's style. They were her father's. The only thing in the corner that spoke of Himiko at all were some soft silk pillows that she'd commissioned for the seats, one in red and one in yellow; Himiko's favorite colors.

Isashi grabbed the red one and set it under her. She was out in the forest often enough that she'd learned to appreciate a soft seat.

"They shouldn't have had any issues with you. You were the junior hunter in that situation."

"I'm a full hunter and I survived, where she didn't." Isashi reminded her, sharply. She hadn't been a junior hunter in over a decade and proud of it. She immediately looked away though. "Sorry. I'm just… there was crying, wailing… her father just walked away from me at the end. Her brother… he just looked disappointed."

Himiko sat down in the bench across from her, holding the yellow pillow. Her fingers picked at a loose thread, idly. "There was nothing more you could have done. They know that."

"I should have seen the signs earlier, agreed to Hana's original plans. I should have realized that…"

Himiko reached over the table and grabbed Isashi's shoulder, shaking her. Her fingers were warm and soft. "You did what you could. If you're going to place blame, put it at the right person's feet."

Isashi shook her head. "It wasn't Kuzunoha's fault."

It made sense that Himiko would blame her sister though. Himiko tended to single-mindedness sometimes and she had asked Isashi to go out to find her sister.

It hadn't been Kuzunoha that had gotten Hana killed though. The monster had been searching around for days before Isashi had gone out there, hunting something only it had understood. When it had found Kuzunoha and Richard's tracks, it had decided to hunt them, even if it hadn't attacked until after Kuzunoha was nearly dead of her disease and it was clear that they would be inside the walls soon.

Isashi had peppered it with arrows, but it had been Richard and Hana who had been doing the up-close grunt work of beating back the monster, keeping it distracted. They'd needed someone long-range to distract it, but…

It was that 'but' that haunted her now.

Himiko snerked, an adorable sound halfway between a giggle and a snort, something all her own.

"It may not have been directly her fault, but she is the only idiot, fever-ridden or not, who would pick up a sword and run towards danger, not away."

Isashi took a deep breath. "She wasn't well."

A polite way to say she'd been dying at the time… and that was something that her friend was still having trouble accepting. Himiko would talk big, she would bluster about how angry she was at Kuzunoha, but in the end, she was terrified of being left alone, with no family around her. Only ancestors. One woman standing amongst the dead, waiting to join them.

Himiko's started picking at the yellow pillow again, with hands gone bloodless.

"Have you gone to see her again?"

Himiko bristled. "We said everything that needed to be said the last time I was there."

"I know that Kuzunoha was rude…"

"She was more than rude, Isashi. I gave her what she wanted, against my better judgment. She threw it back in my face."

She didn't know much about Kuzunoha, other than that Kuzunoha set her teeth on edge… a trait Isashi apparently shared with much of Hidan. On the other hand, Himiko's sister wasn't doing anything odd… not really. She was having a rebellious phase. Odd for a

Sian Ku, perhaps, but not for the Norin that made up the other half of Hidan's population. From Himiko's stories, Kuzunoha had always held that nugget of rebellion in her, even when they'd been very young.

She wasn't going to say that to Himiko. Her friend would be even more pissed.

"She shouldn't have. As the family matriarch, taking care of her is your right."

Himiko rubbed her forehead. "Can we not talk about her tonight?"

She really should be talking about it. Isashi had let them ignore the creature that had killed Hana and that had turned out very badly. But this was Himiko. She always knew what she was doing. And so, for her friend, Isashi would stay quiet. She may have been the older one, but Isashi certainly didn't think she was any wiser.

Isashi shrugged, wishing it looked more casual than it felt. "What were you reading when I came in?"

Work would be a casual enough topic until Himiko wanted to bring it up again. She'd always said that she hated the work her father had left her, but Isashi had seen her dealing with the never-ending task of running the businesses that employed nearly half the people who lived in Hidan. She cared about her employees, their families, and the businesses. It was hard work, work that Isashi herself could never have done. Himiko made it look easy.

Himiko turned to look at the bookshelves as if she could see through them to her desk. Her expression was guilty rather than dismissive like she normally was.

"Part of the treasure that detestable man brought back with him were the journals I told you about. I'm still reading them. I finally found what I was looking for last night though."

"The ones that Richard gave you?"

Richard wasn't detestable. In fact, he was kind of nice. Attractive, almost. She remembered catching him looking at her ass. She still wasn't sure how she felt about that. And there was no way she wanted to tell Himiko about it either.

Fortunately, Himiko had stood and walked around to the desk. When she came back, she had a giddy expression on her face and was carrying the leather-bound book carefully in both hands.

Himiko handed her the book with a sound like a squeal of delight. It took her off guard and she looked down at the book intently, taking the utmost care while she opened it to the page Himiko had been reading. Then she realized that she couldn't read it and raised her head a little, glancing at Himiko.

It wasn't in Cantouk, the language that was spoken most commonly in Hidan. Her mother had wanted her to learn to speak and read Siangu, but she never had, and after she'd changed, becoming an Eleden… well, even her mother hadn't thought she would ever need to know. She would never join the ancestors… and the ancestors wouldn't talk to someone like her. They might hear her prayers and they might intercede for her, but she wasn't considered a descendant anymore.

"It's fascinating, isn't it?" Himiko asked. She hadn't noticed Isashi's confusion.

Isashi could feel a blush forming and was glad that her hard skin showed so little color other than the grayish-silver that was her normal shade.

"Um, Himiko, it's in Siangu." She closed the book carefully and passed it back over to her friend.

Himiko knew that she'd never learned the language. She'd forgotten in her excitement. Her friend flushed and turned to the page she'd marked, biting her lip.

"Sorry about that, Isashi… I didn't mean to…"

Isashi smiled at her to continue. She did.

"It starts here…" Himiko said, pointing at the characters while leaning the book forward enough that Isashi could see the complicated symbols that made up the bulk of the language. "with, 'Fumimaro has always been a headstrong young man, though if a humble servant may have an opinion, going to the trouble of changing his name to Tanaka simply to spite his father was a foolish decision. Our illustrious master brought his wife and I, his humble servant, with him when he traveled to this new world. But the master's eldest son didn't want his father's heritage, though he could have had both fortune and fame with the addition of Kankatta mines to the family holdings. Still, according to my sources, Fumimaro has succeeded in breeding silkworms outside of Sian and her neighbors, so perhaps one day his empire will be the equal of his fathers. Every child of the Morioka family has a good head for business, just as they have always had height equal to their nobility'."

Himiko perked at the implied compliment to her lineage and set the book down on the table, pushing on the spine gently with her fingers.

"He was coming with birth gifts for my father on the ship they found and was supposed to mend the rift if he could. He said my great-grandfather had come to understand the value of family on his sickbed."

Himiko wanted a family. Here was information on one that could be hers. Isashi could see how enticing that idea could be.

"From where?" Isashi asked her.

Himiko blinked in confusion. "What?"

"This servant must say where he's come from, right? Wouldn't the rest of the family still be there?"

Himiko stared blankly before she yanked Isashi up by her hand and into a tight hug. Isashi couldn't breathe and for the first time, she noticed the curves against her, Himiko's arms holding her tightly. The feel of her friend's breath on her neck.

She drew in a breath and held it, almost scared to breathe.

Himiko pulled away and Isashi felt a whine of disappointment in the back of her throat. She pushed it away.

"You're a genius." Himiko crowed. "I may have family out there!"

Brandy Ackerley

"Well, of course. Kuzunoha is-"

"My half-sister. And I love her, but… we could have aunts or uncles, cousins that we didn't even know about..."

That hurt and Isashi wasn't even the one being talked about. She was about to call Himiko on it but her friend suddenly looked contrite, as if she'd just realized what she'd said.

Isashi knew Himiko and Kuzunoha had never been close. Like everyone else in Hidan, she'd seen the way Hayate had played them off each other. The moment Himiko wasn't performing up to his standards, he'd used the threat of Kuzunoha taking her place to push her harder, all the while showering his trueborn daughter with affection, making Kuzunoha push that much harder just to be noticed.

Isashi wished she'd been older. Then she could have told him off for his mistreatment of his family. Even Isashi's own family had never treated her so badly, and she'd stopped being human.

"How would you find them?" She asked.

"Well, the ship had to be coming from somewhere. Like you suggested, he must say somewhere in here."

Himiko picked up the book, beaming at Isashi.

"If he doesn't, then I can ask Kuzunoha if she knows where the ship came from or where they would have picked up Nakamura. It will give me a place to start."

Isashi smiled, still a bit breathless as she looked at Himiko, as if she were seeing her the first time again.

"Then we need to celebrate. Come, we'll have dinner at the Koi."

Himiko nodded, still breathless.

"Let me grab my coat."

Chapter 4

*K*uzunoha batted her eyes at Richard. He didn't look impressed.

"Do you think that fluttering your eyes at me will make me change my mind?" he asked her.

She let out a grump.

"But Richard, look at how long I've been healing already." It annoyed Kuzunoha that her voice turned into a whine. "It's been nearly two weeks and I'm not asking to go far."

"You mean, it's only been two weeks, not nearly." He corrected her. "You should be staying in bed."

If Kuzunoha could have flopped back on the bed she would have. But she would have needed help even to do that. She could probably control the height of her pillows now… if anyone would let her try.

She looked around the room. She'd never liked the healing room. When she'd been dating Deckard, she'd helped him by bringing him water, or the occasional tools that were in the other room. She'd hadn't been able to come and visit Richard when he'd been ill which had been a blessing in disguise. As much as she'd disliked it before, she had liked it more than she did now that she'd been stuck in it for over a week.

Yellow walls, with three beds, one filled by her, covered with fading yellowed blankets. There was a thin shelf attached to each of the walls and a set of candle holders above it, hanging from the wall. The only other bit of color was her brownish bag in the corner and the blue blanket that hung on the back of the chair Richard sat in, in case she got cold. The room stank of medicinal herbs and old blood. Why hadn't she ever noticed that before?

"Resting in a chair would still be resting. And then I could see the yard if nothing else."

Richard looked at her. "Do you think the yard will be that much more exciting than the room?"

"No, but it would be something different."

"You have to be patient." He told her. "I didn't find it fun when I was confined here either."

He paused and they both heard a faint knock. Not on the door to the healing room though, so it must have been on Deckard's front door.

"I'll bet you five it's another person trying to get magical healing out of Deckard," Kuzunoha said quietly.

That had happened no less than twice every day she'd been here so far. She was starting to think that they were trying to injure themselves in the hopes of getting him to heal them.

Richard smiled. "Silvers, yes. It won't be that… I think it will be a visitor for you."

She'd been thinking coppers, but silvers would do. Especially since she was going to win. She could count on one hand the people who had come to visit her since she'd been brought here. Of those, the only one that had come more than once was already sitting beside her.

Richard looked pretty confident though. What did he know that she didn't? They heard the front door open and Deckard greeted someone, a melodically muffled voice returning his greeting.

"I win," Richard said.

"How can you already know? We can't even tell who's out there."

"They don't sound injured." Richard pointed out.

"That still doesn't mean it's a visitor for me."

Richard leaned down and put his lips on hers as she heard her sister's voice nag her before they even entered the room. She swore into his soft lips.

"Kuzunoha, don't swear. It isn't appropri- Richard! What are you doing? She's injured."

He pulled away, but it was Deckard who answered. "A kiss isn't going to injure her further, Himiko."

Deckard looked annoyed, but not at her or Richard. Instead, his near-anger was directed at the vase filled with blue, red, and yellow flowers that he held in his hands.

The flowers were pretty but common, and her gaze slid over to the expensive red and white blooms that Jack had brought her when he'd come to visit. He'd left uncomfortable, and quickly, from his visit two days after she'd been injured. Partially because she was still falling asleep all the time and partially because seeing her laid out like this seemed to distress him.

"What are those?" She asked. She couldn't imagine that Jack would be sending her more already and she didn't know anyone else that would even consider it.

"Flowers," Deckard grumbled before he relented. "Sorry. They're for me. Unfortunately, the rest of the house is full… I can't put these anywhere but in here."

"They do brighten up the room," Richard said.

Deckard set them down across the room on the ledge. The colors stood out against the pale yellow of the walls, and while the bouquet wasn't as full as it could have been, she approved.

"Why don't you have room out there for them?" She asked, furrowing her brow.

Deckard's face darkened.

"Since Deckard's ability came out, a lot of the villagers have felt that whatever thanks they gave him before weren't good enough," Himiko said, uncomfortably.

Deckard broke in. "Which is silly. I am just a healer. I don't want to be treated differently. They should know that."

It wasn't going to happen. Even Kuzunoha could see that. He was blessed and could magically heal people as he'd done to her. She wished she'd been conscious enough to see it. Richard had described translucent gold snakes shimmering between the two of them when Deckard had healed her. It sounded beautiful.

On the other hand, she'd seen the way he hated it when people walked in with a sprained ankle or a banged-up shin or elbow and asked him to magic the pains away. Some had been snide and nearly violent when he'd used normal healing only, while some had cried as if his refusal was somehow much more personal.

She thought the truth was much simpler than that. He hadn't used his powers before and wasn't going to use them again until someone was dying. Why waste a gift of the gods on a scraped knee? It gave Kuzunoha the uncomfortable realization that she had been dying by the time Richard had brought her in. Cold settled around her and she shivered.

Richard wrapped another blanket around her and kissed her forehead. She wanted to tell him it wasn't that sort of cold, but his kisses helped to warm her, so she stayed silent.

"If I had a power like that, I think I would want people to know it," Kuzunoha said without thinking.

Deckard gave her a dirty look. She shrugged. "You can help a lot of people with it, no? If I could do something amazing that would help everyone, I would want to help them."

If she were different like that, it would give a reason for everyone's animosity. Even so, she would help them. Make them all have to swallow their pride a little when dealing with her.

On the other hand, maybe it was good that she wasn't the one with the power.

"You couldn't have," Himiko told her. "Father would have wed you off as soon as you were old enough, arguments or no. Then you would have only healed those your husband decided you were allowed to."

Kuzunoha's face burned. She knew that her father had only considered her worth what he could get from her. She also knew that all of the blessed she'd heard about were living with nobles or royalty… but she'd thought that it was their choice.

Then again, she knew what it was like to live where who you were was less important than what you were. She should have known better.

Deckard finally walked over to the bed, gesturing Richard out of the seat beside the bed. He sat down in it and put his hand on her forehead, making sure that she wasn't too cold.

"To be clear, I like the power. I only wish I never had to use it. That everyone I knew stayed healthy; safe. But now that people know, they are demanding that I use it to heal them. They just want to see it, to brag that they were healed by a blessed, that they've been touched by magic. The others seem to not know what to do with me. They want my power, my ability… but having it attached to a person is inconvenient for them. People have opinions, have needs, beliefs… they don't want to deal with that."

Brandy Ackerley

She reached out and touched his leg and he smiled faintly at her before he patted her hand and tucked it under the extra cover Richard had thrown on her.

"Better to just not tell anyone, I agree," Richard said. He'd moved over to where Himiko was standing. "Use the power when you need to, but nobody can try to demand things if they don't know about it."

"Of course, you would think about it that way." Himiko snorted. "All of this aside, Kuzunoha, we need to talk."

"About?"

"What your plans are when you're well."

Kuzunoha glanced at Richard then back to her sister.

"Why?"

"I may have found you a job."

"But…"

Himiko's lips turned down in a faint frown.

"I know you were considering leaving, but you haven't even decided where you want to go. I decided it couldn't hurt to look while you were still healing. Master Alfric has said that he may be looking for a new student later this summer to help with the new foals in the stable."

Kuzunoha's breath caught in her throat. She had loved riding when she was younger. It had been her escape. On the back of her mare, Star, with the wind blowing through their hair, she'd felt that she could do anything. Master Alfric had even allowed her to start helping in the stables. Her eyes filled with tears. Her father had sold Star and told Master Alfric that she needed his permission every time she was going to ride. Master Alfric had folded to his demands. He hadn't even let her ride after her father's death two years before.

She had loved working with the animals.

"Didn't you mention that you did have somewhere you wanted to go?" She heard Richard say.

"Kalvettika." She almost whispered the word. As much as she loved horses, her reasons for wanting to go there trumped them… mostly.

"Why would you ever want to go there?" Himiko asked.

Kuzunoha's lips thinned and she didn't answer. Her sister continued talking as if she hadn't expected one.

"It's dirty and stinks to high heaven. Plus, the people there are rude, constantly."

"That's where your mother was from, right?" Deckard said.

Kuzunoha's face flushed bright red as Richard and Himiko turned to stare at her.

"You know where your mother is?" Himiko said.

It came out like some sort of accusation. Richard didn't say anything. Just nodded as if her choice suddenly made sense.

"No…" She shot Deckard a dirty look. "Father told me where she came from. I don't know if she returned after leaving Hidan though. I'm hoping to find information about her there."

She didn't know how to do that, of course. Beyond asking around to see if anyone had heard of her. Besides, she still didn't know if looking for her mother was a good idea. She'd left Kuzunoha with her father… wasn't that enough to prove that she didn't want anything to do with her daughter? Still, Kuzunoha wanted to talk to her, to find out why she'd left her with nothing, without even a name of her own.

"Kalvettika? That's the city our ship came from." Richard said. "It's a big city. How would you find her in it?"

"I was hoping you might have some ideas…" she whispered.

"By my ancestor's decree… It's your lucky day, Kuzunoha." Himiko told her. "I have to make a trip down there for business sometime this summer. If you want to search for her before you settle into your new job with Master Alfric, I don't see why I can't take you with me."

Kuzunoha bit her bottom lip. She hadn't wanted to go with her sister. She glanced at Richard.

He smiled at her. "Don't let me stop you."

That hurt. She hadn't been looking for permission, but for whether he would still want to go there with her. Kuzunoha looked to Deckard.

"I don't even know when I'll be able to leave."

As usual, Deckard cut right to the heart of the matter. "You're healing, but you still need time to rest and someone to watch over you. You aren't ready to be on your own yet."

"But for how long…" she asked him.

"A month or more. I couldn't say just yet." He told her.

Kuzunoha looked at her sister and thought about it.

She didn't want to throw the gift back in her face, but… Richard, her mother… she didn't want to stay in Hidan, did she? But what could she do out there? What did Richard do? She refused to go back under her sister's control; would letting Himiko pay her way there be the same thing? What if Kuzunoha got there and decided to stay?

"I don't know yet. Even if I'm healthy enough to go… I can't make that decision right now."

"Think about it. I've only just started planning the trip, so you have time. Unfortunately, I'm going to have to get back." She touched Kuzunoha's foot. "Get better, alright."

Himiko shook her head as she left the room.

"I'm going to have to go as well, Kuzu. I have a meeting with some men at the docks."

"Kuzunoha." She corrected. Then she heard his words about the dock and her heart sank. "You can't be leaving already?"

He smiled at her. "I won't be leaving tomorrow or anything, but I do need to start thinking about it."

"Why now?" she said. She glanced at Deckard. Richard had promised to stay, to try a relationship with her for a while. How could he already be thinking of leaving?

"It won't be immediately. I need to talk to your dockmaster first, see what ships he's expecting in, how soon… that sort of thing. It will take a few weeks before I can find a ship to take me on anyway."

"But you are leaving."

"Eventually. I promise I won't leave without saying goodbye first."

With that, he walked out after Himiko.

Kuzunoha's lip trembled. She didn't want to be left alone. She felt like the world was passing her by, while she hid healing within Deckard's walls. She'd known that Richard wouldn't be staying forever… but she'd hoped for more time before he left. He'd been willing to wait before his trip with Isashi back into the swamp around Hidan. What had they found out there that he was already thinking he had to leave?

"Are you okay?" Deckard asked her.

She didn't trust her voice not to betray her but grunted an affirmative. She wouldn't show Deckard how much she was hurting. He'd said her emotional welfare wasn't his concern before and he was right. She had to take care of herself. Like she always had.

"Do you still want company?" he asked her.

She looked up at him, not sure how to answer. Part of her desperately wanted to say yes… and that was dangerous. He'd leave her alone again. Like he had before. She would deserve it this time too, just like she had the last. Did she have the right to ask him for that?

Before she could answer, there was another knock at the door outside. He sighed.

"Let me deal with that, and then I'll come right back."

"No, I'll be okay on my own." She told him. The moment had passed, and she could feel her walls coming up around her again. "I'll just get some sleep."

He nodded and reached towards her pillows when a second, more insistent knock at the door came. His eyes narrowed and he glanced at her.

"I'll be right back to fix those for you." He said as he walked out the door.

Kuzunoha closed her eyes, glad for the quiet. She reached down, her hand finding her sword. As always, something about the blade calmed her. She settled into her pillows to rest until Deckard came back to help her again.

Chapter 5

Deckard walked into the square, glad that no one stopped talking, or turned to stare. It was getting to be a problem, especially since he wasn't sure how to stop it. But the market was at its busiest time, the morning rush, and no one noticed him. He was simply another blonde-haired man walking in the square. Even if he was one of the tallest.

He basked in the relative anonymity.

Tieni shook her head at him, a smile tugging at her lips. She was dressed down from her normal cacophony of color that most of the Corvidae preferred. Instead, she was wearing a blue cotton shirt and leather trousers that would keep her warm enough through the chill wind that was still coming in off the ocean.

"That's enough. We came here to pick up supplies..."

"Just let me enjoy this, please."

A blonde-haired child turned his way, smiling, but when she opened her mouth to greet him, he put a finger to his lips. The girl grinned and turned back to her mother, though he was sure that she was still watching him from the corner of her eye.

Tieni kissed his cheek and he looked over at her.

"You win. Stay as long as you need to. I'll start our shopping at the general store and then go to the butchers for our extra stewing meat. Come and find me when you're ready."

He warred with his conscience but let her go. She knew what they needed as well as he did and everyone in town knew her well enough to give her what she asked for under his name, whether they approved of the relationship or not.

She kissed him again before she strode away. He let out a breath and smiled. It was a guilty pleasure, but he wouldn't let this opportunity pass him by. He would enjoy this for however long it lasted and then join her to finish the shopping.

He couldn't remember the last time he'd walked through the market without having anyone interrupting him or staring at him. Everything was a relaxing balm to his soul, from the soothing scents of fish and vegetables that were always on display, the garishly placed clothes, fabrics and tools, and the myriad of voices and conversations. He didn't listen in, just appreciated that the mumbling tones weren't talking about him.

"Healer, you need to come see my daughter." A voice said behind him.

The tone was pleading, but thick and for just an instance, Deckard hoped that he was speaking to Healer Bryant instead. Only for an instant, though, then Deckard's shoulders tightened.

"Jonas," Deckard said evenly, turning. "We spoke about this yesterday."

Jonas's dark eyes were nearly as wild as his disheveled hair. He was short, stout, and covered with light muscles that came from going out with the boats to fish every day. His skin below the neck was a deep orange shade, colored by the waxy sap the sailors used to make their clothes repel water.

The day before, he'd been able to see that Kuzunoha needed someone. He'd wanted to help her. It had been clear to him that Richard was unreliable at best. She'd only seen the good in the stranger though. Having him simply leave her like that had to have been a shock. He'd left to answer the door and found Jonas waiting for him. The man had kept him busy for over an hour with increasingly erratic demands that to cure his daughter.

"You're supposed to help her. She's still sick." Jonas told him.

"The only thing that will help is drinking the herbal tea I told you to prepare for her."

The herbs would help with the symptoms but couldn't take away his daughter's addiction any more than Deckard himself could.

"That isn't the only thing–" Jonas said, grabbing his arm.

"What do you think I can do?"

"Use your power on her."

"Jonas, I can't do that."

"Hypocrite. You're a healer, but only that weird daughter of Old Tanaka gets the help. Is it because of her family's money? Or is because you're still dipping your ink at the well? Swore to help everyone, but you won't lift a finger to help my daughter."

People from the square were turning to look, the rumble of voices disappearing, until there was only his and Jonas's. He could feel their eyes on him. Deckard had to stop himself from grabbing Jonas and throwing him as far as he could. Even when he'd been dating Kuzunoha she hadn't gotten favored healing from him. He'd used his ability on her because she'd been dying. Jonas's daughter wasn't dying… and healing her with his power might kill her.

People from the square were turning to look, the rumble of voices disappearing, until there was only his and Jonas's. Still, he could feel their eyes on him. Deckard gritted his teeth and spoke levelly.

"I can't help her because she isn't sick, Jonas. Not that way. Her symptoms are caused by the plant she smokes."

He didn't know what Jonas wanted him to do. Lock up the girl so she couldn't smoke it anymore? Even if Deckard had thought that was the best course, he'd have to lock her up for years to get all the toxins out safely. He couldn't be sure she wouldn't fall back to using it all over again once he let her go either. She'd confided that the leaves in their worst moments were still better than the depression she could never seem to shake. Better to feel pain than nothing at all. He'd told the priest of Kittin to visit her. He could heal the body, but it was the job of the priests to soothe the mind.

"Fish shit. You –."

A flash of red ran past Deckard's eyes. "Kuzunoha was injured and near death. Your daughter smokes cannite blossoms... everyone in town knows what they look like and knows what they do. She isn't sick. She's addicted. The shakes and other symptoms will fade as the toxins fade. Which the herbs I gave you will help with. She'll be fine as soon as the toxins caused by it are gone."

Cannite blossoms could be smoked, leaving the user in a state of bliss for a few hours. When it wore off, the side effects were horrible; vomiting, red eyes, blue streaks appearing on the skin following the veins in the body. It was bad, but Deckard couldn't help.

The most he could do was to help expel the drug faster and that wasn't pleasant or safe. He'd only tried it once, stopping when the power had started pushing the drug out through the pores in her skin, causing her so much pain that he'd thought she would die.

He felt sick remembering that had essentially been what he'd done to Kuzunoha when he'd forced the pus and poison out of her veins. The only thing that had kept him going then was the knowledge that if he stopped before enough of it was out, she would die regardless.

Jonas pushed him with the tips of his fingers, sending Deckard back a step.

"And then she'll want more. She always wants more. You could take it away; you could make her better permanently."

The man's blue eyes were feverish, mad with hope. Deckard sighed as the power within him remained dormant, quiet.

"Even if I were to use the same power on Moira that I used on Kuzunoha, it wouldn't work. I might be able to take the toxins out, but I can't heal her addiction. The priests would be better able to help you with her."

He wished he could use it safely to heal his daughter. It would satisfy the hunger in his soul. When he was near someone he could help, his power burned deep inside until he released it, filling him with relieved satisfaction. He used it, in little bits, here and there, to help all of his patients heal faster, to have their pain lessened when he could. One thing he'd loved about Kuzunoha was that she had been exceptionally healthy. He never felt the need burning in him just sitting with her, as he had with others, even when they had something as minor as a cold or a muscle ache.

Suddenly, his head was yanked back and the sharp snick of a metal blade sounded near his ear. He yanked himself away, pain flaring across his skull. Turning, he saw Jonas' brother holding a huge chunk of blonde hair and a pair of scissors.

"I've got it," Albert called out.

"We'll use it to heal her since you won't do what's right," Jonas told him.

His hair lost its sheen, drooping in the man's hands like a dead rat. Deckard felt his scalp, unsurprised to see blood smeared across his palm. The fire filled him, bringing soothing warmth in its wake as it closed his wound.

The length of a Norin's hair was directly connected to how much honor the Norin had. Honour was a loose term of course, but Deckard had been growing his out since he had taken over the task of healer completely after his mother's death. He had lost very few patients since then, and most of those had been to nothing more than old age. He'd never had a reason to cut it before.

His mother had told him, early on, to expect this sort of response if they found out. They would try to take what you couldn't give, thinking you were withholding it from them. Jonas probably had some idea to feed the hair to his daughter. As if dead hair would help her at all.

It was stupid, like the people who came to see the shrine and left with chicken bones that the unscrupulous thieves sold to visitors as Saint's finger bones. He'd always believed that no one could be naive enough to think that bones of the dead had magic within them. He misjudged them all.

Deckard felt cold flow through him, the idea that to these people he wasn't even a person anymore, freezing him more than a rough winter wind. In their eyes, he was nothing more than an object to be used. That was probably overstating it. He was more like a horse to them. A beast to be used until he couldn't give anymore, at which point, he would be killed, divvied up for parts.

"Now what's going on here?" Deckard heard Mayor Deiter say. "Step aside, what's this all about?"

Tieni ran to his side. She didn't step in front of him to guard him, her hand at her side where a sword would have sat. The seriousness brought him back to the present.

"Are you alright?" Tieni asked him. Deckard shook his head, not trusting his voice to answer yet.

"Calm, everyone, calm down! You didn't need to go to this length, Jonas. Of course, Deckard will help Moira. A blessed can fix anything."

"I can't help his daughter," Deckard told them again. "She isn't sick or even hurt. It's a problem of the mind, not a problem of the body."

"There isn't a difference," Jonas said. "Sick in the head, sick in the body... it'll still kill her in the end."

"There is for my abilities." Deckard ground his teeth. "She has to want it. I can't fix her addiction."

"Of course, she wants to get better," Jonas said, hotly.

"She says all the time that she wishes she wasn't like this. That's want enough." Albert added.

"Deckard, please. Stop being churlish." The mayor scoffed. "If you can help our town's nobility, I'm sure you can help its lower sect as well."

For the briefest second, he wished he hadn't healed Kuzunoha out on the road. He could have told them to take her to his office or the grocers or... anything other than healing her on the street in front of the entire town.

Himiko's voice rang out.

"Stop using my family's trauma as a way to boost yourself, Mayor Dieter. Deckard is a healer and he has always done his duty. Whether that is using the blessed's gifts or whether that is using herbs and time; he would never leave another in pain if he could help them."

Himiko stepped to the front of the circle that had formed around them. She was wearing an impractical set of silk clothes, pleated and pressed in a way that he was sure wouldn't last through the day, her brown hair hanging straight to her shoulders. Her expression was cold, like it usually was whenever he'd had the pleasure of dealing with her. Right now, he could have kissed her for her intervention. Especially since she usually avoided any conversation that involved the mayor and his erroneous idea that she was eager to be his blushing bride.

Predictably, the mayor's entire demeanor changed.

"Miss Tanaka! I am sorry that you perceived my discussion of your family's tragedy that way."

Himiko looked to the heavens, frustrated, and stepped up to Albert, pulling the hair from his grasp.

"You can't take that." He cried, grabbing at it.

Himiko glared at him till he backed off.

"Hush, you superstitious fool. The hair wasn't yours in the first place. You stole it and attacked our healer to boot."

The Mayor stepped up to her. "You're right, quite right, Lady. We are civilized folk. I'm sure our healer has done all he could for the girl..."

Himiko smiled sweetly, though the expression didn't reach her eyes.

Deckard wasn't sure what he should do when she walked over to him and handed him the hair. He looked down at it. It didn't look like his anymore, the chunk hanging dead in his hand. A breeze started to make the ends dance and he tightened his fingers around the dull locks, longing for something he couldn't define, trying to ignore the gnawing worry rippling through his belly.

Chapter 6

*R*ichard had been in this small town too long and he knew it. The problem was that he'd found people he didn't want to leave behind; at least, not without getting to know them better first.

In his mind, Kuzunoha's distressed expression came to mind and he felt guilty all over again. He hadn't wanted to hurt her, but the creature he and Isashi had found was weighing on his mind. He'd been cruel, telling her that he had to leave, after telling her that he wanted to stay, to be with her. He hadn't been lying. Was it heroic to leave her in tears if it saved her life? Part of him said yes, but a larger part was conflicted. Kuzunoha had handled herself well out there, but if the bitch who'd taken him for years came for him, she would step in the way. She would get hurt herself, or worse, taken. He wouldn't wish that on anyone, even an enemy.

"Watch where you're going…" a voice broke through his concentration and he skittered out of the way before looking to find a thick man carrying boxes taller than himself taking up much of the walk. Richard hugged the wall and touched his side when pain flared there.

He ducked his head, sending an apologetic wave at the man, hoping to not be recognized as a foreigner. It was easier to avoid conflict when the other person had no extra reasons to be annoyed with you.

The man grunted and continued on his way, leaving Richard to feel take stock of his injury. Deckard had healed the bolt wound, but he'd torn the muscles near it fighting the monster. A week and a half wasn't enough to heal, and he hadn't done it any favors when he'd helped Isashi dig a deeper grave for the creature.

He made a mental note to stop off at Deckard's later to ask for some more of that hideous tea. While it may have tasted of sulphur and sadness, he'd slept very well, and his chest had healed faster when he was drinking it. He could talk to Kuzunoha while he was there, try to explain why he had to leave. Maybe if he helped her understand, it wouldn't hurt as much when he left.

Looking around he realized he'd made better time than he thought, the warehouse where Master Leigh wanted to meet him at was just ahead. He quickly rubbed his side, massaging the torn muscles into relaxation again and continued.

The door was open when he arrived and he slipped inside, surprised to see Isashi standing primly near the center of the starkly bare room. Dark wooden walls and floors contrasted with an unfinished ceiling nearly two stories high. A small desk sat against the wall to Richard's left, stacked with paperwork. Two doors led out of the tiny room, one to the right and one straight ahead, almost certainly going into the warehouse part of the building.

"Isashi, what are you doing here?" he said as he walked up to her.

She smiled at him but seemed nervous for some reason.

"Master Leigh wanted to ask me about something. You as well?"

He nodded. "It probably has to do with our little adventure then."

The door to the right opened up and a thick gravelly voice said, "Tangentially, at least."

Master Leigh was a heavyset man, with a thicker belly than anyone Richard had ever seen. Despite that, the man was nearly pure muscle from what Richard could tell. He was also the elder brother of the Kerlow family, the closest thing to nobility Hidan had aside from Kuzunoha's family.

Richard nodded politely as Jack and a pretty Sian Ku girl that had a secretary type look to her, despite the overalls and t-shirt she wore, followed Leigh out. She showed Jack to the door, chatting with him casually the whole way. Leigh gestured both him and Isashi into his office.

The office was tiny, only half the size of the secretary's room and filled with metal filing cabinets, a desk, and three chairs. The walls had been painted a lighter shade than the dark outer walls and the roof was only a couple of feet above his head. On the wall behind the desk, there was an impressive painting of a saintly man in armor cutting the head off a gigantic fish.

Once they were all in, he shut the door and gestured them towards the desk.

"I asked you here to find out about this cave you found on your trip," Leigh told them while they all sat down. "I'm wondering if it would be worth it to try to open up and take advantage of."

"Advantage how?" Richard said with a glance at Isashi.

"Well, according to one of our captains who passed by it on their way here, it's quite large. I'm wondering if it would be worth it to open up as a secondary dry dock."

"It took us days to walk back," Richard said, thinking. "That might be too far for an extra dock. Are you that pressed for space here?"

Leigh shook his head. "Not yet, but in ten, fifteen years, I hope so. I'd like to see Hidan grow."

"It's far enough away that it might be better to build a second township there." Isashi put forward. "It would be hours away by ship and we're more favorably set here than we would be there."

Richard could see the wisdom in that. "If you just want to claim it, you might be able to build an inn at the location and have just a few other shops go in."

"Far enough to let some of the younger generation take the lead while keeping them close enough to protect them," Leigh said. "I can see the wisdom in it. Why would they set up an inn though?"

"If you can block off part of the water inside there was a natural hot spring leading to it."

"Is that what made it smell so bad when it fell in?" Isashi asked. Her nose wrinkled in distaste.

Richard nodded. "I've never been at one, but I know that some of the rich love going to such locations. The inlet would provide some security until you had time to get a wall around it."

Leigh made a harrumphing noise. "Would you be able to lead my ship there, Richard?"

Richard nodded. "I think so. Kuzunoha and I went overland, but I should be able to show you the location."

"Good. Isashi, are you well enough to come along and guard the ship and my men as they look over the area?"

"Me?" She asked, surprised.

"Why not? You've seen the area before, correct?"

"Yes, but how long would we be there?"

"A day, perhaps two. I'll send along a few of my engineers and a few of the mayor's people to see if we can do anything."

"I don't expect any problems out there, but yes. I would suggest we take a second hunter, as well."

"Really?" Richard asked. It wasn't that big an area to guard and she should be able to keep track of everyone there.

She nodded. "Richard and Kuzunoha were attacked by a cleris crab there. Those creatures are dangerous. While they're normally solitary, some live near their mates. This one looked too big to easily leave the cave by the access we know of. That suggests another larger hole, somewhere in that cavern. Therefore, a chance of a second one being there.

Secondly, if we're going to be watching overnight, I'll want someone above as well as in the cove itself."

"It will mean that we can split up the workers as well, while we're there." Leigh mused.

Isashi nodded. "I'd rather be prepared than lose a man."

"How long would it take to arrange with one of the other hunters?" Leigh asked.

"I can talk with them tonight and hopefully we'll have an answer for you in the next day or two."

"Wonderful. That will give me the time I need to get the workers together and prepare a ship." Leigh stood up. "I'll be waiting to hear back from you, Isashi. Richard, I'll send you a message when we have more solid plans. Thank you."

"I have a question about my pay," Richard said. "I'd rather there be no confusion later."

"Oh." Leigh seemed surprised. "I suppose it is true that you aren't a hunter. How much would you need?"

Not much, if he was only showing them to the location. They would find it themselves at this point, with or without him. It was just a matter of whether they wanted to take the time to search for it.

Brandy Ackerley

"A day's wage or two depending on how long we're out there. With danger pay."

Leigh frowned. "Danger pay? Only people who can fight get that."

He looked to Isashi, who had stood up when Leigh had.

"He is a good fighter, sir. Worth having on your side. He isn't a hunter, though." Isashi said.

It was true, but Richard hated that the distinction had to be added. He'd fought big monsters and succeeded. With her, two weeks ago.

Leigh thought about it. "I'm only paying for your time. I pay my workers 5 sentine a day and ten if danger pay is necessary. You won't be doing any other work than just leading us... Say, seven sentine? It's what I would pay for a guard."

"Acceptable."

Leigh held out a hand. "We'll shake on it now and I'll write up the contract for you to look over at your leisure."

Richard nodded. "Of course, send me a message at the Koi and we can go see your justice later to authorize it."

A moment later, he and Isashi were back in the sunlight.

"We seem to be taking a number of trips together," Isashi commented.

"We are." He agreed. They walked silently another moment before she turned to him.

"Richard, why did you look so angry in there?"

"I'm not a hunter." He said. "I know I'm only a mercenary, a guard, but… I don't like the distinction."

"It isn't anything against you." She told him. "You're a good fighter. But I need someone behind me that I've fought with before."

"We've fought together." Richard snapped.

"Once," She snapped back, "and one of our fellows died during that battle."

Richard stopped walking. She was right, of course. She turned to face him.

"Richard, I would need a lot more hours in the ring with you before I am comfortable with you fighting at my back. We both know enough not to get in each other's way, but not enough to fight together yet."

"At least, not effectively." He said. "Sorry. You're right. I've gotten so used to being the outsider, the one that doesn't fit, I forgot how much fighting with someone you've trained with changes things."

Isashi smiled at him. "No offense taken. You're a good man to have at my back."

"Fortunately, that is something that is easily corrected."

She frowned.

"When do you have time to practice? I assume there's a training space here." He asked.

"As easy as that then?" She snapped her fingers.

"Well, I assume that you won't lose every bout." He prodded.

Her eyes burned with welcome challenge and she laughed.

"That will be the other way around, Richard. You're good, but you aren't that good yet. But sure, why not? I could use some extra hours in the ring. I'll put our names on it for an hour tomorrow. I'll stop by to let you know what time."

"For dinner?" he suggested.

"Rogue." It was an insult but said with a smile. "What about Kuzunoha?"

"I thought that she was still at the healers. Was she released when I wasn't looking?"

Isashi frowned. "No, but shouldn't you save your dinners for her?"

Richard rolled his eyes. "I should clarify. Having dinner is not an invitation to my bed. I don't have many friends here yet. Actual company would be appreciated."

Perhaps he could explain his goddess's tenets as well. It would also help her to understand that he wasn't cheating on Kuzunoha. He would prefer to have that belief of hers cleared up as soon as he could. She flushed.

"Dinner then."

"Tonight." He promised.

Chapter 7

Deckard closed the door and leaned his head against it, listening as Nanami Rin huffed her way indignantly down his walkway. He'd never had to throw out a patient before. While he hoped he'd never have to do it again, he wouldn't hesitate if that old bat ever came calling again.

He'd never had to deal with her before. She'd always insisted that no apprentice could serve her well enough and even after Master Lin had declared him fully trained, she'd chosen to go to Hidan's other healer, a Norin by the name of Bryant, for her health needs.

Bryant was welcome to her.

She'd come in, disparaged everything in his home, before refusing to sit in the same room as "glorious Tanaka's unfortunate by-blow". While he had to admire her inventiveness in avoiding naming Kuzunoha directly, it had left him wishing just once that he could tell the woman off before throwing her out. He'd forgotten just how much the rest of the townsfolk ignored Kuzunoha or disparaged her if they couldn't ignore her. Once, it had been his job to stand up for her. Now, he supposed it wasn't anybody's, but her own.

"Deckard, are you alright?" Tieni asked.

She was standing at the door to their room, where she always retreated to when he was healing. Thank the gods for that.

He'd been a full healer for six years now. He'd never once felt that he was Hidan's only healer. Since his being a blessed had come out, he was starting to wonder though. Bryant had been silent on Deckard's 'new' powers and everything else. Deckard hadn't even minded having so many of Bryant's patients come to see him. Until now.

Nanami hadn't asked him for help. She'd come, demanding that he heal her since Bryant was busy. She insisted that she had a cold and that the only way, at her age (which he wasn't respecting either,) was to heal her with his power. Considering the fight she'd put up to see it, he had been perilously close to giving in, just to get her out the door.

"Deckard?" He felt Tieni touch his shoulder and turned completely, grabbing her up in his arms.

He wondered how insulted Nanami would have been to know he'd had a Corvidae in his room the whole time she was there. It almost made him wish he'd told her.

Tieni pulled him closer, putting her head against his neck. Her scent, a mix of his own herbal soap and something sweet that was all her own, comforted him. He felt like she could handle the weight of his problems, bending with them, but not breaking.

"Thank you." He whispered.

Her tone was as low as his. "You need a break."

"I can't."

"Everyone needs to every once in a while."

"No." He pushed her away, gently.

She let him go and he walked over to the stove. A broth was heating on the hearth for Kuzunoha. It was late and he hadn't even been able to start his own supper yet.

"Why not? You've done it before."

"I've gone away for a meal," He corrected, "or gone to the market. But I have to be here. If I'm not, people could die."

"The only people coming to see you are people who want to ogle at you, like some exotic creature in a noble's garden." She dismissed. "I'm sure Kuzunoha will be fine if you leave her alone for a few hours."

"An hour or two. Maybe we could go for dinner after I've gotten Kuzunoha settled for the night."

"You need an entire night, not an hour or so at the Koi." She pushed. "Can't you get someone to watch the invalid for the night? Between idiots trying to scalp you and having to deal with everyone in town acting like you're going to start shitting magic everywhere, you need a break."

His hand moved up to touch his hair and didn't find it. After the incident in the market, he'd shorn it as close to his skull as he could. It was odd. He felt every breeze that passed, a kiss on skin that had never felt such before.

It also announced to everybody that he was questioning. His honor, his choices, what he thought was right… everything. It shamed him and freed him, at the same time.

"Who could take over for me? Bryant? He has the other half of Hidan to deal with." He pointed out.

"What about that Sian woman who watched over Kuzunoha that night when we had dinner at the Koi last week?"

He paused. "That was my old master, Lin. She's retired now."

"Which means she probably doesn't have any plans. If you ask her, she might be able to watch for you. And being your master, she must have training in everything you need her to be able to do, right?"

She wasn't wrong. "Where would we go? The Koi is really the only place we have for entertainment in the evening."

"You may not have heard since you've been in here all day, but my cousin, Danior, arrived just before I got back."

Deckard's nose wrinkled. "The Corvidae? But we can't go out there now. The gate closes in an hour. Once it's closed we'd be out there all night."

She tapped his nose. "Exactly."

"How is that supposed to be relaxing?"

"The caravan will ring the wagons for protection and will have a few people on guard. The rest will be in the center, sitting by the fire, talking late into the evening, making music, dancing, and sharing stories. We would be welcome since I'm family."

The idea of being out of town for a night still sent cold shivers down his spine. On the other hand, the idea of looking up at the stars with Tieni in his arms while music played in the background was temping. So tempting.

"I'll see if Master Lin is willing to watch the house for an evening."

* * * * *

Of course, it hadn't been easy. Nothing worth it ever was. It took another two days before Master Lin could give him an entire night. He considered it fortunate since Kuzunoha had finally started looking better. Her skin wasn't looking as grey, and her eyes weren't as lightless as they had been. She would be safe until morning.

Tieni had used some of her earnings and purchased a large roast to give to the Kompania as a gift. As he and Tieni walked out of town, Kei, a Sian guard a few years older than Deckard himself, stopped them.

"Healer. You're heading out late. You know that we lock the gate up soon, right?"

Though Kei's tone sounded pleasant and inquiring, Deckard could see the dark looks on the other guard's faces.

"Yes. Tieni has family out here. We're joining them for dinner."

Kei nodded, reminding him. "You only have an hour though. We won't be able to open the gate after that. Even the latecomers are coming in already."

"We were planning on staying with her family tonight."

Kei pulled him roughly away from Tieni. "Not to be rude, but do you trust them, Healer? They're Corvidae."

"I trust Tieni. Especially since her family has no idea what I am."

Kei flushed, having been caught out. It wasn't Deckard's profession as a healer that he was worried about.

"I still think it's dangerous for you to go."

"Am I a prisoner?"

Kei looked concerned and looked around. The man was wishing he had a commander here, someone who did have the authority to tell Deckard he wasn't allowed to leave. Finally, Kei moved back.

"Of course not. I'm just concerned about your safety. You know that. It's my job."

Deckard nodded but the movement was too sharp to be considered gracious.

After they were well away from the wall, Tieni looked at him. "That was why I thought you should just not tell them."

He sighed. "I'm worried that if I didn't, they'd come out, armed, looking for me."

He'd never felt trapped inside Hidan before, but then, the guards had never had a problem with him leaving before. Of course, he'd never told them he planned to stay out overnight before. He let out a breath. He could ignore it, but this was just another way that his life in Hidan had changed.

Tieni pulled him toward the wagons. There were two concentric rings of them as far as he could tell. Outside both rings, the Corvidae were pulling down their stalls. Most were selling things, cloth, jewelry, and even some rare herbs that they collected from other townships. The gaudiest cart was blue, speckled with bright embroidered stars and a sign that proclaimed 'Madam Morjiana knows all'. The scent of fire and worked iron hung heavy in the air.

"You don't have to stay, you know."

"What?"

"The Kompania. We can go with them when they leave if you want. You could get a clean start." She shrugged.

"What about the people in Hidan? They need me."

"They have other healers, Deckard, and it's clear they don't appreciate all you do for them."

Deckard put a hand to his head. He didn't want to have to think about this, not tonight.

"I don't…" he couldn't answer. Part of him agreed that everything would be simpler with people who didn't know him, but he couldn't just run, could he?

"You don't need to answer, right now. For tonight, you have no worries. We can think more about it later." Tieni kissed him.

"What worries?"

The question had been asked by a man, dark-skinned with similarly dark hair and eyes. His hair was wavy, rather than curly like

Tieni's, but he sported the same three braids she did, though the beads covering his were dark green, grey and red, rather than dark green, blue, and red. He reminded Deckard of Richard. The same too-smooth smile spread across the man's face.

"The guards were worried about their healer coming out for the night." Tieni joked.

"Well, maybe they have a reason. Are you worth ransoming, Healer?" The man looked him over. "No, I can already tell, you'd be more trouble than you're worth. Danior's the name. Tieni's cousin, and leader of this kompania, by trade."

"Deckard," he said, clasping the hand than Danior held out, "troublesome healer, and consort of your cousin, Tieni."

"Not of Hidan?" Danior frowned, leading him in.

Deckard felt self-conscious. He shrugged. "Healer and consort are all I wish to be."

Tieni's gaze was soft and hot. Danior was not impressed.

"Well, you must be quite a healer if they want to keep you that badly," Danior said.

Deckard shook his head. "I'll be honest. Our guards tend to rely on stereotypes rather than knowledge sometimes."

Danior shrugged. "Many townspeople are like that. Honestly, Tieni, I am surprised you've lasted as long as you have."

"A testament to my willpower." She said. "Also, that few kompania's come near here in the winter."

Danior laughed. "The roads of the swamp never freeze solid. They get ice on top and stay mud underneath. Will you be hitting the road again soon?"

"We were considering it. Do you have extra spots?"

Deckard wished he could turn back time so she wouldn't ask that question. He hadn't even thought about it yet.

Danior's gaze turned shrewd as he saw Deckard's discomfort. "There is always room for family, but… we'll have to talk about the foreigner. That will be a question for tomorrow though. For tonight, enjoy yourselves. See if your healer can even handle being outside of the walls at night."

Danior offered a pleasant smile that didn't include Deckard and left. He waited until Danior had left before turning to Tieni.

"Are you thinking about leaving with them when they go?"

"I thought we might." She said. "I know you didn't want to talk about it yet, but I needed to talk to Danior if you decide we can go. I was just taking precautions for you."

"Yes, but I hadn't even…"

"Just think about it. Danior will be here for a few more days."

He nodded and grit his teeth. "Would he need to know about…"

She pulled him close. "He knows you're a healer; a damned good one. He doesn't need to know more than that."

Deckard let out a breath. He'd never considered leaving Hidan before. Not seriously. He glanced back towards the gate. He'd also never thought that the city guards would try to keep him from ever leaving for a night. He squeezed his hand into a fist. He didn't want to live life in a cage, gilded or no. If Hidan was going to force him to stay here against his will… he had to decide soon whether he would leave. If he waited for them to make their move, he might find his wings clipped before he could fly away.

"Alright, I'll think about it. I don't think Danior likes me though."

"Part of growing up Corvidae is learning to deal with people from the towns we visit. He thinks you're nothing more than a polished, stuck-up man who's worried about being outside the walls. It will pass as he gets to know you."

"What about the rest of your extended family?"

Tieni winced. Many Corvidae didn't approve of their members having relationships with people outside of their race; with people that might convince her to abandon the road.

"You haven't proven yourself trustworthy yet. You aren't family. But once they see that I trust you, they'll start, too. Once they get to know you, it won't be an issue."

He nodded. "Well, let's see if I can't improve that first impression. Introduce me to your cousins. They're the ones we're taking this meat to, right?"

Tieni grinned. "Even on short notice, you'll love what our cooks will be able to produce. As for the rest, be the best you can be and they'll fall in love with you, too."

He let her lead him towards the circles, hoping that she was right.

Chapter 8

*K*uzunoha blinked the sleep out of her eyes, noting that the sun was already low in the sky. She felt less groggy today than she had the last couple of days, and she was hurting less. She still felt like she couldn't do anything but nap all day. Irritating, but Deckard kept promising that she'd heal better if she allowed herself to rest more. She stretched and then moved her fingers and toes under the blanket. Even with the weight of the extra blanket Deckard insisted that she keep over her calves and feet, her toes were still cold and sluggish. However, the sluggish feeling was almost gone from her fingers. Deckard had told her that the remaining poison in her system would gather there, the last places to let go of the damage that had been done to her body.

She could hear Deckard moving outside of her room, talking to somebody. The door was nearly closed… he must have been talking loudly for her to hear him through it.

"Do you think we should take it?"

"I don't think that it will matter on the road. And you said it was going bad, right?"

"Only because people don't want to accept herbs when I when I can just…" Deckard's voice faded into an intelligible mumble.

Kuzunoha pushed herself out of bed, for the first time feeling like she wasn't going to fall back into it. She waited for the lethargy to overtake her and cheered silently when it didn't. Still, she was careful as she walked to the door, her toes feeling odd as if she were walking over water with glass in it; sharp pains followed by cool wetness, then back to pain. She moved slowly over the wooden floor. There was no need to push when she was finally starting to show improvement.

She opened the door and saw Tieni's hands roaming Deckard's back as she pulled him into her embrace. Kuzunoha's stomach lurched and she stumbled towards the bed, collapsing onto the soft folds. It creaked under her.

He'd been over her for years now. She knew that. So, why did it feel like a kick in the teeth to see him with someone else? She swore, her gaze blurring. She'd never had someone make her feel so comfortable and happy, before or after him. She wiped the tears away angrily before they could stain her cheeks.

It was different with Richard. Could it be just as fulfilling? She touched her chest. Maybe. She didn't know yet. She hadn't known him long enough and this relationship had been anything but proceeding regularly.

Suddenly, Kuzunoha realized what else she'd seen with Deckard. Backpacks and sacks stuffed full on the too-thin table that Deckard had been given when he'd requested one eight or nine years ago. Red silk blankets, thinner and starting to look threadbare in places, hanging over the backs of the apprentice-made chairs. His healing tools, the oddly shaped knives, hammers, and scissors, set on the counter, his travel kit packed to bursting beside them.

Deckard was leaving. Not just her, but Hidan entirely.

Part of her cried disconsolately, a fourteen-year-old who had finally found a place to belong demanding that her future-self fix what she'd broken. Kuzunoha ruthlessly shoved it back to the darkness where it belonged. She'd been without Deckard for years, and she'd never thought of herself as a lost little puppy without him beside her. She'd watched him move on and had moved on herself. Hell, she was planning on leaving Hidan, too. What was the difference between her leaving and him?

She knew the answer to that. It was proof that Hidan wouldn't remain the same either. She wanted to believe that when she left, everything and everyone would be the same. That nothing would have changed except her. Deckard leaving told her that wouldn't happen. If she chose to return, everything would be different.

Her mouth set in a line, unconsciously mimicking her father's severe expressions. Could she still leave, knowing that?

The goddess Bokuro said that every love, family, friend, or lover, was connected to you by a red string. Those connections were the threads used to weave your future.

She let out a breath, hearing someone come towards the bedroom door. Leaving would mean never returning. Or at least, it wouldn't be her Hidan anymore. It might be the same village, but it would never be hers, the one in her memory, ever again.

Her soul felt like it was frozen. She could accept losing Hidan. She could live with no family, abandoned by her ancestors if she had to. Could she also accept losing the first man she'd ever loved, permanently?

She shook her head, leashing the tears that threatened to tear at her resolve as the door opened. Deckard had saved her life, even though she'd hurt him. He deserved more than tears and a thank you.

Paying him in money would be rude, she knew that. What else could she do? If he wasn't leaving immediately, she could pick herbs for him. The sunny petals of the hiton flower could be dried and crushed; properly applied it could help with everything from headaches or mild pain to fevers. It was one of the few blooms she could still identify after so long. Would it be blooming already? She couldn't remember.

"Kuzunoha, I thought I heard you moving around. You should still be resting. Did you need something?" Deckard's voice shook her out of her thoughts.

"No." She paused and then went for the heart of the matter. "I saw the bags. Are you leaving?"

He looked away and she ruthlessly suppressed her tears and looked away, too. Deckard walked over and grabbed the wooden chair from against the wall, dragging it to her bed. He slumped into it, watching her. Kuzunoha didn't move until he touched her knee.

Brandy Ackerley

Even with his hair damnably short, he was still one of the most attractive men she'd ever met. When she'd first met him, she'd been sure that he had to be part-angel. She almost laughed. She hadn't considered that as a blessed, he sort of was. It hadn't been his strange power or even his beauty that had caught her though. It had been the damnable adorable growl he'd used whenever he was salty about having to do his job. She had joked that he was only angry that he had to work. He'd agreed, since him having to work meant that "someone had been stupid somewhere along the way."

"I didn't know it would be happening this fast, but yes. Tieni and I will be leaving tomorrow night with her cousin's kompania. I was going to tell you in the morning. You aren't well enough to be on your own yet." He let out a ragged breath. "I know you don't want to live there anymore, but I want you to stay at your sister's until you're well. I've asked Master Lin to check on you until you're healthy again."

As if her health was what concerned her right now. It would, of course, be his concern, though. But, leaving tomorrow? She wouldn't be able to do anything if he was leaving that quickly. She wouldn't even be able to get somebody else to pick her enough hilton flowers; at least, no one that she could trust to know how to pick it correctly. Hell, the only reason she knew how to ball up the loose petals and pluck the fragile base from the stem was that when they'd first started dating he'd taken her to collect herbs. Time spent together where her father, angry and against the romance, couldn't interrupt them.

"That won't be necessary. I just need rest, right?" He frowned and she continued. "Deckard, I want to do something for you before you go."

"You don't need to. You aren't well yet. Master Lin will be coming to see you. Promise me you'll stay at your sister's."

"I'll stay until I'm healthy," she promised. "No longer."

He'd saved her life. In return, she'd ruined his. Had she ever done anything to make his life better? She didn't know anymore.

"You didn't ruin anything." He told her, using that gift he'd once had of being able to read her like an open book. "That was everyone else."

"If I had told Richard that he couldn't take me to you, you wouldn't hav –"

"He didn't bring you to me because you'd asked. He called me because I was the one you took him to when he was injured. If he hadn't brought you to me, you would be dead now."

He looked like he wanted to say more and shook his head instead.

"Can I clean? Or help you pack?" She asked.

He laughed harshly. The silk clothing he wore made a slithering sound. Since when had Deckard ever worn silk? He'd always preferred cotton, saying he didn't need anything that expensive.

"Kuzunoha, stay in bed. You aren't well enough to help and you'll be more of a burden if you try. Don't make this more difficult for me than it has to be. Please."

Kuzunoha flushed. She had never gotten along with Tieni, but she'd been willing to put that aside and work with the woman if it meant paying her debt to him.

Her thoughts turned to the coin in her pack. She had nothing else. Rude or not, it was the only avenue left to her.

How much was a life worth?

She wasn't anybody special. The nobody daughter of a self-important jerk, noble-born or not. Even counting her adventure with Richard, she hadn't done anything extraordinary. She'd done only what was needed. She hadn't saved any lives; in fact, she'd cost one of Hidan's hunters their own. Everyone agreed that she shouldn't have gotten injured, shouldn't have been out there inconveniencing the hunters. Nobody said it, but she knew that she never should have gotten Deckard involved either.

Ten coins. That should cover any expenses he'd have for a year if he was frugal. He deserved more than frugality. Twenty? Well, it would help, but… no, forty. That would be enough. It would be enough to set him up in any town or city he ended up in with everything he'd need to start a new life.

"Wait, please." She pushed herself out of the bed and he swore, reaching for her. She grabbed the money box from her backpack and returned to sit on the bed. She was breathing deeply, but she didn't think she'd felt dizzy at all. Good. She fished out the coins and started grabbing them by the stack. Fifteen each… she may as well make it thee stacks to be even. She dropped them into the green money pouch Richard had included with it. Green was bad luck for a Sian hoping for prosperity, but the Norin considered the color lucky.

"Take this with you."

Deckard hissed as she thrust the closed bag at her.

"What are you doing?"

"I have to do something. You're leaving, you'll need money for…"

"Do I look like a whore? Selling my blessing for money?" He stood over her, threateningly. She flinched.

She hadn't meant it like that. "What other choice do I have? I have to do something."

He put a hand to his face. "No, you don't."

He turned again and she stood up. Her head spun this time. She ignored it, steadying herself with a hand on the bedpost. "You accepted silk from my sister. How is that any different?"

His voice lowered to a hiss. "Your sister presented me with a gift that she knew I'd need. Everything got from the city has to stay here, you know that. A healer doesn't own anything, except the gifts they are given. Everything else has to stay here. This was a gift. Not a payment. Sit, please."

"Deckard, if I had something else, anything else, I could do, I would. But I don't have that time. Take my gift. Please." She pushed the bag into his chest. She did feel like she needed to sit. She would as soon as he took the bag from her.

He backed away as if the coins were venomous.

"You never had to do anything, Kuzunoha. You never understood that. Now, sit down and stop causing me trouble."

When she didn't move, he reached for her, pushing her down onto the bed. The bag dropped from her hand, thudding to the floor. She ignored it, seeing him rush for the door. She pushed herself to her feet, using the bed to keep her standing long enough to chase him.

He reached the door first, slamming it behind him. Tieni called out to him. He snarled at the Corvidae woman.

"Drop that and come outside. I need some air."

Kuzunoha launched herself at the door and opened it, putting her weight against it. Deckard was holding Tieni's wrist. He turned and saw her.

"Since you have all this energy, you may as well pack your bags, Kuzunoha. You're going home first thing tomorrow."

Kuzunoha watched him drag Tieni out the front door. When it slammed shut, she stumbled to the bed and sat down. Her eyes were stinging and her head felt like someone had dipped it in a tar vat. She wiped away the tears in her eyes and saw the green purse laying on the ground by the bed. She grit her teeth and focused on forcing the dizziness back. She wasn't going to stay in this house one minute longer than she had to. He'd told her to pack and she would come hell or flood.

She grabbed her bags and quickly changed out of the cotton nightshirt he'd provided and into one of her robes. Sick as she was, it still felt good to be in silk again. She left the nightshirt on the floor beside the purse. It was his now and she didn't want anything of his. She walked over to the window and took one last look at the room.

It hadn't been painted in years and the yellow paint was closer to a cream-shade than the sunny yellow it had once been. The sconces in the walls were bronze, holding tallow candles. Only one was lit. She walked over and blew it out, plunging the room into darkness. She walked to the window and opened the wooden slats.

The sun had set while she had been talking with Deckard. The stars shone, with a half-full moon and the smallest amount of purplish-orange on the edge of the western horizon. The scent of herbs and freshly-turned earth was overpowering. She glanced at the fence that led around the house and shook her head, throwing a leg over the sill and climbing outside. The road was a bad choice. If Deckard saw her leaving, angry or not, he'd force her to return. She jumped the fence into the alleyway behind the house instead, still keeping to the shadows.

She hadn't gone a full block before she had to stop. She had a stitch in her side and was breathing a lot heavier than she should have been. She was holding the dizziness at bay for now, but she didn't know how long that would last. Her shoes felt wet inside, with rocks or glass poking her sensitive toes. She didn't see anyone else on the street, so she leaned against the nearest building, and put her hand inside her right shoe, waiting for her breathing to even out. The shoe was dry as a bone and so were her toes.

With another sigh, she pushed the shoe back on, tapping her toes on the ground twice to settle the shoe right. She took a step and her legs wobbled under her. They were just starting to hurt like they had the first day or two of walking she'd done out of town with Richard. She leaned against the building again. How long would it normally take her to get home from here? Ten minutes if she walked; five if she jogged.

There was no way she could jog. She wasn't even certain she could walk that far without help.

At this rate, rumors that she'd left Deckard's without his permission would make it home before she did. Not that the manor was her home. Not anymore. Deckard might be right that it was the best place for her to finish healing, but she didn't want to arrive like this. Tired, sweating and ill, in need of a bath before she fell onto her mattress. Himiko would have a fit, not to mention the trouble that she would cause for the maids. Worse, if she went there Deckard would find her… if he bothered to look once he figured out she'd left.

Where wouldn't he look for her?

She was only a block or two away from the Koi. Most likely, Richard was still there. An errant thought made her smile.

I'll want you on a bed before I leave…

There had been a delightful purr in his voice when he'd promised to stay, to wait for her. Flushing, she pushed it out of her thoughts. Tired and sick as she was, there would be no fun of that sort tonight if she went to him. Still, even if she spent the night just lying beside him on the bed, his arms wrapped around her, she'd feel safe, wanted. She wouldn't feel the need to cry herself to sleep.

It was worth the risk of finding him there with someone else. More than a partner, she needed a friend… and he was the only one she could think of. She leaned on the dirty wall again and pressed her forehead against the cool stone, steadying herself. She'd been trying to thank Deckard. The thread between them had been cut, not tied off. It would be fine though. She was fine. Resolutely, she pushed herself away from the wall and started stumbling her way towards the Koi.

Chapter 9

"*C*alla, you are beautiful," Richard told her, pulling his lips away from hers.

Her return kisses were softer than he expected from her. That first night, when Himiko had hosted her majority day celebration, Calla had been eager and somehow sweeter than the spun candy clouds they made back home. Tonight… she was holding back from her desire and he didn't know why.

She pulled back and bit her lip, lightly. "Stop sweet-talking and undress me."

In response he tugged her shirt over her head, throwing the flimsy material to the floor.

"You don't appreciate the play? That's half the fun," he said, lowing his head to her full breasts.

Calla, for all her eagerness before they'd come upstairs, had been giving him conflicted signals since he'd closed the door to his room. Richard had been hoping for an active partner; both drinking the other down like a chilled coffee in a Jisian afternoon. He slowed down further. Maybe he was moving too fast, despite how eager she'd appeared earlier. Though, if she hesitated any further, he would have to put a halt to the fun until he understood why.

Her hands were playing with his belt, but she made no move to tug them open.

"Richard? How long will you be staying?"

"Long enough for tonight." He whispered against her neck.

"You could stay longer than tonight." She said, her hand moving up to play with the hair on his chest.

He pulled back as though she'd slapped him… and not in the fun way you might slap your partner's ass.

"Not forever," she amended. "Just… longer."

"I can't. I have… promises to keep."

He pulled away. Apparently, what she wanted was to talk.

"I know… but Hidan is a good town, with good people. It would be nice to know how long we have. You have. That's all."

"I don't make promises I can't keep." He reminded her.

He would never make that mistake again.

She opened her mouth to answer when there was a knock on the door. He glanced at the door, ready to ignore it when the handle turned. Finding it was locked, a feminine voice called from beyond the door.

"Richard? Are you here?"

He froze. What was Kuzunoha doing here?

"Who is that?" Calla asked, sliding further from his grasp.

"Kuzunoha." Richard stood up.

"I thought she was still sick," Calla said, reaching down for her shirt.

She looked more than a little annoyed that he was even going to open the door. Well, she would have to deal with her dislike of Kuzunoha. He wasn't going to leave a friend outside, especially when that friend should have still been at the healer's home.

She tried the door again and he heard her voice, a new tremble in it that hadn't been there before.

"Richard, please… I'm sorry… if you're busy… maybe you're not here though… I'll just… leave…"

"Just wait a moment, Kuzunoha," Richard called as he reached the door. He waited until Calla had gotten her shirt on before he opened it.

Kuzunoha was leaning against his doorframe, looking like she couldn't stand up straight if she tried. Her complexion had been looking normal earlier today when he'd seen her. Now she was grey and little beads of sweat covered her forehead. She had her backpack sitting on her shoulder, half-open with the box he'd bought her to keep her gold in poking out. In her left hand, so white it looked devoid of blood, she held her short sword. The blue and black material of the blade's sheath just emphasized her paleness.

"What are you doing here?"

He regretted the harsh words but Kuzunoha wasn't like other women. Instead of shrinking into herself like a wilting rose, color rose in her cheek. That little bit of pink gave him hope, even if it was too red for the grey of her skin.

"Deckard released me."

Deckard would have never let her leave looking like this. On the other hand, Kuzunoha didn't lie often. Her preferred way of dealing with things she didn't want to deal with was to only tell the part of it that suited her. He could appreciate that misdirection.

Maybe if Kuzunoha hadn't looked half-dead, he would have appreciated her attention to distinction more.

"And you felt the need to see me before heading home?" He asked, knowing that wasn't the case. Even if Deckard had approved her leaving, Himiko certainly wouldn't have.

She looked away gulped, taking in a shaky breath. Her eye fell on Calla and she met his eyes again.

"I only wanted to tell you I was going to my sister's." She glanced painfully at the stairs. "And maybe, if you could help me downstairs? I can sit for a few minutes before I head over there." His disbelief must have shown on his face because she snapped. "Never mind. I got up here on my own. I'll get down on my own, too."

If she tried to take the stairs herself, she was going to fall down them. He reached for her and Calla pushed him away from the door.

"We'll talk later," Calla said, kissing his cheek.

Then she glared at Kuzunoha and slid past her, forcing her to move away from the stairs. He noticed that Calla did everything possible to avoid touching her. Another time he would have called her on it, but today he had other things to concern him than her attitude.

"Goodbye." He looked at Kuzunoha. "Come on in, have a seat."

She swayed a little when she shook her head obstinately, so he grabbed her hand and pulled her into his room, sitting her down on the bed.

"No, Richard... I didn't mean to cause you any trouble, I'll just go downstairs. It's quiet down there. I can stay in one of their spare beds if I need to."

He walked back over to close and lock his door. He wouldn't trap a woman against her will, but he was going to find out what had happened before he let Kuzunoha go anywhere.

"You are not staying in those lice-infected sacks they have downstairs." He told her. He shuffled her over on the mattress just far enough that he could join her. "What in the dark happened with Deckard?"

"He told me that he'd be sending me hom… back to my sister's tomorrow." Kuzunoha began. By the time she finished, Richard thought she might cry. Fortunately, she was made of sterner stuff and settled herself, taking a deep breath.

"I just don't know why he reacted so badly." She was looking better, but her voice still trembled.

Richard pulled her into a hug. Deckard had to know what she'd been trying to do. His reaction must have been about Kuzunoha specifically. Maybe he'd been insulted that someone he'd once loved thought that he needed money to heal her. Or maybe it had been that his secret was out and accepting the money felt too much like a step towards latching himself into the cage he so wanted to avoid. Either way, Deckard was being an idiot.

"I'm certain he understood what you were trying to do," Richard said. "Would it help if I took you out of town tomorrow? You can pick a little bag of the herbs you mentioned for him if you'd like."

"No." She looked away. "It's going to be bad enough when he comes looking…"

She pushed away from Richard guiltily.

"You will have to deal with him before he leaves." Deckard might head to the manor first to find her but either way, he'd be here before long.

"I'm… not going back, Richard. I shouldn't have come here, but I… didn't feel like I had anywhere else to go. Now that I've rested, I can probably make it to my sister's."

Richard shook his head, suddenly understanding the other part of her confusion. Deckard had wanted to send her to her sister's. She didn't think of that as her home anymore, but almost certainly that's what the man had been calling it. It was all too clear that she'd finally accepted that she would be leaving Hidan.

Deckard may have caused this, but her reaction wasn't all about him either. That knowledge was a relief.

"It's hard the first time," he said.

"Leaving?" she asked.

He nodded.

Her eyes were wet, though she hadn't started crying yet. "Does it get easier?"

Richard bit back his first response, a jilted ill-timed joke. It was never easy. You think that you'd finally made a place for yourself and then that place was gone. The thing that he'd found most helpful was not calling it home. If you were always moving, always in the process of leaving, it was much harder to become attached.

He couldn't tell her that. She wouldn't always be on the move. Adventure may have been in her blood now, but she would want to find a permanent place one day. When she found it, she might run away for a few days, but she wouldn't up and leave forever.

She nodded. She looked much better now, but she still needed to rest.

"Richard... Can I stay here tonight? I know I ruined your evening with Calla and I'm sorry, but I don't want to have to deal with Deckard, or my sister, tonight."

She would have to unless he ran interference for her. There was also the inconvenience of having such a desirable woman in his bed. He had been expected to have a willing and able participant tonight. While Kuzunoha was certainly willing, he wasn't going to take advantage of her like this. On the other hand, he wasn't going to send her to her sister's with or without Deckard's interference, either.

She continued, a nail in the coffin of his arguments. "I don't want to be alone."

He hid his bitter laughter. Two women had been on his bed and he still wasn't going to have any satisfaction tonight. Mind you, considering with the way the conversation with Calla had been going, he didn't think it had been likely he'd have found relief anyway.

He picked up Kuzunoha's hand and kissed her fingers.

"You're staying tonight. I'll go downstairs and get us something to drink. I think I'll ask them about bringing us some breakfast tomorrow too, so if I'm not right back up, don't worry. Just settle in and warm the bed. I'll be back soon."

Kenneth was manning the bar when he got downstairs. "I thought you'd be down. What do you need?"

The inn wasn't as quiet as Richard had been hoping for. Four patrons, older men, were sitting around one of the big tables, throwing cards around. It sounded like they were playing Hold Out, a card game where you tried to get the best hand of cards, trading cards with others, sight unseen, bluffing to make others think that you had a better hand than you did. As much as he enjoyed the game, he could already tell that they were playing a regional version that he'd have to learn if he wanted to join in.

He turned back to Kenneth.

"Some mulled wine for me, chamomile tea for her, and one of those fancy water heaters, please."

"Of course. She'll be staying the night then?"

Richard sighed. "Yes. Can you send up some breakfast in the morning?"

Kenneth made a note. "Of course. I can send up one of the boys with everything later if you're heading back up."

Richard glanced at the door. He could wait in the common room for Deckard and Himiko. Neither of them was going to get to Kuzunoha tonight.

"I'll be down for a few minutes still." He said, settling in to wait. "Just bring it over here when you have a moment."

He wished again that the bar had been empty. Especially since he couldn't imagine Himiko or Deckard would be polite when they came in.

Chapter 10

"*D*eckard, we could leave tonight. There is no reason for you to deal with that infuriating woman again." Tieni reminded him.

"The gate is shut already." He reminded her.

"There are ways over the wall that don't require a gate," she muttered.

Deckard had never taken advantage of those, but he knew Kuzunoha had, on occasion. The hunters knew about them and kept them protected from monsters finding it. With a sigh, he opened the gate and walked through, holding it open for Tieni. She resolutely stayed on the opposite side of the fence.

He let out a breath. "She is frustrating, but she's also a patient. Being vulnerable like that doesn't make for good decisions. Whether I like her or not doesn't matter. I just have to deal with her."

The argument hadn't been his fault, not entirely. Kuzunoha should have known how much he hated the idea that his gift was only worth what someone would pay for it. A healer working legally had every acceptable cost covered for them and their families. The town mayor paid for their supplies, but excepting the leanest times, it was the locals paying in anything they had. A good healer never had to fix his roof and he always had food in his cupboards

A blessed could have that and more, of course. They would have gold-threaded cloaks and the best tools, food equal to the noble's they served.

He had become a healer to make sure that no one died, that no one suffered if he could stop it. If he had simply wanted wealth and prestige he would have relied on his blessed status. But the blessed didn't have the freedom to share their gift with everyone. The last wandering blessed had been Valkyrie the Rebel. She had snubbed all of the nobles and raised the populace against their leaders when they'd tried to trap her. As soon as that was done, she had disappeared again, wandering the land, healing those that needed her gift and living piously off their thanks.

That had been centuries ago.

The worst thing he could think of being sent to war, forced to work himself to the bone, forced to heal soldiers only to send them back out within days to the front to nearly die again, over and over. He would not do that. He wouldn't have his gift abused that way.

"She is a patient who could be shipped back off to her sister without issue tonight instead of tomorrow morning. She's healed enough for that." Tieni snarled.

Deckard let the gate slide close and turned away. He'd only wanted twenty minutes to cool off and he'd been out here longer than that now. He would tell Kuzunoha why he was so disappointed in her and leave it at that.

"It's my responsibility, Tieni. This is my duty. It's difficult enough to leave my entire life behind, without giving up on my last patient."

Tieni didn't say anything else, but after a few moments, he heard the gate swing open, banging on the other side of the fence as she took out her frustration on its hinges.

He headed for Kuzunoha's room and opened the door. The room was dark and he grabbed one of the lit candles in the main room to check on her. His stomach dropped. She was gone and the window was open. He swore internally and ran over to it. She wasn't well enough to be walking around on her own.

The back of the house was silent and still as a painting. The moon was less than half full, giving the yard a faint blue light. He looked, trying to see into the shadows, hoping to find her, even though it wasn't likely. She wouldn't have stayed anywhere she could have seen herself and in the darkness, her vision was second to none. She could traverse a moonless night as well as she could the same area at noon.

His vision was good, but not that good. Just as he started to turn back, movement caught his eye and he saw a tiny tuft of something wave on the fence.

"No." He whispered. She couldn't have made it over the fence on her own, could she?

"Deckard, why are you staring out the window? Where's your ex?" Tieni asked from the doorway.

"She's gone." He said, turning back into the room. On the floor by the bed, he saw the green bag of coins she'd tried to give him.

"Then she must be feeling a lot better than you thought she was," Tieni said, coming up behind him and looking out the window as much as she could.

Deckard picked up the bag and looked inside it. Gold coins, more than he'd ever seen in a single place. She had left it for him. He put it in his pocket.

"Apparently." He grumbled, climbing unceremoniously out the window.

It took only a couple of steps to get to the fence. He'd been hoping the tiny flutter on the fence had been a broken spiderweb.

Of course, nothing was that easy. Caught in a slight crack of the fence was a broken silken thread. He couldn't tell the color in the darkness; he had been lucky to see it at all in the dim light. Unfortunately, he didn't have to see what color it was. Kuzunoha wasn't in her room and she wasn't in the yard. If she had left through the front, he or Tieni would have seen her.

"I have to go find her." He said, turning to Tieni.

His girlfriend had her hip up on the windowsill and was hanging half out of it, watching him. She crossed her arms, her expression hardening.

"Deckard, the girl ran away. If she's well enough for that then she's well enough to be on her own."

Part of him wanted to admit that Kuzunoha wasn't his problem. But Tieni didn't know Kuzunoha as he did. She always over-estimated what she was capable of. So, if Kuzunoha wasn't going to make it to her sister's and she wouldn't, not in her condition, then where would she go? She had very few people who would take her in for the night. Jack, but his house was nearly the same distance. Besides which, since Richard's arrival, she'd been distancing herself from the other man. He snorted. He'd answered his own question.

"She's gone to the Koi. I'll go get her," he told Tieni.

He had never hated his ability to read Kuzunoha more than he did now.

"If she's with Richard, she'll be fine," Tieni said.

"Stay here. I'll be back in ten or fifteen minutes. Kuzunoha is my duty until tomorrow morning. I'll bring her back and then we can finish packing."

He heard the snort of derision Tieni made, but almost missed her muttered, "Take your duty and tie it to an ebon strand."

He frowned but didn't turn around. That was a pretty severe curse for one of the Corvidae. The Ebon strand was how they believed their dead deity would find the world when he wished to destroy it. They believed that if they could fill that connection with unpalatable items, perhaps he wouldn't return to raise the dead and eat the living with them.

He would deal with Tieni's anger when he got back. There was a chance that Kuzunoha wouldn't make it as far as the Koi and he'd have to search the city for her. Hopefully not.

When he reached the Koi, it was quiet. Perhaps the rest were tired out from having been out of town all day. From what Deckard could tell, everyone had made multiple visits to the Corvidae over the past four days. The streets had been much emptier than usual and their arrival was all people seemed to want to talk about. He wasn't surprised. For small towns like Hidan, the mix of strangers, danger, and entertainment drew them like bees to flowers.

Deckard had never felt the draw to the fairs the Corvidae set up though. He liked his quiet life too much to pine for that sort of thing. Which only made him less sure that he was on the right path.

Only six people were inside the inn. Kuzunoha wasn't one of them. Four were sitting at a table together, near the center of the room where the fireplace's heat lodged away from all the windows. They looked over at him and their faces darkened before they returned to their cards; they were elders of the town. Their ears would undoubtedly be open for gossip, but they wouldn't bother him otherwise. Kenneth stood at the bar, chatting with the last person, Richard.

"He shouldn't have gone out with that girl of his, to begin with. I mean, all night? What if he wastes his power, healing one of them? We need to protect our investment." One of the men said.

Deckard bristled. Yes, leaving was the right decision. He'd tell the guards after he was out tomorrow. They would run to get the mayor, but by the time they came after him, he and the Corvidae would be long gone. They could send men to try to convince him back, but to try to hold him would be against the law.

"Deckard, what are you doing here this late?" Kenneth asked him, putting down his cloth. He moved to pick up a glass, taking it to the tap to fill.

Richard turned, his lips curled in a snarl. He strode towards Deckard, some dark creature of malice and destruction. For a single moment, Deckard's heart sped up. It had been years since he'd gotten into a fistfight with anyone. He shook off the fear and straightened. Of all the things he should fear, this pallid shade wasn't one of them.

Richard didn't punch him, but he did push Deckard back towards the door.

"You and I need to have a conversation."

Deckard fell back a step and then caught himself. Richard's next push didn't move him.

"Where is she?"

Richard's eyes were narrow slits, but he didn't push him again. Deckard knew that if he and the stranger did get into a fight, he probably wouldn't win, but Richard would understand that it wouldn't be a one-sided fight unless he wanted to bring his knives into a fistfight.

"I'm saving you the trouble of having another argument tonight. Kuzunoha is up in my room, but you won't be seeing her. Go home."

"Excuse me?" Deckard said, affronted. The conversation in the bar died.

Richard didn't let him continue. "Kuzunoha found out you were leaving and tried to thank you. You threw it in her face and made her run here. You know how sick she is."

Deckard's face burned. "She didn't thank me. She tried to pay me as if I'm a whore who performs for coin."

Richard snorted. "What else should she have given you? Could she clean your house? Help you pack? Find you herbs you might need outside the walls? You're leaving tomorrow."

"She could have found some other way to thank me," Deckard said. He knew he was wrong, but he would not admit that to Richard.

"Perhaps she should have baked you cookies and you could have chanced death trying to eat one to please her?" Richard suggested.

Deckard winced. She'd tried to help him make a soup for a sick patient once when they'd been dating and he'd been too busy to start in on it immediately. She'd added sugar instead of salt, burned the broth and he still didn't know how she'd gotten into the derrina berry stock he kept in the healing room. Added sparingly, the berry could aid sleep and help reduce pain. She'd added enough to kill and had thought it was only dried fruit at that. Even if it had been the dried fruit she'd thought it was, who would ever add it to soup?

Richard pressed his advantage. "She couldn't have done any of those and you know it. I also know that if I had offered you money, you wouldn't have liked it, but you wouldn't have kicked me out."

Deckard looked away and remembered that they had an audience. His hands curled into fists and he gestured for Richard to follow him out to the dark street outside.

Richard closed the heavy door behind him.

"You're a stranger… she isn't. Look, I'll accept that I may have over-reacted, but she should have known better." Deckard ground out

"She did. Had it been anyone but you, she probably would have thought her thanks would have been enough. Instead, she felt the need to do more."

Deckard ignored Richard on that point. Kuzunoha was no more carrying a torch for him than he was for her. Sometimes it seemed as if she thought he was still angry with her, but he'd gotten over that. He wasn't perfect, but he'd forgiven her for breaking his heart long ago.

"Fine. I over-reacted. I'll apologize. But I will be taking her back home for the rest of the night."

Richard's hands tightened into fists. Deckard felt a tiny thrill at finally getting to him.

"No."

"No? She's my patient."

Deckard's eyes narrowed as Richard stretched out a crick in his neck and then opened his fists with deliberate intention.

"Deckard, I do not want to have to tell her that I laid you out flat outside the Koi when I go back upstairs. She is in my room and she's going to stay there tonight."

Deckard's eyes narrowed. "You think you know better than a healer how to take care of her?"

Richard didn't move, but his lips smoothed into a sneer.

"What I think is that she deserves better. She asked me for nothing more than to be held by a friend tonight. You're hardly even willing to swallow your pride enough to admit that you're wrong. You said it yourself, what she needs is rest. She won't find any with you."

"You think she will with you?"

Deckard knew he'd gone too far there. He didn't like Richard. The man was shady, too smooth, ready and willing to seduce any woman he met. But he did care about Kuzunoha… more than just as a toy; no matter how much Deckard didn't want to admit it.

Richard's hand went to his dagger. He didn't draw it, but when he pulled his fingers away, it was with a jerky, repressed fury.

"What you are, Dick," Richard hissed, deliberately pronouncing the first part of his name wrong, "is angry and insensitive. Go home. Talk to Himiko's maids in the morning and I'll take her to her sister's myself after you're gone. She doesn't want to see you and I agree with her."

The words hurt as much as a punch would have. Maybe he had been harsh, but she should have known better; should have been better.

"She said she doesn't want to see me?"

"As you're so fond of reminding everyone, you have a girlfriend and it isn't Kuzunoha."

Richard turned and strode back into the Koi. Deckard considered following him in, forcing his way into Richard's room to talk with Kuzunoha. Instead, he resolutely turned away. If she didn't want to see him, he didn't need to see her either. He would go see Himiko and her maids at the house at dawn. With luck, he and Tieni could be at the caravan by mid-morning.

Chapter 11

*I*sashi walked into the impromptu campsite just as Samuel, the eldest and leader of Hidan's hunters, finished lighting the fire. As usual, they were meeting outside of Hidan. Samuel didn't like having all of them in Hidan at once. He said it was just asking for an attack to happen.

Isashi chose a rock seat near the fire and smiled at Ichigo. The Sian Ku man nodded and went back to sharpening his weapon, a thick bastard sword. He was thin and his hair had a reddish tint that had always reminded her of nearly ripe strawberries. The only other person in the clearing was Chris, a Norin just a few years older than her. As usual, he was standing a few feet away, his jacket thrown carelessly to the side. His arms were bare, the golden hair on them thick as fur. Maybe the enormous amount of hair was the reason that even on the coldest winter nights, he never wore anything than cotton and leather.

"Now that you're here, we can start the meeting," Samuel said. He stood up, taller than anyone else in the clearing, his dark clothes making him sink into the shadows around him.

Isashi looked around for Hana, without thinking. Then she looked down, tears burning at her eyes. Hana had been a hunter since Isashi had joined.

She wasn't the only one feeling the loss.

"Hana was always too damned eager for a fight," Chris said. "But gods be damned if that didn't make her a solid partner."

"She was so irreverent." Ichigo sheathed his blade. "But her mind was always on task."

"It feels wrong starting without her," Isashi said. She wrapped her arms around herself and moved closer to the fire, crouching near its flames.

"She'll be missed," Samuel said simply. "But she wouldn't want us to dwell. Grief is for the living, not the dead. Did anyone notice any incursions since?"

Ichigo shook his head. "No. I haven't even seen the birdos stir from their nests as far as their normal hunting ground. If we wanted to, we could try to attack and take the whole nest out."

Samuel nodded slowly.

Chris grumped. "Better the devil we know than the devil we don't. Keep them and their damnable blade birds. We know how to deal with those."

"They're too clever by far. I wouldn't mind if they were dumb, like the sahaugin." Ichigo complained. "Those fish are dumb. Their strength doesn't mean much since they can't attack the town without coming onshore."

Samuel looked to Isashi. "What do you think?"

Isashi frowned and threw an extra log on the fire now that it was large enough.

"Killing them all wouldn't help. It would leave a vacuum that I'd rather not watch get filled with something a lot more dangerous than the birdos."

"We don't know what would fill that vacuum. It might be something a lot dumber and easier to trick than the birdos. Something that wants to come in but can't because the birdos keep them out." Ichigo argued.

"Possibly, but we've only been seeing larger creatures lately. I'd rather keep the ones we know how to deal with. We could cull their pack earlier this year." Chris moved away, a thin sheen of sweat on his brow.

"What if we cull them and something else then comes in that they were keeping down?" Isashi asked.

Ichigo shrugged. "Then both sides take casualties, making it easier for us to cut down whatever takes their place. Culling now will make their autumn breeding cycle much easier to deal with."

Samuel looked to Chris, who frowned but didn't add another argument.

"We're down a hunter, which makes culling them earlier the safer prospect. Clear out everything near Hidan, and we'll head to their nests in five days." Samuel said.

Isashi frowned. "Can we make it sooner? Leigh and Dieter have Chris and I going with the ship to that new inlet."

Chris nodded. "It would be better to make it sooner rather than later. The birdos lethargy won't last long."

Samuel crossed his arms. "Good point. Ichigo, can you keep an eye on them over the next two days. We'll clear this area for our departure, but if the birdos start moving before then, come back and let us know. Otherwise, we'll join you in three days."

"I'll leave directions to my camp in the usual clearings," Ichigo said.

"Is there anything else to report?" Samuel asked.

Chris crossed his arms over his chest as well. "The creature that killed Hana came from the north, but I don't know from where. We have no information on them. I've sent requests to the towns of Calsentia and Erokswald to see if they've seen them before."

Ichigo asked. "From what I could tell, it was a real flesh-eater. Didn't care if it was eating birdos, blade birds, or regular animals. The only reason I think it waited so long to attack Isashi and Hana was that it seemed worried about there being four humans and wanted to be sure it could defeat them first."

"It came too close to killing both of them as it was," Samuel said.

Isashi's head fell. She'd done everything she could but it hadn't been enough. They needed more.

"We need more information on all the creatures that could be nearby. I went back to the area with that thing that killed Carlos' nephew. I'd buried it deep, but something had dug it up and eaten part of it. Plus, the grass around it was growing weird, it almost looked like it was glowing."

"You didn't tell us immediately?" Chris said. He pulled out a pad and a graphite stick from his pockets. He was their chronicler, and his notebook was never far from him. He always said he would ink all of his notes into a solid book one day.

"Fortunately, Richard, the stranger that fought the creature with Hana and me, knew how to deal with it. I went back to it earlier today. Whatever it was, mixing cold-touched iron into the ground stopped whatever it was the creature was doing and it remained buried this time."

"This Richard isn't a hunter, is he?" Samuel asked.

"We know he's a killer of men," Ichigo said. "I don't know how much we can trust his words."

Isashi let out a breath. "I think he's trustworthy enough."

"Not enough for my notes," Chris grumbled.

"I did have an idea for that." Isashi rose slowly. "I had mentioned to Samuel that the eldest Tanaka has requested I join her when she travels to Kalvettika."

Samuel broke in. "I said you wouldn't be going. If she wants a guard, she can take a few from Hidan's walls. Hunters don't guard a single person before no one life is worth more than somebody else's."

He had said that, but Isashi hadn't given up hope yet. It was against what Samuel thought a hunter's tasks were, but Isashi took a broader view of it. Plus, it was Himiko who had asked her to go. No wall guard would do as good a job as she could.

"But we do need information and sending one of us to Kalvettika isn't a bad idea." Chris mused. "They have an entire hunter's guild house up there, I've heard, not just hunters. They're supposed to have information on everything in the entire country."

Samuel frowned. "We just lost Hana. This isn't the time to send somebody on a two-month trip just to find out some information."

"It's exactly the time to send someone." Chris pointed out. "We've already agreed to cull the birdos early. The creatures will be reeling for months if we're able to clear out enough of the adult members of the pack."

Ichigo raised an eyebrow. "If we have to lose somebody, there won't be a better time. Though I still don't think it's necessary. Calsentia and Erokswald may not have as much for us, but they'll have enough."

"I don't like Himiko taking advantage of us," Samuel said.

When there had been five hunters, if most of them had disagreed with one of Samuel's decisions, he would usually reevaluate the choice. With it being an even split, it meant the discussion was over. Isashi couldn't let that happen. She wasn't going to let Himiko make such a long trip on her own. Certainly, mayor Dieter would send guards with Himiko if she asked, but she wouldn't ask. Why would he?

"Samuel," she began.

He made a slicing motion with her hands. "Enough. I have made my decision."

She should stop now. If she pushed too far, she could receive some punishment. Staying away from town for a month or some other unhappy job. She blew out a breath.

She couldn't stop now. She wouldn't.

"No, Samuel. I don't think you've considered everything. We should send one of us with Himiko."

Samuel's eyes narrowed but it was Ichigo who responded. "What do we get for sucking up to her?"

Everyone was looking at Isashi. She didn't like being the center of attention. She sucked in a breath that threatened to get caught in her throat.

"Protecting the people of Hidan, especially one who brings so much to our town is exactly what we should be doing. The Mayor will want her safe, since her safety safeguards the town. It will show a level of dedication on our part."

"Dedication to what?" Samuel said.

Chris smiled. "Our dedication to keeping Hidan healthy and happy. The lady Himiko employs over half the town. If she were to get hurt, Kuzunoha would take over. She wants to leave. She may close down the business, or worse, sell it to an outsider who doesn't care about Hidan. The family and business would be gone."

"The mayor will be so pleased with our decision, he may even give us extra money for the trip," Isashi said.

"What do you think we need?"

"Info is good. But I could see if they have a book on the other monsters as well. We wouldn't have to rely on hearsay. I'll still talk to the hunters, of course, and take notes, but…"

Chris's eyes gleamed eagerly. "Yes."

Samuel looked like he still disagreed. "You think you can get the mayor to pay for a book? They're expensive."

"I think he'll do that and pay for my trip there and back. I won't be hired by a single person. I'll be hired by the mayor."

"Certainly then he could explain to the others why Himiko warrants a hunter guard to accompany her and they don't," Ichigo said. "How much would this book help us?"

Chris looked eager. "If she can find one that covers the continent, we could have a resource that will last. We wouldn't have to worry about other monsters migrating. Even if we can't find the exact type of monster, we should be able to find out what it's most similar to. It would take out a lot of the guesswork."

"You want the book, then you should go," Samuel said.

Chris shivered and shook his head. "I don't want to be gone that long."

Ichigo crossed his arms. "Don't look at me. I am not volunteering. I still think this is a bad idea. Involving big cities always is."

Chris looked at Samuel. "That means it's you or her."

Isashi held her breath.

Samuel glared and then shook his head.

"My place is here in town. Isashi, I approve this, but only if you can get the mayor's permission."

"Proof of that will be him opening up his coffers," Chris said rubbing his hands together. "Now, let's move on to the other things on today's agenda."

Isashi breathed a sigh of relief and moved to sit back down on the stone, finding it pleasantly warm against her ass. Himiko would know how to convince him. She could ask her when she returned home.

Chapter 12

*D*eckard blew out a breath while he pushed the bellows together and breathed in as the device refilled with air with an acrid scent that reminded him of charged air during a storm. He let out another breath, before starting over again. Sweat was running down his back, making him feel dirtier than he probably was. Working with the forge was strangely relaxing, in a way he hadn't thought such a physical task could be.

He scratched his back, getting rid of a drop of sweat that was tickling its way down his spine. He wouldn't have had to deal with them if he'd worn a shirt, but it was much cooler without it on. Plus, he could avoid burning holes in the material this way.

This was his second night out with the Kompania. He was surprised just how much work went into packing and unpacking anything on the wagons, but he had to admit, the ability to set up camp, or take it all down, in under an hour was impressive.

They had stopped about two hours ago, just as the sun started to set. The sun was below the horizon now but there was still plenty of light. He'd expected the night out of a city to be dark and forbidding, but between the warm glow of the coals and the fading vestiges of sunlight, the forest had managed to remain bright.

"You can stop now," Ruslo said, removing the hot metal from the ceramic box. Ruslo had reddish hair that sat like scraggly straw on top of an eggplant-shaped head. His arms and chest were wider than any other man Deckard had ever seen and his belly was almost as wide. "I should be able to finish forming the new shoe now."

Deckard nodded and stepped back, wiping himself off on the towel he'd set aside earlier. He'd made it of soft rags his first day on the caravan. The cloth was rough and much of it didn't work, only sopping up liquid if it was left sitting against it, instead of sucking it up as a proper cotton cloth would have. Hanging the towel around his neck, Deckard walked back to watch as Ruslo finished banging the metal into shape. It was brutal, harsh, but his soul vibrated with every clang. He still wasn't sure if that was a good thing or a bad thing.

Ruslo glanced at him and then went back to his work.

"You'll want to be careful with that towel. If you aren't, you'll have a fire around your neck. Fire, especially out here, can be dangerous."

"True, but it would help keep away most of the dangerous creatures."

Ruslo held the horseshoe up, nodding before he took it back over to the forge. Locking the shoe in place, he gestured for Deckard to continue working the bellows. With a smile, Deckard tossed the towel back to its space and picked up the blast-bag.

"The fire tells the creatures out there that we're carrying enough metal to be more trouble than we're worth. Though, the forests aren't as dangerous as you kennick believe. Mostly, the creatures only attack if they want something."

Kennick, Deckard had learned, was how the Corvidae referred to anyone who lived in a town. It was derogatory and no different than the people in Hidan calling Tieni a crow. He hadn't approved of the people in town using the term crow, and he didn't like this slur being applied to him either. Still, showing it bothered him would simply make them take even longer to accept him.

"They are always hungry for human flesh," Deckard said. Walls alone had never been enough to keep everyone safe. Kuzunoha's father had fallen to an attack when the goblinoids that lived near Hidan had burrowed under the walls and tried to destroy the town from within. Only the hunters' quick actions had saved as many as they had.

"Are you always hungry? Do you eat even when you're not?" Ruslo said, checking on the horseshoe. Unhappy with it, he slid it back into the forge to heat again. "Do you always take the time to cook something extravagant? Or do you decide that leaving a simple stew on the stove is a good enough choice some days?"

Deckard took a step back, horrified. It was blasphemy. Monsters weren't people.

"They are not like us." He spat, vehemently.

Ruslo opened his mouth, but it was Tieni who answered.

"Some instincts are more than human, Deckard, they're bred into everything with more than an animal's intelligence. Even monsters want easier prey to hunt. Being in a group as large as this one is protection all its own."

Deckard turned and saw her walking towards him. She'd cut her dark hair short the morning before they'd joined up with the troupe. It was odd seeing her with hair nearly as short as his shorn own, except for three thick strands that she'd left long enough to stick her colorful beads on. He liked it though. She leaned in to kiss him on the cheek and he moved to catch her lips instead.

Ruslo laughed. "Alright, get on with you. I'll finish this horseshoe and then come for dinner."

"I should stay until you're done." Deckard offered, though to be honest, his arms were already starting to ache. He kept himself in shape but using the bellows and banging out the metal took constitution and strength that he had never needed before.

"You're needed before dinner. My cousin was training Rukeli and the boy managed to get a good slash in. He wanted you to check it out."

Deckard nodded and thanked Ruslo while he grabbed his shirt and the mobile healing kit he'd made for himself before leaving Hidan.

"Where is his wound? How deep does it look?" he asked, following Tieni closely.

"Rukeli misjudged and knocked him one on the skull. I'm not a good judge. He'll certainly need stitches. It was bleeding a lot." Tieni made a beeline toward the circle of carts.

All five of the biggest vehicles were driven into a tight circle every night. The walls provided the fire and those within the walls some protection from the weather. Outside of those five were seven more that wound a larger circle around them. He still didn't feel comfortable being outside of town walls, but he was doing his best not to let it show.

Deckard shook his head. "Most head wounds bleed profusely and look worse than they are. How cognizant was he?"

They entered by the lead cart, a monstrosity with chipping paint in five different colors and no discernable pattern that Deckard had been able to make out. Danior was sitting near the fire on the dinner benches. Deckard jogged to his side, not waiting for Tieni's answer.

He and Danior had gotten off on the wrong start, but Deckard still wasn't sure that his original assessment of the man was wrong. Certainly, he would never turn on his family… but Deckard wasn't family. He was living on the grace of their guesting laws until he was accepted or kicked out.

Danior was sitting on a bench surrounded by four boys, desperately dabbing at his face with a cloth. The one that looked proud and sick must have been Rukeli, though he didn't know for sure. All four of the boys were too old to be called 'children' but weren't old enough to have attained their majority. Their relation was obvious, all had the prominent dark hair and eyes of the Corvidae people. One of the boys looked like the stubble on his chin may have been dirt rubbed on for effect rather than actual hair.

"Ho, Danior. What were you getting up to? Boy, I need this bowl filled with water." Deckard picked up one from the table behind Danior and handed it to the one with dirt on his chin. "Fresh is better. You," he pointed to the next, "help him bring the water and," he pointed to the third, "you can find me a cloth to wash your master's injury."

The boys' eyes were wide as Deckard removed a tiny white cloth from his kit and pulled the wet, red cloth away. The blood welled and began to drip again. Deckard used the white bit of cotton to put pressure on the wound. He handed the last child his medical kit.

"You're Rukeli, right? I need you to hold my case open while I work, can you do that? Stay there, I'll need light to work. You others, why are you still here? Get moving."

Rukeli nodded while the other three went running. Deckard looked at the wound, wiping at it. It would need stitches, Tieni had been right about that, but probably no more than three or four.

"That was well done." Tieni's cousin told him. "Rukeli, be careful with those supplies. The cost will come out of your hide if you drop them."

Rukeli stopped leaning forward to see and stood up straighter. Deckard narrowed his eyes and strung some thread while he talked.

"I've dealt with boys like that before. Everybody does better with something to do."

He took out his canteen and cleaned the wound with its water. Pulling the wound shut, he looked at Danior.

"Have you had stitches before?"

Danior waved, dismissively. "Many times. How many do I need this time?"

"I'll put in four. It's jagged enough without making it worse. Be careful; you'll have a new scar if you're not."

"I'll ruin my good looks is what you're saying."

Danior's grin reminded him of Richard's when he was trying to be charming. Deckard refrained from telling him that the blood caked on his face ruined the effect.

"I'm sure you'll have no trouble coming up with a story to tell the girls; perhaps you took it fighting ten goblins in the woods," Deckard said, not quite able to keep the growl out of his voice.

Danior snickered, then winced as Deckard started to stitch the wound closed.

"There were sixteen of the buggers and all I was wearing was my knickers, it being nighttime and all that. All I had for a weapon was a rusty dagger that one of the creatures had dropped."

Brandy Ackerley

Deckard tapped a bit of power and pushed it into the wound while he pulled the threads tight. The power snuggled in like a cat near a smoldering fireplace. The stitches would start pulling at the healed skin in a few days, but it shouldn't tip anyone off. He reminded himself that he did have to be more circumspect than he had been. That had been what destroyed his life in Hidan.

His mind jumped back to Kuzunoha. He'd wanted to apologize, but he'd missed that chance. There was no going back now.

It only took him a few moments to finish stitching and Danior jumped off the table to look at Deckard's work in a bronze mirror, nailed to the side of the lead cart. He pressed at the stitches and turned, this way and that, judging the work. He grabbed the cloth from the boy that had returned and used the water Deckard had told the other two to get to start wiping the blood away. Despite cleaning himself, Danior didn't pull any of the stitches. He clearly hadn't been lying about having them before.

"You are good," Danior said to him, "and, that's the last time I let you get in that close, Rukeli. It's your job to wash the cloth and dispose of the water. Make sure you take the water a couple of hundred feet away before you dump it."

It wasn't a good idea on the road to have the scent of blood on the ground near their campsite. Taking it well outside the caravan's enclosures made sure that any creature following the scent wouldn't end up in the middle of the caravan by accident. Hopefully, most of them wouldn't bother, instead, sniffing or licking at the unfortunate tree all night.

"Sorry again, sir," Rukeli said, picking up the bowl and cloth.

"Means you're finally learning. Now get on with it." Danior huffed, gesturing someone forward.

Deckard turned and saw an older woman, darker-skinned than the other Corvidae, her grey hair streaked with black, walking towards them. She was dressed in the most garish outfit he'd ever seen, oranges, greens, and red shades that fought like cats in a bucket. She was holding a long wooden pipe that had been polished to a golden gleam. She took a puff and let it out slowly while she looked at the injury.

"Well, Morjiana?" Danior asked her.

It took Deckard a couple of seconds to realize that the woman wasn't speaking something foreign but the same language as Deckard himself. Her accent was so thick that people who had stuffed their mouths with cotton would have spoken more clearly. She was older than Danior, probably in her forties, maybe her fifties. Time had not been kind to her round frame, but she commanded respect from those around her.

She took another puff. "Ez az goot az when I steetch."

"Good? Or better?" Danior asked.

"Bedder, though his steetches smelk vike fyr." Morjiana said. "'De' kennick doo well, if he stay."

Deckard suddenly realized they were talking about his handiwork and couldn't stop the shard of anger that made him grind his teeth.

"You got yourself hurt deliberately? With a head wound?"

Deckard growled at the stupidity. Head injuries were never something to underestimate, no matter how insignificant they seemed.

"I'm not daft, man," Danior told him. "We had a perfectly natural kitchen accident planned to test your skills. This just meant that we didn't have to cut someone else to find out what we needed to."

Deckard's hands clenched to fists. Tieni touched his shoulder.

"It's a normal way for my people to confirm someone's skills."

Despite her words, Tieni sounded pissed. Most likely her irritation was due to them not believing her assessment of his skill in the first place. Though he'd wished Tieni had told him this was a test before he worked on Danior. After all, he'd used some of his healing ability to set the wound. This woman might be able to tell that it was healing faster than it ought.

Morjiana whispered into his ear, her breath smelling of ash and a spicy fir tree sap. "Ah I tee it, boy. I ain' gonn' tell."

Tieni and Danior continued as if they hadn't heard her while the short woman waddled away.

"… now I've seen those skills for myself, Tieni," Danior said. "Speaking of which, how do you like working on the forge, Deckard?"

"Good." He said. He stretched, loosening up the ache in his shoulders.

Danior smiled. "You won't feel that way in another week. It's hard work. Still, learning from Ruslo will be your task unless someone is hurt. I haven't seen you on the practice field yet. What weapon do you use?"

"I don't. I'm a healer."

Danior frowned. "Out here, you will. Let me know what you would prefer; I will find a practice weapon for you. You will start with the boys and spend two hours on it every night after dinner. I want you proficient as soon as possible."

Deckard blinked, shocked, as Danior walked away. He was a healer, not a killer.

One of the young boys ran up to Danior and tugged on his sleeve pointing. Danior glanced up, and Deckard saw Danior's face light up in an unrestrained smile at the beautiful woman waving to him from the window of a cart. He jogged over to the fair-haired beauty and reached a hand up to cup her cheek.

"Who is that?" Deckard asked.

"Zujenia is Danior's wife," Tieni said. "We won't be properly introduced to her or the newborn for another two weeks or so."

Deckard must have looked confused.

"I forgot, you allow your wives to go wherever they want. We restrain our newborns and their mothers to their carts. Just until the threat of changelings is gone."

"Changelings?"

"Some monsters can take our form if they wish. They hunt us by looking like us. Whole families were eaten by not noticing that their child had been replaced early enough."

Deckard watched as Danior's wife touched her husband's head, checking for herself to see that he was safe.

"They take our form? Pretend they're human?"

"A perfect duplicate. No one knows what their true form is." Tieni said. "But all the tales say that you'd never be able to tell that they were only human on the outside."

"Well, that's terrifying," Deckard muttered. "Why haven't we heard of their type in town?"

Tieni shrugged. "We say that buildings have a magic all their own. For monsters like that, they have to be brought in or invited. Walls share that and make cities and towns impregnable to them."

Deckard prayed that creatures like that didn't actually exist. There were few races that lived side by side with humans, without being human themselves. The eledar were the most common, though he'd also heard of a type called Pirobolm; a sentient burning rock; those were more than he needed.

"Odds are that you'll never see one. Even most Corvidae don't know anyone that's actually seen one." Tieni said. "What weapon will you want to learn?"

"Tieni, healers don't fight; they heal those who do."

"That's what happens in towns. Not on the road. Out here, our walls are our homes and if we have to hide in them, we've already lost too much."

She was right, and he felt fear at their being unprotected again. Not only that but if the creatures got this close? What then? People could die and he wouldn't be able to help till the fighting was already over. He didn't have to be a killer though. He could choose to be a protector, someone who only fought when there wasn't another choice.

"What sort of a weapon do you suggest?"

She smiled encouragingly and gestured to the weapons area. "I'd suggest a blade over a staff. Let me show you why."

Chapter 13

*K*uzunoha grasped the wooden blade tighter and her teacher, Master Howse, sighed.

"No, Miss Kuzunoha, don't hold it like you want to throttle it. Lighter. Softer. You are not a barbarian from the 'Bowl. You are a slight woman using a blade, even smaller and more delicate than yourself."

Kuzunoha tightened her grip but growled. "Cats are small and delicate, too, but they kill when they want to."

"Kuzunoha, you don't have to push yourself," Himiko said, from the other side of the training ring.

Howse glanced at her sister but kept his gaze on Kuzunoha. "True. Cats are perfectly designed killing machines. Dangerous, no matter which end you get. However, you are not. Not yet, anyway. Now, do you think you can do one last run on the dummy?"

Howse's thin, fuzzy hair, floated on a thin breeze, white and soft above his age-marked skin.

She let out a breath. It had been a week since Deckard had left and two days since Master Lin had told her, point blank, that if she was healthy enough to complain as much as she was then she was healthy enough to start exercising that extra energy away.

That said, Kuzunoha had to admit that she was tired. Was she pushing it too far? Master Lin had warned her that if she pushed too hard or too fast, she'd be back in bed for twice as long. She glanced at Himiko. Her sister looked frustrated and gestured for her to sit down.

"Yes. I can."

She held up the wooden weapon, ignoring that her arms were shaking. They had been that first night out with Richard as well. One more attack wasn't pushing it.

She focused on the dummy. The one Richard and she had created in the woods had at least resembled a human, if only in silhouette. This dummy was just a log stuck in the ground, thick enough that it could take a pounding. The stick had lines painted on it, showing where the throat, heart, and stomach of a person would be. The wood had been smooth when it was first made; now hundreds of tiny little chips and grooves were carved in its weathered surface.

Trying to keep herself light on her feet, Kuzunoha surged toward the dummy, lunging with the weapon and jabbed as close to the heart circle as she could. She moved her blade up, slashing at its unarmored sides. The last movement in the set was thrust into the neck.

At the last second, she saw Deckard's face on the dummy and she yanked back on her weapon. She took a deep breath, took her stance again, and filled her mind with thoughts of the troll that had hunted her through the woods. That had been on her land, in her home, threatening her people. Bloodlust rose easily and she dove in to finish the move the way she'd been taught.

The wooden blade slammed into the wood hard enough that her arms vibrated. The force pushed her wooden blade back towards her and she fell back. She took a deep breath, feeling her arms shake with the power she'd just expended. It was unsatisfying to realize that she hadn't even dented the log. Then she glanced down at her weapon.

Down the center of the wood, a crack a millimeter or two wide and a couple of inches long was running down the blade. She felt mildly better and smiled at her audience. Himiko looked taken aback, her eyes wide and horrified. Howse stepped forward and took the weapon from her, tracing a finger along the crack.

"Very good, Miss Kuzunoha. Quite a lot of power in that last swing." He said.

"Thank you. It felt good." She admitted with a smile.

"Maybe you are a barbarian…" Himiko muttered. "Are you done your training now?"

"Yes, Himiko. Give me one moment. Good morning, Richard!" She waved at him quickly as he entered the training yard before turning back to Howse. "Thank you, sir, for the training."

Howse smiled and handed back the weapon. "It's my job to make sure that when you do go, you're prepared. Keep this. Breaking your first weapon is a big event. Perhaps it will remind you to not use your actual sword against stone again. Not that a bit of practice is likely to break a blade like that. A master's work. Still, no point in tempting the fates. I'll see you the day after tomorrow."

She smiled and took the wooden sword from him. Howse had been horrified when she'd told him about using a named blade created by a master, to break a rock. He'd joked that the only reason he had agreed to train her was to make sure she'd never treat a blade that way again.

"I don't think it's likely to happen again. See you." She turned back. Her sister was standing near Richard. Neither looked particularly comfortable.

"What are you doing here?" Himiko said to Richard.

"I'll be leaving with the boat in an hour. I wanted to say goodbye to Kuzunoha."

"Good. She needs to get back home to rest soon."

"Himiko, I'll be fine," Kuzunoha said. Richard grabbed the blade from her, noting the crack.

"Very nice. Your first cracked weapon?"

She nodded. Richard grinned. "So, that must mean you're getting your strength back."

"Slowly." Himiko cautioned. "You've only been up for a few days."

Kuzunoha rolled her eyes. "Is there anything else, Himiko?"

"Yes. I'll need to talk to you later today. About the trip." Himiko said.

Brandy Ackerley

"No problem. Head to work. I'll head towards the dock with Richard and then go home to wash up and rest. I'll stay there until you get back."

Himiko glared at Richard but spoke to Kuzunoha. "Don't go all the way to the docks. Master Lin said that you'll need quite a bit rest still and you already worked with Master Howse today."

Kuzunoha was ready to argue, but Richard stepped in. "Kuzunoha, I agree with your sister in this case. We'll walk, but only to the market. You can rest by the well if you need to and then head back."

Kuzunoha wanted to argue but knew that if she did Himiko would insist on walking with her until she got home. There was little that would kill a romantic walk more than having your sister who hated your boyfriend following and throwing in mean comments and asides.

"Fine, fine. I'll go to the market and then return home."

Himiko nodded to her and then to Richard and left.

"Thanks a lot." She grumbled at Richard. "It's bad enough having my sister baby me. I don't need you to do it, too."

He smiled, but it didn't quite reach his eyes.

"I'm not babying you. There have been a couple of people that I think are dangerous hanging around the docks. I'd rather you not be there."

"You think I can't handle myself." She bristled, taking back the weapon.

Richard put his hands up in a gesture of surrender.

"Kuzunoha, I don't want to take them on. Please, just take my word for it. Stay away from the dock for now, okay."

If Richard was worried, they had to be dangerous.

"Are they after you?" She asked.

He shook his head and gestured towards the gate her sister had left through a few moments before. "Not unless you do something to make them turn my way."

She nodded. Some form of bounty hunter then. And as much as she wouldn't mind seeing people that Richard considered dangerous, she wouldn't press. She started walking beside him.

The training ring was near the southeast wall. The roads weren't fully cobbled in this part of town but were made of wooden slates placed over the boards to keep the dirt from getting too muddy during the storms. The homes in the area were tiny, entire homes a little bigger than her bedroom.

Most of the people on the road were the working families of Hidan. They stepped out of her and Richard's way. Even with the distance they put between themselves and her she could hear their voices.

"She scared him away…"

"Our blessed left because of her…"

"That Kompania wouldn't even let the hunters Dieter sent talk to him…"

"She'll be gone soon enough…"

"Wish she'd leave the man though…"

"Not every attractive foreigner needs to fall under her spell…"

She tried to ignore it. She hadn't realized that Mayor Dieter had sent anyone after Deckard to try to convince him to return. She should have. Losing Deckard would have been a huge loss for Hidan, even if they'd only just found out what they'd had. As for the other part; she turned to Richard.

"Have you thought more about it?"

"About what?" Richard asked her. She wondered if he could hear the voices or if he was just playing dumb for her sake.

"Coming with us when we go."

Her sister had managed to convince the mayor to send Isashi with them for protection, but Kuzunoha hadn't had time to convince Richard to accompany them.

"Ah… Where were you going again?" He asked.

"Kalvettika." When he didn't respond fast enough, she started filling the silence between them. "It's the biggest city on this side of the continent, nearly the size of Jiza. It's Norin-controlled but they have a huge dock from what I've heard. We could probably get a ship to take us anywhere in the world from ther-"

Richard stopped her with a kiss. "Kuzunoha, you don't need to sell it so hard."

"Does that mean you will?"

"I don't know." He said. "It's to the north… and I don't know if that's the direction I should be heading in."

"Richard…"

"Do you know if you'll be coming home again after the trip?"

She bit her lip. She had gotten permission from Alfric to ride again. She was going to tomorrow, though she wouldn't be able to take care of the animal. It was disappointing since she'd enjoyed it when she was just a girl. She wouldn't even be able to attempt it until she regained her strength. Despite the confidence Himiko had presented the idea with, he'd seemed very hesitant about taking her on. She was still good with the horses; no matter how long you were out of the saddle it only took a couple of rides to get the skill back. His hesitation couldn't be due to her father's threats, not if Himiko had managed to convince him to consider it.

It probably had to do with her reputation. Why would he want someone that most of Hidan hated working for him? And while whether she worked there or not probably wouldn't change his bottom line, he would have to deal with the repercussions from the townsfolk; the snubbing of a member of their community for being with her. Even Deckard had dealt with that when they'd dated. It had been his obvious distaste of her after their relationship ended that had made them come around to love him.

Somehow, she couldn't figure out how to put all that into words.

"I don't know if working at the stables is where I'm supposed to be. I love riding the horses but it may be better for me to just buy a horse to travel with."

"You certainly still have the coin," Richard said. "Though they will get expensive eventually."

Kuzunoha stayed quiet. He let out a breath.

"This has to do with your mother, doesn't it?"

She looked away.

"Kuzunoha, if you get there and find your mother I don't mind if you stay. We promised that we'd talk about our relationship when we needed to…"

"If not now, then when?" She pressed. "I'm going to be leaving in a week and I don't know if you're going with us. Do I need to tell my sister to get you a ticket, as well? Do we need supplies for you? Will you be paying for yourself? Or will I have to pay for the privilege of having you there?"

She stopped talking, embarrassed.

They weren't too far from the market now… if she turned on the next road, she would have a straight walk to her house. Considering how she felt right now, she didn't need to rest. She'd just head home from here, crawl into her room and lock the door until she found a way to melt into the floor beneath her bed.

"Kuzunoha, are you worried that I'm just going to leave you and not tell you?"

She started walking faster and he grabbed her hand, pulling her back towards him.

"No." She couldn't meet his eyes.

He pulled her into a hug. "I wouldn't do that to you. I just don't know if Kalvettika is the best place for me to go."

"When will you know?"

Her voice was muffled by his armor. It was nice to have his scent all around her, even if the armor still stank of sweat and copper to her.

"How about this? We will be coming back into town either tonight or tomorrow. We'll have dinner at the Koi and I'll have my answer for you then. Not on our whole relationship, but at least, whether I'll accompany you to Kalvettika."

She nodded and kissed him. Kuzunoha didn't know him well enough yet to know if she wanted him forever, or if she just wanted him for the moment. What she did know was that she didn't want to lose him quite yet.

"That's all I ask."

Chapter 14

Richard drove his blades at Isashi's face, taking advantage of her moment of weakness, toppling her to the ground. He extended, pushing himself further than he normally would have, determined to land a point. Isashi swore when her elbow hit the ground and her weapon went flying. Unfortunately, she didn't wait for his attack and rolled to his far side, kicking up sand behind her. She'd left without her weapon though. Richard knocked it as far behind him as it would go and chased after her, growling when she made it to the cliff and managed to stand before he got to her. Fortunately, he didn't think even Isashi could climb it. Not here where it was nearly fifty feet of grey shards to the top.

She avoided his first attack by knocking it away with her arm braces and simply dodged his next, dodging to his left. His stick hit the rocks behind her and vibrations rocked his hand. He didn't let go of the weapon, but he could already tell his shoulder would pay for that misstep later. He bounded away from Isashi, giving them both space to breathe. It wasn't a good idea, but he needed to get rid of the sharp pain shooting from his shoulder to his wrist. Fair enough. If he could keep her away from her weapon, he'd still have the upper hand, even if that hand was effectively out of the battle. She glanced at her weapon and he leaned that direction, showing her he was ready to move the moment she did.

Isashi, damn her, leaped the other way, keeping a good six feet away from him, catching her breath. Things would have been much easier for both of them if she'd just move closer.

He stretched his fingers, spinning the stick around, trying to rid his arm of the tingles in it. Clearly, he still needed the power in it. Isashi saw and moved in, faster than he could take advantage of, aiming a kick at his left foot, still weaponless. He avoided the hit but swore as she jumped up and over him, tossing a handful of sand in his face. He sputtered, trying to use his ears instead of his eyes to find her. The sand muffled her steps and a stick thrust into his side hard enough to make spots dance in his vision.

He dropped the stick he'd been using as a weapon and raised his hands in a gesture of wordless surrender. Necessary, since he'd breathed in some of the sand and could feel the grit lodging in the back of his throat.

"Good job on trying to crowd me on the wall. If you hadn't backed off, you could have kept me on the defensive." Isashi told him.

He nodded, clearing his eyes of sand. The grit in his mouth made his defeat taste worse. Isashi was standing about two feet away, smiling at him. She was breathing heavily but hadn't worked herself into a sweat yet. He wiped the last of the sand away in disgust. He had a long way to go before he was going to be ready to face her seriously.

"The last five points have gone to you." He grumped.

Four men were watching them, taking a break from their work breaking open the cliff face. Two were exchanging money, again. The larger man was determined to make all his money back by sticking with Richard. While Richard was honored, he pitied the man's coin purse. Still, it wasn't his place to stop a fool and his money from parting.

Isashi smiled, unabashedly. "You're good, but you haven't been a hunter as long as I have."

She finished wiping the sand off the flotsam that she'd chosen as a weapon and sheathed it in her belt loop, gesturing towards the makeshift table they'd set up upon arriving. Richard walked with her. He was better at fighting than most town guards, which was something, but not enough. He would have to train harder.

Their audience looked away, now that the show he and Isashi had been putting on was over, wandering back towards the opening to the hidden lagoon.

He'd been surprised by the state of the inlet, enough that he almost hadn't recognized it. There were perhaps five or so feet of mud still caught at the top of the cliff. The rest had fallen into the water, filling the beach around it with stick mud. The deep waterway they'd swum to get into the inlet had disappeared, only a few feet high now.

While the workers thought they'd be able to open it up easily enough, it was clear that they'd have to fight the wildlife to do it. All the tiny crabs that had been living in the wall were filling the beach and dragging the mud back up the cliff in an attempt to rebuild their homes. One of the men had set traps. He was going home with no less than seven large ones already.

"You're an eledar. You could have been a hunter longer than I've been alive."

She glanced away and looked suddenly uncomfortable.

Richard smiled apologetically, realizing that he'd messed up somehow and set his own flotsam weapons on the table. The men had been eating at it and there were still crumbs on its top from the buns and fish-filling they'd all shared.

"Sorry. I suppose I should take that as the compliment it is, coming from you." He said.

"I'm not that old." Her voice was hardly more than a whisper. "Only 28 years old."

He blinked. He'd expected a century or more. In a race that could live for over a thousand years, how often would you expect to meet one only a few years older than yourself?

"Wow. You haven't had time to get used to the whole forever-thing then, I gather?"

Her smile returned, almost despite itself. "I've never heard it put that way before. Honestly, I'm not looking forward to it." She sat down, still not looking at him.

"Forever is good, so long as you have people you care about to surround yourself with."

She glanced up. "When I've found those people, perhaps. Until then... it's easy to procrastinate when you know you have forever to get things accomplished."

"Is that a nice way of saying you don't want to train anymore?" He picked up his sticks and spun them. They were lighter than he preferred as a practice weapon, but he hadn't thought to bring his own. He'd thought they would be too busy guarding the workers to practice. Isashi had said that she and the other hunter, a tall Norin, were taking turns scouting, but she could take some time to work with him.

"This has been fun." She admitted, rolling her shoulders back. "You have a style that isn't like anyone else's. Certainly no one around here."

He nodded. "It makes sense that if you're always fighting the same people or the same monsters, your style will stagnate."

He leaned over and opened the basket with the left-over food in it. Lifting up the heavily watered-down ale they'd been served with lunch, she nodded gratefully. He poured them each a glass and handed her one. She gulped down half of it and then slammed the cup back down on the table. She leaned forward, stretching her back out. The movement allowed him to see down her shirt and he admired the accidental view.

She was attractive, though it was clear that he was alone in his appreciation here. Isashi's bark-like skin shone a soft grey that felt like freshly sanded wood; soft and smooth as sin. At least the back of her hands were; they were the only place he'd been able to touch without intimacy during their training. He wondered if it would be the same in her more private areas.

She glanced up and saw where he was looking. Her cheeks didn't flush, but her eyes widened, and she grabbed her shirt, pulling it up around her neck. She didn't look angry... more pensive and embarrassed.

He growled at himself. She'd been opening up to him and in a moment of weakness, he'd sent her crawling back into her shell again.

"I'm sorry. I seem to be making mistakes all over." He filled her cup again. "I was trying to think about how to ask you about Himiko. You're her friend, yes?"

She nodded, still holding her shirt to her neck.

"She's arranging a trip to Kalvettika. I heard you were going, as well."

Isashi nodded, letting go of her shirt, though she made sure the shirt didn't fall back into its prior position.

"She's been obsessed. It's a Tanaka trait, I think… I can't say I blame them though. Family is very important to the Sian Ku. Why are you asking?"

"Kuzunoha asked me to accompany them."

"Himiko wouldn't like that." He must have looked surprised because she sounded defensive as she continued. "Don't take this the wrong way, but she doesn't really trust you."

"She thinks I'm untrustworthy?" He may not have had the best of intentions all the time, but he thought he'd proven himself worthy of her respect, if not her friendship.

Isashi winced. "That's not what I meant. She doesn't think you're going to stick around."

He shuddered. "Around Hidan? She's right. That doesn't –"

"Not Hidan, Richard. With her sister. She thinks that you'll drop Kuzunoha as soon as we arrive at a big enough city for you to lose her. And while she doesn't want you around her sister…"

"She thinks her sister will be lost, trying to follow me," Richard said.

She wasn't entirely wrong. He wanted to leave Hidan, and it had to be sooner rather than later. And he didn't know how he felt about Kuzunoha yet. She was confident and beautiful, but he felt something when he was around Kuzunoha; something he couldn't identify. It wasn't love or fear, but an uneasy feeling, like butterflies fluttering in his belly. Until he understood it, he didn't want to make any rash decisions.

"Kuzunoha knows what she signed up for. That said, I don't intend to disappear, leaving her wondering where I went. I don't abandon the women I see that way."

Isashi put up a hand to stop him. "How you run your relationships is none of my business. I am not Kuzunoha's keeper and neither is Himiko, though she'll fight you for the honor. Either way, it's your business, and Kuzu's."

He'd never heard anyone but Deckard call Kuzunoha by that nickname before. He supposed she probably avoided using it when Kuzunoha was around.

"Good enough. What do I need to know if I come?"

"Nothing that will concern you, directly. Though I should warn you… Himiko is counting on her sister's return to Hidan. If you try to take Kuzunoha any further, you'll have made an enemy."

"Legally?"

Isashi shook her head. "Personally."

That was something. It meant that there was the possibility of having to deal with bandits taking personal bounties against him, but it also meant that he had legal recourse if it happened. With it having no legal standing, no official bounty hunter would take it and it meant that he could apply to any city guard for protection within their borders.

That was a small thing, but comforting, though no matter how powerful Himiko thought she was, her reach was nothing compared to the reach of the one already after him. That one had minions of her own, and he wasn't sure if her reach had a limit. By the light of the Courtesan's Sailor, he would run until he'd found one.

He glanced at Isashi, noticing that she almost looked bored.

"You don't sound convinced of Himiko's plans."

Isashi's shoulders fell again and she glanced around. Richard wondered if she was subconsciously checking to make sure that Himiko couldn't hear her, even knowing that she was back in Hidan. Isashi had it bad, even if she hadn't realized it herself yet.

"I'm not. Kuzunoha... she doesn't fit here. She never has."

Richard felt his brows scrunch up.

"I was wondering about that. In any other town, no matter how eccentric a girl like Kuzunoha was, she'd be well thought of. Rich family, beautiful, intelligent, brave. She isn't kind, but everything else is there. Yet, everyone treats her like a leper."

Isashi narrowed her eyes. "She's... different. She doesn't react like a normal person would. She's always reacted wrong, more so when she was young though... like she was trying to learn how to respond, but never quite got it right..."

She paused, her words failing her.

"I don't understand," Richard said.

Isashi's sigh was explosive. "It's gotten better now that she's older. Almost like she's learned to pretend better. But most people in town remember those awkward years too well to forget."

"Good enough then, I suppose. What about Jack?"

Isashi looked away embarrassed. "Most react the way I mentioned. He reacts the other way; fascinated by everything she does."

"As you feel about Himiko?"

His tentative question bought him a glare, which he thought was an overreaction.

He'd first met Jack when the man had tried to convince Richard to hide any treasure they found from Kuzunoha so he could force her into a marriage. Since he hadn't, Jack had clearly decided Richard was an enemy to be squashed.

If Jack had been anyone else, Richard would have simply fought the man, embarrassed him during the battle, and left it at that. But he didn't trust that Jack wouldn't bring a knife to a fistfight. There was also the fact that he was related to the other rich family in Hidan. If you didn't work for the Tanakas, you worked on the ocean or in the docks for his family. An affront, even to a bastard of that sort of family, wouldn't be taken lightly.

Also, when Richard had seen him, paying off Kuzunoha's debt and selling him the treasure they'd found as their deal had bound them, he'd mentioned that Kuzunoha was staying at Deckard's while she healed. The look in the man's eyes had seemed unhinged, promising death as soon as he could arrange it. Jack's anger was getting worse, from what Richard could tell when he'd seen the man around the docks.

That had been why he'd asked Kuzunoha to stay away from the docks. He didn't know what it would take to finish pushing the man over the ledge to madness, but he didn't want Kuzunoha to find out firsthand.

A scream from the far side of the camp broke Isashi's glare. She balled her hands into fists and snapped around, running.

Two of the men were running to the cliffs in a panic; one had already reached them and seemed to be trying to climb it. All were keeping an eye on the water as if they expected something to drag them into the deep water against their will.

"What happened?" Isashi called to them.

She stayed between them and the water's edge, drawing her bow. Richard stood near her, just a few feet closer to the cliff. He drew his daggers, trying to see what had panicked the others.

"Auberlin… some watery tart popped up and drown him." One of the terrified men said.

Isashi and Richard raised their weapon, scanning the water's edge. Suddenly, Richard's breath caught in his throat. Thirty feet out, as a woman seemed to rise up from the waves. Dark-haired and grey-skinned, she smiled at the beach and his mind started shrieking in terrified burbles that he kept from his lips only with effort. She was holding the last sailor out of the water. The man seemed to be drowning, coughing out more water than Richard thought he could have held in his lungs.

"Auberlin…" Isashi shouted, shooting. The arrow hit the woman and the area around the wound splashed, water falling from a broken container. Then the container reformed.

The woman's torso shook as if she was laughing and she licked Auberlin's throat. Richard felt like she was staring into his soul, like everything she was doing was a show for him. Then she dove back under the waves, taking her dying captive with her.

Isashi swore, her next arrows hitting the water. The first skipped off the water, like a rock thrown just right. The rest fell into the surf.

Isashi backed away further away from the water, calling instructions and yelling for her partner.

Richard's back touched stone and his heart nearly burst from his chest. He'd backed up to the cliff without realizing it. As if there would be any defense if one of her kind were here. The beach, only ten to fifteen feet wide wouldn't stop one like her.

He'd overstayed his welcome. It was time to leave Hidan.

Chapter 15

*I*sashi was sitting on her rocking chair, her legs up to her chin, when her front door opened. She uncurled herself, turning away from the door, gritting her teeth.

"Isashi?"

"I don't want to talk about it, M –" Isashi stopped snarling when she saw Himiko. "Sorry. I thought you were my mother."

Isashi loved her parents, but while her father was proud of her profession, her mother was all too ready to console her and suggest that she didn't have to be a hunter if it was too difficult.

She turned away again. She wasn't in the mood to talk, but she'd long ago told Himiko that her door was always open for her friend. She was the only one given the privilege. Considering that Isashi had kicked even her mother out on more than one occasion, it wasn't a small thing.

"Isashi, what happened?" Himiko ran up to her, pulling her up from the chair and looking at her.

She looked away, wishing she could hide her face. She looked a mess and she knew it. Of all the people Isashi wanted to never see her like this, Himiko was her top choice.

"We lost a sailor today… Auberlin."

Part of her hoped that Himiko would turn away, would curse her out for the useless non-human that she was. Instead, Himiko opened her arms wide and pulled her into a hug. Isashi shivered. She should push Himiko away. But she needed it. Tears filled her eyes again and she turned her head, letting the tears fall onto Himiko's shirt. She sniffled, and Himiko tightened her grasp, pulling her even closer. She could feel Himiko's heart, steady and pure, beating against her chest. Her own heart felt like a rabbit, pounding its way through her.

She deserved to be alone, but at least one friend would never let that happen.

"How?" Himiko asked.

She wished she had a better answer to that. She hadn't been the only hunter there and no one should have been near the water. Isashi had been watching from the seat she'd been on and none of the sailors had even been that close to the water.

"Auberlin… I was watching all of the sailors while I talked to Richard. Everyone was safe, no one was close to the water. I didn't even see anything. According to the other sailors, he suddenly turned towards the sea. Something flashed out and dragged him in."

Isashi sniffled again and shifted. Himiko held on. There was no way for her to escape, not without doing something unforgivable to Himiko. Despite how uncomfortable she felt, she couldn't make Himiko let go of her. Considering how she was starting to feel, it would have broken her heart.

"What was it?" Himiko leaned away, just far enough to catch her eyes.

Brandy Ackerley

Isashi pushed away, trying to hide again. Himiko yanked her closer, pulling Isashi's head on her shoulder again. Isashi smiled despite herself. And sniffled. Her nose was plugged, even if her eyes had dried again. That was what Himiko did to her. Wrapped tightly in her business-oriented friend's arms, she shouldn't have felt protected, shouldn't have felt stronger herself. But she did.

"Something new."

"Again?" Himiko sounded horrified. Isashi sighed.

"New creatures aren't unknown; we usually see a new type every year or two. Three completely different creatures in as many weeks… It's too much. We've never seen this before."

Himiko's arms tightened as she pushed away again.

"You need this…" Himiko's voice was tight. "Don't push me away."

Isashi sniffled again and pulled away just far enough to look into Himiko's beautiful eyes. Whoever said that dark brown eyes weren't as attractive as lighter colors had never seen Himiko's. They were the more expressive than her own green eyes and held depths of black and orange in them, sun and moonless sky in equal balance.

"I won't push you away," Isashi's voice caught in her throat, "but if I don't let you go, you're going to have snot in your hair."

Himiko shook her head and leaned against Isashi's chest.

"I can wash my hair if I need to. Hold me as long as you need."

Isashi felt her lips break into a tiny smile.

"Thank you." She lifted Himiko's head up so they could see each other again.

Such a tiny distance between them. It was still too large for her to cover.

"You're smiling now." Himiko's mouth curved into one of her own. "That's better."

Isashi nodded. This time when she let go of Himiko, her friend let her.

She was a coward.

"Did the creature tempt him closer to the water's edge?" Himiko asked, looking around.

Isashi followed suit, suddenly embarrassed. Her house always had an unlived feel to it, since she only lived in it when she was staying in town. Her bed couldn't hold more than one and she hid it behind a plain paper wall. She had a rocking chair and a stool that didn't match with each other, or the simple table just beside the black metal stove that heated her house in the winter. Her single shelf had two statuettes on it, clay things she'd made when she'd been young.

She had an armor dummy set up in the corner with a tiny rack beside it for her weapons. Normally she put each item pristinely in its place, but today, everything, including her kit, had been tossed in a pile in front of the rack.

The one thing that stood out from everything else in the room was an old book, tucked up against her alcohol that she'd found years ago in a forgotten box in the swamp. Decrepit with age, the lock had nearly fallen apart when she tried to clear off the rust. From what she could tell, it had been abandoned by someone decades ago. She'd tried to find the owner, but no one in town had ever seen it or even expressed interest in claiming it aside from the Norin church, and that had been because it contained lesser-known myths of their religion. While she followed the gods of her mother, her father's deities still interested her, and she found the myths comforting and had kept it herself.

"I don't know. None of the men were sure. One said he'd heard some sort of music, but the others heard nothing."

She gestured for Himiko to take a seat. Both were of hard plain wood, with only a few beginners' carvings on them. Though both seats had cushions tied to the seat, neither the colors nor the designs matched.

She waited until Himiko had sat down in the stool before she poured out a drink for both of them. The whiskey was cheap but strong, and she served it in the only cups she had, a ceramic interior set into a wooden base carved with tree vines.

Himiko took her whiskey and sipped. If she didn't think it was up to her normal standard, she didn't say anything.

"Have you talked to Samuel yet?"

Isashi had only just placed her cup to her lips. Instead of sipping she drained her cup in a single gulp and slammed it on the table.

"That good?" Himiko asked.

Isashi refilled her cup and stalked to her favorite chair. She sat and pulled her knees up to her chin again, letting its rocking motion soothe her.

"I'm off duty until we return from Kalvettika."

"Off duty?"

"He doesn't trust me to protect people anymore."

"Himiko, I'm sure he only has your best interests at heart."

Isashi snorted at that. Himiko leaned towards her.

"You've seen two people die before your eyes. Aren't you usually given time off anyway when that happens?"

"Sometimes. If we can afford to lose a hunter."

They couldn't now though, not with Hana gone. Yes, Isashi leaving still left them with three, the number of hunters a place Hidan's size would normally have, but they were used to having more than that.

"The others haven't needed it."

"The others haven't been dealing directly with the dead. Didn't you find that other body too, Carlos' nephew, before all this started?"

Isashi nodded, not liking the picture that Himiko was painting. It sounded reasonable. It felt everything but.

Himiko let out a breath. "It's been a damned difficult around here lately, hasn't it?"

"It's never easy to lose someone we're trying to protect."

"And even harder to lose a friend." Himiko reached out for her.

Isashi smiled, and put her feet on the floor, reaching her fingers out too. Their fingertips brushed lightly together before Himiko leaned back, Isashi following suit.

"I have had enough of talking about my life though. How was your day? I could use the distraction." Isashi said.

"As distractions go, you were mine. I was planning for the trip. We should be able to make four different stops on the way, so I want to bring enough gifts for everyone on our list and a few extras, plus some stock. Logistics, which is boring as hell, though the trip itself should be fun."

"Logistics? That sounds worse than boring."

"I don't mind them, though I admit, it isn't the favorite part of my job. I've already worked with Tim planning everything for the next few months while I'm gone."

"I spoke with Richard," Isashi said, noting Himiko's uncomfortable glance into her cup. "He hasn't made a firm decision yet, but I think you can plan on him coming. At least, on the way there. Honestly, you could do worse than offering him a position as a guard."

"You think he's that trustworthy?"

Himiko immediately regretted her snarky question. Richard may not have very honorable intentions, but he wasn't the criminal she'd originally thought him to be.

"Yes. Plus, it would make your sister happy."

Himiko snorted. "I think Kuzunoha could do with less accommodating, but you're probably right. Whether I like him or not is beside the point."

"Speaking of, did you ask Kuzunoha about that thing on her sword?"

She'd mentioned something about wanting the little ring from Kuzunoha's sword. Something about it being one of the family signets. Himiko looked away.

"You have to ask her."

"But, I… I mean, we know she's going to bring the sword. It'll be fine. I can ask her anywhere between here and Kalvettika. Plenty of time."

"Why are you doing this?"

Himiko stared into the cup. "If I ask her now, she'll think it's the only reason I asked her to come. It will push her away. She won't come back."

"You think she'll react better if you wait until you're in Kalvettika?"

"I think I might be able to put it to her as something I didn't realize I'd need. I mean, our family… they won't know us or my father's name or anything. If I want them to trust me, I can't go with just the book. It won't be enough. I'm taking other proof but I'll need the signet too. So long as Kuzunoha doesn't find out later…"

Himiko let her words fade away.

"She's probably already considered it, Himiko. If you don't want her to think you were just using her for the blade, tell her."

Himiko avoided answering by taking a large drink of her whiskey.

"I'll think about it."

"Will you at least talk to Richard?"

Himiko rolled her eyes, then she opened them, looking crafty.

"Wait. You said he's good in a fight, right?" Isashi nodded. "I'll ask him to join us, as an additional guard there."

"Why?" Isashi asked, insulted that Himiko might agree with Samuel that she wasn't able to do her job.

"It will help to put space between him and my sister," Himiko said with glee.

"What? How?" Isashi was confused now.

"If she thinks he's only there because he's been paid to stay with her, she'll lose her attraction. No wedding bells to worry about."

"Kuzunoha seems uninterested in marrying. Period." Isashi said.

"That's just Jack she has no interest in… which honestly is a disappointment. If our father had been less stuck up, he would have realized that connecting both our families in town would have given both of us a lot more power to work together than we have now. It would have been good for Hidan." Himiko said.

"Himiko..." Isashi started. Himiko cut her off.

"Well, I can't very well let her run off with Richard, can I? What will my ancestors think if I let the only other member of the family run off on her own?"

Himiko drank down all of her whiskey and set the cup on the floor beside her chair.

"They'd think you did the best you could with a very bad hand," Isashi muttered.

"If only she'd been born male…" Himiko murmured, "Father could have sent her away to join the army or something. No dishonor there."

"She could have gone anyway. Women fight nearly as often as men do. The real problem is that Kuzunoha has never followed an order in her life." Isashi said. Himiko made a strangled sound and Isashi leaned forward. "Himiko? What's wrong?"

Himiko looked on the verge of tears.

"Isashi, if she doesn't belong here, then where? She was my father's mistake, and everyone knew it. There was no way I could give her any control over the family businesses. Even placing her as an equal could muddy the line of succession later." She took a deep breath and closed her eyes. "Kuzunoha may not like it, but regardless of her majority, it's still my job to take care of her."

Isashi stood and refilled both cups. She handed Himiko's back and sat down, raising her cup.

"To impossible tasks?"

Himiko reached forward so they could clink their glasses together.

"To impossible tasks."

Isashi lifted her cup to her face and watched Himiko sip her own, resisting an urge to reach out and hold Himiko as if her arms could solve Himiko's problems as easily as she'd helped Isashi with her own.

Chapter 16

*D*eckard huffed his way through the weapons set. If nothing else, the workout was meditative. He always felt more focused afterward. He had known living without walls would bother him, but he hadn't realized how much. Walls meant protection, safety, and comfort. The sword at his waist didn't. One day, it might, when he'd gotten used to having it there, but for now... it just felt wrong, especially as he'd only just managed to stop bumping it into everything he walked by.

His unease made him doubly glad that they hadn't been attacked yet. He'd known that being outside the city wasn't an automatic death sentence. After all, he'd gone out of Hidan multiple times each year, wandering the swamp for an afternoon, usually looking for fresh herbs. Yet, he'd always felt certain that the cities were the lights in the darkness, rather than the monsters being spots of dark marring the light.

He reached the end of the set, and breathing deeply, placed the tip of the wooden sword on the ground. He'd thought he'd been in shape but, between the weapon training and the forge, he was coming to see just how out of shape he was. His shirt was sticky with sweat and he pulled the offending garment off. While he drank some water from the open barrel, he heard a collective sigh. He froze but didn't turn, continuing to drink as if nothing had changed.

Only after he'd finished, did he turn to look at his audience. Six women, all of marriageable age, single and generally attractive. There was only one stood out to him, a dark-haired woman with full red lips. All of them had hungry gazes locked on him. One, wearing blue, yellow, and orange, wet her lips with her tongue while she watched him.

Most of the men nearby shook their heads, annoyance at Deckard for taking their attention writ large on their faces. They continued with their sets, but Ursa, a bear of a man near Deckard's age, took off his shirt as well, smiling at the ladies as he did so.

Danior walked up to the women. "Honestly girls, he is simply a man with his shirt off. Nothing new. You don't all watch me when I train with the blade."

The girl with multiple gold hoops in her ears replied, "We might if you ever took your shirt off."

One woman's red lips turned in a frown. She was dressed brightly; bits of something reflective accenting her voluminous multi-colored skirt.

"We're related to you, Uncle Danior. No one is related to him."

Danior rolled his eyes and clapped his hands. "That's it. Everyone back to work. You can gawk later when the work is finished."

Most of the girls scurried away, but the woman who'd spoken last didn't move. Danior scowled at her.

"You too, Charani."

Charani glared at Danior and stepped away, catching Deckard's eye. She gestured towards one of the caravans on the outer circle, most likely her own. He shook his head. He was with Tieni, though even if he hadn't been, he had never been one for random dalliances. Danior's eyes narrowed and Charani pouted as she turned to leave.

He would have to thank Danior when he got a chance. But Danior's glance now suggested that he'd better continue his work.

Deckard walked back to his place and drew the weapon, drawing the weapon through the air to the left, holding his pose long enough to make his arm ache. His arms weren't burning yet, but they would be later.

He started another practice set; a series of slashes and movements designed to look like a dance but teaching good movement for the weapons as well. As graceful as it was, the weapon wasn't quite for him, but he couldn't say why. Tieni had said that it was because no weapon felt right yet. She could be right. He had chosen a super-thin blade made to stab rather than rend an opponent; maybe the traditional weapons of the Norin would feel better in his hand than the slimmer blades that Danior's kompania preferred.

"Get to work, Charani. He's taken." Deckard heard Tieni say.

Deckard turned. The girl had returned to the water barrel again as soon as Danior had walked away and had been watching him again. He ignored her and smiled at Tieni, nodding at her as he continued to move through the movements.

"For how long?"

Charani's words slithered in the air, much like the rattle of a snake might. His hands tightened on the hilt. He knew Tieni could defend herself, especially against words. It didn't stop him from wanting to go over and step between the two.

"Langer than de boy be wid us," said Morjiana, loudly enough that Deckard's ears rang.

He ducked his head. That was what he deserved for listening in on conversations, even if they were about him.

Realizing that he couldn't pretend he wasn't paying attention anymore, Deckard turned and smiled at Tieni again, even giving a quick nod to Morjiana. Charani's eyes widened when she realized he'd snubbed her. She flounced away; a cascade of red, blue, and green bits reflecting everything.

"Let me finish this and I'll join you," he said.

His arms felt like jelly when he finally finished his sets. He put the fake weapon on the rack, next to the others, and grabbed his real blade, hooking it into his belt. His shirt was dry now, though he'd still need to wash it soon. He tossed it over his shoulder. He could wash and hang it later.

"He's getting much better." Tieni was telling Morjiana. The older woman nodded and Tieni asked in a false hushed voice. "Will we be traveling long enough for him to get really good with the weapon?"

Morjiana's eyes closed for a moment before she spoke again. "He'll be here lang 'nough to save a life n' take one."

Tieni frowned, clearly annoyed that the healer hadn't gone along with her coy question. He was much more concerned about her words.

"Killing someone is always a last resort," he reminded both of them. Death was nothing to joke about.

"Even if it be a monster?" Morjiana asked. The way she said the final word made it sound like maan-star.

His lips tightened to a line. "Monsters don't deserve our sympathy."

He had never forgotten running for Hidan, desperately trying to keep up with his mother and father. A group of birdos behind them, screeching and howling, the tiny skulls and bones they wore cracking against each other, when a group of guards had appeared with two warriors at their head. His father tripped hard, crashing against a stump. Deckard had tried to turn, chubby hands reaching out, but his mother had dragged him towards the walls. Samuel and another hunter had started firing arrows as the goblins leaped onto his father's back, snapping and chewing at his flesh.

The last thing he'd seen had been the birdos' skulls covered in his father's blood. Samuel had told his mother that he'd shot Deckard's father himself to save the man pain since there had been too many creatures there to rescue him. Only he and his mother had arrived to take the empty healer's house in Hidan.

The woman shook her head. "You won't kill the monster. You'll mourn it and damn the man."

Tieni sucked in a breath. "Morjiana... you can't mean..."

"That part's been written, Tieni. Can't change it now."

Deckard's blood ran cold. Some of the Corvidae were supposedly gifted with visions of the future. He hadn't realized that Morjiana truly had the power to see the future, he had thought it was an act she put on for the people they swindled into paying for knowledge of their futures.

His own people's god, Kittin, was able to see the future but she granted that knowledge imperfectly and then, only to her priests. The priests said that there were keystones in every life, events upon which an entire life was based. While the priests could ferret out those secrets if they tried, they warned that even Kittin herself had misunderstood the first prophecy, bringing herself nothing but pain.

His fists clenched, though what he wanted to do was to show Morjiana his palm like Kittin's avatar had done when it had banished the first monster. The gesture was said to protect against evil.

Morjiana wasn't evil though. She was simply a follower of the Dead like Tieni was. A different set of beliefs and values, no matter how odd or wrong they sometimes seemed.

"Thank you, Morjiana. I will do my best to stop it from occurring."

He didn't think he could avoid the pronouncement since it had already been said, and he knew he'd never mourn a monster. All he could do was stick to his beliefs and try hard not to kill.

Morjiana shook her head, muttering, "Won't work, but everyone's gotz ta try."

She walked away, leaving him and Tieni to themselves.

"Is she..."

"She is real, one of the best of the Corvidae clans in the country. You're taking this well."

Tieni's expression told him that she, at least, believed in Morjiana's power.

He shrugged. "Not a lot I can do then. Either it's a keystone and will happen, or it isn't and may not."

Tieni's eyes flashed. "Your priests may not read the future correctly, but our seers…"

Deckard pulled her close. "I'm not trying to be dismissive, Tieni. But all she said is that I will have to kill somebody while we travel. We both know that there are bandits who hunt these lands; they hunt everywhere. That's why I'm learning to use this sword, right?"

"She also said that you'll mourn a monster."

"Which makes no sense. Mourn not killing it faster, but mourning its loss? It makes no sense. Worrying about it won't help."

Tieni sighed. "True. Still, if anyone could mourn a monster, it would be you. You're compassionate beyond reason sometimes."

He mumbled amused agreement against her lips as he kissed her. Tieni fell against him and he felt her hands lift to his chest.

They both heard a yell and stepped apart. One of the younger boys, Tyler ran up to them.

"Deckard, sir. Ruslo needs your help with the furnace." The boy called to him.

Deckard nodded and kissed Tieni once more. "I love you. No killing your cousins over me."

Tieni glanced towards the distance where Charani had disappeared. "You didn't even look twice at her, did you?"

He grinned. "With that personality? When I already have you? It's not even worth considering."

Tieni's eyes shone as she pulled away. "I promise. See you at the meal."

Deckard grinned and left to find Ruslo.

Chapter 17

*R*ichard slammed Isashi's weapon with his own, twisting his blades to make her lose her weapon. The wooden weapons cracked together, and he hoped her weapon would break and that only his would remain. His ears rang and all of the weapons remained whole. Isashi's grip didn't even waver. He fell back as she pushed, giving her room to breathe.

He wanted to growl, to go from practice to real and take her down. Only the reminder that she wasn't his true enemy, wasn't the one he wanted to hit, held him back.

It had been a week since the attack, and he was still in Hidan.

Locked in a town no bigger than a single neighborhood in Jiza, he had spoken to everybody about when the next caravan leaving was, where the nearest towns were, or even if there were any Corvidae nearby that he could reach with little to no traveling. No one had any answers that didn't include leaving by sea. The only option left open for him was to take the ship with everyone that evening. Though at least now he was being paid a guard's salary to go.

Richard tossed one of his wooden knives in the air and caught it at a different angle, turning it into a throwing knife. He threw it at her head. The blade was less than a finger's width from her head when she turned, leaning away to avoid the attack. He pressed forward with his remaining blade, hoping that the distraction would give him the upper hand.

She caught his weapon with her own again, before he could even score a point and he pulled another wooden knife out from the sheath on his back, arming himself again.

She pulled in a hard breath and struck for his spleen. He used his new weapon to deflect hers, glad that he wasn't the only one being pushed by this battle. The moment he knew that momentum would carry her blade away from him, he yanked his right blade away and drove it at her. She just managed to avoid it and slide out of his reach.

"Sneaky..." She wheezed at him. "Always getting in my space."

In a fight against someone with a blade nearly three times the length of his own, it was the only tactic that would let him win. He had to get so close that she wouldn't be able to swing her blade. He had to make her weapon too unwieldy to use.

"If you think you can't win, I'll graciously accept your submission." He said, gulping for air every other word.

She frowned, but he didn't give her a chance to respond. Leaping towards her, he feinted right and then cut back to the left once she'd committed to the block. With a sense of elation, his blade smacked her in the side, the first solid, deadly hit he had gotten against her.

"Point!" he crowed, almost missing her blade striking at him. He leaped out of the way, frustration filling his features.

"Wrong." She told him.

He glared, gripping his knife harder. She was right, darkness damned.

By their agreed rules, it wasn't a guaranteed kill-point on an armored individual and the blow from the weapon might not have been hard enough. He slid behind her, stabbing low. She slid out of the way and he saw her blade coming in from above. He rolled to the right and slid a few inches on his back, watching while her blade smacked the ground where his neck had been just moments before. She was grinning now, enjoying the fight more now that she thought she had the upper hand. Richard leaped for her leg from a crouch, slashing a line from the back to the front. He took a deep breath, vulnerable, while Isashi worked to stay on her feet.

"Point." He said.

"Armor." She argued again.

Half of his blow had been across the front, but the sliding to the back of the knee could have caused her a loss of mobility, slicing through the arteries that could have been a killing point. That was too much to say while he was out of breath.

"Half-point," he growled, kicking her leg to bring her down to the ground.

She dropped her blade and collapsed on him. Richard's breath fell out in a huff. It was fortunate that he was already breathing so heavily that the extra gasps he needed to get air were only a little more difficult.

Isashi muttered under her breath and tried to grab one of his knives. They wrestled, and he growled distractedly as she pushed her hips down on his. Isashi finally managed to steal a knife and held it to his throat.

"Kill-point," she said, breathing heavily. "I win."

Richard pushed up and Isashi forced his shoulders back to the ground. She wanted to hear him admit defeat before she'd let him up. He hated the superiority on her face. He moved his hips beneath her.

"If you wanted a ride, m'lady, all you had to do was ask." He panted.

Her smile vanished and so did her body, faster than she would have if she'd had no interest at all. He lay back, wheezing. He had thought she'd only been interested in Kuzunoha's sister, not him. He glanced over. Isashi's shoulders were curved forward and she wouldn't meet his eyes. He silently swore. He hadn't meant to hurt her. Or at least, he hadn't meant to do anything more than make her a bit uncomfortable.

"We aren't dating." She told him. Her voice was steady, even if her body language wasn't. "We are training. If you don't understand that, we stop. Now."

"I'm sorry." He said, sitting up. "I didn't mean it that way."

"Yeah, well..." Isashi stood, her eyes going to Kuzunoha. She'd come to get a few pointers, but she wasn't watching them. Instead, she seemed to be contemplating her sword.

"I just don't think it's appropriate." Isashi finished

She wasn't wrong, if not for the reasons she thought it was. He nodded, waiting. Isashi let out a breath and moved forward, giving him a hand up. He grinned and took it.

"What is it about my relationship that bothers you? She and I have talked about it and neither of us wants to be tied solely to the other."

Isashi shook her head. "That isn't it."

"You feel that you can only love one person at a time?" He gestured for Kuzunoha to come over. She didn't seem to notice. "I know the gods here demand it for piety's sake."

Isashi shook her head.

"My father's gods think lust is wrong if that lust isn't directed at someone you want to be with. Permanently. If you haven't proposed in a year… there had better be a reason. My mother's gods, the same as Kuzunoha's, are worse. Even a generation ago most marriages were arranged. Especially if you're rich or belong to an important family."

Richard shook his head, still trying to get Kuzunoha's attention.

"Marriages are arranged all the time in my homeland, but most include a clause where you are allowed to stray. Sex is sex... it can be part of love or it can be separate."

He was about to yell at Kuzunoha when Isashi asked, "So, you don't love her at all?"

Richard turned. This needed his full attention. No hurting her, no confusion.

"Kuzunoha and I have known each other for what? Two months? That's hardly long enough to get to know somebody, let alone fall in love with them."

"Yes, but…"

"I care for her. I risked my life for her." It was unfortunate that Isashi wouldn't understand how serious that was. That was too private to explain. He saw Kuzunoha finally look up and start jogging over. "Don't trivialize my feelings. I care for her, deeply, but where I come from, marriage has nothing to do with love. One of the reasons I do feel as I do is that she understands this."

"Who's in love?" Kuzunoha said as she got close enough.

"I shouldn't have asked," Isashi muttered, giving her a pointed look.

Kuzunoha paused for a mere half-second too long before she laughed, realizing they'd been talking about her. Richard winced inwardly. The laugh wasn't forced, wasn't false, but neither was it self-confident enough to convince him that she was completely sure about their arrangement.

"I don't see either of us falling for each other," Kuzunoha said. "Certainly not this fast."

That sounded much more self-assured and he let out a breath that he hadn't realized he'd been holding. He liked Kuzunoha, respected her, and he didn't want to hurt her.

It was hard to trust though. She wasn't a follower of the Courtesan, though she also didn't have the shame that so many others here tied up with their intimacy. Still, he would talk to her later about it. He wanted her to understand, not just accept. He didn't want to lead her on.

"Your sister… wouldn't approve." Isashi said. She sounded unsure of herself. "But, either way, it's your choice to make. I need to go to the baths now if I'm to have time to make sure everything is packed for the trip. You two are ready to go?"

Richard's teeth ground together. Everything led back to the water and this boat. He didn't like it.

"It was easy for me to pack," Richard said, gesturing to the spot Kuzunoha had been sitting. It wasn't as though he'd had to make hard decisions on what to leave behind. Everything he owned was in those two bags.

Kuzunoha didn't look guilty, but she did look unsure. She waved to her weapons master as he entered the circle. The man gestured for her to continue her conversation. He probably wanted time to set up the training dummy for her. She was getting better, but still not good enough to work on anything more than the basics.

"I'm packed," she said.

"Afraid you're leaving something important behind?" Richard asked.

Isashi frowned and Kuzunoha gave him a dirty look.

"I see I shouldn't have asked," Isashi said. "I'll see you on the ship."

Richard waited until she was out of earshot. "You're still unsure?"

"Of us?" She shook her head, a little too violently. "No… I… my sister worked to find me a life here. I keep thinking… The stablemaster understood when I spoke to him yesterday. He was willing to consider me, even though I'm about six years older than a traditional apprentice would be. At the same time… I don't think I can be happy here."

Richard shook his head and grabbed her hands. "Kuzunoha, I have bound you to no contracts or agreements. If we get to Kalvettika and you decide that you decide this is where you need to be, I'll support that choice. No regrets. Don't let your sister stop you from finding the life you want."

Kuzunoha glanced towards her family's home. Sadness and loss fought for space on her features. Richard suddenly understood what was bothering her.

"Did you just realize that today may be the last time you'll see Hidan?"

She spun away from him, her eyes wet.

"If I leave, nothing will change for them. Nothing. They won't even remember me later."

"Kuzunoha." The weapon master called for her. "Come, it's time to show me what you've learned before you go."

Richard leaned forward to kiss her.

"I'll wait here. Afterward, we can go through what you've packed. I'll do my best to make sure you're not forgetting anything that might be important. We'll talk. Happiness isn't a place. It's being comfortable, safe and loved, and knowing that's true wherever you are."

She nodded, and a real smile caught at her lips finally.

"Thank you, Richard." She said and wiped at her eyes once before heading to greet her weapons master.

Richard thought of the few items he'd taken with him when he left home. All of them were gone now; his mother's necklace, a worthless bauble that she'd always left with him when she went to 'work' for her pimp, the poem his first crush, Chandana, had written for him, and the knife his father had given him the day before he was killed.

One day, he'd find out what happened to all of them. For now, he'd do what he could to make sure that Kuzunoha wouldn't be left feeling like she'd lost everything when she left Hidan. Perhaps he couldn't get his past back, but he could make sure that Kuzunoha didn't lose hers.

Chapter 18

*D*eckard smiled at the children as they screamed in delight, feigning fear, running towards their parents. Their pleasure was infectious, even if it was tempered by the knowledge that their fearlessness wasn't universally shared. The unhappy expressions of the children's parents told him that much. He waved once more. None of the children dared to wave back once their hands were grasped tightly by their parents and they were summarily dragged back inside the village's walls. One of the children looked back though, a boy no older than Deckard had been the first time he had left home.

It was the same in every village they stopped in. People liked the wares they brought, loved the interesting sights and sounds of visitors, but they didn't trust the Corvidae. No more than six of them were allowed in the city during daylight hours. Less than that at night. You had to be ready to show that you had stolen nothing at any turn and if you dared to buy anything from their market it was twice as much as a member of the town would pay. It was galling and worse to realize that everyone in Hidan had been this bad as well.

He had never bought into that belief that those who chose to live outside the safety of a walled city were untrustworthy or thieves; he would never have gotten to know Tieni if he had been that sort, but he'd never tried to stop the rumors about them, either. It was worse being on the other side of the equation, knowing that every one of these kids would be listening to stories of children taken in the night by wild crow magic, sacrifices for their dead god by this time next week.

Deckard wished he could change that but knew he would have to be satisfied that at least one of those children would question the tales told over the next few days.

He stretched and walked closer to Morjiana's tent, a dark blue cloth with strange sigils that looked like tiny stars painted upon it if you were further away than a few feet. As soon as the children were inside the walls he was in charge of helping Morjiana pack it up.

In town, everyone had more than one job. His was to provide a welcoming friendly face for those wishing to have their metal ware fixed. The Norin population responded nicely to him, assuming that he was simply paying his way, helping them while he traveled. He wasn't trusted, but he wasn't considered immediately suspect.

Morjiana's task of the fortune teller was always popular. More often than not there was no magic; just a watchful eye and helpful advice. He understood that it was mostly perception and tricks used to provide comfort, but he felt bad for the girls who flocked to her wagon, seeking a future and truth that was as more likely to be fake than not.

Deckard made certain that he was far enough back that the two girls Morjiana was talking to wouldn't notice he was there. The girls were enjoying their 'taste of danger;' leaning forward, their eyes wide as they took in every word. When Morjiana finished, she clapped once, glittery dust billowing dramatically from her hands. The girls passed a knowing, eager glance with each other before removing thin bracelets off their hands and passing them over.

Morjiana took these with the proper solemnity, though almost certainly the bracelets were nearly worthless. Deckard now knew that they would be cleaned and sold for a pittance the next town over. So much of the danger that townsfolk feared was just smoke and mirrors. Nobody would fear the Corvidae if they could travel with one for a few weeks.

He smiled and nodded at the girls as they walked past him, until the taller girl looked at him. Her expression, her posture. It was like the first time he'd seen Kuzunoha all over again.

He'd been trying to find his way to the general store for more bandages for his mother. He had never found out where she was going that day, or why she looked dour, he only remembered her expression and her beauty. He'd wanted to help her, to make her smile.

He turned away like he had that first day. It had been nerves that had stopped him. Today, it was the memory of everything after. Kuzunoha had cheated on him, broken his heart. He hadn't thought she could hurt him worse until the day he left. That wasn't her fault, he knew that even if it felt that way. A hand touched his shoulder.

"You ain't 'ngry t'at her." Lady Morjiana said, her accent as thick as ever. "You sad you ain't going to see dem again. Won' ease your heart to know, but you ain't gots to worry 'bout dat."

He nearly snapped; nearly lost control. He was very proud that his voice was only tight.

"I highly doubt that. I never plan on going back to Hidan."

Kuzunoha, for all her bluff, would stay there. She was proud of her home, her heritage, even if he'd always thought her father wasn't worthy of it. Also, he needed her to be there, to stay. Something had to remain there for him. In case, he ever had to return.

She shook her head. "Deckard, you be 'ngry, so 'ngry. It burn de air 'roun you and make a corona 'a hate. You gonna destroy youself. An' I worry you gonna take that gurl over de edge wit you."

Deckard was struck silent for a moment. "I would never do anything to hurt Tieni."

Morjiana turned to the other side of the field where Tieni was pulling down the stage. She played the part of a beautiful princess as well as a humorless warrior. The irony of her wasn't lost to him. She would have preferred a priestess position or maybe one of the magi sidekick characters, but of course, those were the prized roles. Being such a new member of the Kompania meant she hadn't earned her right to play one yet.

Morjiana raised an eyebrow. "You a'ready made da choice.... you chus don know it yet."

"How would you know?"

She raised an eyebrow. "You don believe de gods that gave you your powah would let you be free, do you? De gods... de be harsh mastahs when you don listen."

Tieni moved towards them, carrying a huge bag in front of her.

"Deckard, Lady Morjiana? Are the rest of the kennicks gone? We could use your help in camp. In particular, Ruslo will need you with the forge, Deckard. A lot of stuff for us to fix by morning."

Deckard waved at Tieni and turned back to Morjiana's cart. "I'll take this down for you. You should get into camp."

As if listening to the gods would help. They didn't direct… they listened. He didn't have a priest to talk to about it. With that avenue gone, all he had left were his dreams… and he didn't think that resting his future on a self-interpretation of a dream was any way to live his life.

Besides, if he ever did talk with them, he'd tell them exactly what he thought of their blessing to him; he'd throw it back in their faces and leave.

The cart was quick to pack up. He was still feeling hurt when he neared the forges and threw himself into the work, putting on the thick apron and gloves with pleasure. By the time he was done, he knew he'd be too tired to think more about things he couldn't change.

He'd just managed to get his second piece, a fork that needed to be reset, onto the anvil when the peal of a bell chimed over the caravans. Deckard held his breath. One chime was for an immediate group meeting and two meant strangers approaching. This late, he couldn't imagine anyone leaving town, which only left the road or the forest surrounding the field they were in. Deckard paled as the bell rang a third time.

"Mongrels," Ruslo swore.

Deckard turned, hearing a guttural barking, like sick foxes, behind them. Coming towards him and Ruslo were four creatures, a little bigger than a child of eight, with brown mottled skin, big floppy ears, and teeth dyed orange with old blood. Their clothes looked like they'd been pulled out of the garbage, stained and ripped, none of it matching.

Deckard's hand reached down for his blade and found nothing. He swore and decided the hammer would be a better weapon than the hot tongs. Ruslo shook his head, bearing a curved sword in his right hand.

"Careful. The tool is worth more than their hides." The blacksmith growled at him.

Deckard's response was lost in the howls as the monsters dove in, their teeth and claws gleaming red in the forge light.

Deckard gripped the hammer tight in his hand and swung hard as the first creature neared him. The creature didn't even slow as it easily dodged the weapon. Deckard cursed, trying to bring the heavy weapon back around. It was difficult to control but he managed to get a glancing hit in on the next. The thing shrieked and jumped back grabbing its ear and screaming, its cry vibrating like glass. The air itself seemed to shatter under its weight. Despite the lack of clear air, Deckard appreciated the sound. As long as the thing was screaming, it wasn't fighting. Which meant he only had to deal with the other one.

A rash of claws down Deckard's back made him hiss with pain and for a moment, the only thing he could see was golden dragons dancing to the tune of the inhuman scream. The cuts burned almost pleasantly. He pulled back on the power before he was healed completely. There would be questions enough about this battle if anyone other than Tieni ever saw the cuts... he didn't want to deal with the questions that would come of a shirt ruined with claws and his back completely uninjured.

The stinging pain seemed to give his arm strength. He used it to aim the hammer at the creature's face.

Terrifyingly, the creature didn't seem to notice the hammer strike, or its dented skull, as it hissed and pushed its way past his weapon. Deckard pulled back the hammer, but too slow to stop the creature from chomping at his hand. Fortunately, the creature's teeth weren't sharp enough to tear through the thick leather gloves in one bite.

Deckard dropped the hammer and pulled his knife. It was made for paring fruit and cracking open tough herb shells; Deckard didn't even know if it could hurt the thing. On the other hand, anything was better than letting the thing figure out that his gloves were already starting to strain under its teeth.

Fortunately, the knife slid into the creature's neck with ease, parting bone and sinew like jelly. The creature bit down even harder, but it started gurgling blood and Deckard knew it couldn't last long.

Behind him, there was a violent yipping and Deckard turned just in time to see the last creature die as Ruslo's blade sliced through its oversized head.

Deckard felt the bile rise as the bones seemed to boil, melting into the thing's body. He turned, throwing up as he smacked at the creature attached to his glove. Ruslo caught him and used his sword to pry the things teeth off of Deckard.

While he tried to catch his breath, Deckard heard the bells ringing again. The pattern seemed familiar, but his mind couldn't translate them. Was it more of the creatures, coming to hunt them in deadly waves, till the caravan was overrun? He waited, his breathing fast and hard but no more came.

Bile rose in his throat again, burning like acid and tasting faintly of the cheese that he'd eaten with his meat at lunch. He took a deep breath and swallowed slowly, trying to ignore the taste in his mouth turning his stomach while he stared at the corpses on the ground.

Ruslo's heavy hand on his back helped.

"It's alright, man. We repelled the attack. Finish throwing up. The first time is always the most difficult."

Deckard didn't, but he did spit, trying to clear his throat of the bile still bubbling there. Ruslo passed him a small bowl filled with water. Deckard rinsed his mouth out, spitting again before he drank some. It didn't settle his stomach, but he could handle it. He handed the bowl back. Ruslo refilled it for him.

"Thank you. I was fine until I saw..." Deckard gestured towards the creature and Ruslo nodded.

"The mongrels do that whenever they're hit. They form back up solid soon after, but it makes them almost impossible to kill with a hammer." He handed the water back.

Deckard shook his head, staring into the bowl. "I meant the... melting."

Ruslo's response was casual. "Yeah, most monsters don't leave behind bodies. The mongrels are worse. They melt, leaving nothing but the junk they were carrying, pitted and scarred to hell. Where is your sword? It's a stupid thing to forget somewhere."

Everybody was expected to defend the caravan during times of attack. He knew that. How could he have left it somewhere? Was it still in his room? He remembered taking it off at lunch. Deckard nodded.

"At lunch, I left it..."

Ruslo stopped him. "Find it before dinner, if you don't want Danior and the others ribbing you all week. Head into the center and make sure nobody needs to be stitched up first though. I'll take care of the bodies over here. Tell Danior you left your sword here if he asks, in the creature you killed. You'll still get ribbed, but less than if he knew you'd forgotten it completely."

Deckard nodded. His heartbeat was slowing finally, but his stomach was still roiling. He took a deep breath. He had work to do. He could process what had happened when people weren't injured.

"Hey, you're bleeding. Why didn't you say something? You okay?"

Deckard glanced at Ruslo. The man was staring at his back. Deckard stretched out his shoulders and tried to turn as if he were trying to see the injury.

"I didn't even feel it. I'll ask Morjiana to take a look after we've taken care of the caravan."

Ruslo nodded, and Deckard headed towards the center area, stopping only long enough to grab his healing kit and a new shirt.

Chapter 19

*K*uzunoha looked off the edge of the ship again, staring out at sea. The water bubbled past the ship, showing the coral reefs beneath them. Those reefs meant safety, as much as was possible for Hidan. Only smaller monsters lived inside the reefs. The larger monsters, creatures that could destroy ships within moments never came inside. Kuzunoha didn't know why, though surely one of the sailors would have enlightened her if she'd asked. Considering her interactions with them so far, she was doing her best to avoid them all.

She'd always thought the Bludhol reef was more of a solid wall, rather than interlocking puzzle pieces of blue, green, and white that they seemed to be as the boat skimmed the water over them. It was thrilling. Yesterday, she'd even seen something huge outside the reef; fins and antennae coming out of the water. Despite her thrill, the captain had acted like sailing this close to the edge of the Bludhol and the monster sighting was normal. She wasn't sure she trusted anyone who took seeing a monster that large as an everyday occurrence.

"Mistress Kuzu, it's good to see you above deck today." Leo, the youngest of the sailors, said.

Kuzunoha nodded coolly towards him. She's already told him not to call her Kuzu, but he had no interest in even trying to learn it. The boy had decided that she was beautiful and would fall to his charms. The problem was that the boy had none. She'd decided that ignoring him was the best way to handle the situation since talking only seemed to encourage him.

He frowned and tried again. "It's a nice day, but the Bludhols been quiet all day. We'll have to find a cove to shelter in tonight."

She stared at the waves beyond the reef. A fish, as long as she was tall, jumped out of the water in the distance. She watched as it continued skipping out of the water and finally realized that it seemed to be running from a large black shadow moving ten feet behind it.

She shivered. She loved the taste of fish but was so tired of the tame varieties they had aboard. She wondered what that shadow was, and whether it was edible or a monster.

"It's going to be cold tonight though, Mistress Kuzu," Leo said, moving closer to her. His voice was husky now.

"My name is not Kuzu." She stepped away.

She had corrected him once already and she wanted to slug him for it. Deckard had been the only one to earn that favor from her. This one, she wouldn't even do the honor of pretending he had.

"Kuzu-ha-nam-ka then." He said, throwing random syllables together as if she wouldn't recognize her name. "Anyway, it's going to be cold, right? So, the best way to keep warm is to lay with a lover beside you. I'll even let you have my share of the whiskey tonight if you're still nervous."

She rolled her eyes before returning her gaze to the coral below.

"I'm not nervous. What I am is uninterested."

His frown deepened. He was apparently used to getting his way, though how she didn't know. Perhaps it was due to his Captain's warning that any trouble on his ship would be met by leaving all of them on some tiny deserted isle or inlet with whatever was left of their fee and supplies. Despite the captain's threat, she couldn't let this useless boy intimidate her.

"I can't imagine why not. A little girl from a little town. You should be grateful for my attention." He grabbed her hand. "If you don't want me telling the captain that you're causing trouble, you'll come with me for some fun now."

Kuzunoha ripped her hand out of his and pulled her wakizashi an inch out of its sheath, making sure he saw the wickedly sharp blade.

"Keep your hands to yourself or lose the use of them. Your choice." She slid the blade back home with a click.

He smiled like he found her defiance arousing.

"You think you can wield that. Adorable. Let me guess? The eledar is teaching you?" He shook his head as if he couldn't understand it. "Enough is enough. Put the toy away."

"Toy? I assure you it's quite real."

He rolled his eyes. "Please; who would make a blade that flimsy for anything more than decoration? I understand that you might want to keep dangerous men away from you. That brute you're traveling with must hound you incessantly."

Her mouth peaked a smile at the corner as she saw 'that brute' coming towards her. Richard joined her in her room most nights and even enjoyed cuddling up afterward as well, something very few men did. She liked having someone to curve her body against.

"I wouldn't mind if he would hound me a little more." She said a bit loudly, catching Richard's eye. He turned towards her.

"Am I not doing my job properly already?" Richard said.

There was pleasure in his tone until he saw Leo. The boy took a step away, glaring daggers. Kuzunoha smiled.

"I'll see you tonight, Kuzu," Leo said. His voice had a touch of restrained malice to it.

She snapped around, pulling her wakizashi, but Richard touched her shoulder in warning.

"He isn't worth the trouble," Richard told her. She watched Leo walk away, growling, before she slapped the blade back into its sheath again.

"Should I ask what was happening between the two of you?" Richard asked.

She sighed. "He's under the impression that no means yes, and get lost means take me, I'm yours."

Richard rolled his eyes. "You need my help?"

"I have it under control," Kuzunoha said. The man could harass her, but couldn't do much else. Forcing someone was one of the crimes worthy of banishment. She frowned. Could that be why he was a sailor? Forced to sail the seas after being banished?

Richard shrugged. "I have dealt with women like him. Sometimes they are annoying, but sometimes they push too far. If you do need someone, let me know."

Richard, with his dark skin, expressive eyes, and perfectly trimmed hair and goatee, was handsome. He may not have had Deckard's perfection, but yes, she could imagine him having problems with women. His features were rugged and friendly, but most of all, he moved with all the grace of a cat and had the manners of a lord when he needed to.

Deckard was never charming. He was beautiful, yes, but always direct. There was no subtlety to him. If he liked you, you knew it. Which made the reverse true.

"Why the frown, Kuzunoha?" Richard leaned close and brought her head to him.

"I was thinking of Deckard. I was so angry... but I wish I'd seen him. That we'd left on better terms."

Richard had tensed up when she said Deckard's name and she pulled him closer, melting into his embrace.

"You can't be afraid of a man that isn't even here." She told him.

He relaxed. "Afraid? Of Deckard? He is a skilled healer and pretty, but a contest between us would be no contest at all."

Despite his words, he sounded less sure.

"Then why pull away?" She let her desire show. "I am in your arms, not his."

He smiled. "You think I have nobody that I miss from all the places I've been to? Even I like being alone with my memories sometimes. I thought you wouldn't want me to disturb your peace."

"I prefer having you near." She said, tangling her hand in his shirt. Loneliness could kill you as easily as a sword. She liked Richard. He was a friend, handsome, and a good lover. What she didn't need was somebody promising forever. Which made him everything she needed right now.

Richard kissed her. "I did come out here with news. Have you heard that we'll be arriving in Kolhana late?"

Kuzunoha blinked. "Oh, is that what the boy was fumblingly trying to tell me while propositioning me?"

"Leo," Richard said, tasting the name. He had a dark expression that looked like it fit too well on his face. He smiled at her and the darkness seemed to evaporate as if it had never been there. "Your sister requested we stay an additional night so she could deal with her business."

"Asking the captain for an extension?" Kuzunoha asked. Their captain didn't seem the kind to appreciate any delay. "Did she threaten to find another ship?"

Richard nodded. "The captain told her that was fine. He'd leave us in Kolhana."

"So, we'll be getting off there?"

"No, but it was a near thing. I wanted to warn you against trouble." Richard said. He ran a hand through his hair and turned to look the direction Leo had gone. "For what good it is."

She shrugged. "Some trouble you can't avoid."

"You sound like you've known ones like him, before?"

She shrugged, "My father may have not wanted me near his companies, but he did leave a nest egg for my future husband. To be given so long as the family approved the match. Some were more interested in the money than me."

Richard grinned. "How big a bonus is that again?"

Kuzunoha checked to make sure he wasn't being serious.

"You know, I don't think my sister will ever give up that money, not unless I marry somebody well-situated to help the company."

"So, I shouldn't start picking out curtains is what you're saying."

Kuzunoha laughed. He was always able to lift her mood, always ready to stop her from taking everything so seriously. She loved that about him.

"Well, either way, we'll let her have her fancy dinners and you and I will have fun carousing the local inns."

Kuzunoha curled into him again. "Together? Or not?"

"Why decide now. We can see if either of us finds someone of more interest while we're there."

Kuzunoha bowed her head. It was going to be like that tonight. "Of course."

"Are you not okay with…"

She waved him off. "Of course, I am. I was just thinking that Kolhana is nearly as small as Hidan. Boring. And I tire of pathetic men hitting on me."

Maybe she could just stay on the boat this time around. Richard grunted an agreement.

"At the very least, would you like to walk their market together? It won't be the black market of Sakre, but you may find something fun."

She perked up. "There's a black market in Sakre? Will you take me there?"

"If you like. I've never been to Sakre, but it may be fun. And if it isn't, we can make finding one our next goal. Traveling everywhere, viewing all of the best markets, legal or not."

It was nice to laugh again. She didn't know what she wanted long-term, but for now, she just wanted Richard beside her.

Chapter 20

*R*ichard stood outside of Kuzunoha's door, listening. The water covered the sound of her light breathing and almost covered the faint nasal sound she made at the end as she almost snored. Despite the comments she'd made earlier about wanting him to hound her more often, she hadn't invited him to sleep with her tonight. He respected her more, even if it meant that he was wandering the ship rather than finding his rest. Before he turned to leave, he quickly glanced down the hallway. It was quiet too, with all of the sailors either in their rooms or above deck. He reached forward and touched the door, checking to see if it was locked.

When it didn't budge, Richard closed his eyes leaning his forehead against the wood of her door. She wasn't taking her safety for granted, but she also wasn't waiting for him tonight either. The first was good, the second was better. He stole away, quietly sneaking up to Himiko's door.

He didn't hear Himiko at all, but Isashi was snoring away quietly. He grinned, wondering what she wore to sleep. During their harried return to Hidan, she hadn't bothered changing, had only washed and then put her clothes back on, but he rather thought that she was the sort of girl who wore nothing when she was in her own home. Himiko was almost certainly wearing some silk menswear that cost more than he brought back from the ship. He snorted and pressed his ear to the door while he turned the handle. It was locked too, and the sound of breathing in the room didn't alter, suggesting that both were asleep.

Well and good, he thought, moving towards the deck of the boat. The women he traveled with were safe and thus, he could relax too.

"Richard, that minx keeping you up again?"

Richard recognized that voice and his hand moved away from his dagger. He'd been asked, privately, which of the girls were available and willing the first night on board, and all had been pleased that he'd only claimed one as his own, even if the other two never showed any interest. He smiled widely as he turned to Andre.

"I think I may have finally tired her out," Richard responded amiably.

Andre was one of the better men on board. Blue eyes that shone even in the dim moonlight and hair even lighter than Deckard's had been, he favored the Norin side of his heritage, though there was something else mixed in if his scrawny size and wiry physique were any indication. He went barefoot on the deck while he was working, swearing that he worked better feeling the deck beneath his feet. Andre had shown him the thick-furred boots he wore when he wasn't on duty, or whenever he went off the ship, so perhaps there was some truth to his claim.

Richard inwardly shivered though. He'd swam in that water a month ago; after no more than a few minutes he'd been shivering so hard he'd thought that he may have been dying. How the man didn't mind it freezing his toes every day, Richard couldn't even imagine.

Andre's voice boomed in laughter and the man slapped him on the shoulder, causing Richard to fall forward a few steps. Despite his size and stature, he was much stronger than he looked.

"Good man. The best way to keep them quiet during the day is to have them yell all night, eh?"

Richard joined him in the laugh. In this case, whether he agreed or not didn't matter. It was a matter of pride to be good enough in bed to please your women and every man was willing to pretend he believed you had those skills, so long as the favor was returned.

"So, what are you doing up here so late? Need to use the deck?"

The ship had no room set aside for a washroom so most of the sailors simply leaned over the side to do their business. For the 'skittish' women, they'd found chamber pots with locking lids. Richard used the pots as well, but he'd leaned off the ship's side at least once on his first day.

Growing up as a dock rat in Kaleka City, he had quickly learned the necessity of blending in and inserting himself seamlessly into nearly any group. The simple ritual of dropping trow on deck and pissing into the waves had done that here. He'd been adopted as one of their own. It wouldn't win him any favors if there were trouble, but it would earn him drinks, a place to gamble and his "entitlement" to protect the women he'd brought on the ship without anyone calling him on his right.

Normally, it was a way to lay claim to whomever he was with. Here, he was protecting the crew. If any of them took their desires too far, it would be the sailor that wouldn't survive the encounter. Kuzunoha would maim any who tried to touch her without her consent and Isashi would slaughter the person that forced themselves on Himiko.

"No, I just need a bit of air to think."

"Good man," Andre said again, nodding sagely, gesturing him towards the aft end of the boat.

Sailors considered themselves great thinkers, having so much time to devote to the passion, and Richard wasn't going to be the one to try to dissuade them. Especially since on a ship, you could expect to have quiet while you did so unless there was a pressing need for all sailors to be on hand.

Richard gave him a quick nod and left, glad to see that the 'sage spot' wasn't already filled. Due to its almost hallowed position among sailors, most ships had one and it was the one place where a man could sit and expect to not be disturbed. Even the captain of a ship would obey that law, at least if he didn't want his men disturbing any private time he hoped to ever have again.

Like the ship itself, the seat was made of simple unadorned wood. The only difference was that the seat had been worn smooth by the bottoms of all the men who'd sat upon it. Small indentures where the butt could rest comfortably were all too noticeable, and he wondered if perhaps it hadn't been worn smooth just by use. It was attached to the deck by sturdy legs, bolted down tight. Instead of sitting, Richard leaned against it. He'd never understood the idea that you had to sit to think.

He shook his head. Whether he was sitting or standing wasn't the problem. The problem was the gorgeous woman down in the room beside his that he didn't want to hurt. He was almost certain that her cunning plan (he snorted at the idea) was to stay with him once they reached Kalvettika.

He'd dealt with women like that before. One, in particular, had scarred him so badly that the idea of any woman latching onto him gave him hives.

But Kuzunoha was different. Something about her made him want to stay... and that was the problem. Made him... he shook his head again. She wasn't the like the queen, he'd made sure of that. But still, every time she frowned, he felt something near a compulsion to make her happy. It bothered him.

He couldn't remember if that was normal or not.

He also didn't want to be tied down, even to Kuzunoha. He wasn't sure if the life of someone on the run was something she could adapt to. Richard couldn't stop running; not even if he'd found someone worth fighting for.

What if she stayed? What if she didn't mind running forever? Could he keep his dark side at bay that long? She wouldn't like what his impulses drove him to want, any more than he'd liked it when the tables had suddenly been turned back on him.

He sucked in a breath, surprised that there was no pain. Had he finally figured out the trick? Thinking about the problems, without thinking about a person?

"Thinking of the past?"

The silky voice spoke in a language so much older than human that it bore no resemblance to any other tongue he'd ever heard. He remembered learning it painfully and breathlessly at the knees of the one who wanted him back. Richard's eyes went wide and his breath locked in his throat.

The term 'woman' could have applied, so long as you used it very loosely. Her lower body was nothing but a snake-like whip of water that undulated under her, while her upper body simulated a human woman's, naked with large breasts that hung unnaturally high. Her skin was a greyish-blue, like the ocean in this frigid land. Her dark, shoulder-length hair dripped, as though she'd just popped her head out of the ocean. He hadn't met this woman before, but if she was like the others of her kind, it would still be dripping hours later. Her face was the most disconcerting, round and soft, with impossibly large black eyes that had no irises. Her ears were fins that drooped constantly, like a fish's pectoral fins when it was starting to drown in the air it couldn't breathe.

Her smile showed only the hint of coral shaded teeth.

A thrill of fear and desire burst in him. Before it could take hold, he'd drawn a dagger and thrown it into her chest.

She didn't stop smiling.

"*Ricca*, that wasn't necessary. You know how difficult it is for us to hold these forms while in this world."

Richard's heart skipped a beat when she called him Ricca. The queen had insisted that it was his name, that Richard didn't exist anymore. The sight of his knife gliding slowly through her skin, as though it were only sinking through a wave chilled him more than even the water here could. He'd known the attack wouldn't kill her. Fey touching their element were nearly unkillable. For a creature like her, of the water domain, looking solid and being solid were two very different things.

Even so, he had a new blade in each hand already, this time his cold iron ones. There was always a chance she would make a mistake and allow him the satisfaction of killing her that he craved.

"It's an automatic response to being startled," he told her, speaking the most common language on this side of the world, rather than his native language or hers. She knew the languages here... she could work to translate just as much as he could. "What do you want?"

Not that he needed to ask, but he had to keep her busy. Her real body would be connected to this one, hiding somewhere under the water that nourished this reflection. He could hurt her if he could lure it to the surface. But he had to be subtle. If she suspected, she would hide her true form deep enough that he would have no chance of killing her at all.

"I just want to talk," she pouted but used the same language he did. "Besides, it's been so long since the Mistress has seen you. She worries."

His knife drifted into her lower region and he watched it sink, his despair following it. If he got close enough to touch her, she would grab him and drag him back with her. Even if the shadow itself didn't have the control to grab him, she could knock him off the ship and into her domain, like any other wave.

"There's no need for us to talk. I'm not a hero. As per the promise, I can't come back yet," he said, sounding bored.

The shadow frowned at him.

"I hardly understand how that matters, Richard. You are not fey; you do not have to hold yourself to the promise."

"What sort of man would I be if I didn't?" His mind screamed that he would be a twice-broken one to return with her. He answered more politely, "I doubt that I would be as interesting to her highness if I was not."

If only that were true, he would consider it. If she were bored, she wouldn't want to 'play' with him any longer.

"Break your rule. She wants you back." The fey said. "You know your duty."

Richard nodded. "I do. She told me to become a hero. I will return when I am."

He could make that promise because a hero might be strong enough to slay her, and if he had his way, he would never be one to find out.

Her eyes narrowed, though in frustration or cunning he couldn't have said.

"You saved the life of another. Does that not count?" She asked.

"Of course not." He answered quickly. "One life is not equal to another and the girl was quite unimportant."

Richard had believed that once; still almost did. Fortunately, while Kuzunoha wasn't unimportant, at least to him, the fey would consider her so. Even to Richard, their rules deciding how much somebody was worth were... convoluted at best.

"Return to where you belong." She told him, no longer willing to cajole.

She was being very set on this one point and he couldn't figure out why. If she wanted to take him, she most likely had the power to destroy the ship and force him to come with her. When she was attached to her element there wasn't much that could stop her. Why did she need him to agree?

Suddenly, he understood. The fey were very good at enchanting victims, but this one had no power to keep him alive if she took him. The only portals she had were probably deep in the ocean, a distance he wouldn't survive without drowning. Even they had limitations. His knife slipped lower, past her belly and Richard smiled. Its loss wasn't as bad as he'd thought, even if he couldn't kill the blue bitch right now. Still, he was careful to keep his eyes on her for any sudden movement.

"Could you take me there?" He asked, wanting to test his point.

She smiled. "Of course, but it would mean so much more if you went yourself by one of the land portals."

He didn't let up. "But I could go with you?"

"She would not be pleased," the creature frowned, watching him through narrowed eyes.

He stepped close enough that she could grab him if she wanted to. When she didn't, he smiled, and it was anything but charming. He hadn't felt so much like himself since he'd escaped. He reveled in it.

"You could take me, but you couldn't do it and get me there alive. You have no teeth here." He reached out and took hold of the knife, yanking it out of her. The water released it with no resistance. The fey's water-form watched him as he took out a cloth and dried the blade, sheathing it. She was furious. "Now that you've delivered your message; you can leave."

Her eyes widened at the dismissal. But she couldn't take him back to the Lady without killing him and if she did, the queen would destroy her. She wouldn't mind another 'playing' with him first, but someone would die if he did. At least, if he died before she could kill him herself.

"Leave?" She said as if she'd misunderstood. Richard didn't say anything more to her, just turned and started walking off. "Richard? Come back! Your life is in my hands, I will destroy this floater you are on..."

Richard walked under the deck, breathing easier now that he was safely in the hold. Surrounded by firm walls, he could be a little more certain that he hadn't put everyone he knew in immediate danger. He let out a breath. They couldn't stay on this boat though. Fey were unkind, cruel, and they were masters of destroying their toys. She would respond with retribution... just as soon as she figured out a way to do it without killing him.

Chapter 21

*H*imiko looked at the city of Sakre and kept her jaw firmly closed. It was so much larger than Hidan, so much wider, so much everything... she could hear the noise of so many people and they weren't even at the docks yet. She couldn't imagine how many people lived in it or how many hunters it would take to protect so many. Part of her was excited to be somewhere so vibrant, but a larger part wanted to skip this city and continue on their way.

Even the walls were different. In Hidan, they were no more than twenty feet high. The bottom five feet was made of a solid stone while the rest of the height was made with strong wood. It was easy to repair and replace, especially since they didn't have access to a local mine for good stone. Here, the walls were double the height of the ones in Hidan, made of cold, dour stone secured by metal bands the whole way up.

What sort of monsters could they be dealing with here that the walls needed to be forty feet tall and made only of stone?

"It's so large. And there are so many people. Do you think they'll still have space at the inn?"

Kuzunoha was acting like a bumpkin tourist, and Himiko was embarrassed standing next to her. Still, it was nice to see Kuzunoha happy, smiling with a rare, unguarded expression on her face.

"There will be multiple inns and they'll certainly have space. It's not their busy season." Richard answered her.

Himiko didn't even want to consider that this wasn't the city's busy time of year. It was too full as it was.

"How can you tell?" Isashi asked. "It looks plenty busy to me."

Himiko saw a ship come closer to them and Isashi signed something with her hands to them. The man in the boat stood up and then flashed the same hand signal back. He must have been one of the hunters positioned in the water to warn of water monsters converging on the town.

The only place a creature would be able to attack easily was the dock since the walls stopped thirty feet past the land's edge. If an invader could get there unnoticed, they would be able to do significant damage before the hunters could reach them. If she remembered correctly, there was a gate that they could drop leading into the town that could be dropped, but that would leave all of the people outside to die until the hunters could arrive.

"That dock is only half full, so unless they have a very active fishing population that we didn't see on our way in, it means that they're prepped for way more ships than are docked right now. During the busy season, all the docks will be full." He pointed to colored balls floating on the water. "And there will be ships anchored all around the bay."

The idea of a city this size doubling in a matter of months sent chills running through Himiko. Humans weren't meant to live like pickled eels packed together in a jar.

"It will be even easier to find an inn to stay at for a few days," Kuzunoha said, contentedly.

"We won't be taking a room in the city," Himiko said. She may have to go into that disgusting hive, but she'd save everyone else the horror of having to go with her.

"Why not?" Richard said. "It's a good idea."

"No point in paying extra, but the boat is harder to defend than a single room in the city," Isashi said.

"Maybe you won't…" Kuzunoha muttered.

Isashi disagreeing with her hurt. Himiko focused on Kuzunoha's grumbling.

"The ship needs to dock for supplies, but we don't need to leave since I'm the only one with business in the city," Himiko told them.

One of the sailors, a dull-looking older man with greying hair and leathery-brown skin looked at them. His smile was strained.

Richard touched her shoulder lightly and led her a few steps away. "Lady, it certainly isn't necessary, but I think all of us need a break from each other. Not just us from the crew. Besides, I know that Kuzunoha was hoping to hit one of the markets while we were here."

"Kuzunoha will stay where I tell her to." Himiko snapped.

Richard, gods damn him, just smiled, as if she were the one being unreasonable. Which, she considered, may have been the case if she was assuming that Kuzunoha would ever follow a direct order from her.

"I am not being paid to be your yes-man," Richard said. "Also, you can't keep me with money, and without someone there to watch her, your sister will be in town within minutes."

Himiko opened her mouth to argue, but Richard shook his head, continuing.

"I'm not here to argue with you. My job is security. With all of us getting off this ship, I would rather not leave our things here unguarded."

"You think an innkeeper would be more honest than the captain and his men?"

"I think that one of the ship's boys has been bothering your sister since we boarded, and that means that the captain has less control over his crew than we'd like. A good innkeeper will allow us to use our own locks."

Himiko didn't want to agree with him; she didn't want him to be right. On the other hand, she had seen the boy that had been sniffing around Kuzunoha. He'd sniffed around her too, but Isashi had dissuaded him. Since her sister had miraculously had better taste than to sleep with him, Himiko hadn't bothered with reminding Kuzunoha to keep her distance.

"You want my sister away from the boy? Are you worried she'll decide to stay with him, and not you?"

She could see her sister doing it out of spite if she'd known that Himiko thought that Richard was more acceptable to her.

Richard shook his head. "Your sister stays with who she wants, as do I. What I do worry about is the captain deciding that we're causing too much havoc on his ship and sailing away with our things on board or leaving them on the dock in a pile."

Himiko's eyes widened. "Can he do that?"

Richard nodded. "It's his choice to accept us as passengers or not."

"How will staying off the ship help?" Himiko asked as Isashi joined Kuzunoha at the bow of the ship.

"First, if we're out of sight, we're out of mind for the crew. That boy won't obsess over her, the captain will have another day or so of not having to worry about the crew. And with the crew not acting up while we're here, he'll be much less likely to leave us behind since you still have the second half of his pay."

Staying in town would mean trouble that she'd wanted to avoid, but Richard had a point. Was there any reason not to stay at an inn, aside from her not wanting to spend one more minute in that city than she had to? No. More than that, she was remembering her father, pushing her to succeed, to make the family proud. If she had to sleep in this town to do that, then that was what she'd do.

"Fine. Can you arrange for a dock boy to carry our luggage?"

Richard nodded and looked towards Isashi. "Of course. I'll get Isashi's help packing up."

Himiko frowned but nodded. Then she glanced over at Kuzunoha again. She was pointing out part of the ocean to Isashi with a worried expression. She rolled her eyes. It was probably nothing more than a fish and Isashi would tell her so. Himiko sucked on her teeth. She wouldn't get a better chance than now to talk to Richard.

"Richard, wait." He turned back to her. "I want you to stay with Kuzunoha, every moment while we're in town."

He looked perplexed. "Why?"

"Because she's my sister and I don't like the look of this town. I hired you to keep her safe."

Himiko didn't want to point out that he was the one who should want to protect her. Fortunately, she could see on his face that she didn't need to.

"She'd be fine in the city... but I promise I'll stay as close as I can."

Himiko blew out her breath.

"That's all I can ask."

Chapter 22

*R*ichard looked out the window. Himiko had left twenty minutes ago, Isashi in tow to make sure she would be safe from pickpockets and less savory types on the road. Himiko had grumbled about it, but he'd supported Isashi when she'd told Himiko that she would see her to and from the location. Himiko's father may have tried to teach her about how to not be taken for a bumpkin while in a city, but it was clear that she didn't know how to handle herself in a city this big any more than Kuzunoha did.

To be fair, neither did Isashi. But she could take him on in a fight; a regular thief or even a couple of thugs should be no issue for her to take on. Plus, Isashi could be nearly as stealthy as him when she was trying. The only difference in their skills was that she had practiced that stealth in the wilds, while he practiced his skills in a more urban environment.

Richard hadn't been in a place this big no more than a handful of times since he'd left Jiza. His heart wanted to yank him out of the room, to find the busiest market and walk around, picking pockets like he'd done when he'd been growing up. Of course, back then he'd had to steal… his mother didn't make enough to keep both of them fed. If he didn't steal, then she would starve herself, which led to even the few customers that she had been getting turning her aside, leaving her for those who wanted to hurt their evening's dalliance.

Not to say that he hadn't come to love it. He'd been a damn good thief. Good enough that the guild had taken him in after his mother had died. He shook his head and looked out the window again. He couldn't afford to live in the past.

The room Himiko had found was simple but functional. Four beds with a moderate-sized chest at the foot that they'd immediately put their own locks on. The floor was stone, odd for a building with more than a single story, but the walls were wood. The finish they'd used was old and needed to be redone and the sun shone in through a few of the areas where the wood had pushed itself out of alignment. In winter, he was pretty sure that this room couldn't be heated and would be sold cheap for anyone stupid enough to think that they would be able to cover up enough to keep out the cold. Fortunately, it was summer now, which meant the room would only be mildly chill after the sun went down.

The room was on the third floor which was a pain to climb to but gave them a perfect view of the street in either direction. It was busy and dirty, with garbage, mud and other detritus on the road. Despite that, the people he was seeing were clean and well off. Merchants, business owners, crafters, artisans. Even the sailors looked better off than the average. He caught sight of four pickpockets walking among them.

Sakre was a dream for those who hid under the law, an entire town where anything, legal or not, could be bought or sold.

The fashion was based on sea wear, and he could tell who lived here by who was carrying, if not wearing, a waxed leather jacket with dozens of brass buttons going down the front and side in various colors. They also all had long hair, worn without ties or wraps.

Kuzunoha grumbled and he glanced back at her. She was on the bed beside the window, tucked up right next to the wall. Isashi and he had taken the ones closest to the door just in case there was trouble, even though they weren't expecting any. Kuzunoha had a book open in front of her, the journal he'd given Himiko, but he didn't think she was reading it. She'd only turned one page since she'd opened it, moments before her sister left.

Kuzunoha grumbled again and he let out a sigh. She had unwillingly constrained herself to the apartment when he'd told her that the night market wouldn't open until after dark. However, considering how she kept glancing up at the door, if Richard suggested that he needed to leave the inn for any reason, she would push him out the door and try to wander the city alone.

In a city that played loose and fast with the rules like Sakre, pretty women could find themselves in a lot of trouble. If that wasn't reason enough, Himiko had employed him to keep her sister safe. A task that should have been simple enough if she hadn't been chaos incarnate.

Kuzunoha sighed again with a slight whine to her voice, "Richard…"

He'd put a plan in place when they'd landed. As soon as they'd landed, he'd hired a dock boy to carry their luggage and run to the taxes office to report their own ship for contraband. Sakre was full of corruption and most were willing to turn a blind eye for a few coins, but the tax office still had to collect their taxes. They had to pay for the walls, the repairs, the hunters… all of it. They were willing to take less, but they wouldn't take the paltry amount the captain had paid. They would check what the Captain had said he was bringing in against how much he'd paid and visit when the fee didn't match what Richard had implied the man was carrying.

Now all he had to do was talk to the captain and tell him he'd heard the taxmen talk about coming and raiding him boat while they were here. As soon as he saw the men coming, the captain would take his ship and head right back out to sea whether he had the contraband items or not, since it was all too easy for a pirate to lose his ship. The Sakre officials would lose him unless they had a ship of their own ready, which they wouldn't for a surprise raid. The captain and ship would escape and the fey would find out quickly enough that he wasn't on board.

However, the plan had one flaw. There were other ships here, dozens. Surely of those, one would be willing to take passengers with them. It had been luck itself that he'd been able to convince Himiko to stay on land instead of the boat. There was no way to keep them on land unless Himiko decided that boats, in general, were unreliable.

Not only that, but he still had to get down to their ship. If the Captain didn't hear about the taxmen coming, he wouldn't flee. He'd just stay there, having to pay the money which would make him even angrier at their group.

He turned back to Kuzunoha. Her expression was dark and angry, and he immediately sat up, wondering what he'd done wrong.

"Look if you want to leave, just go already," Kuzunoha said.

"What makes you think I have anywhere to go?" He said with a smile.

She frowned. "We've been sitting in complete silence while you look out the window and then back to the door. You're either waiting for someone to come up here or you want to go out."

He sighed. He really shouldn't have tried to deny it. Not when he was being that obvious.

"I think I may have forgotten one of my knives on the boat. I'm trying to decide if I need to go grab it."

Her brow creased. "A knife? Why not just wait until the day after tomorrow?"

"It's sentimental. I don't like having it anywhere but on my side." He shrugged and she looked over to her wakizashi, nodding.

"So, go. I'll be fine here." She said with an eager glance out the window. She wouldn't be able to see much outside from where she was sitting, just the tall buildings around them and blue sky above that, but her eyes had stars in them, while she dreamed.

"You'll be out of here the moment I leave." He retorted.

She bristled and finally put down the book. He noticed that she hadn't bothered to mark the page.

"So, what if I did? We're in a city, I'd be fine if I went out and looked around."

"Kuzunoh–" he began. She glared at him.

"As I recall, you were the one who wanted us to go our separate ways and 'see if we found other people' while we were here."

Her tone was snide and he realized she thought he was just trying to stop her from finding her own company for the night. He was defending himself before he thought.

"It isn't that…" he winced.

"Then what is it…" she suddenly growled in irritation.

With an all too dramatic flair, she flung herself to her pillow. As her head hit the pillow, two tiny gray down feathers shot into the air. By the gods, she looked sexy, even if it was the silliest attempt at a tantrum he'd ever seen. Kuzunoha ignored the feathers as her voice rose from between the thick pillows

"I don't believe this. My sister told you to be my nanny, didn't she?"

He wanted to deny that, but she wasn't wrong. "It doesn't mean…"

"I don't need you watching out for me. I can handle myself."

"It isn't you, but the people you meet that I worry about."

She shot a glare his way.

"I notice my sister got to go out."

"Not alone. Isashi went with her." Kuzunoha still looked rebellious. He continued before she could argue more. "It isn't that I didn't want you with me, or that I think you can't handle yourself. But if I'm going to the boat, there's a chance you'll have to deal with Leo."

"Well, that's at least an argument I can get behind. But if that's really your only issue, why don't I just stay on the dock? It's not like I'll get in trouble in the minute or two it will take you to grab your knife, right?"

She had a point. If he took too long, he could tell her he'd had to ask the captain about it. Even if she told her sister about the trip and she pressed the captain about it, the captain should be pleased enough to hold to the story about the knife.

"Alright then, get yourself ready. We'll head out to the docks and then look around the town until dinner. After that, we can leave your sister and Isashi at the inn and head to the night market."

Her grin was infectious as she ran to her bag and used her small mirror to put on some light makeup.

Richard grinned. While she was dressing herself up, he would be dressing himself down. He didn't want to be remembered in case the taxmen asked about people heading to talk to the captain after it fled.

Fortunately, Kuzunoha was gorgeous and there weren't many Sian Ku here. She would command a lot of attention. He would command more if he was as meticulous with his appearance as he normally was. He hadn't seen a single person in town with skin as dark as his and that would be noticed. He opened his makeup kit.

He quickly decided on a pale powder mixed with a tiny bit of grey. It wouldn't make him appear light-skinned, but it would make him look older and a bit sick. Then he fluffed up his beard and hair to look a bit worse for wear. To finish, he used an eyedropper. In five minutes, his eyes would look unfocused and liquidy, almost like he was drunk or had eye problems.

Small changes, hopefully enough that Kuzunoha wouldn't notice until they were on their way back. He could claim a stomach issue and return immediately. A quick bath and a restive nap, and he'd be fine for dinner.

"Are you ready to…" she paused, looking at him a bit critically. "Are you feeling all right?"

"I'm just worried about that knife," he said, getting up. Apparently, the makeup was a bit overdone. He would remember to put it on lighter the next time. "It's a silly thing, but you know how it feels."

She nodded and glanced at her sword. She couldn't take it around town. Weapons longer than a foot were prohibited. She sighed and locked it into her chest. "I do. Let's make this quick then."

Chapter 23

*K*uzunoha stood up on her toes to see above the crowd at the dock. She could already see the ship coming into sight. She jumped up trying to see further and growled. Leo was on deck. She thought she could see his lascivious smile from here.

"I will stay up here," she offered. "I can already see Leo."

They were just outside the docks, which were busy this late at night. She didn't see many fish coming into the city like there would have been in Hidan. Just box, after sealed box. This city must have a huge amount of people they traded with. Especially since, if she remembered correctly, there was little to no farmland here.

Richard shook his head.

"I'd feel safer if you came onto the docks. This isn't a great area to be standing on a street corner." She flushed, realizing that there were streetwalkers among the crowd. Richard smiled kindly. "Trust me, you don't look like you belong, but it would be just my luck to have someone drunk not realize it. Just stay on the dock and ignore Leo. If he gets off the boat, you'll have an actual grievance to take to the captain."

She flushed and followed him in. Fortunately, nearly as soon as they were in, the crowds thinned enough that at least she could see more than a few feet in front of her. When they reached the dock, he kissed her. "I'll be right back out."

She watched as he jogged toward the plank, speaking easily with the men on board. Leo caught sight of Richard and saw her a moment later. He sauntered her way.

"Couldn't stay away, huh? I got some time if you want to come up here."

She bared her teeth again. She'd dealt with obsession before, but Leo had it worse than anyone else she'd ever know.

"No, thank you. I'd rather stay on land and walk all the way to Kalvettika than spread my legs for you."

"That can be arranged," Leo told her. He leaned over the ledge, looking at her. His eyes and nose were a puffy red. Could he be drunk this early? She stepped away and he frowned again.

"I think you just want to keep those pretty panties of yours from getting soiled by associating with the likes of a sailor. Are you traveling to meet your lordly intended husband? Can't let a mere sailor interfere with that marriage." Leo said. "Not that you don't want to. Or have you been fulfilling yourself with your guard and you're just hoping that the lordling don't find out? I wonder how he'll feel about knowing you've been disgracing yourself with that boy?"

"Is that a threat?" She asked, struck by the audacity.

Not that she had a lordling waiting for her and she certainly wasn't saving herself for anyone. Still, the fact that he thought he could threaten her burned. She wanted to turn the boy into bloody ribbons and her hand went to her side. She felt naked without her sword. Her fingers twitched into claws.

"Hardly a threat if I'm telling 'im the truth, is it?" He smirked, putting a hip on the side of the ship. "You'll come on board and pleasure me, or I will make sure your lord finds out."

Kuzunoha forced a laugh out, cruel and cold.

"There is no man, as you'll find out when we reach Kalvettika. If you speak to me again, I will take my blade and feed you to the fish though, your captain's threats be damned."

She turned and walked to the end of the dock and walked across to the boat on the other side, a sturdy low ship that used rowers rather than just sail to get them across the seas. She wouldn't leave Richard here, but she wasn't going to stay and let the idiot make her angry enough to do something she knew she wouldn't regret.

"You are being exceptionally kind to the human spouting lies. I have never understood the way your kind puts up with it." a voice asked.

She looked away from the ship and saw a girl hiding in the shadows by the pier. She had dark stringy hair and wore a blue outfit that showed too much of her sallow complexion. Kuzunoha's stomach twisted, and she almost reached down to grab her abdomen. She didn't usually have serious cramps and it was a week early for her normal flow.

Could she have eaten something that had just decided to go bad? She'd never had food sickness before.

As she walked nearer she realized it was the woman, not some offending bit of uncooked meat, that was making her stomach curdle. She didn't know how, but her instincts screamed that this woman was dangerous. That Kuzunoha would die at her hands if she didn't bow and scrape at the stranger's feet. Kuzunoha stood straight and took a step back. She had nowhere to run and if she stepped further than that, she would.

"I am not being kind," Kuzunoha said. "I am being expedient. The man and his ship haven't fulfilled their debt to us. After that, his ship can burn with him in the crow's nest for all I care. But I won't kill him while I still need his master."

Too much truth, Kuzunoha's mind shrieked at her. Why was she even answering? As she watched the woman's hair dripped more onto her oversized blue jacket? Or was it grey? When had she washed her hair that it was still dripping? She hadn't seen any bathhouses on the main road and only someone desperate would try to wash in the dirty seawater that lapped the hulls of the ships.

"Politics is always so dull. Can't you just capture the captain and tell him to off the offal? Tell me, *Vixia*, what would you do to him if he tried to touch you?"

The women stepped out of the shadows. Her hair caught the light and shone like it was blue, rather than black. The woman's skin did not change, and Kuzunoha realized that the shadow hadn't made this stranger look sallow and grey; in fact, the shadows had hidden strange bumps dotting her face, neck, and hands, looking almost like scales. She stank of ocean brine, even more than the ocean itself did.

"I would slice his throat open, revel in the bloodshed, and throw him overboard. He could feed the monsters. A sacrifice to keep them away from our ship." Kuzunoha said, realizing that she'd backed up a few steps.

Of all the ways to answer, why that one? Some part of her had needed to let the woman know that she would kill if she had to.

She was almost to their ship again. She wished Richard would come out already. She wasn't used to feeling threatened and that included the battle with the men who had tried to kill Richard.

The woman clapped her hands together as if Kuzunoha had said something funny. They made a sloshing sound. How wet was this woman if her hands sloshed when she clapped them?

"What fun." The woman said, showing a glint of teeth. "Your people aren't prone to violence, but you act more like one of us. I can see why he chose you to dally with."

"Richard?" Kuzunoha said, her stomach fluttering again. Was he why this woman had sought her out? A jilted ex-lover of his, perhaps?

"Of course. But tell me, why did you come back to the boat?"

"We'll be leaving town in just a day or two. On that." She gestured towards the boat, annoyed that she hadn't been able to keep the bite out of her voice. Was she jealous? Could it be simple jealousy that made her hate this woman? No, she'd hated her from the first moment they'd met.

The woman froze, looking supernaturally still. "This boat?"

"Yes," Kuzunoha said. "As I said, I still need that man's master. We have places to be. Places that don't include you."

The clothes the woman had been wearing, flowed off her as if they'd turned liquid, leaving her naked. The scaly skin condition covered most of the woman's body and her skin started turning dark blue. Kuzunoha's stomach dropped and the air was too thick to breathe. The dark part of the woman's eye spread out, covering every speck of white within them, and they glittered as if her eyes were covered with a thin sheen of oil.

The woman blinked and two sets of eyelids came together from the sides, the innermost one clear and the second the same color as her skin. Not up and down… side to side.

The woman shouted. "Release him, *Vixia*."

Kuzunoha's throat closed, hurting from a desperate need to scream that she physically couldn't fulfill. The woman's body shivered, and Kuzunoha heard a gasp from behind her. She watched with horror as the woman turned to water, sloshing through the cracks in the dock to the filthy water below.

Kuzunoha fell to her knees, not certain why she felt like the end of the world had come. Moments later, she heard a bell sound and the ship beside her started rising out of the water, tilting back and forth wildly, while a whirlpool thundered below it. The whirlpool didn't pull the ship into it but lifted it out of the water. Kuzunoha couldn't tear her eyes away. A dark form leaped from the ship and Richard landed beside her. She gibbered something as he grabbed her arm. It hurt and she whimpered. Richard hauled her to her feet.

"What the hell happened?" He demanded.

Kuzunoha opened her mouth and found the words stuck in her throat. The ship turned vertical and three people fell off the ship into the water at the whirlpool's base, where the ship ran over them. Leo screamed and followed the trio of men. He wasn't lucky enough to land in the water. His head shattered on the dock, thick blood seeping out of cracks wide enough that she could have fit her fingers between them. A sudden clarity hit her, and she could focus. He smelled…

She took one step towards Leo and nearly fell as Richard dragged her away from the carnage. To her horror, she saw whirlpools forming beneath the other ships, small at first, but growing larger. Sailors were abandoning their vessels and others, too far from the deck to do so, were screaming while they tried to pull up anchor and run.

They wouldn't escape. The white foam under the other ships wasn't whirlpools of water like she'd first thought, but ice that froze them in place, climbing the sides like a malignant blue moss. Richard pulled her around a corner, breaking her line of sight and Kuzunoha felt like she could breathe again; Had she drawn breath at all since that woman had screamed, splashing through dock planks to join the water below?

Kuzunoha felt brick behind her and cobblestones beneath her feet and slipped down the wall, falling on her ass onto the cool, dry ground. Richard heaved a few breaths and then collapsed beside her.

"What was... that?" She asked. They were away from the water. How far had they come?

"That was a monster, one of the water fey," Richard whispered.

Monster? This creature had been more a force of nature than any monster Kuzunoha had ever heard of.

"If it was a monster attack, shouldn't we have stayed to help?" she asked, tentatively. The question seemed mad, but people were dying out there. They had fought other monsters together.

Richard looked at her as if she'd gone mad.

"Kuzunoha, I can't take one of the fey. Even if I could, I was tasked with keeping you safe." Richard shook his head. "Come on, we can find a guard or magistrate to warn on the way back to the inn."

Kuzunoha nodded and stood, feeling a little like she was drunk, but she didn't want to run. She wanted to fight the bitch that had put her and Richard in danger.

"Kuzunoha, come on. We have to go."

"Fey..." she said, memorizing the word. "Are they always that talkative?"

Richard froze, and he turned, "What do you mean?"

Brandy Ackerley

"This one talked to me. It seemed to know you."

"What did it say?" His eyes were wide and worried.

"I don't remember... What does it matter?" Had it been
something about how it wasn't a surprise that Richard had chosen her? "I
think it knew you."

He looked like now he couldn't find any air. "We need to get
away from the water. Fey are obsessive. If this creature has chosen you
as its new obsession, then your life will be in danger in the waters
around here. We need to get back and tell your sister. There's no way we
can take a boat now."

"Me? It was your name it said."

He looked at her, pityingly. "If I had been the object of interest,
it would have talked to me. Not you."

Kuzunoha felt a chill run down her spine and she followed
Richard down the city streets, leaving the water and its horror behind
her.

Chapter 24

*T*he city was larger than any Deckard had ever seen before.

They'd stopped outside of the city so that Danior could talk to everyone about the 'rules' of how to handle the larger settlements. Deckard tried to pay attention, but his eyes kept being pulled to the tall walls. When his parents had been taking him to Hidan, every town had been large and exciting to him. Hidan had been just the size he'd needed… there had been a limit to the new things he had to deal with.

Sakre supposedly had over ten thousand people living in it, and apparently, that number could more than double in the fall. Deckard couldn't understand how they could protect that large a place. The walls were a good first step. The only other thing that people mentioned constantly was that Sakre was the black-market capital of the country. Deckard didn't approve of pirating or thieving in general, but he could appreciate their drive to carve a niche out for themselves.

He was hoping he would have a chance to go further in than the "staging area"; a bubble in the wall they used to hold caravans when they came through. Tieni had told him that only half the caravan typically got to go into the big cities like this. It was a reward that most of the Corvidae reached for at every stop they made.

"Remember, city folk aren't like town folk. The smithy will be on, but no work will be done tonight. It's close enough to nightfall that the townsfolk will want their rest. They will not bring us their business tomorrow if they feel we kept them up tonight. As well, no weapon training. The sound of battle makes them skittish, thinking there is an enemy outside the gates. If there is a panic, the guards will turn against us. We do not allow that to happen."

Danior had been telling them the rules for cities for nearly ten minutes now. In that time, Deckard had figured out that the rules were pretty much the opposite of dealing with the smaller towns. For Hidan, trusted or not, the Corvidae's skill with weapons meant they were an extra line of defense. Instead, people in cities believed that in the case of an attack, their walls and protection just meant that others were clamoring for protection.

"What about going into town?" One of the younger boys asked.

Danior caught the young man in a penetrating stare that made the boy blush and look away. Deckard almost smiled himself at the boy's brazenness and stretched trying to see exactly who it was. Unfortunately, aside from having light-colored hair, he couldn't tell.

"If you are lucky enough to go into town, be on your best behavior; don't do things that will get the rest of us in trouble, yes? Tomorrow, the regular rules will apply. Watch your money, expect to pay a premium on everything and if you aren't properly respectful, expect that the townsfolk will insist that you have the correct currency, and tax you for the favor. Lavinia will be going into town tonight to exchange our coinage into their most common currencies. We will exchange until we are out, as close as we can to cost. If we have not enough and you need to exchange it in town, pay less than five percent. Any more than that and the Kennicks are conning you."

Deckard walked back to his cart while Tieni planned what she would like to see or pick up if they were allowed in town. Personally, Deckard would just be happy to be inside a city's protective walls again. He'd been with the Corvidae for three weeks now. He'd hoped he'd been less dependent on the idea that he needed walls to feel safe.

Everything went wrong the moment they reached the outer walls. The hum of the city rose and he could hear horseshoes clomping across cobblestone. The yelling he heard sounded like guards trying to quell a riot. Danior was talking to the guards at the entrance when one, a stout man with a receding hairline rode up, looking over all of them warily. Danior tapped his apprentice on the shoulder.

"We gon' need our kits, Boy. This city gotz a problem with a monster tonight." Lady Morjiana told him. He turned and saw that she'd walked up just behind him.

"How do you know?

"De wood'n be so worri if it weren't monsters. Dis one, she dangerous; Power surrounds her like a cloak. They taint goin' want peoples sitting outside dey're gate tonight."

Deckard looked around. "Wouldn't they feel more worried about having us inside?"

"You nutz, boy? We taint goin' to be hon'rd guests. Dey goin' put us to work. And if the monstar come back, it take us, not dey're own."

"Danior wouldn't..." Deckard began.

"We've been invited inside... but there's work to be done. Lady Morjiana, I'll need you and Deckard to help them. They have injured. Tieni and Ruslo will be accompanying you as guards." Danior said as he walked closer.

Never mind, Deckard thought dejectedly.

"O 'coorse." Lady Morjiana said.

Deckard and Tieni were ready to enter the town within minutes. As soon as Morjiana and Ruslo joined them, the stout guard took them inside and passed them off to a young recruit man wearing leather armor and a blue cape with a fish emblem on it. Panic was in his eyes as he drove them through the city at a breakneck pace.

The only thing Deckard would remember later from that rushed ride was the impression of orange burlap stalls and people wearing dark clothing, hawking junk that promised to safeguard the wearer. The worst sort of thieves preying off people's fears.

Deckard's stomach turned when they reached the docks and he saw the carnage. For a moment he was reminded of the birdos attack on Hidan only a few years ago. There were bodies everywhere, more than he could easily count. As he watched, two more men were dragged ashore by some of the townsfolk. There were no boats in the harbor anymore, only wrecked hulls.

Everything was surreally silent around them. Something cracked loud enough to be heard for miles and he turned to see one of the boats suddenly break free of the ice holding it down. Its bobbing motion seemed obscene in the stillness. He sucked in a breath that froze in his chest. None of the ships were moving with the roll of the water.

Debris moved, the water moved... but the ships didn't, each surrounded by a white icy crest that held them fast. The few men he could see in the boats looked dazed. What the hell was ice doing here during this time of year? It was Blonimem, the fifth moon of the year already. While snow could freeze ships this close to land during the winter in hideous storms, he'd never heard of it doing so in the summer months. Snow? Certainly, that happened often during the rest of the year, but he'd only seen a snowfall during the summer once before, and never bad enough to freeze ships, locking everything into an eerie tableau that defied imagination.

"Healer?" The caped guard touched his arm gently. "Please, there are people who need you."

Deckard shook his head and closed his eyes. He couldn't do anything about the impossible things. He had to focus on what he could do... healing those that remained. He opened his eyes with a nod to the guard.

"Of course. Where is your first healer?"

Even in Hidan, the eldest or most experienced healer took leadership in a situation like this, directing everyone's efforts so healers and regular people weren't left running on top of each other trying to do their work.

"She's this way."

The woman he was led to was nearly as young as himself, with skin dark as pitch. Little beads woven into the woman's complicated little braids clacked quietly while she worked, reminding him of Tieni. He glanced around and saw his girlfriend taking direction to help out near the beach. He nodded, glad to see her getting ready to help as well.

He knelt beside the healer and assessed the patient. Frozen from the legs down and a wicked slice down his chest. It wasn't bleeding fast enough, which meant that there was something wrong other than the cut. He looked over the patient's legs. The ice was cold enough that it was slowing the blood as it traveled through him. If they didn't fix that, he would freeze before he could die from the untreated blood loss.

Deckard put his hands out and she let him take over massaging the man's legs activating a whisper of his power, working to repair the damage, warming him up with his own body

The healer sat back and put her hands on his arm to warm them. Her hands were nearly as cold as the young man laying before them, but she didn't show it a moment later when she lifted her hand, drying them on a cloth at her belt. Then she took a needle and thread out of her healer's kit. When she spoke, her words were clipped and harsh, but they were in his native Norin.

"Hold him still if you can, while you massage."

"I'll hold him."

He leaned on the patient's chest, sharing his heat and kept massaging his legs. She nodded her head in pleasure at his resourcefulness. The man flinched when she put the needle into his flesh, and Deckard put more of his weight down. It was oddly comforting to hear the clacking of her beads as she worked. By the time he was done, the man had some feeling in his legs again. The woman called over a young boy and gestured him to take the man to a large bonfire that someone had thought to start. Though Deckard would have loved to have a moment to take in the heat, he followed the other healer when she gestured for him to follow.

"You are clearly trained. How good are you?" She asked.

"I have been a full healer for ten years now. Village-taught, though I currently travel with a kompania."

She nodded and began to clean the blood off her hands. "Good. I'll need to handle the sailors. Most will speak Norin; if you find one that doesn't, call for Frairwick or Igraine. They are both very clever with languages. I must stay and heal these men first; they're city folk."

Deckard knew about the subtle dance every healer had to engage in with foreigners. Despite how many could be saved by healing those most badly injured first, a city healer generally had to heal the members of their community before they started in on others. Sometimes it didn't matter, but this wasn't one of those places.

Since he was also a traveler, he could see to the most badly injured travelers without causing any of the drama he had always hated most about being a healer.

Turning, he walked to an older man with sandy brown hair and grey eyes who was directing the recovery of sailors from the waterfront. The man's thin frame didn't give the impression of strength or fortitude, but that could have also been due to the dazed gleam in his eyes.

"Where are the most badly injured?"

The man stared at him blankly, as if he couldn't understand Deckard. He touched the man and asked his question again, trying to ground the man in the here and now. The touch seemed to wake the man up.

"Sorry, sir. Sorry. This way. These are the ones that look the worst. This man, he was on one of the boats. He has been stabbed through by debris and frozen in the ice. One of our men had to cut him out..."

"Thank you." Deckard cut him short. The man needed to talk, needed help too, but not as badly as the men on the sand. If Deckard could find a priest, he would send him to the man later. He would need to talk it out to somebody. "I'll need an assistant."

The man hesitated but nodded and then yelled. "Roe, get over here."

A young boy no older than 15 or 16, pimpled and colored like the Corvidae, ran over to him.

Deckard arranged Roe's hand on their patient's skin around his shoulder. "Squeeze as tight as you can."

Roe nodded, gagging when Deckard pulled the debris out of the man, causing blood to well in the wide holes.

"Do we know what happened here?" Deckard asked casually. If the boy was going to be any use, he had to be able to handle the horror. Distraction would work better at this point.

"Two women were hanging around one of the boats earlier when one of 'em suddenly started screaming her damn head off. Someone said they saw her get yanked into the water. A few seconds later and all the ships in the harbor started freezing and cracking in half."

"Did the other woman escape?"

"Yeah. They're still looking for her."

"For what?" Deckard asked.

The most the woman would be able to tell them was what the creature had said. Knowing would be useful only if it was going to return. He glanced around at the damage again. He supposed he could see why people wanted her. Another attack like this and there wouldn't be a harbor to return to.

The boy gagged again and turned away when Deckard's needle pierced the man's arm. Deckard tugged on the thread and asked his question again, with more authority in his voice. A trick that his teacher had taught him to break through shock.

"The usual... They want to give her to the creature."

Deckard's hand almost slipped, and he swallowed hard, mouthing a silent prayer to Tormu, the god of innocence and the innocent. *May the poor woman escape, unharmed and into the arms of those who will protect her.* No one should be sacrificed to appease monsters.

"Don't you think that sacrificing her would be wrong? What happens when it wants another person?" Deckard asked, continuing his work.

The boy shrugged, trying not to look around.

"Her life isn't worth this. It isn't worth the possibility of this ever happening again. No one's life is."

Chapter 25

*R*ichard was trying too hard to sit in one place and look casual. His posture was too stiff, he was sweating in places that made him glad there was a bath included with their room and he was being too quiet by far. The only saving grace was that with three beautiful women as his companions, nobody would be looking at him with anything but pity or admiration. Isashi would argue the number saying that either she didn't count as beautiful or as a woman, but he wasn't making the call aloud, so she couldn't complain.

"It isn't as though I did it on purpose!" Kuzunoha hissed at her sister.

"Did you even try to stop it before it happened?" Himiko hissed back.

Both were trying to keep their voices down, which in a bar like this, got you noticed. It would be better if they were to have this argument in their room rather than out here, but he'd already been silenced with a look by both Kuzunoha and Himiko for speaking up. When those two agreed, the heavens themselves would quake in fear.

The entire harbor had been destroyed to hear people talk. Docks, tools, people… little if anything had been spared. One woman who'd stumbled in had said that the monster had raged until an honest-to-goddess magi had stepped out, using pillars of flame to rain down destruction upon the creature's head.

Magi were worth the expense if a town could afford them. Not only could they bring actual magic to aid the settlement, but they had other skills to offer, everything from discerning truth from lies to easing the damage storms could do. They couldn't do everything, but their powers could save lives and give the people they protected a better chance to survive.

"What was I supposed to do? Shriek and run away? I didn't even know that she wasn't… like us, until it was too late." Kuzunoha said.

"Of course, you wouldn't. You never notice anything important." Himiko shot back.

Isashi covered Himiko's hand with hers. "Himiko, please, we are drawing attention."

Himiko turned on her friend, but Richard leaned forward as well, supporting her with a voice perfectly pitched to carry.

"I agree. If you two can't stop arguing, then we should take this upstairs. There's no need to air our dirty laundry about the city."

One of the men who had been listening close snorted and turned away at Richard's words. He didn't think it would help, but hopefully, some of the crowd in the bar would assume they were talking about catching one of their spouses cheating.

Himiko glared at Richard, but Kuzunoha stood up. "I don't think we have anything more to say, regardless."

"Where do you think you're going?" Himiko said, using the table to propel herself upwards. Kuzunoha looked frustrated and Richard could tell she hadn't had any place in mind.

"I was promised shopping and that's what I'm going to find." she finally said.

Richard dashed out of his chair to grab Kuzunoha as she stomped to the inn door. Just before she could grab for the door handle, it opened to admit a tall fellow, pale-skinned with dark shorn hair and the most vibrant red and orange robes Richard had ever seen. He carried an old lantern of blackened copper and glass; a flickering flame danced on the coal inside.

"Magi." The bartender breathed and bowed. "Welcome."

Richard grabbed Kuzunoha before she bumped into the man. He'd never been this close to one before, but the ones in Jiza could be worse than any entitled noble brat about things like that.

"No need for that." the Magi told the bartender. His voice was thick and ominous, but there was a smile hiding in its rich tones, as well. "I'm just here to talk with these beautiful strangers."

Then Richard looked at the flame, dancing orange and red with flickers of blue at the tips. He blinked and suddenly realized that the flame was watching him like he was watching it. Richard stopped breathing and watched as the creature reached out and used tiny hands of flame to grab a piece of coal that had rolled to the edge of the glass. The unblinking eyes of the fire stared into his soul as it popped the coal into a mouth that appeared as suddenly as the eyes had. The coal cracked and turned to dust as if the thing were chewing it.

Wish-givers, his people called them, but the term they used here was Magi, for the tools they used rather than what they could do. Not to say that all his people's wish-givers helped people but only an idiot told a man that could burn his face off with a thought that he was being an ass when he denied a request.

Kuzunoha smiled and then walked around him as if he hadn't meant her. The man stared and she crumbled like a hunted animal under that stare. She turned and returned to the table. Richard bowed and gestured for him to join him while smiling at the innkeeper.

"I'll need a drink of whatever the honored sir usually takes," Richard said, his breath caught in his throat.

How had this man even found them? The best way to remain hidden was to have no one interested in you, now everyone would want them. The innkeeper poured his best wine into a glass and shoved it at Richard. Everyone was standing around the table, greeting their guest. He handed the drink over with care.

"- and this is Richard. I assume you came here to talk about buying some of our silk or glass." Himiko said. Her tone sounded slightly desperate.

The wish-giver's lips raised in a tiny smile and he nodded. "Of course. It is not often that quality goods such as you and your sister have brought with you come into town."

Himiko nodded. "We can show you our stock upstairs."

"I would appreciate privacy to conduct our business." The Magi said.

Himiko gestured for him to follow her, though only a blind man could have missed the glare she sent her sister's way before turning to the stairs.

Richard took up the rear and felt his breath catch again as he looked around the room Himiko had gotten for them. It was small enough with the four of them and their bed, but with the addition of the wish-giver and his living fire's presence, the room felt even smaller. Himiko had pulled out a chair for their guest and then sat herself down on the only other chair in the room. Isashi sat on the nearest bed. Kuzunoha had the look of a caged animal as she took her place by the open window. Her eyes didn't leave the Magi, even while the man himself seemed to shrug off her attention.

"I'm glad you came up with a better explanation." The Magi pulled a ceramic bowl out of his suit. "Excuse me a moment."

They all watched him as he filled it with coal from a hidden pocket. Richard shut the door behind him and then moved to his bed, watching as the man coaxed the fire out of its lantern and into the bowl. It crackled for a brief moment before consuming one of the coal pieces and flaring to life. Though the creature's size didn't change, the sound coming from it had intensified to something more akin to a bonfire than a flame smaller than one you would use to cook with. The Magi whispered to the spirit and then dashed some herbs onto it. The spirit burned them up greedily and Richard's ears felt like they popped.

Kuzunoha whined and held her hands to her ears as if the popping had hurt. The Magi seemed taken aback but turned as Himiko told Kuzunoha to stop whining. Their guest made a motion as if working out a crick in his neck.

"Now we will not be heard by those wishing to spy on our meeting. I am Vitricious, Magi of the flame. I am here because a few hours ago, a very powerful water demon pulled itself onto our harbor and was provoked into causing havoc."

"I didn't provoke it." Kuzunoha snarled. She jumped up to sit on the windowsill.

"Kuzunoha, shut up," Richard whispered. Wish-givers were powerful, and those sorts of men usually took to being told they were wrong badly.

"Then what exactly did?" He asked.

Kuzunoha sucked in an angry breath and didn't speak, looking instead to Richard as if he could bail her out of this mess.

"My sister didn't provoke it... or at least, she certainly wouldn't have done so deliberately." Himiko's voice rang out, distracting the

Magi. "She said it became infuriated at the idea that we would be leaving the city soon."

The Magi shook his head as if that made no sense.

"You killed it?" Richard asked. He had been going for casual, but the question raced out of his throat burning like the little fire in the dish. He coughed, pushing down on his emotions. If he paid too much attention to them, he would die here.

The wish-giver glanced at him. "I am very powerful, and I did hurt it. Unfortunately, so long as its body is attached to the water, it cannot be caught or killed. When she realized I possessed the power to burn the water below the surface as well, she fled."

Richard hid his fists with the sheets of his bed, trying to look like the answer didn't terrify him as much as it did. She'd been threat enough when she'd simply been annoyed. Now that she was injured, she would want to capture him and kill everyone he was with, in the desperate hope that one of them would hurt him, or that one would be interesting enough to distract her from her pain.

"Why have you come to us?" Himiko said.

The Magi turned his glare on her. It softened, but only slightly.

"I am not a patient person." he said, "and I have never tolerated fools well, even before I became magi. This does not mean that I am cruel, or that I am without mercy."

Richard sucked in a breath but didn't say anything. He knew where this was going. He would have been more pissed off at the audacity of the stranger to think they'd go down without a fight, but he supposed that the Magi did have the power to back up his words if they didn't obey.

"This creature didn't come out until you arrived. The ship you arrived on took the most damage and multiple people saw the 'pretty girl' talking to it." He looked harshly at Kuzunoha. "I don't believe in coincidences. The thing wants something from you. Whether your lives, your deaths, or something else, I don't care. What I am concerned with is that if you are here, it will return. I can't, and won't, protect you when it does. You should leave town, quickly and by land."

Himiko had been holding herself calm enough, considering the situation, but at his words, she stiffened. "One of our members was attacked, targeted by a creature you have admitted to not being able to kill, and your response is to make the victims leave the safety of thick walls?"

"I said I am not cruel, and you do not look like fools."

The wish-giver would have sounded more sincere with that compliment had he not modulated his tone just as his eyes ran over Kuzunoha. The man's gaze fled from her and back to her sister as if there were something about Kuzunoha that repelled him. Was it simply that he thought she was the fey-touched; the one beloved by such a dangerous being?

"My people are not as wise, nor as patient, as I am. Even your beauty, and hers, isn't up to this challenge. The damage done was more than considerable. We have had attacks by roving bands of sahaughin and taken less. When enough people find out that it was a member of your group talking to it, they will decide that she should be sacrificed to satiate it. If you try to stop them, they'll feed all of your bodies to the waves in a misguided attempt to stop the creature from returning and causing more havoc."

Richard didn't want to agree, but he had seen people lynched in Jiza. It was never pretty. He couldn't let the girls be hurt because of his curse. Isashi stood before he could.

"Travelling on land is difficult enough in a small group. I am the only hunter of us. If we can't take a boat, how do you suggest we leave?"

The man pulled his eyes to Isashi. Those eyes suggested that because she wasn't as beautiful as Himiko, or even Kuzunoha was, that she was inconsequential. Richard had a sudden urge to punch the man. Like fae, a woman's appearance had very little connection to her strength or power.

"A Corvidae caravan arrived in town soon after the attack. Their healers are helping out at the docks, but no strangers will be welcome now. I would suggest traveling with them. The water demon must remain connected to the water or face the possibility of its own death. So long as you don't travel in or over water, the creature shouldn't be able to reach you."

"For how long?" Isashi asked.

"The Corvidae?" Himiko said at the same time. Her nose twisted in disgust.

"They are trustworthy, in their own way." Richard offered. He'd traveled with a group between towns before. "You have to set the boundaries, but after that, you couldn't ask for a tighter crew."

"I don't know, Hunter. I have never seen one of these before, only read about them in tales. It could be days or years. I simply don't know."

"We'll go and talk to this crow and his crew tomorrow then," Himiko said. Her tone suggested that the control she was trying so hard to cultivate was slipping.

Vitricious smiled at them once more and placed his fire back into its lamp. "I may seem harsh, but I am merely trying to keep the peace. It is your group that has left your paddles on the dock and placed yourselves under the power of forces beyond your control, not me."

As soon as the Magi had left, Himiko turned to the rest. "Does anyone have any other suggestions?"

When nobody answered, she sighed. "Isashi, I'll need you to come with me tomorrow. If I need to talk to the crows, I'd rather do it with you at my back."

Chapter 26

*H*imiko looked at the roof of their room. She'd been awake since Kuzunoha had slipped out, Richard following behind her, asking where she was going. She'd expected both to return within moments, but instead, the door had remained closed. Himiko had to simply assume they were gone now, out to buy black market items in a town that would lynch them if they knew who they were.

Himiko growled and flipped over, pushing her face into the pillow. If she'd been at home she would have gotten out of bed, read a book by candlelight, gotten some tea, or even gone for a walk outside. In this strange town, holed up in an inn that wasn't in any way like her home, she couldn't do any of those things.

Her fingers clenched harder around the pillow, squeezing the down feathers. It may have been soft, but it tasted dusty like it hadn't been cleaned properly. She forced her fingers to let the pillow go. At this rate, she would owe this third-class useless establishment for the destruction of the thing.

Truthfully, it wasn't what she wanted to destroy anyway.

Kuzunoha had been put in danger again. She had literally had a guard with her, been inside an obnoxiously large city, surrounded by people and thick walls. She had still managed to find the one place that a monster could get through the defenses. It was some sort of hideous joke. Like the world was trying to correct a wrong that had been made years ago when Himiko's mother had taken in her husband's by-blow instead of letting it die on their stoop.

Himiko was tired of it. Regardless of what sort of family might be waiting for her in Kalvettika, Kuzunoha would still be her closest living relative. That counted for something. She didn't get along with her sister, and it was likely that they never would, but she would be damned before she just let the world have its way.

She let out a heavy sigh and hit the straw-filled mattress with her fists. She didn't know what more she could do though. She'd hired someone to do nothing but protect Kuzunoha and even that wasn't helping. Maybe Richard was the problem? Her sister had always been uncanny and odd, but the world had never targeted her before. Not like this.

"Himiko?" Isashi said. "Are you still awake?"

Himiko opened her mouth to reply, stopping when she realized how silly that would be.

"I'm having trouble sleeping."

She heard Isashi shift in her bed and Himiko glanced over. It was dark, but what light there was from the open window illuminated Isashi's bunk. Her friend was leaning on her arm, looking across the room at her. Her face was lost in the shadows, but her hair reminded Himiko of hot coals; a bit of red among the deep shadows.

"What?" Himiko asked.

"I've known you for over ten years now. The only time you can't sleep is if you're sick or worried," Isashi said. Then she pointedly looked at Himiko. "You're not coughing."

Himiko closed her eyes.

"My sister is trying to get herself killed. It's my job to take care of her. What am I supposed to tell my ancestors when something inevitably succeeds in killing her?" Isashi wrinkled her forehead and Himiko went on. "And before you argue that she isn't, I'd like to remind you that she was also the focus for that thing that killed Hana as well. This isn't an isolated incident now... it means something, and I don't know what."

She shivered and Isashi slipped out of her bed, crawling under the covers to sit beside Himiko. The bed wasn't really large enough for two, but when Isashi's arms wrapped around her, she felt calm settle over her. Himiko wrapped her arms around her friend, ignoring the burning in her eyes as she burrowed against Isashi's shoulder.

"You heard her. She said it spoke to her." Himiko whispered.

"She also said that it seemed human to her. You know there are ones that can hide among us. Nobody could have seen the danger until it was too late. If even a hunter could miss it, how can you blame Kuzunoha for doing the same?"

Brandy Ackerley

Himiko could feel Isashi smoothing her hair and grabbed her friend tighter. Isashi was always willing to listen to her. She shifted so her head was leaning on Isashi's chest.

She continued, in a whisper. "This town is huge. Yet the foreigner is the first one that sees this creature and pisses it off enough to attack?"

Isashi took in a breath.

"That might not be what happened. Kuzunoha said that it got angry when she said they would be getting on the ship again. It could be new to this area and doesn't like ships passing over what it considers its territory."

Himiko pulled away, annoyed. Unlike her own skin, Isashi's caught all the light, shining faintly. It was beautiful.

"That isn't any better. We're still left with an obsessed monster that a magi couldn't defeat on his own."

Magi were dangerous and powerful. She'd tried to entice one to come to Hidan since the attack that had killed her father. Unfortunately, the yearly retainer for one had made the gross profit of her family's businesses look paltry in comparison. She hadn't found one willing to waive that fee or even negotiate with her.

Isashi smiled, ignoring her last comment. "Kuzunoha does attract attention."

The words pissed off Himiko. It was petty, she knew, but she hated that Kuzunoha was so pretty. Short, graceful, soft; their father had never let her forget that while Himiko may have been the trueborn daughter, it was Kuzunoha who had looked the part. Not that Himiko thought she was bad looking... just that comparing her to sister was like comparing a draft horse to a noble's racing steed. Both may have been beautiful, but one was clearly a work of art while the other was not.

"You're suggesting we scar her to make sure that she's more unnoticeable in the future?" Himiko griped.

Not that she ever would, of course. Even if she did it would probably turn out rakishly haunting in a way that played up her sister's sharp features.

Isashi rolled her eyes. "No. Your sister just isn't like everyone else. She stands out in a crowd."

"So, what can I do? Even a dedicated guard didn't help."

Richard had promised to take care of her, to keep her out of trouble.

Isashi shrugged. "Richard isn't the problem here and I don't think we can solve the problem that is Kuzunoha by talking it out in the dark. What we can do is take the problem step-by-step. The monster is tied to the water. So, we don't travel by water for a little while. It may be safer within walls, but it isn't as though stepping outside a city will get you killed. I do it all the time. So do the Corvidae. If we travel with them, like the Magi suggested, they'll know what we need to be on the lookout for."

"If they're willing to take us with them..." Himiko let out a harsh breath.

Isashi changed her position so that they were sitting side by side under the covers. Her fingers unerringly found Himiko's cheeks and wiped away tears that she hadn't realized were falling.

"Now, you're just being obstinate. Why? Is it because of your dad?"

Panic rose in Himiko. She'd been with him when the creatures had burst through the wall in the basement of the silk farm. He'd been complaining about how she couldn't do her job properly when she'd noticed an odd scratching noise and the wall behind them had burst, releasing the tide of creatures. They'd both been running for the main floor and the locked gate that served as a door there when he'd screamed and fallen. She hadn't slowed down until she was out and slammed the gate shut, locking everything in. She'd watched just long enough to see five of the creatures yanking the flesh off his bones, the bird skulls they wore painted red with his blood. She'd started heaving and heard more scratching below her, along with howls in Hidan.

She'd fled. It had been Isashi she'd found, wielding her arrows and slaughtering the creatures in droves around them.

Isashi pulled her close again and Himiko realized her heart was trying to beat its way out of her chest again.

"No one should have had to see the way he died," Isashi told her. How did she always seem to know exactly what Himiko was thinking about? "Think instead about that quote of his… Farmers farm, tanners tan, and traders…"

"… trade, no matter what." Himiko sighed. "Fine, we'll go and see if we can convince the Corvidae to see us to Kalvettika."

Isashi grabbed Himiko's pillow and slipped it behind her back. Then she pulled Himiko in close again. Himiko quivered, releasing another sigh and relaxed against Isashi's chest. Idly, she wondered if she could convince Isashi to stay with her a little longer. Her friend was brushing out her hair with her fingers. It felt… nice. A little odd, but nice.

"Himiko, I…." Isashi suddenly stopped. Himiko glanced back up at her but the light wasn't catching her anymore. She was just a voice in the dark. Isashi's voice was full of promise. "I promise, I'll always be here."

Himiko smiled and settled back on her friend's chest again. Of course, Isashi would always be there. Her friend was practically immortal. Her eyelids started drooping almost immediately. Then, she fell asleep faster than she had in years.

Chapter 27

He'd heard multiple times that they were lucky that only six boats had been destroyed while the rest had 'merely' been damaged; if not by the original frost, then by the fire that he'd learned the Magi had used to scare off the monster.

Deckard shook his head. Unlike the boats which could be conveniently counted using fingers and toes, there had seemed to be no limit to the bodies dragged from the water. He'd counted nearly a hundred, and over sixty of those had been beyond anyone's ability to heal. Even his powers couldn't bring back the dead. Kuzunoha had been the closest he'd ever managed to pull somebody back from. He'd been exhausted for days afterward.

He was tired now, too. Even just using his power to subtly reinforce the physical healing he'd done had taken his power to its limit. The last time he'd been that tired had been when the birdo goblins had snuck their way into Hidan.

There had been a lot of dead then, too.

The wagon he was riding on stopped and Tieni poked him gently. "This is our stop, Lover."

Deckard shook himself and looked around. They were still inside the walls, and the caravan had been brought inside.

"Thank you," Deckard said, yawning. He kissed her, then turned to the cart driver and thanked him. "I don't know if I would have made it on my own."

The burly Norin in the driver's seat nodded sharply at them, waiting impatiently for them to get down. His beady eyes glared at everything but he didn't respond. He hadn't been pleased to have the town guard ask him to return the healers to their caravan.

"That's one of the reasons why a guard is sent as well as a healer," Tieni told him. She had acted as though she hadn't expected anything more from the driver. Deckard hated the coldness he'd received since he'd joined the Corvidae. "Though I'm surprised you lasted that long."

Lady Morjiana and her guard had returned an hour or so before, having done all they could. Deckard could have returned then, but he had wanted to make sure that some of his patients were stable before he left. He wouldn't have felt that he had done his job if he'd left their care to others before they were out of the woods.

He yawned again as he walked up to the caravan. One of the boys, Deckard thought it was Drake, ran by him, carrying the grills they would put the cooking on when they stopped. Odd that they'd be cleaned up before they were leaving.

Then Deckard looked around and realized that the entire caravan was packing up.

Tieni whistled like a chirping bird and one of the younger girls came running over.

"Rowan, what's happening here? Weren't we going to stay for a few days?" Tieni asked.

The girls every motion shone with anger. "We were. The Kennicks want us gone. They didn't threaten, of course, but from what Ebon heard from Troll who heard it from Danior, we'll be safer the sooner we're out of town. Especially with the trouble our lord and master is bringing down on us."

Rowan jacked her thumb towards where Danior was overseeing the takedown of the smithy cart, unnecessarily.

Someone had told him that the city folk want them gone quick. He hadn't believed them; not when the Corvidae's healers had spent an entire evening helping Sakre's wounded. Deckard clenched his fist again. He enjoyed some aspects of traveling with the Corvidae. Then there were things like this that he'd hated. Deckard had hoped that he'd be able to see his patients once more. Unnecessary guilt tore at him. He reminded himself that he'd done all he could last night.

"What's the reason this time?" Tieni said, her tone wry. "Let me guess. Their own injured were too loud and it was our healer's faults."

Rowan shook her head. "It wouldn't be the first time, but no. Some stranger was seen talking with the thing before it attacked. More than a few want some strangers to sacrifice if it comes back."

"That's the most ludicrous idea I've ever heard," Deckard told Tieni as Rowan started rushing away. Suddenly Rowan turned back.

"I almost forgot, we're going to have some guests. They'll be taking your wagon."

Deckard turned to Tieni while she swore in a tirade so crude that a few of the sailors he'd known would have been taken back. While he was just as annoyed at the inconvenience as she was, he had to admit that she was going overboard.

"Ah, Tieni. I see you've heard about our guests." Danior said.

"This is a travesty and you know it." She growled at her cousin.

"You are the most junior members. You know that in these cases it's the most junior members who are moved."

Deckard kept his mouth shut. He'd thought that Danior and he were finally starting to come to a compromise. He'd thought that friendship couldn't be far behind. But he couldn't think of anything worse than losing the wagon he shared with Tieni. Where would either of them sleep?

"I'm your cousin, and way older than a junior member, you *cobalti*…"

Deckard put a hand Tieni's arm and held her back. "Tieni, I don't think anyone deserves to have that said about them."

Brandy Ackerley

"You may be my cousin, but you and he have been with us less than a season," Danior said, ignoring Deckard completely.

"I've been on the road since I was born." Tieni's frown was terrifying. She threw off Deckard's hand.

"Aside from your year with the boy," Danior said. Tieni's mouth flattened to a line. Well, that did answer Deckard's question.

Though it was a rare occurrence, a few of the Corvidae did settle down in the cities they passed through. Most gave it a try, at some point, usually for a season, or maybe two. Tieni's father had been angry, but Deckard hadn't thought Tieni's own family would treat her like a child over it.

"Who will we be staying with?" Tieni asked, hollowly.

"Is that the wagon we'll be staying in?" Deckard heard a familiar voice say.

He swung around, shocked to see Kuzunoha, her sister, Richard, and Isashi walking into the camp. Drake, the scamp that had run past them on their way in, started answering her. Kuzunoha turned his way and stumbled, her mouth hanging open like a fish, gasping as they did when first landed, but not dead yet.

Richard caught her before she could tumble to the ground. Then he turned and saw who she was looking at. He tilted his head in a subtle acknowledgment.

"Deckard?" Isashi said, walking over as she spotted him, too. Himiko followed with a frown.

"What are you doing here?" Tieni asked before Deckard could find his voice.

"We stopped in town for business and our ship was wrecked," Isashi told Tieni and him. "We didn't know—"

"Deckard," Kuzunoha blurted out, cutting off Isashi. "I hadn't expected to ever see you again."

Her thankful glance at Richard while he got her settled and led her over rubbed Deckard the wrong way. He was too tired to be dealing with this today.

"Oh, you know each other?" Danior asked. His tone was all smiles and rainbows now.

Deckard glanced at the caravan master, realizing that these were their new passengers.

"I thought you'd still be in Hidan. Are you feeling well enough to be traveling?" Deckard asked Kuzunoha.

She looked away. "Master Lin isn't as skilled as you, but she gave me a clean bill of health."

Had Master Lin said that? Or had she somehow convinced his teacher she was ready to be on her own? He turned to Himiko.

"Has she been resting enough? Getting enough fluids. What sort of exercise is she doing?"

"I'm fine. I've been doing some gentle sword-work," Kuzunoha told him.

Brandy Ackerley

Himiko's eyes narrowed in untamed frustration. "She's still irritating every monster she can find. It's why we had to contract your kompania to see us the rest of the way to Kalvettika."

"This isn't the place to discuss—" Danior said.

Kuzunoha's back straightened and she argued. "I am not..."

The rest of her words ran together into an incomprehensible torrent but all he understood was that she had caused the trouble. All those people…

"You were the cause of everyone's death," Deckard whispered.

She looked stricken and stopped talking. He stalked forward and grabbed her.

"Do you even know how many lost their lives? Over sixty. I was pulled in just after sunset and worked until they kicked us out as the sun rose. I haven't even been able to wash yet." He let go of her, gesturing towards his ruined clothing.

Kuzunoha's shoulders slumped. Deckard rubbed at his face and stepped away when Tieni tugged his sleeve. The monster had probably been just looking for a reason to attack; something to justify the havoc she had longed to cause. Deckard sighed. It wasn't the victim's fault when someone attacked unprovoked. He had been awake too long. He would have to apologize.

Richard pushed Kuzunoha behind him and stepped up to Deckard aggressively.

"That was uncalled for, Deckard. I expected better from you." Richard snarled.

Kuzunoha needed an apology, but he wouldn't give one to Richard in her stead. "You're one to talk."

Kuzunoha pushed Richard out of her way and growled silently; an expression that was all teeth and anger. He felt a moment of triumph, expecting her to turn on Richard. To defend him. She didn't.

"I didn't kill those people, Deckard. A monster did."

Deckard's back straightened. How dare she chastise him? She was right, but she wasn't blameless enough to reprimand him.

"Even if I'm being honest…" he said.

Richard glared at him. "You're not being honest. You're being casually cruel."

He looked at Richard again. Everything had gone wrong when he had arrived in Hidan. Deckard didn't know why would he expect her to find any difference between the monster in her bed and the unnatural ones outside the walls?

"You've made your bed, Kuzunoha." He said. "Or, more accurately, you've stolen my bed, so go lie in it."

Deckard stalked away to grab his things from the wagon he'd started to think of as his. Behind him, he could hear Danior trying to apologize for his rude behavior. For once, Deckard didn't care. Tieni stepped beside him as he opened the door. She reached and pulled him into her arms.

"Tieni…" he growled.

"You're right, Deckard. She needs to start taking responsibility for her actions."

Gods be damned. He'd spent weeks wishing for just one more chance to talk to her to not leave things as he had. Now he'd made it worse.

He would have to apologize. As soon as he'd slept.

"Danior won't be pleased." He told Tieni. He was tired. So tired. All he wanted was to wash the blood off and fall asleep against her. To forget there was a world outside of her arms, at all.

"He can fight in the final war for all I care," Tieni swore. "Let's pack and head to our new wagons to sleep for the day, Love."

Chapter 28

*R*ichard couldn't deny that his traveling companions had slipped into his heart somewhere along the way. Even Himiko had found a place for herself in there. But, he'd been on his own for so long… staying with them all the time felt cloying.

He had managed to slip out of the wagon without anyone noticing… now he just wanted some time alone. Nighttime with the kompania was quiet, but even so, four people sat around the central fire, sharing ale, one strumming a stringed instrument. Too many for him tonight.

The darkness wrapped around Richard like the bed cloth of a lover as he slipped away from the circle of protection the wagons formed. It felt good to get out of sight, to be on his own. Until a set of the shadows to his right moved.

Tieni held up her hands, her fingers laced together in the symbol of non-violence.

"Richard? You're still up?"

He'd forgotten she was on watch tonight. That reminded him that Deckard was somewhere out there in the dark, too. Alone. Richard owed him a private conversation and an even more private 'gentlemen's disagreement'. He may have muttered a half-hearted apology to Kuzunoha when he'd woken up to join the group for dinner, but that wasn't enough for Richard's peace of mind.

"I've always disliked small rooms. How are the woods tonight?"

She rolled her eyes. "Having a guard on tonight is a waste of a good night's sleep."

That surprised Richard. "Why would you say that?"

She gestured in the direction of the church.

"That is the church of the Penitent Astrologer. It's a safe zone."

"I thought those were myths," Richard said with a frown.

Safe zones were places that monsters couldn't, or wouldn't, travel on, or through, and he'd never found one in his travels before. Supposedly, monsters forced into a safe zone died, and in one tale a monster had entered one and been changed into a 'holy' mount for the count of Tory; whether you remembered him as the Bloodthirsty Count depended entirely on which side of his war you'd been on.

"They're very real. The Corvidae have them all mapped out." She told him.

He would have to get a copy of those maps. They would sell for a pretty penny... after he'd copied them, of course. "Yet, Danior still has people on watch?"

She rolled her eyes. "Danior's rules. We have a watch on, every night, even here. That doesn't make it less of a waste. What are you doing out?"

Richard shook his head. "I was hoping for a private walk. Will it be safe enough for me alone?"

Tieni shrugged. "In a different area, I'd suggest you take a partner with you, and maybe a third to watch your backs for when the two of you get distracted. Here though? Have fun. Don't go past the shrine to the north or the graveyard to the east though. The safe zone ends there. You might always want to watch your feet if you head to the graveyard. The cliff is high, and the water takes a little more every year. What's left is likely to land you in the ocean with no way back up."

Richard waved goodbye, heading east. The Courtesan didn't put much of her time or energy into dealing with the dead and the bodies were either buried namelessly in the desert or given to the ocean; both cleansed the soul as well as the body, either by fire or water. The idea of burying your dead in ground that could be used as perfectly good farmland or grazing land seemed like such a waste. Still, he had come to appreciate the beauty of the stones they laid at the feet of their dead here.

Unfortunately, the graveyard was small, only fifteen or so bodies were so marked. Near the other end of the graveyard, there was a larger stone edifice that looked like a stubby stone slab, about as high as his chest, big enough to lay a body on. Fortunately, there was nothing macabre there, only some sort of shallow bowl resting on top. Richard picked his way across the graveyard to it.

Brandy Ackerley

The bowl was carved out of a simple sandstone; probably the cheapest the church had been able to afford, which still would have been expensive considering its size. On the right corner, part of the rock seemed to have dissolved away, leaving only a sharp edge sticking dangerously out. Its base was inscribed with faded markings. Most were smoothed, as though the wind and the sea had gotten to them. He found one where the markings were almost clear and bent down, wishing he could pull the moon closer or make the starlight brighter so that he could read it.

Would you want to?

The answer didn't seem to matter as much as the question itself did and he couldn't quite tell why. Standing he turned to look at the cliff. The nearest bodies were about ten feet inland from the edge, but at the rate that Tieni said the cliff was deteriorating, the bodies and their stones wouldn't remain there much longer. He shivered, seeing the ocean water ripple as another wave rolled up against the land.

Would the fey be able to make it up here if she wanted to? Should he leave and go to the shrine which was higher up? It was better to be safe than dead. Still, he turned to the bowl. He'd look at it and then go.

He was surprised to see that the bowl wasn't flat like he'd thought. There was some sort of figure carved into the bottom, but half-filled with black, brackish water, he couldn't make it out.

Richard tried to pick it up and found the bowl heavy, but manageable. He tilted the water out and used some from his canteen to finish cleaning it. The carving on the bottom of the bowl was well worth the effort.

It was beautiful, a young figure carved to look as though it was a body, rising out of the white of the bowl. Its legs and arms had been carved athletically and the chest was slim and mostly flat. The face was exquisite work, round and kind, eyes closed, hair, carved strand by strand to fall back into the bowl. He decided the figure was female, probably a young woman of 15 or maybe 16. He touched the face softly. Not much younger than he was now... and maybe a year older than when he'd left Jiza.

He put the bowl back onto the pedestal and touched the face once more. Then he took out the rest of his water, took a small sip, and poured the rest into the bowl.

"Pain is gone and those who loved you keep that memory within. May the spirit rest and you find your release in the embrace of the gods."

The wind picked up, flipping his hair around him and he grinned. He felt better as if he had helped to lay her spirit to rest. Perhaps she didn't have anyone to bless the place where her body rested and had been pleased with his work. Either way, he didn't regret it, or the pleasure he felt from doing a job well done.

Pleased? You are pleased?

That was... odd. He shook his head, wondering if he was more tired than he'd thought. He turned from the pedestal.

Not pleased?

He stiffened, realizing that the thought had not come from him. He turned slowly back to the pedestal and saw a tiny creature standing by the bowl, no taller than a doll, looking into it as carefully as he had been not long ago. She was naked and her body was exquisite. Her form was an hourglass, plump in all the places that he liked, though her waist was so small that he wondered how it could hold her up. He couldn't tell what color her hair was, only that it was dark, like that slim area that surrounded the full moon, a warm blueish grey. Her skin looked blueish too as if she'd been painted the shade of the sky from his homeland; the exact shade it would have been at high noon when the sun was beating down on you, but the hottest part of the day was still to come.

The air went out of him and his daggers flashed into his hands. If it was another fey bitch, he'd kill her, gut her before he was taken again.

The creature reached into the bowl, touching the water he'd placed in it, not looking at him at all. The water sparkled where her hand touched, making it look like stars were hiding in its depths. A breeze that felt unnatural, but perfectly cool blew across it, causing tiny ripples to form on the surface, making those stars dance.

The creature turned to him for the first time. Her eyes looked like the sky above, or the water beneath her hand, dark with brilliant twinkles of light in their depths. The too-large eyes blinked at him, the eyelashes fluttering more like insect wings, a flash too quick for him to separate. Her expression was strangely familiar, almost as if she were pleased that he'd figured out something. Then she turned back to the bowl and reached in and he saw the wings on her back glittering in the moonlight. They looked like insect wings, delicate but powerful.

Her expression was wrong on her oval face, though he couldn't say why; the perfect pout not quite conveying how she was feeling. Despite that, he could tell she was worried. She flew up to him, zipping to his face. When her hands touched his cheeks, they were cool like the breeze.

You have no breath. Why do you have no breath?

She whimpered as if the thought of him not breathing was a nightmare of epic proportions.

He drew in a breath and she looked so relieved he felt bad for worrying her. She hugged him and he could feel her relief wash through him.

He didn't want to kill her, he wanted to protect her... but he had to ask.

"Are you fey?"

The creature tilted its head as if it was deciding how to answer the question.

Fey? What is Fey?

Terrifying creatures of lust and worship who destroy those who fell within their grasp. Dangerous beauties who 'broke' their toys simply by not knowing how much damage somebody could take before they died. Like a child that broke their doll, not realizing that compared to them, the toy was fragile.

It was so easy to be broken that way.

He didn't say anything aloud, but her expression changed to one of sadness. He pulled away gruffly and raised the bigger of his daggers. It wasn't one of the ones he would normally draw. It was nearly a foot long and over an inch wide. He pointed it at her. The queen had taken him by kindness at the beginning as well. It hadn't lasted. It never did.

"They are monsters, and all look different. The one thing that none of them can do is touch cold iron."

The creature stared at him and then flew up to the dagger, landing skillfully on the broad side of its blade. She might have weighed a full pound, soaking wet. Too light for her size. Her bare feet took no damage and she crouched, lowering her hands to caress the blade. Her nose turned up in disgust.

Earth metal. With no flame inside, it remains brittle and hard. Earth cannot be moved.

Suddenly, she flew up, stopping just a few inches away from his face. Tilting her head, she smiled at him again. She moved forward slowly, her body smelling like the air after a thunderstorm, dry heat, and soothing mint. Her head was no larger than his nose, but he could feel her lips burning, like desert sand at midday, when she kissed him. His lips tingled under her faint pressure.

Mine? Mine?

He reached out and touched her back. He felt the spike of desire in her and her wings beat even faster. Her hands moved, calling into them a bubble.

Breath?

He opened his mouth and she moved forward, pushing the bubble into his mouth as she kissed him again.

The taste was like nothing he'd ever tasted before. Cold mint mixed with vanilla and the faint scent of the swamp. Richard gasped as the taste settled low in his lungs, and for a terrifying moment, he wondered if he would ever feel like he had enough air to breathe again. The sensation settled, and he was suddenly aware of her chest rubbing against his lips and the soft heat coming off her body.

Fly? Please?

Richard had never wanted to give in to something so much in his life. If he let her, she would show him everything he'd ever dreamed of. She would drag him along behind her, flying until he had nothing left to give her.

He'd been in a relationship like that before. If he accepted, he would never want for anything, he would do anything she asked, no matter how depraved. In the end, he'd crave the destruction she forced him to cause.

He'd nearly lost himself to that fey bitch. He wouldn't let it happen again.

He took in a deep breath, forcing himself to ignore the taste of mint, still on his breath. "No, little one. I must stay firmly on the ground. For now."

She looked like he'd just kicked her puppy. It felt like he had.

No? Fly with me?

He shook his head, firmly. "Not today."

His head suddenly felt clearer, as if he had been light-headed or dizzy, though he hadn't noticed anything before. She touched his face, an intensely sad expression on her own.

One day?

He nodded, mutely. One day... a day that his heart wished would be tomorrow. He shook his head, promising nothing.

"I have to return to my friends. Will you come with me?"

The creature nodded, her expression brightening.

Now if only he could figure out how to explain to them what she was.

Chapter 29

"*W*hat is it?" Deckard asked, looking at the creature with distaste.

The thing that Richard had brought back with him was a little under a foot tall, blue, and made in the mockery of a real woman; her body too perfect to be natural. Nothing sagged or drooped, and her waist was too thin. She was pretty but wrong. It was like she'd been carved by a painter who knew what women were supposed to look like but had never actually seen one naked. And she had wings. Similar to a bug's, they looked fragile and glasslike, nothing more than a thin spiderweb of veins holding them together. It seemed impossible that she could use them to fly, but she did, all too often for his tastes.

"More importantly, why did you bring it back with you? Kuzunoha, stop that. You don't even know if the little thing will bite you." Himiko said.

Kuzunoha and Isashi had been trying to tempt the little creature to eat berries since Richard had returned with it, though she'd just upgraded to a dollop of cream on her fingertip. The little creature was looking at the food in confusion like she wasn't sure what she was supposed to do with the offerings.

"It can't be a monster," Tieni said. "We're in one of Gren's holy places."

She had been the first one other than Richard to see it and she still looked flummoxed.

"It's not human, so what else could it be?" Himiko said.

Kuzunoha gestured towards Isashi, "By that reasoning, neither is she, and I would never say she wasn't human."

Isashi sat up, tense and unhappy, curling in on herself.

Himiko flushed. "Kuzunoha! I didn't mean it like that. This creature is all of a foot tall and blue. What else could it be?"

Richard held out his hands and then bent low. The moment he moved, the creature's eyes were on him, wide and pure. Deckard almost thought he could see a bit of a desperate air to them as if the little creature was hoping Richard would save her from the giants who kept trying to give her pieces of food as large as her head.

"What are you?" A moment later, Richard continued, looking at everyone. "Well, I've never heard of it. Have any of you?"

If Richard was trying to convince them that the creature hadn't driven him insane, he wasn't doing a very good job of it.

"Richard, she didn't say anything," Isashi said, almost sounding apologetic.

Richard looked annoyed and then looked at his creature again.

"Why can't they hear you?" He frowned and glanced at his friends again before turning back to the creature. "I mean, can you speak out loud? So that they can hear you, as well?"

The creature grimaced. "Sylph."

He had expected the creature to sound like a mouse, squeaking, just based on her size. In reality, her voice was closer to a purring cat, so low it seemed to vibrate in the air. It wasn't uncomfortable... but at the same time, it wasn't unpleasant either.

Richard seemed to melt into the sound like cheese on freshly baked bread.

Tieni took a step forward, looking at the creature more closely. "Sylph? Well, Morjiana will know what it is."

"The real question is, how dangerous is it?" Deckard asked.

Kuzunoha glared at him. "Dangerous? She's barely a foot tall. She's no more dangerous to us than Richard is."

Deckard caught Richard's eye and wondered if the man were thinking that there was more truth to her statement than she realized. Richard didn't seem to mind killing, and he held too many secrets too close for Deckard's comfort.

"What if this thing can control his thoughts?" Tieni asked. "We don't know what it can do and it talks to him in his head."

"Weren't you the one who said it wasn't a monster?" Kuzunoha said.

"It could be a danger to everyone though," Tieni said. "We have to know. Danior will want to know."

"I'm certainly not feeling any control, but if you want, I'll shoo the little thing away," Richard said.

He looked like he didn't care one bit about the creature. Certainly, if he were being controlled by it, he wouldn't seem so calm at the idea of tossing it out on its ass.

Richard picked up the sylph and put her on his shoulder, like some sort of demonic parrot.

"I say we let Richard keep his pet," Isashi said, standing up and dusting herself off. "At least until we get to Kalvettika. Then we can look through the library there for more information."

"Library?" Deckard asked.

Himiko was sitting against the wagon, her arms crossed in front of her. "It started as a library of holy texts. It's grown since then, and people say that you can find the answer to any question you have there."

Deckard blinked. Now that she mentioned it, he remembered his mother going to Kalvettika when she'd realized what he was. Had she gone to the library? How large would it have to be to answer any question asked of it?

Would a library that large be able to solve his problem? Would it have a way to fix him, remove the power so that he could live without fear of it?

"I'll allow it for tonight," Tieni said. "If we find out anything that we don't like though, we're tossing the creature out, and all of you with it. I expect you to keep that thing away from everyone else in the meantime, Richard."

Richard patted the sylph softly and nodded. "I promise you that she won't leave my sight."

"Come on, Deckard," Tieni said.

Deckard started walking her way when Kuzunoha popped the cream into her mouth and stood.

"What are you going to name her?"

Richard turned to it. "Name her? I don't even know what sort of personality sh- it has."

Isashi shrugged. "Why not ask the creature itself?"

Deckard looked at her horrified and he wasn't the only one. Himiko's eyes had bulged as well. Isashi looked away and her voice was less sure of herself when she spoke next.

"It just seems to me that if she knew what she was, then she should also know her own name."

Richard laughed. "Good point. Well, little one, you heard my friend, Isashi. Do you have a name?"

The creature looked around at them all quickly but then looked back at Richard. The creature's hand reached out and his cheek. After a moment, Richard shook his head, gently.

"Say it out loud, please."

The creature looked uncomfortable. "Zaiya."

Deckard saw Richard touch the creature's shoulder and thought he saw an unguarded pleasure in Richard's face.

Kuzunoha grinned. "Zaiya. I like that. Well, let's start by asking the next question... What, exactly, do you eat?"

Deckard left without hearing the answer and caught up with Tieni. Her shoulders were tight and he stopped her. Without saying anything, he touched her back and started massaging out her stress. She wasn't putty in his hands, but she did move her shoulders, directing him to all the knots that were making her tense. She moaned a little as he rubbed out a particularly resistant one.

"Yes, that one... It's been bothering me since they first showed up." She told him.

He nodded, even though she couldn't see it. "They'll be gone soon enough. Kalvettika is what? A week away at the most?"

She nodded. "The only way it will be longer is if weather locks us down during the trip."

He didn't think that was likely. He knew that in early spring and late winter, they could get very impressive snowfalls this far north, but it would be decidedly odd if it happened in the middle of summer.

"Do you think Danior will let Richard keep his toy here for the whole week?"

Deckard had seen the look of adoration in the little thing's eyes... he didn't think it would leave Richard without a fight, even if they wanted it to. He was more concerned that Richard wouldn't let it go; regardless of his brave words tonight.

Tieni sighed and a bit of her tenseness returned. "Most likely."

"What about the danger?" Deckard asked. "You said yourself, we don't know what it is."

She nodded and turned to look at him.

"That's why Danior will let him keep it."

He must have looked confused because she continued.

"The Corvidae don't have the resources of a town if we run into trouble, so we hoard what we do have. Sometimes, one of the children will find something that no one in the clan knows about. A new bug, a new animal, sometimes a baby monster. When that happens, the child is allowed to keep it, so long as they agree to watch it and tell their elders everything about it that they learn. Generally, one of the young fighters is given the task of watching over both to see if the new thing is dangerous. Sometimes, even young monsters can be tamed and used effectively, and other creatures may have a hidden use."

She shook her head. "The last new thing was a small monster that looked like beetle the size of your hand. If you fed it blood, liquid or dried, of any species, it would glow red for hours. When we can find them, we keep them in cages and feed them the blood from our meat or injuries we take. It's a safe way to have lights in our wagons, without having to worry about having a fire."

"Danior was the one who found it?"

She shook her head. "No, one of his friends. He was envious though. Even now, he'll want to find a use for Richard's little creature, and if he does, he'll try to keep it to show the other tribes when we cross paths."

Deckard shook his head. "That doesn't sound safe."

"Safe isn't the point, Deckard."

He didn't like where this was going.

"Safe should always be the point," he told her. When it wasn't the point, people got hurt.

"Either way, we'll see what Danior says. Do you want to come with me?"

"You're going now?" He asked. "You said you wouldn't be going until morning."

"Safe may not be the point, but that doesn't mean that we're going to be stupid about it. We wake him now so that he is the first. He'll wake Morjiana and ask her what it is. If anyone knows, it should be her."

Deckard nodded, happy that something would at least be done to protect everyone before the night was finished.

"Let's go."

Chapter 30

*K*uzunoha smiled as Danior called for her but finished pulling her blade back with a whip-like snap and twisting to it across an imaginary enemies' neck before she turned to face him. The man seemed immune to her charms, but he was willing to talk to her. Very few in the caravan, that didn't also have an urge to be between her legs, had been willing to. Fortunately, Kuzunoha wasn't hoping to find a warm bed here; regardless of what Deckard seemed to think.

"Danior, how can I help you?"

He smiled, meeting her gaze. It always struck her as a bit odd when people did that. Growing up, it had been beaten into her that meeting someone's eyes was personal; something that you only did if you were very close to a person. Otherwise, it was a challenge to their authority; to His authority.

Her father was dead, she reminded herself. She didn't have to worry about enduring his disappointment ever again.

"The weather tonight is beautiful, no?" he asked.

She nearly rolled her eyes. Perhaps it was a Corvidae thing to talk endlessly around your questions, rather than just asking them straight. Whatever else it was, she found it annoying.

"It's beautiful." She answered.

The forest swamp around Hidan was moist and thick, and even where the land was firm, you could smell the faint scent of life, rot, and salt. Here, the scent of salt was fading and with it, trees firmer and straighter than those at home had taken their place. She'd grown to love cedar since her injury and had been pleased to find that it grew more commonly in the firmer soil. She had claimed an entire bough of the last one they'd walked by, hanging it by her bed in the wagon. The scent filled the entire area, relaxing her whenever she was inside. It made sharing such a tiny space with the others manageable.

Danior smiled. "I have always liked this part of the forest, as well. Though I have never had the luck of your guardsman for finding beautiful things within it."

He'd been envious over the creature Richard had found. Kuzunoha didn't mind the little beastie, though she thought Richard's attachment to the creature was odd. She fancifully thought that she'd felt it the moment he'd found it, although she couldn't have said why. The little creature didn't seem overly fond of her either.

"Yes. Your fortune-teller said the creature was a spirit of some sort?" she said.

"Tied to the elements, though they all look different. She's never seen one that took the form of a person before. She said this one is a creature of the air. A sylph." He said, the unfamiliar word catching on his lips. "At any rate, she said it poses no threat to us. So long as we don't push to remove it from your friend."

"That doesn't tell us much." Kuzunoha pointed out.

"She's a fortune-teller. Her job is to whisper sweet nothings and empty promises to Kennicks. She may have seen a lot in her time, but it doesn't mean she's one of those books that know everything."

"An encyclopedia." Kuzunoha said, with a smile, pleased to be considered more than just a 'Kennick' in his eyes. "True. I just heard that she had an almost encyclopedic knowledge."

"There are some things she does know that well. Just not this. Do you mind if I ask you a question?"

She tilted her head and he let out a breath.

"I don't like Deckard much; my cousin deserves better, you understand." She nodded and he continued. "However, I noticed that you seemed to know Deckard more than passingly well."

"He came from Hidan, where we're from."

"More than that…"

She flushed. "He and I used to date."

"Any chance you still want him?" he asked bluntly.

Yes, she thought. Kuzunoha blinked and flushed more. It wasn't that simple.

"No."

He frowned. "Pity. That would have taken care of Tieni's attachment quite nicely. In that case, I must ask, your prior attachment to him won't be a problem, will it? If he is my man and not yours I'll have to ask you to not cause trouble with him."

She shook her head. "Deckard does not approve of me or my choices, but I suppose I gave him a reason-"

A bell started ringing throughout the camp. Kuzunoha hadn't even had time to ask what it was for before Danior yelled at her, "Enemies. Stay here."

Like hell, she thought, running after him.

She had been expecting a creature like the goblinoids that lived near Hidan and nearly stopped dead when she saw Danior attack an armed woman dressed in a dark, undyed robe.

The blade hit hard, and a reddish spray filled the air.

The blood, its thick metallic scent surprised her, bringing clarity with it. Not monsters. They were under attack by humans.

"Bandits," she breathed.

Two more men, dressed in the same type of clothing, surrounded her and Kuzunoha felt that breath catch in her throat.

"Pretty little thing," the first commented.

"She'll fetch a pretty price too, so long as we don't dirty her up too much," said his companion.

"Don't even think about it. She's one of them sing-song girls. Might be the one we're looking for."

Kuzunoha felt her lips pull back in a snarl. She'd heard strangers to Hidan use the slur sing-song before. They used it because they couldn't even be bothered to remember the name of Sian Ku. She hadn't appreciated it then and she certainly didn't now.

"Little pretty thinks she has teeth..." the first started to say.

Kuzunoha didn't let him finish. She leaped at him, pulling her blade quickly to try and slash his chest. The bastard brought up his weapon, some sort of harvesting tool with a curved blade, deflecting her blade.

He sounded incredulous as he said, "Bitch tried to cut me."

Kuzunoha heard his friend coming up behind her and didn't bother responding, just spun, catching his spear with her weapon. She dodged right, and he followed his spear a step closer to her.

"Can't blame the pretty for reacting when you scare her. You shouldn't have smiled." The spear man's words were light, but the expression was cold.

Perhaps he hadn't expected her to be able to move that fast. She ignored the man behind her and sent a few jabs at the one in front of her, pushing him back. Fast was one thing she could do. She heard a grumble from behind her and moved to the right, beside the spearman, just as the farmer's tool the other man had been wielding slashed across the spot. The tip of the blade caught the spearman's leg and he turned away from her, grabbing his leg. She pulled her blade across his back and he swore obscenely as he fell to the ground

She didn't think he was badly injured but hoped his injuries would be enough to keep him down. She felt a blow land across her back and hissed. Unlike the bandits, her armor was still in one piece and stopped the blow from dropping her. She swore. Even with armor, attacks like these would still bruise her to hell. She'd hurt for days afterward if she survived this attack.

She dodged out of the way of a second cleave, but not by enough. The armor strap on her shoulder took a slice but stayed attached. She swore again. She had to finish this battle quickly. Her sword was already feeling heavier than she liked, and she knew she'd only been fighting for a minute or so. It was strange that she could do this while practicing against a wooden opponent for ten minutes or more but put her against a real opponent and she was already gasping for air.

There was no more time for rumination as the guy tried to jab her in her ribs with the pommel of his weapon, just catching her side. Her breath shot out in an 'oof' of air and she panicked for a second while she tried to suck in another. Her second breath was deeper, but it hurt.

She ignored her lungs as much as she could and caught his weapon on hers, pushing him away. He stumbled back a foot or two and suddenly Danior was there, his blade sticking through the man. The bandit's eyes went from dark and menacing to confused; lost. He dropped his sword and tried to look behind him, his hands reaching up to the weapon.

Danior ripped his sword out and the bandit fell forward as if his legs couldn't hold him anymore. He coughed a few times, blood falling into the green grass beneath her feet.

Kuzunoha opened her mouth to say something, but the sudden stink of released bowels filled the air, making the heady scent of blood vanish. She blinked when she felt an arm around her and felt Danior's hands on her, keeping her from falling.

"It's okay, girl. Don't pass out on me."

"I'm fine..." she said. After a moment, she took a deep breath. The air tasted fresher this time. She wasn't sure if that was good or bad. "I feel much better now?"

Kuzunoha hadn't meant to phrase it as a question, but Danior seemed to understand it better than she did.

"A lot of women get sick when they're forced to kill somebody. It isn't anything to be embarrassed of. You fought very well."

Kuzunoha narrowed her eyes. "I've killed before."

"Monsters. My lady, it is always different when it's another person." Danior turned as one of the younger boys called for him. "Roe? Report."

She wanted to correct him, wanted to tell him that it wasn't some moral holding her back, but didn't dare. She was starting to suspect that there was something very wrong with her. Until she figured out what it was, she had to keep that knowledge private and safe.

"No deaths or major injuries. One bad cut, but Morjiana says not to worry, that head wounds always bleed like a gushing rainspout, even when they're not deep. She's stitching her up already. The villains took three boxes of supplies and one of them managed to grab Morjiana's trinket drawer."

"Who took a head wound?"

"Lavinia." The boy told him. Danior grinned.

"Oh, I am going to have fun with this… after I check with Morjiana, of course. Start cleaning this, please."

"Yes, but sir… you need to go see Deckard first. He and Tieni insisted."

Danior frowned. "Insisted?"

The boy nodded and ran off. Danior turned to her. "Were you hurt? It looked like they got in a hit or two in."

Kuzunoha shook her head, trying to clear it. "A few bruises, that's all. Go, I'll check on my sister and our other companions as soon as I've caught my breath."

He frowned. "They were near the center of the caravan. Wonderful idea. Please stay at your cart when you get there. I'll send a healer your way to make sure you are all undamaged as soon as I'm able."

Kuzunoha nodded and waited. As soon as Danior was nearly out of the field, she walked over to one of the men. The scent of blood and offal was strong, making her stomach clench. Growling, she dipped her fingers into the man's wound and brought the bloody fingers to her nose.

As soon as the fingers were near her nose, the scent overpowered the offal. She swallowed hard, salivating at the smell of the coppery liquid. Her tongue flicked out to lick her lips. She wanted to lick the blood off; she wanted to find out if it would taste as amazing as it smelled. She could always plunge her fingers back into the corpse afterward, like taking cream from a ja–

She fell back onto the grass and rubbed her fingers against the leaves and dirt, removing the blood. She wasn't an animal; she wouldn't do this. She looked at her fingers, tiny flecks of rust among the dirt now. She could still smell the blood on them. She needed to find some soap and fully wash her hands off.

If only she could find something strong enough to wash away the sickness inside her as well.

Chapter 31

*R*ichard watched while Kuzunoha pushed her head back against the bare walls of the cart again. After the hits she'd taken in the battle, she'd asked to borrow his blanket to sit on rather than try to balance on her hammock or sit on the wooden cot that they'd provided. He'd tucked the unused hammock up and out of the way.

Kuzunoha gave another little growl as she tried to find a more comfortable way to sit. They were adorable, though he didn't say that out loud. Nobody would have appreciated the opinion, Himiko least of all.

"You're covered in bruises, Kuzunoha. What were you doing fighting? You're not good enough to be taking that sort of risk."

Himiko's voice was well on her way to yelling. Both she and Isashi were sitting side by side in Himiko's hammock. Richard uncharitably thought that Himiko might have chosen to sit there deliberately just so that she would be above her sister. Isashi didn't say anything, just touched Himiko's arm again. At this point, her presence seemed to be the only thing keeping Himiko calm.

She might have been calm, but that didn't make her right. If Kuzunoha had survived the fight against two opponents, even if she had gotten help at the end, then she was more than skilled enough to be taking up her sword, especially when threatened. Her sister might want her to be as good or better than a hunter to be called half as good, but that wasn't the lowest bar for fighting.

Zaiya's voice rang in his mind, soothing his annoyance and he relaxed. He was glad that Danior hadn't tried to make him get rid of her. He liked the sweet little thing.

One comes.

Richard nodded to himself and changed his position from sitting to a half-kneeling position, one of his hands near his weapons. While this was most likely Morjiana, it might be Danior giving another excuse for why the healer still wasn't available to look at Kuzunoha. Though honestly, aside from a tea for the pain, Richard knew they wouldn't be able to do anything for her.

"I am more than skilled enough," Kuzunoha said, sitting forward, wincing.

Richard was just as glad he hadn't taken any hits since the battle had been done by the time he'd gotten his armor on. It took hours for bruises to properly settle into the muscles.

"Kuzunoha, lean back. The more you rest today, the easier tomorrow will be."

Kuzunoha smiled faintly at him. Himiko continued her tirade.

"Even if you were, you shouldn't have been there. We are paying Danior and his troop to take us to Kalvettika. The only time we should be joining them in battle is when they ask for it."

"If I had run, it would have been three against our Kompania leader. We could have lost him."

Her sister looked like she was about to snap that it was an acceptable loss when the door opened. Richard schooled his face to impassivity the moment he saw who had opened it. When Danior said he was going to send a healer, Richard had assumed that he meant Morjiana. That would have been the kind thing to do. Instead, Deckard's stern face looked in on them.

"Danior said that some of you hadn't seen a healer yet." Deckard's tone was chiding and frustrated. It was also aimed specifically at Kuzunoha. She wiped her fingers against the baseboard again. Richard wondered if she was still feeling the blood from the men on her hands. He'd never suffered nightmares about the things he'd done, but he wanted her to sleep easily. She'd been defending people. No one should feel guilty about that.

"Don't get started, Deckard. If I hadn't, Danior could have died. Three against one aren't good odds."

"Danior thanks you for that, but your sister is right. You should have run from the battle, not towards it." Deckard told her.

"Because I clearly can't fight?" Kuzunoha growled.

Deckard shook his head and started to climb in with his healer's kit. It was a tight fit and Richard slipped out, leaning against the door. It was surprising just how much space there was inside the little wagons, but five was still too many. Deckard picked up Kuzunoha's wrist to begin looking her over.

"Whether you can fight or not is immaterial here. What matters is that these people have been fighting together for months; years in most cases. Without that practice, you become the weak spot in their defense."

"Thank you, Deckard," Himiko said.

Richard snorted. She sounded even more arrogant than usual. It was surprising just how much she sounded like Kuzunoha, actually. He looked around and realized that someone was missing.

"Where's Tieni?" Richard asked.

Deckard rolled his eyes but gave a thankful nod for giving over his seat.

"We are separate people."

"Debatable," Richard said.

Tieni may not have acted like a puppy following her master around, but he could count on the fingers of a single hand the number of times he'd seen her without Deckard around. He'd probably have some fingers left over.

The healer grumped and turned back to Kuzunoha. Why had Danior sent him rather than Mojiana? He had been there and knew she wasn't injured enough to require a blessed. Unless they hadn't told Danior… in which case sending Deckard was a slight against Kuzunoha. Unlikely, if the battle had gone down like Kuzunoha had said. He would have appreciated her following him, even if she'd only been good enough to distract the two men.

Why had two men gone for the less skilled member anyway? That was bad tactics and bandits should have known better.

"Ouch. Do you have to press that hard?" Kuzunoha yanked her arm away.

Deckard's movement looked harsh, but Richard could tell his fingers were only touching Kuzunoha softly.

Deckard was trying his best, but he would blow up eventually. If he didn't then it would be Kuzunoha. The only combination more volatile was Himiko and Kuzunoha, an unescapable mixture at the moment. Put all three together and every eye would be turned to them, if only because of the amount of beauty in one place.

Richard smiled. Deckard was a distraction.

"Zaiya, where is everyone?" He whispered to Zaiya as he stepped back from the doorway. She hesitated and he clarified. "Everyone else in the caravan."

Danior is talking to them past the big fire.

Richard smiled, slipping away from the door. The only person who noticed was Isashi. She sent him a questioning look and he mouthed back the word, bathroom. It was the easiest lie. Hopefully, he would be back by the time anyone else discovered him missing.

He did feel guilty for leaving Kuzunoha on her own though. Women were usually better at social situations where talking was necessary. It was doubly strange that neither she nor her sister were very good at it. Being raised by a merchant, they would have learned from him, wouldn't they?

"Zaiya," he gestured her to come with him, "can you hide yourself for the time being?"

He'd expected her to fly into the nearby trees. Instead, she nodded and her body faded, becoming little more than a ghostly outline against the darkness. A moment later, even that was gone. He coughed lightly to hide his surprise.

"Good enough. Stay on my shoulder, please."

She landed lightly; a comfortable weight to keep him balanced. That was such a useful ability. He wished he'd had her back when he had been a thief in Jiza. She would have made his reputation as one of the greatest the city had ever known. One day he'd go back. He'd claim his own and take revenge on the ones who had forsaken him.

He shook his head. To tell it true, he would be lucky if he ever returned home again. At any rate, now wasn't the time to worry about those who had wronged him. It was time to think about how he was going to walk into a potential lion's den and not get caught. Zaiya was useful, but he didn't think she could hide him the same way she hid herself. Fortunately, he'd grown up on the streets. The first thing you learned as an apprentice thief was how to hide in a crowd.

As he walked, he changed his gait to match that of the men in the Kompania. It was unique, an interesting gait, like they were constantly tired, but couldn't stop, and bounce-stepped to give their feet relief. He bent at his chest, changing his hairstyle with a few quick brushes of his hand. Then he paused at the fire and took off his heavier jacket. He dropped it by the fire, mollified that by the time he got back to it, it would be warm from the blaze. Maybe it would get warm enough to burn away the chill that infested these northern lands for a night.

He grabbed a straw hat from a table near the fire and pulled it low over it his forehead. Finally, he grabbed two mugs of ale and walked to the clearing the kompania had crowded into.

Hop-skipping confidently, he nodded to the closest man without raising his hat and handed him the fuller of the two mugs. The man looked surprised for no more than a second, at the drink instead of Richard's face, before he took the mug gratefully and started drinking. The few people who had looked his way turned away as well. He would have smiled if it had been in character. It was so easy to make people think you belonged. Get one of their own to identify you, even with just a nod and that was all it took.

He lifted his mug and took a sip. The moment the swill touched his tongue he regretted it. He'd been expecting a pale ale that might be politely compared to horse piss. Instead, the pale orange liquid had come from the dredges of the barrel. Bar owners knew that if they mixed the dredges and watered it down just enough to make it a liquid rather than syrup, it would be stronger than the strongest whiskey. Rotgut they called it, because that was what it did; rotted your gut while you tried not to remember why you were drinking it in the first place.

Regretfully, he pressed the mug to his lips again, pretending to drink. He would need to drink a full cup of cooking water before he returned to the wagon. He was certain that if he didn't, the fowl brew would eat through his stomach before the sun rose.

"What are we supposed to do with him?" One of the men near the middle said in response to something that he'd missed from Danior. "It's bad enough you've got us hauling travelers, but now we're hauling criminals?"

"Yeah, we've always just killed the buggers before!" A woman added.

"Calm. We've already done the deed. The man won't be coming with us." Danior said, placatingly. "But we needed to find out who they wanted, and why, before we did."

The group seemed confused, but Richard frowned. He'd thought the men were just bandits. Had one of them been a bounty hunter? Their authority was taken for granted in all but the most lawless of places. If one of these men had a lawful bounty, they would have said so, rather than just attacking.

He figured it out just before Danior spelled it out for his crew.

"They weren't bounty hunters."

"One of our passengers?" That was said by a woman in her thirties. She was round with skin closer in shade to Richard's own than he'd seen in a while.

Danior sighed. "One of our passengers… and one of us."

"Who?" The demand was called out by four or five different people.

"Deckard."

"Why would they want him?" A tall man with a hooked nose said.

A woman near Richard muttered under her breath, 'I know why I'd want him…'

Tieni put a stop to the mutterings. "He's one of us, new or not. He's shed blood for us and stopped our own from being lost."

Danior kept his face neutral. Hmm, maybe Deckard had been sent to them as more than a distraction. Interesting. Perhaps he'd been hoping that the group wouldn't share Tieni's feelings?

"The passengers ain't ours though." A man Richard couldn't see called out. "And Tieni has never liked them anyway."

Richard ducked lower, assessing the situation. If they decided to give up any of them, Richard would have to get back unseen and convince the others to run. Zaiya's cool touch on his ear steadied him, even as her words chilled him.

Task? You have a task for me? We will fly.

She seemed eager, too eager. He shushed her as quietly as he could. Morjiana had told him that she was some sort of spirit. Spirits apparently needed something from the people they chose, a purpose or quest. Richard didn't know what she was asking for, but he'd made a promise without doing his due diligence once before. He would never do it again. There was a library in Kalvettika, and a magi guild if that didn't work. He wouldn't accept anything until he'd done his research.

"They aren't going to stop with one, now that they know we have both," Danior said.

The overweight black healer that pretended to read fortunes held up an arm. Everyone quieted almost immediately. They considered her sacred or scary, superstitious lot that they were. Richard was pretty sure that Danior just appreciated her sound advice.

"Once we get them past the bridge, neither will be our concern," the old woman said, her voice crotchety and rough, so heavily accented it was difficult to understand her. "Those bandits, they stop at a gate that big."

One of the men crossed himself with the symbol of a star and circle.

"How many of them can there be?"

Richard shook his head. Too many. For every miserable little town and decent-sized hamlet, there was a small group running around thinking they were tough, willing to prey off stupid farmers, not realizing there were less of those than you'd imagine. Generally, monsters destroyed the stupidest of these groups. Sometimes, though, enough bound together to become dangerous.

The men muttered and Richard answered the growl with the sad truth. "Bandits dealing in slavery won't give up just because they lost a man or two."

Slavery happened, but there was paperwork, forms that had to be filled out in triplicate, filed with the local Master's Union, and checked independently before one could be made a slave. Bandits that took men to sell were just kidnappers and nothing good would ever happen to their new property. In Jiza, they were usually sold with no tongues and the tips of their fingers cut off. If there was no way for them to communicate about their old life, no one would be able to fight for their rights because there would be no way to return them back to a life stolen from them.

Danior's eyes caught on him. He was sure that Danior recognized him, but he didn't call Richard out. Instead, he frowned but nodded. He was a good man. If Danior had said anything, he could have been lynched.

"They can't let us go now. If we arrive in Kalvettika with this knowledge, the guards will call for the army to clear them out. At this point, it's us or them. If nothing else," he grinned, "the passengers should be grateful."

"I certainly hope so. It ain't like they've been grateful yet."

Danior's smile was fake. "You could have tried treating them like real people rather than a doll you pay for. A solidly new idea for you, Crunch, I know."

Good-natured laughter rang out for Danior's comment and one woman with a thick baritone called out, "You deserved that tigress Eleden's beat down and you know it."

"So, what will we tell the princesses?" one of the kids asked.

The poor kid was probably young enough to still be led around by what fell between his legs. He wouldn't want to lie to women that looked like Kuzunoha and Himiko; whether he would mind lying to Richard or Isashi was another matter.

Danior turned his gaze to Richard and said in a deceptively civil tone, "I wouldn't want them unprepared, but there's no need to worry them before we get to Kalvettika."

Richard gave a slight nod back and answered in a voice accented like the men in the kompania.

"Better to not tell any of them about the man till later. Say that we found out his leaders want some of the caravan's treasures. They'll understand the need for traveling fast, without trying to take it into their own hands."

Danior nodded and turned his gaze to the rest of the kompania.

"I'll work out a schedule of guards and plot the most direct route we can take. Pack up tonight. We're going to have an early morning ahead of us."

Chapter 32

"*W*hat about your society?" Richard asked.

He kept the woods in view out of the corner of his eye while he talked to Zaiya. She was flying beside him, occasionally flitting down to sit on his shoulder. She was the most beautiful woman he'd ever seen in his life. Even Kuzunoha and her sister didn't compare. Not that beauty was all that mattered, not by a longshot. Still, even if Zaiya's conversation wasn't as engaging as theirs, she was still exquisite. He loved her wings the most. They made her seem even more ethereal then she already was.

Society? No. We flit, we fly, we enhance, WE ARE.

She was talking in his mind, a feeling that he had decided was similar to the time he'd over-indulged on a mixed liquor called Castle Crusher... It was a fuzzy feeling, and like everything else about her, he loved it, even if he wasn't quite sure he could trust what he heard.

"Why is it I can hear your voice in my mind, but you can't hear mine?"

As distracting as her body was, he forced himself to keep watch on the forest around them. It had been nearly twenty minutes since the last bird had stopped chirping, so he was expecting something to happen soon. Three days of travel while being followed had made them all irritated, if alert.

Then he saw it. A hand movement, against the leaves on a bush. A signal; low, quick, and dirty, but there was also nothing else it could be.

You have not flown yet. Until you fly, we are too far apart.

She could have meant he needed to physically fly first, but he didn't think so. Even the wish-givers didn't actually fly, to his knowledge. She probably meant something else, though what he didn't know. As much as he wanted to, the imminent attack would take precedence.

"Can you do something for me, Zaiya?"

She smiled and was suddenly too close, less than an inch or so from his eyes. Her own blatantly inhuman ones blinked at him.

Request? Request.

"Can you do the invisible thing and head into the forest? I think the caravan is being surrounded. I want to know how many of them there are before they attack. I don't want you seen though."

He didn't want her in danger at all. Invisible, the men might know she was spying on them, but the odds of one of them hitting her with one of their bows was very unlikely.

Count. Humans in woods? Trap! I go.

Her form paled out in front of him until it was nothing but whitish lines. It was... odd... seeing through her. There was no other word for it. He saw her move up into the sky and within a moment, she was completely gone from his sight. He blinked for a moment and then looked around as if he expected her to suddenly reappear in front of him. It was almost unsettling when she did that. At the same time, so useful. He wanted to test it, see just how far that power could go.

She didn't reappear and he shivered. She didn't think like him; didn't even act in a way he could understand. He hoped she would return. Having her was like holding a firebomb in his hand when she was there, but not having her within arm's reach left him feeling like part of his soul had run from him. He hadn't realized how much the little creature had gotten to him since he'd found her less than a week ago.

Kuzunoha slowed down and started walking beside him. "Where did the flit-flit go?"

He shrugged his shoulders. "The woods, I think."

She sent a worried glance towards the woods then looked back at him. "You don't think she saw something, do you?"

Not smooth, he thought. Fortunately, the men out there had not been subtle and even Kuzunoha had seen them at this point. Danior had told him personally that they'd left the remains of the guard out for the bandits to find, hoping that band would be cowed. It seemed to have worked since they hadn't been attacked yet. At the same time, they were still following, which meant they certainly hadn't given up yet.

"Kuzunoha, you should be careful. It almost sounded like you were worried."

She sent him a dirty look. "Not for me. My sister is here and so are non-combatants like Deckard and those kids. They may have been trained, but that doesn't mean that they are skilled or that they want that responsibility. Plus, Danior said these were humans, not monsters." She looked concerned over that, but he couldn't tell why.

"Is there a difference? The knife goes in either way." He said. She shook off her concern, trying to look blasé about the whole thing.

"That's my thought, but apparently, most people do find that there's a difference."

It was adorable that she included herself in that mindset. Richard knew what she was talking about though. Even mercenaries and bounty hunters didn't like killing humans, which was one reason even bandits tended to subdue their prey, rather than moving straight to murderous intent. People like him, those who saw the killing and enjoyed it, were the odd ones out.

Kuzunoha wasn't like that. If anything, her problem might be that she cared too much. She even treated monsters as though they were just another perspective to keep in mind. A more violent one, but nothing more than a different opinion on how the world should work.

A sudden wind blew past him bringing with it the scent of cool rain and summer breeze with it all at once. A moment later, he felt the reassuring weight of Zaiya on his shoulder. She didn't reappear, and he reminded himself to thank her for the discretion.

"Anyways, I'm going to go and check with Danior and see just how much longer this is going to take. I can smell water nearby, so we must be near the river again."

He'd hoped it was just the scent of Zaiya until he realized that he could hear the sound of running water too. Damn it. They may not have seen the fae since they'd left the Sakre, but he didn't want to chance meeting her again, especially not when they were already on the run.

Kuzunoha lifted her nose to the breeze and sniffed deeply before she shrugged. "If you say so. I can't smell a thing."

He gave her a quick kiss and then walked away.

"Don't go visible, Zaiya. Report."

There was a moment's hesitation and then she said, *41 people breathe in the woods.*

"Do they surround us?"

Yes. I help?

He grimaced.

"Yes. Any of those people ours?"

Yes. She paused. *There is less breath now.* Another hesitation, then she asked again, *I help?*

She seemed saddened by the loss of air. One of the men out there was no longer breathing. He made some soothing noises to calm Zaiya and quickened his pace. If Danior's men were out there and taking care of the following bandits, it was all to the good. On the other hand, if they were the ones losing people, the caravan master needed to know now.

Richard may not have cared about the men or felt guilty for their loss, but he knew Danior would. Also, he would need to change his strategies accordingly. The caravan only had thirty-three members that were old enough, healthy enough, and skilled enough to join a fray like this, which meant that unless Danior had pulled another twenty out of midair there were more enemies out there than their group had at full strength.

He caught up alongside the front caravan and swung up onto the roof of the wagon before he walked up to the front seat where Danior sat.

"Richard? What do you need? I'm a little busy." the older man said.

"We're surrounded and you're losing men. How long until we reach Kalvettika?"

Danior did a double-take at that and shook his head.

"How did you...? It doesn't matter. We have another hour or so at this speed."

"If we rush?"

"We're already rushing. Horses can't walk all day without a rest. They'd be stressed before we arrived."

"Dying will suit them better?" Richard asked.

Danior glared at him. "I don't think it's as serious as all that. Not yet."

"Zaiya says that they are killing your men now. There are forty of them out there, Danior. We're in trouble."

Hearing her name, the little creature faded in much as she had faded out. Blue skin and all, she sat on his shoulder, her too-large irises blinking back at Danior.

I help? She asked again turning to him.

Danior stared at her and then at Richard.

"Useful little thing, isn't she? If we survive, would you be looking for a new job after we get the girls to Kalvettika?"

Richard smiled at Danior. He just might if Deckard could be convinced to shove off.

There is less air now. There are no more of his in the forest. Zaiya pressed herself against Richard's neck, shuddering.

For a moment, he was distracted by the feeling of her miniature body against his. It was new and familiar at the same time. Wrong, and all too right.

"What's she doing now?" Danior asked.

"She says that there are no more of yours in the forest." He said.

Danior swore. "By that which dies eternal, how many of theirs are still alive?"

Only one no longer breathes.

Richard closed his eyes and told Danior what she'd said.

The caravan master swore as the path started to open up. Richard could see the nearby river, over forty feet wide, the water rushing by in torrents, nearly thirty feet down a cliff no more than five feet from the edge of the road. As the trees cleared, Richard also got his first view of Kalvettika, built wide around a high wall that looked out over the lower one. Just a little away from the outer wall, a thick stone bridge crossed the river. It looked as though there was enough room between the walls to park their entire caravan three times over.

The guards might be able to see them from here if they were walking the tops of the wall... but they almost certainly wouldn't stir until the caravan was close enough for the guards to tell the players involved.

Flee the Goose! Zaiya suddenly screamed in his head.

Richard leaped forward and heard a thunk in the wood behind him. An arrow with grey feathers was standing straight up from where he'd been. He looked into the woods, along with Danior. They were out of time.

Danior turned to his men.

"Get everyone up onto the wagons... Send Talos to wake our night crew. Get our travelers inside the wagons if they'll go. If they won't, get them on top. We'll be running the rest of the way."

The men turned to leave, and Richard added. "Get your fastest scout to run to the city. We'll need their aid as soon as possible."

The man looked from him to Danior and then waited. Danior sighed and nodded curtly. The man bowed his head and ran to start giving orders.

Chapter 33

*D*eckard blinked his eyes, trying to figure out what had woken him up this time. He had never been a particularly deep sleeper and being on the night shift of the caravan had only made that tendency worse. The caravan had a way of bouncing, no matter how flat the road looked and the bed box he was sleeping on was too small with the privacy walls set up.

The knock came again, and he sat up, shaking off sleep.

"Tieni, Deckard. You're needed. Now." Talos' voice was thick and roughened from the cigars he smoked.

Deckard started grabbing his clothes and heard Tieni open her door on the other side of the wagon.

"We're under attack?" she asked.

The door outside opened.

"They've fired on us, yes. We'll have to dash and defend the rest of the way. We're going to need both of you out there with us."

Deckard opened his door, pulling his pants up. Tieni had told him what had happened at the meeting. The bandits had decided that they wanted some treasure that the caravan had picked up. He'd believed her at the time, but he'd noticed too many things since then. No one would say what this treasure was. Not only that, but at least one conversation had stopped dead as soon as he came close enough. He'd been careful, burn it all, but the only other option was that it was something Kuzunoha or her crew had done.

Both options were bad, but he had to know. He had to know where the danger was, what they were looking for. He couldn't defend it if he was blind to the truth.

Which meant he had to ask Tieni.

He hated this part. It had been why he'd sworn off dating until he'd found someone that he'd been so attracted to that he couldn't deny it any longer.

"Tieni… what do they want?" Deckard asked her.

Tieni hesitated, holding her leather armor in front of her. She pulled the shirt on and started lacing it.

"Nothing… the item that Danior was talking about…"

Deckard wasn't hurt by the idea of Danior lying to him. The man didn't know Deckard, other than as a kennick who had kept his cousin in a town for a year. Tieni's lie cut deep, right through the same wound that had been left from Kuzunoha's. He reached out and took her hands in his.

"I'm not an idiot, Tieni."

She wouldn't meet his eyes. Kuzunoha hadn't been able to either when he'd asked her difficult questions. The only difference was that Tieni wasn't cheating on him. He let out a harsh breath. She still thought she was sparing him something though. Had that been what Kuzunoha had thought she was doing?

"If we're being attacked, I need to know who to guard." He told her.

She pulled her hands from his and tucked in her shirt, already reaching for her armor, carefully not meeting his eyes.

"It doesn't matter. Just watch out for yourself out there."

He closed his eyes.

"So, it's me?" Deckard said. He leaned against the wall. "How did they find out?"

Tieni winced. "They don't. The man that was captured… He said he had been hired to find you."

"From somebody in Sakre?"

She shook her head. "It sounded like they were hired before then."

"Who hired them?"

"He didn't know. He just knew that bringing you back would include a bonus for the one that did." She said.

He shook his head. "Why would you lie?"

Tieni squirmed. "Danior decided that. He didn't want any heroics on your part. No leaving the caravan in the middle of the night or something."

"That's stupid. Unless I led them away and made a point of getting caught, they wouldn't have left you alone." That was a dumb idea… and Danior didn't strike him as dumb. Rude and unlikable, but not dumb.

She raised an eyebrow. "And the stupid heroics part? I think he was afraid you might do something trying to keep anyone else from getting hurt when it was you they wanted."

"I might do something like that to save someone I care about." He admitted, touching her arm.

"So, his argument wasn't completely unfounded." She kissed him. "Just don't go getting me in trouble by telling him that you know, please."

He nodded and she sighed in relief. "I've got to get out there. Come out when you're ready. If they are attacking, we'll need you."

"Stay safe." He caught her eye as she opened the door. "I won't be pleased if you need my skills."

"You won't." She said, grinning. "Just your other skills, once we're safe in town."

She closed the door and his smile fell. It wasn't just him. If it had been, Tieni wouldn't have mentioned him trying to protect anyone else. He would have to pay attention and find out just who they didn't want him protecting.

It took Deckard a few more minutes to get his armor on and his gear properly set for combat. Then he grabbed his healing kit and strapped it on to his leg. There was a rap on the top of the caravan. He called out, "I'm coming out now."

The caravan didn't stop moving when he got out, which was a surprise. Instead, Uther, a bear of a man, helped pull him to the top of the caravan. Everyone else was already up top, the wagons full of people wielding bows and shields. A glance told him that the non-combatants were the only ones left inside. He let out a breath. At least he wouldn't have to worry about them out here.

He ground his teeth together when his eyes fell on Kuzunoha and Himiko still out. Himiko was armed with a shield and a dagger. Kuzunoha had her crossbow out and a man to shield her as well. Himiko had aligned herself with Isashi, at the ready with her bow. Kuzunoha was with one of the men he didn't know as well. His eyes narrowed. She should have been inside. He didn't have the luxury to be worried about her. If only it could be that easy.

"I thought Danior would have told all the non-combatants to get into their rooms," Deckard said.

Kuzunoha had glanced at him when he'd come out but seemed too focused on the hills to care about anything else. Ironically, that pleased him. He was glad that something had finally gotten her to take the situation seriously. Maybe she had learned more than he'd thought.

"Isashi and Richard wanted to help," Uther said.

Tieni glared at the other carts. "As for the others, two extra bodies to fight may be useful if the bandits decide to do anything more dangerous than harry us on our way."

"What have they done so far?" Deckard asked, gesturing at the forest.

The trees were thinner here and he could see the city in the distance, huge and menacing. It was the biggest city he'd ever seen in his life and he couldn't imagine how the city's hunters were even able to protect an area that large. He forced his eyes back to the forest. The city wasn't his problem… hopefully, the city would never be his problem.

"They've shot a few arrows our way; distancing shots. They're just testing the waters until we're out of the woods completely." Uther said.

"Why would they want us to be out of the woods?" Deckard asked. "Wouldn't they prefer to attack us here, where they have the ability to hide and we don't?"

"They may have mobility, but we have nearly equal numbers and in here we can ring the wagons and make them attack our stronghold. On the road, riding, we don't have as many people who can fight, since we need at least one driver per wagon and a dedicated protector for that driver; good fighters all and effectively out of this battle. It's not to their advantage to attack now." Tieni told him.

"So, we're giving them the advantage of terrain?" Deckard wondered out loud.

Uther looked at him as if he were an idiot. "Would you rather stay in the forest and have forty of them come to attack us in the dark?"

Deckard winced. It was the difference between his upbringing and theirs. It would be years before he knew everything the Corvidae seemed to instinctively understand.

"What can I do?"

Uther shrugged. "Right now? Keep an eye out for arrows and don't get shot. Be ready to jump to someone else's wagon if they get hit badly and it's safe to do so."

"Moving across to another wagon isn't safe if we're moving. Ever." Tieni mentioned idly. Her eyes flicked to him, but her gaze was back on the forest right after.

"Morjiana doesn't fight, does she?" Deckard looked around making sure he couldn't see her.

Uther shook his head. "She's upfront with Danior, but she isn't as spry as she used to be. She's inside his wagon if they need her. There won't be a lot of healing while we're fighting. You'll need to use those new weapon skills now. Unless, of course, you'd rather hide in the carts with the children."

Deckard held up his hand, stopping Uther. "I needed to know what my duties were. I've been in a few battles, but nothing like this."

Uther smiled at that. "Ah, first-time jitters. I can understand that. The first time Ulric got into a situation like this he crapped his pants when an arrow nearly hit him. Do better than that and no one will have an issue with your performance."

Deckard rolled his eyes and found his gaze wandering over to Kuzunoha's wagon again. He wished she was on his wagon, that he could protect her, too. He looked at Tieni. At least he could make sure that she would survive this. He let out a breath.

"I will."

Chapter 34

*R*ichard sat on Danior's wagon, watching the woods thin around them with trepidation. He didn't need Zaiya anymore to know how many of them were out there. He could see their shadows through spots where the trees were sparse. More than a few had horses, either riding them or running alongside. They knew as well as Danior did that the caravan would be at its most vulnerable as soon as the road was clear.

"What do you see?" Danior asked him.

Danior was the best driver on the caravan, but at the speed, they were going, even he would have trouble reacting in time if he also had to watch for the enemy. He'd chosen Richard to be his second in this case.

It was odd to have that trust given so quickly, but Richard appreciated the man's judgment.

"They're moving closer. Becoming bolder. We could start sending a few shots their way."

"Save the command until they're clear of the forest. We don't want to waste shots that will just hit the trees if we can help it. Also, you realize that we probably won't end up seeing close combat, right?"

Richard glanced down at the dagger in his hands. He had been playing with it since he'd gotten onto the wagon. It was a little thing he could fidget with while waiting. Most men had something, a string to tie knots into or a rock with a smooth pit shaped for a finger to rest in… For Richard, from the time he'd been five and his father had died, he'd lived with a dagger in his hand.

"I'd rather be ready then unprepared," Richard said.

Danior grunted. "Just makes a man uncomfortable at this spee-"

"Duck." Ruslo, Danior's second interrupted him, raising a thick wooden shield that covered Richard and Danior completely. Richard heard a clunk onto the metal and Ruslo grunted. He pulled it down a moment later. An arrow rattled around on the roof behind them and the shield had a new dent on its pitted surface.

"That was close. What are they armed with?"

"It was a warning shot," Ruslo said. "They haven't gotten serious yet."

Richard ignored that. He didn't want the shots any closer. He scanned the forest. "Zaiya? How many are shooting at us?"

Her huge eyes blinked at him.

Twenty-five feathers. The rest have dead earth or dead branches.

"Twenty-five with bows. The rest are armed with blades and staves. I'm not sure how many horses yet. Over twenty, certainly. Most of them look like nags."

Danior swore. "That's still more beasts than I'd like. How long until they catch us?"

Not if… when.

"There's no chance of getting to the city ahead of them?" Richard asked, swearing silently.

"Not with this short a lead," Ruslo confirmed.

The trees above them suddenly disappeared and Richard realized they'd left the woods. His mouth opened wide as Ruslo shouted for them to duck again. At the same time, Danior swore and spurred the horses into high gear. The sudden burst of speed sent Richard rolling toward the edge of the seat. Zaiya shrieked in his mind and he caught one of the ropes. Arrows rattled off the wagon again. This time Richard could feel the vibration from their impact. He pulled himself back under the shield, noticing that one of his pant legs had been pierced.

"I could have fallen off," he muttered, willing his heart to calm.

Zaiya caught his face in her hands. *I would not let you fall. We would fly.*

"That was them getting serious," Ruslo told him, unnecessarily.

Richard held his breath, waiting for the sound of horse or man screaming but amazingly, no one had been injured yet. That couldn't hold, could it?

Danior snarled at him. "Pull yourself together, man. I need information. How much time do we have?"

Richard shook his head and forced himself to concentrate on watching their opponents. They were following quickly, but their nags pulled at the reins and danced under their riders.

"None," Richard whispered, hoarsely, "we have none."

Danior grunted. "Five minutes and we'll be at the bridge."

Ruslo interrupted again. "Incoming!"

"Blinding bells!" Richard swore. At this rate, they would never make it to the city. "Do they normally shoot this often?"

He saw Kuzunoha and a few of the others try to return fire, their aim marred by the speed of the wagons. One of the bandits screamed as he was thrown. His horse panicked, bucking all over. Richard saw an arrow sticking out of its shoulder. The riders surrounded the beast and grabbed at its harness, while one moved to the rider. The fallen one didn't move.

Richard pulled his eyes back to the enemy. If they hadn't already been riding with purpose, they had it now.

"Riders on the way. We took out one."

"How many? How long till they reach the wagons?"

"Twenty-two, now. Half a minute to one minute." If they were lucky.

The wagons slowed for a moment, the road covered with tiny rocks, that shot up at he and Danior like tiny knives. Thirty seconds at the most, since the men would have to slow as well. If they didn't, they'd have injured horses to deal with. Still, there were only two more rounds of shots before Richard saw the first of the riders pulling alongside the furthest wagon.

"They're on us." He confirmed to Danior and pulled one of his more common throwing daggers to defend them. The other men sent another round of arrows the bandits' way.

Suddenly, Himiko screamed. Richard didn't know where the man had come from, but the muscled man was hauling himself up the side of her wagon. Himiko flashed her teeth, brandishing a short knife that was nearly a foot and a half shorter than the other man's blade.

The man smiled back at her and then took an arrow in the chest. Richard saw Isashi casually aiming at another bandit that was near their wagon. She wouldn't be fast enough to take all of them herself, but she was their best bet for firing on the run.

From one of the further caravans, Kuzunoha shrieked in rage. When Richard found her among the confusion, she was on her knees and one of her legs was covered in blood. The shield man on her wagon was sliding across the roof slowly, dead of an arrow to the chest. Above Kuzunoha stood one of the bandits, a mongrel of a man, with black hair and freckles so large that it made him look diseased.

Richard swore and stood on the thick seat. He threw his blade hard, satisfied when the knife impaled itself in the man's wrist. The villain howled. Kuzunoha took a swipe, but the man avoided it, catching the back of his friend's horse before he fell beneath the carriage. Kuzunoha took another swipe at them as the rider pulled his horse away from the wagon.

"Richard, left," Ruslo said.

He spun and dove, shouting a warning for Danior to duck. A dull knife passed overhead, and Richard saw the bandit just off to his left, still on horseback. The man's grimace was probably a mirror of Richard's own. Battle was always a dirty pleasure. Richard pulled another of his throwing knives and apologized under his breath as he threw. His knife hit the horse in its leg and the beast whinnied, throwing his rider into the nearby trees before it bucked, running into the trees. Richard saw his knife fall and then go under one of the following wagon's wheels.

He swore again. Today was going to be expensive. He checked for the others, just in time to see a rain of arrows coming down at them. Ruslo got the shield up in time, cutting off Richard's view; there was nothing but the sound of wagon wheels and hooves hitting the ground; then the screaming began.

He pushed Ruslo away and found his friends in the chaos. Kuzunoha was holding a small shield above her, but she was swearing. He did, too, following her gaze to Himiko. She was on her knees and he could see an arrow sticking through her right ankle. The driver helped Himiko pull herself under his shield, but Richard knew that wasn't going to help. Leg wounds were nasty, and you could bleed out faster from a leg wound than from anywhere else.

Richard did a quick count of all the wagons then, glad to see the bandits slowing down, pulling behind him. He swore when they started stringing short bows again.

"Seven men down, plus Kuzunoha and Himiko. They're stringing their bo-"

Danior cut him off. "Hold on, we're turning."

Richard grabbed tight and watched as everyone else did too, trying to keep an eye out for the next rain of arrows. It was already coming down and Richard was sure that it was only due to the sharp turn that Danior made that he wasn't skewered by one himself. He saw Kuzunoha rip an arrow out of her arm, grabbing for her shield as it rolled off the wagon. He could almost feel her teeth grinding as she struggled to contain a scream.

"Kuzunoha!" Deckard yelled.

Richard spared a glance at the healer on the furthest wagon. Deckard was holding a shield up, protecting Tieni while she shot an arrow back at the bandits. Fortunately, he didn't look insane enough to try jumping caravans to get to Kuzunoha. At least, not yet.

Richard looked to Isashi, but she was tending to Himiko's leg. She spared a look at Richard. That look said a lot. She didn't think they were going to make it. Another rain of arrows came down and Richard heard a snap as Himiko's shield broke.

Richard moved out from behind Ruslo's shield and ran to the back of the wagon, hurling himself across to Isashi's wagon. Yanking himself up, Richard heard a feminine scream in his mind and looked up to see six more arrows heading towards him. He rolled into a ball, gritting his teeth, preparing to feel the arrows pierce his armor.

It never came. He opened his eyes. All six of the arrows had fallen uselessly around him. They hadn't even hit the wagon hard enough to make a noise as they'd hit.

"What in the world…" he said, blinking.

I help. Zaiya told him as the wagon's wheels clattered, having reached the bridge finally. Her voice was a cool breeze, blowing through him, calming him.

"You helped? You can stop the arrows?"

The little creature nodded proudly though he noticed what could only be sweat and lines on her face from the concentration.

He heard another scream and looked to his friends. Isashi pulled another arrow from her quiver, pulling it back to her ear, while Himiko tried to hold what was left of her shattered shield in place. Kuzunoha hadn't been hit again, but he could see her desperately trying to wind her crossbow up nearly one-handed.

"Can you stop the arrows for everyone?" He asked.

Zaiya shook her head.

Too many, too much…

He swore. There had to be another way…

You could.

"I could what?"

You could use my power to stop them.

He sucked in a hard breath. Was it a trap? Was Zaiya some type of fey after all? Even though she hadn't responded to the cold iron? Another scream tore through the air as Isashi let her arrow fly.

"How?" He grit his teeth. If she was a fey, he could kill her after she'd saved his people.

Zaiya smiled at him, raw elation mixed with a predatory gleam, but it was somehow overlaid with that innocent essence that nearly illuminated her.

Come with me! We'll fly! I help!

Chapter 35

*T*he world suddenly imploded, leaving nothing but brilliant colors floating in its wake. Richard's heart skipped, and he looked around. This was nothing like the fey realm he'd been kept in, but wherever it was, it certainly wasn't part of the real world either. The colors settled down to a dusky purple, like the sunset on a clear day near the ocean with clouds carrying the light far further than it would otherwise go. He felt a presence settle beside him and leaped away, fumbling for a dagger. He yanked one but stopped as Zaiya smiled at him.

Zaiya, who was nearly his height, though otherwise she looked the same. Zaiya's smile… meant something.

For the first time, he knew without a doubt what it was. She was eager, glad he had agreed to come, glad that he had said she could help, glad that he'd accepted her. She'd been waiting so long for someone like him.

The feeling broke and he realized that he hadn't been able to read her expression... he'd been reading her mind.

Zaiya, he stuttered as he said her name. He sounded like she did when she talked in his head. The feeling was close, familiar, intimate.

He moved away from her, remembering another touch in his mind, shaking him to his core. Demanding, caressing, pleading, biting; she'd wanted all of him, not just what he's been willing to give. That voice had demanded submission.

Richard!

He felt a hand touch him and the memory was gone, chased away. A tiny blue spark, somehow part of Zaiya and yet separate, ran it off, settling contentedly in its place.

She can't have you. Zaiya said with finality. Then her shoulders hunched. *You don't want her, right? We don't have to go to her. We're safe here. She can't reach us.*

Richard moved forward pulling Zaiya against him. Whatever she was, she wasn't fey and she wasn't demanding. If he said no to whatever she offered, she would accept his answer. That meant something. He lifted her face to his and kissed her.

The touch was electric, shining through him, pulling her to him, closer and more solid than she'd been before.

She can't reach us here. Richard repeated as he pulled away. *We're safe.*

Zaiya smiled at him and grabbed his hand, pulling him along behind her.

Come, we fly. We'll be happy, there will be nothing to stop us. We can do anything.

They could, Richard realized. His mind opened to the possibilities. If he accepted the offer; *contract*, she corrected; contract then, he could fly anywhere with her. They could search for knowledge, for a safe place. They could see the world, raining lightning down on their enemies, safe from reprisal in the clouds. They could see every land, visit any place. He would never be bored, never want for another's touch. Even if he did, she would be fine with whatever he chose, she would join him if he so desired, leave him be when he wanted to be alone. She would be perfect and because he would be with her, he would be perfect. The colors were so vibrant here, so perfect. Everything would be...

He felt his feet leaving the ground beneath him, his body becoming weightless and Zaiya's hand turning to clouds in his. He struggled, feeling his body tingle and realized that he was becoming vapor too. The sudden shock brought him to his senses.

Zaiya, do we have to do it this way? Is there another? He dropped back to what passed for ground in this world of shapeless color.

Her hand turned firm in his and she turned to him, her mouth pouty.

Richard, can't you feel it? The air, we can fly...

Everywhere, I know. He responded. With a tug, he brought her back down to his level. He reached a hand up and touched her wing.

Powerful fey had wings; theirs felt like firm leather with the thinnest of lace spread between them. They snapped easily. Another blue spark chased the memory away.

Zaiya's were soft, smooth; delicate yet firm. They looked like an insects. He gently touched her wings, his hands chilling as if they'd been created by a cool breeze, frozen into shape by some tremendous cold. She shivered as if she enjoyed his touch.

Stay here, with me. He promised her. *Everything you want up there, you can have with me, down on the ground.*

She glanced up and he touched her chin slightly. Her eyes blinked rapidly, and she looked back up.

We can go there later. He promised. *Right now, come to me. Be with me, by my side.*

He pulled her in for another kiss. She only hesitated for a moment before falling into his arms. His lips parted hers and she reciprocated before flushing and pulling away. Had she ever flushed before? He didn't think he'd ever seen that shade of purple on her cheeks or breasts before. She shook her head and pointed up at the sky.

This. We do this there?

Here? He pressed.

Up? She pleaded.

His breath caught, but he knew, he had to give something to her if he wanted to win this battle.

Up. He agreed.

Her eyes widened, and her smile lit up her face. This time, instead of turning and tugging him up with her, she simply started to rise, her form starting to turn insubstantial in front of him. His flesh tingled and quivered under the touch of a million tiny fingers, taking his spirit out of his flesh; or perhaps more disturbingly, turning his flesh to spirit. Even though he knew what those tingles were doing, it was seductive, stimulating every part of him, filling him with energy, life... breath.

He leaned in close, his mouth closing over hers again. The touch of her now, vapor on vapor, was somehow even more intoxicating. Every part of him, tingling, wanting him to finish the act, to accept the contract on her terms.

If he were to fail here, everyone on that caravan could die. He didn't care about most of them; travelers that he hardly knew the names of. Besides they were physical, mortal. Zaiya's hands touching his body made him feel like he was ascending to godhood.

He ran a hand up her spine and she moaned into his mouth again. She moved to touch his and he pulled back, gasping. He couldn't do this. A hero wouldn't let them die. He couldn't let his friends die. They were physical, worldly, but so was he.

Zaiya, my love, I can't, he panted as if pained. The panting was easy, too easy. Acting as though he wasn't enjoying every moment of it was the hard part. *It's too much... Come back down with me.*

She looked worried and within a moment they were physical again. Her eyes watched him nervously, unsure of what to do.

He touched her head.

It was too much for me. Can we try again, here? He gestured to where they were.

She paused, hesitating before nodding. For an instant, as his lips closed over hers again and his fingers roamed her body, he wondered if it was as different and stimulating for her being solid as it was for him being vapor. He ran a finger up her back again and she quivered in his arms, her legs shaky.

Yes, it probably was.

He sat down, pulling her onto his lap. He kissed her again, making sure that her legs stayed too shaky to stand. He pulled away and kissed the side of her neck before whispering in her ear.

Stay with me here? His fingers traced invisible circles on her skin. She shook, then paused as if his words had taken time for her to understand. His hand slowed to a crawl then stopped.

Punishment? You stop if I don't agree? She accused.

A valid one, seen from her point of view, but he shook his head.

No. I want you to agree without my touch. I want your consent. Zaiya, my friends need me. I can't go with you. I want you to come back with me. I'll need your help.

We are together. Why are they important?

She sounded so angry at being denied. He touched her hand, gently.

They are my friends and they are fragile. They are also in danger. He paused. *If we don't help, they'll die.*

She thought about that.

Use my power to help them and then we continue?

He had her.

Yes. But I will have to be stronger first.

There had to be a way to fly with her without losing himself. It would take time to learn, but he would find it. He would have time enough if they all lived.

Zaiya nodded. *True. I help. You agree to the contract?*

The contract. That was what was important. Every creature that gave its power needed something in return.

I gain the use of all your power... in exchange for this? Here and in my world, if possible.

He touched her again and she shook on top of him. He wished he had the time to take care of her before they left.

Yes. She whispered.

What do you take from me?

All of you. You will be mine and we will fly forever.

He shivered as she pushed him down and he promised. *Yes.*

Zaiya pressed herself against him and Richard gasped. His clothes disappeared, and he could suddenly feel everything about her.

Her emotions, his hands on her body and her body on his. She blinked and her eyes suddenly lost their unnatural iris. They looked human, but still a brilliant blue; a shade that humans would never be able to reproduce.

My friends... He gasped

I know. She said with regret. *Later we will finish.*

When it's safe. He agreed.

She kissed him and lowered herself to him. He fell back, his entire body filled with her energy. Everything fell out of focus and he blinked quickly trying to clear them.

Before his sight cleared, noise assaulted his ears, painful after the perfect silence of that place. He could hear fast running water, horses' hooves pounding on wood, and screams. He pushed himself up and saw an arrow coming straight for him.

Chapter 36

*D*eckard watched as Kuzunoha dodged on her wagon roof again, narrowly avoiding another arrow coming her way. Her roof was filled with the spiny remnants of other shafts. He saw her mouth twist in a snarl, and she took aim again. The shot missed and flew into the water, sinking below the surface.

"Deckard," Tieni snapped at him. Her eyes were kind but pleading. " I know you're worried, but I need you here."

He raised the shield again and nodded an apology at her. The shield got up just in time to deflect the two arrows that came their way. He couldn't protect everyone, but it was harder to concentrate on only Tieni than he thought it would be. He tried forcing concentration like he'd learned as a young healer. Here, like in the healing room, losing focus would mean losing people he could have saved.

He ripped out the arrow that had stuck into the shield and saw that the point had survived. He shoved it into the quiver for Tieni. It wouldn't fly straight, but she was down to three. At this point, quantity had its own quality. While he watched, she calmly pulled the short bowstring back to her jaw and loosed. Her arrow hit one of the far horses and the beast screamed, slowing on the bridge. The rider pulled out the arrow and turned his horse away, looking disgusted.

"There are still riders out there. Do we have any more arrows?" She said, notching another shot. Deckard shook his head.

"Once they realized you were firing them back, most of them stopped firing at our wagon." He looked at the other wagons, looking like pincushions compared to theirs. "We could try to jump."

The bridge was wide enough for two wagons to go abreast if they needed to, though, at the speed they were going, it wouldn't be as safe. The bridge was stone walls with a wooden road set between them, high over the river below, made simply to cross the chasm. Ships could probably travel underneath it if they needed to get further inland.

"I don't think our driver would be willing to slow. How is that hunter friend of yours doing?" Another arrow flew and one of the horses whinnied. Unfortunately, at this speed, it was difficult to make any of their shots hit.

He glanced up to make sure their airway was clear and then looked around to check on Isashi. She had run out of arrows as well and had taken the shield position over Himiko. He could see the blood on her outfit from here, though they'd removed the arrow, so it probably wasn't that bad. He did a mental tally; there were at least 14 people with injuries, and they'd lost another four. It wasn't without loss on the other side, but the tally still seemed too high. Even a blessed shouldn't be worth this much.

From ahead of them, Deckard heard Ruslo yelling. Fortunately, it was in anger, not pain.

"Richard? Dumb kennick, what are you doing?"

"Deckard, watch out, another big volley is on its way," Tieni called out.

Deckard turned, raising the shield. There were dozens of arrows flying towards the wagons. He felt Tieni move closer.

"The guard is finally opening the gate. As soon as we're off the bridge, we're in the Kalvettika's territory. They must be trying to take us out before we-"

In the sky above them, a breeze caught all of the arrows, sweeping them to the left and right of the caravan.

"By the soul secrets, what just happened?" Deckard whispered.

The wind chilled Deckard's soul, so strong that it darkened the sky while the bandit's arrows rained down on either side of the bridge. The sound of a crossbow twanged, loud and clear, and one of the bandits screamed. Deckard's eyes were drawn to one of the bandits falling off his horse, his hands gripped over a bolt in his stomach. Deckard heard Kuzunoha whoop behind him and knew that it must have been her shot.

The sound of the wind changed as the bandits raised their crossbows, pointing their weapons into the darkening wind. The wind turned the smaller bolts, sending them skittering upwards like the arrows a moment before, but one, triple the size of the others, shivered through the wind, staying true to its course. As if the world had slowed he turned with it, seeing the bolt strike Kuzunoha's shoulder, just above her collarbone. Kuzunoha's scream tore through him and she tripped on one of the shafts. He reached for her as she fell, shrieking over the edge. Her eyes were panicked as her hip caught the side of the stone bridge beneath them. Her hands scrambled for purchase, but she bounced off the bridge going over the side towards the river.

Tieni grabbed him, keeping him from falling as the wagons screeched to a halt, horseshoes clanging like broken bells as the beasts skitter-hopped across the stone. Deckard grabbed Tieni's bow from her and pulled the last arrow from her quiver. He turned and shot. Just before the arrow hit the wind wall, the direction of the wind changed. It caught his arrow and pushed it forward, giving it more power than he could have alone.

His shot hit the man with the heavy crossbow in the face. Part of Deckard felt ill, but it was small compared to the rush of anger. He watched the man long enough to see him tumble off his horse to the ground, realizing that his anger was that the man would die too fast to pay for his crime.

The rest seemed cowed and rode back to the edge of the bridge. Most continued running, though just a few remained to the sides, watching to see if there was still a chance to snap up their prey.

Deckard leaped off the wagon, running to the edge of the bridge. He begged the seven that Kuzunoha hadn't died. He found her pulling herself up to a small outcropping of grey-toned rock one-handed in the river below. Her shirt was covered with blood and her arm hung uselessly at her side. Her body quivered, wracked with coughs, even after she'd found solid purchase on the stones.

"Kuzu? Kuzu, are you all right? What's hurt?" he called down to her.

She waved him off and he growled. He turned to look for Tieni or the guards; someone had to have rope they could use to climb down. With that wound, she wouldn't have the strength to climb up herself.

Everyone had a look of wide-eyed panic. But they weren't looking at the bandits. Hell, the bandits that hadn't fled had the same look on their faces. He spun, wondering what the new threat could be.

Richard was standing on top of Himiko's wagon standing over her and Isashi, nearly glowing with power, lighting in his veins, showing even through the black clothing he favored. His eyes were as inhuman as his little creature's. Speaking of the little thing, she flew a foot or so behind him, her stance the same, her eyes glowing with the same power.

The little creature had saved them. The question was how. Had it stolen Richard's life as payment? Or had Richard made some sort of deal? The man had been obsessed since he'd captured his little witch. If the little creature managed to convince him that they were enemies, the kompania would have to take up arms against Richard.

Deckard didn't like Richard, didn't trust Richard; despite that, Deckard could only justify attacking him if he was a threat.

Richard looked at the kompania and the bandits, then away, as if none of them were threats. Until he looked over the far side of the bridge. Then Richard bared his teeth, and the power that seemed to be flowing through him dimmed. His creature didn't stay behind him. Instead, the creature landed lightly on Richard's shoulder, following his gaze.

Deckard heard the bandits fleeing, the sound of horses being whipped but he only spared them a glance to make sure they were running away. Whatever was a threat to Richard it wasn't here. It was on the river, coming towards them.

"Deckard, what are you doing?" Tieni asked him as he pushed by her and ran to the other side of the bridge.

Which meant that whatever the threat was, it was heading straight toward Kuzunoha.

He reached the opposite stone wall and leaned far over it, his eyes snapping on the water below. The water was darker than it should have been this time of year as if it wasn't cloudy midday, but a dim twilight. Standing on a set of rocks was a woman with dark hair and eyes, dripping as if she had been thrown in like Kuzunoha and just climbed out. She was tall and imposing, despite her sallow greying skin. As he watched, the woman flung off her jacket, exposing her naked body to the elements.

Her hips swayed as she stepped off the rocks. The moment her feet touched water, they faded, becoming snake-like, pure dark liquid.

Deckard's breath caught in his throat. He'd never seen a monster like this before.

The woman cried up towards Richard. Her voice was deep and powerful, not like the haunted scream Deckard had been expecting. Her tones sounded like words, almost like speech and they rung in his ears. On the sides of her head, fins rose where her ears should have been and quivered.

Behind him, he heard Kuzunoha shriek a challenge.

Chapter 37

*K*uzunoha watched the world spin around her, her pain shattering everything before her eyes. She tried to turn her head and saw the bolt sticking out of her chest, right up by her neck. She reached for it, every nerve in her body shivering. Her hand didn't make it to the bolt before she hit something hard enough with the opposite shoulder that it made even the earlier pain disappear. She floated blinking stupidly at the dark water, wondering why she couldn't breathe, couldn't move, couldn't feel anything. Her armor broke away from her body and she slowly started rising to the surface.

She tried to take in a breath and water filled her nose and mouth. She blew it out and started struggling, desperate to find air. She couldn't make her body move the way it was supposed to and she flailed instead of swam. Her chest felt like it would burst before her head pierced the water. She coughed out water and tried to draw in a breath. She felt water follow some of the air down and her body convulsed.

Her right hand smacked hard into a hard surface and Kuzunoha flailed at it. She surprised herself by finding a small lip to hold on to. Her left arm wouldn't work, but Kuzunoha forced herself around in the water and realized that she'd managed to find a small sandbar covered by tiny stones. She climbed onto it, coughing up water, and tried to keep her stomach from spilling everything she'd eaten that morning. She heard Deckard's voice and waved ineffectually towards it. His voice stopped and she tried to catch her breath.

Everything hurt and trying to breathe didn't work. She coughed up more water, her eyes full of tears. After another convulsion, she could finally draw in shallow breaths. She was shivering, but couldn't tell if she was cold or not. She turned her head, the movement taking her breath away again, and saw the problem.

The bolt that had hit her, knocking her off the wagon had shattered when she hit the water. Most of the bolt was gone, but a handspan of wood, no thicker than a painter's detail brush, was still stuck inside her. She looked at it, panicking and then reached up. She couldn't draw in enough air again and had worked herself into a panic before she could force her fingers to probe the wound. She felt metal and something round. She dragged the objects out, nearly passing out. Bile rose in her throat again and she focused on what she'd pulled out, trying to stay conscious. The metal point was holding onto what was left of the shaft by the thinnest of sticks. The tiny ball was a faded yellow-white... bone maybe? She couldn't tell and dropped it, letting herself fall to the rocks.

Finally, the pain eased enough for her to let out a breath. She yanked in a few more gasping breaths after it. If she could just fill her lungs, if she could just rest and let the pain ease away, she'd be fine.

A deep voice shattered what peace she'd found, rising over the sound of the water rushing around her little sandbar. Kuzunoha curled up into a ball, but she forced her body out of the position as soon as she recognized it. She had to defend herself against the watery woman and she couldn't do it from her knees.

Kuzunoha forced herself to stand up, grabbing for her sword, surprised to find that it was still tied tightly around her waist. She bit her lip to keep from screaming and fell to her knees again. Moving didn't just hurt, nothing was working properly. Her breath was catching in her chest and she couldn't move her left side without nausea rise in her throat. Her right arm worked, but she wasn't sure how she could fight like this.

She searched for the woman and instead found a horse watching her from the water. Except it wasn't a horse. She didn't know how she knew that, but she did. The eyes… there was intelligence in them. The creature stumbled towards her on the rock. Its body, below the horse-like head, looked humanlike. As it came closer, she realized that what she'd thought was glistening hair were tiny scales, so small that they looked and moved almost like thin fur over the creature's muscles.

The creature opened its mouth and its tongue flicked out. "You do smell good. Old enough. Strong enough; if you don't die."

It took Kuzunoha a moment to realize the creature was speaking to her. It took its first step onto her little island and she saw that while the creature had hands, its hind legs under the scaly fur were thick, sculpted muscle that ended in delicate hooves.

"What do you want, creature?" She spat out, dragging herself to her feet

The horse tilted its head and looked at her. Its nostrils flared again. "You. You are strong. But not too strong. You will be mine."

It licked its lips.

"No." The word came out of Kuzunoha before she'd even thought to do so.

Now that creature was close enough, she could smell it, fish left to rot in the hot sun. She drew her weapon.

"The blue one," it gestured to the dangerous creature behind it, "told me of you. She is too strong. You are not. Enough."

Kuzunoha screamed, defiance and anger in her tone. She drew the blade of Four Feathers and slashed at the creature in front of her. It hadn't been expecting her to move as fast as she did. Her blade slashed the horse's chest, leaving a gaping stripe where it touched. Moments later, blood welled and started flowing. The creature hissed and stumbled back, breathing deeply. Gills on its neck, hidden until now, opened and closed, like a fish out of water.

The attack nearly dropped her, but she forced herself to remain standing. She wouldn't let it take her. She pulled the blade back up to an attack position and waited, hoping her body wouldn't collapse before she could kill it.

Chapter 38

"I told you to return to your Queen through the gate, mortal. I destroyed your ship to remind you of your duty. Why do you still disobey her request?"

The creature was speaking its ancient language. The sound of it reverberated through Richard, making his very bones ache. Part of him wanted to fold up and let her do as she pleased to him. That tone; if you obeyed whatever they were going to do would hurt less. And if he pleased it…

Zaiya's answering scream ricocheted through his head, banishing the fey's call. He bared his teeth at it again. He had escaped. He was never going back. Death would be preferable. He looked down at Himiko. She and Isashi were staring at him as if he'd grown an extra head. Maybe not an extra head… but like he'd suddenly saved their lives with strange magic. Perhaps the terror and confusion were warranted. He looked at Isashi.

"Is she okay?"

Himiko had taken a bolt through her leg, near her ankle. She wouldn't be standing on it anytime soon, but she didn't look injured otherwise. She was shivering and he wasn't sure if it was in fear of him or not.

Himiko turned a pained, angry gaze on him. Her hand caught Isashi in the chest and she answered him. "I'll be fine. I jus–"

Kuzunoha's scream of defiance rang through the air, cutting Himiko off. Richard's heart dropped into his stomach and with an iciness he didn't feel, he hardened himself. He couldn't do anything for her right now. She was in the fey's territory and he would have enough trouble just trying to keep everyone else in the caravan alive.

The water fey looked greyer than it had when he'd first saw her and much greyer than she'd looked when she'd been tearing the ships apart in the harbor. The Magi had injured her. He nodded at Isashi and saw that she was helping Himiko to the ground behind the wagon.

"She'll be safer off the roof," Isashi said. "Is this the creature that attacked the docks?"

"Yes."

"Can you defeat it?"

He didn't know the answer to that yet.

Injury, exhaustion… in their world, fey recovered from these things in hours. Richard had assumed it would be the same here, but from her appearance, he'd been wrong. Could he defeat her, in her current state?

Zaiya, do we have enough power to defeat her?

She looked confused. Like they had been in the other world, her eyes had irises now. They looked more human. While he missed the otherworldliness, he knew that he would enjoy the ability to understand her better.

Enough power? She can't have you.

That wasn't the answer he'd wanted, but really, anything other than, 'of course, master' would have fallen into that category.

Zaiya scoffed. *Master? You are mine, I am yours. No master.*

Had anyone else said those words, they would have felt cloying; confining. He understood that she wasn't scoffing at the idea of him being her master, she was scoffing at the idea that one of them was better than the other. They were partners, nothing less and everything more. He let out a breath.

Isashi stood and caught a new sheath of arrows. Richard realized that one of the people who had been inside the wagon was taking this moment to rearm everyone they could. That would help.

A twang filled the air and a bolt went flying towards the fey. She moved her hand in an upward gesture and pulled ice from the water. The crossbow hit the wall of ice and snapped it. Instead of changing it to water again, the water fey released the wall. It tipped over, falling into the river. She pulled up another bit of water, freezing it into a pointed icicle and sent the shot towards the caravan. It hit the wagon the man had been on, sending a chunk of the roof flying off.

She hadn't brought up that wall when he'd thrown his blade on the ship, which meant that she had something to protect now that she hadn't before. Richard narrowed his eyes. If she was using her actual body to fight and couldn't just decide to flow back into the water at will without retreating, then they had a chance to defeat her.

"Let's hope so." He finally told Isashi. He raised his voice. "Take aim. Anyone with a weapon!"

Shots went flying towards the fey and she brought up another wall of ice. The fey pulled up more icicles and shot them at the caravan. One man screamed and more pieces of the caravan shattered under the weight of the bolts.

"Zaiya. I need to control the winds again."

His beautiful partner looked down at the woman, her expression full of anger and determination.

You have it. Always.

He nodded, calling the breeze to him again.

"You don't think these pathetic weapons can hurt me, do you? Not even your cold iron could save you now!" the fey screamed at him, still in the language and tone that made his knees weak. The water rose around her, two hulking creatures waiting to answer the call of their mistress.

The breeze blowing kept him from panicking. His answer was succinct and said in the language they used on this side of the world.

"Fire."

The twang of linen and sinew rang through the air. Richard growled and pulled at the wind, forcing it to conform to his will. The first shots soared towards the fey, too fast for him to catch. Two of her water elementals caught the shots and she escaped, leaving her creatures to join the water below as she saw Richard's breeze catch the remaining shots and send them flying towards her. She wasn't fast enough and had to call up another ice wall. The shots shattered the ice, letting a single shot get to her.

She screamed as the arrow hit her in the thigh, snapping off a chunk as if she were made of ice. With a wail, she whirlpooled into the water and then spun up again. Her leg was healed, but the look of hate she sent his way sent tingles down his spine. If he didn't defeat her here, he didn't think he would survive her attempt to forcibly return him to her queen.

The others seemed surprised at her ability to heal and then Richard saw the waves under her rise, forming two more elementals while lifting her closer and closer to the top of the bridge. She was trying to get close enough that her elementals could take them down. If he let them close, she would destroy everyone here.

"Take aim again." He called out. "Fire."

The fey woman snarled at him, the water dropping her back down to the normal water level. One of her elementals leaped over her, taking the shots meant for its mistress. The creature burst, like a popped waterskin. Two shots made it through, almost hitting the fey herself.

Richard breathed heavily. Zaiya's power was strong, but he could already feel himself getting tired. He shook his head. He wasn't willing to fall yet.

"Isashi, I need 3 shots from you when you see her. 1 second between each. After everyone else has shot." She nodded and he gave the order again, "Fire."

The fey snarled used another two of her creatures this time. Both burst just as the first of Isashi's arrows released. He sent them down, directing two of the arrows to one of the elementals and the third to the last. The first burst and the second sank into the waves.

Not destroyed but probably injured.

When she'd first appeared, the fey had almost looked human. Now she couldn't have been mistaken as anything but the monster she was. Her hair flowed around her head as if she was floating underwater, not in air. Her skin was solidly grey, dripping with slime instead of water. Her eyes were a solid black and her fingers had become claws.

"I will not be defeated!" She screamed at them.

She drew up the waves again, slamming them into the bridge. Everyone on the bridge felt the hit as it shuddered under them. They fired again, without waiting for Richard's command. She put up another shield to stop the blasts and her attack on the bridge stopped. Richard looked at Isashi. He was probably grey with exhaustion himself.

"Isashi –"

"I only have one arrow left." She told him.

"Then make it count." He told her. "Shoot as soon as she releases the ice wall."

Isashi nodded. The ice wall started slipping back into the water and Isashi released her arrow.

Zaiya was grey, her color gone. Grabbing his face, she breathed into his mouth. The taste of swamp and cold mint filled him again. This time, he felt the world slow down. He grabbed Isashi's arrow as the ice fell, caressing its shaft with his power. He would only have this one chance. As soon as the ice fell far enough that he saw the fey's glaring eyes, he redirected the arrow and pushed every bit of power he had towards the creature. Richard saw the fey's eyes widen and she began throwing up her hand, but Richard could already tell that she would be too slow.

All of a sudden Zaiya fell, and with the contact lost, the power drained from him as well. Richard desperately grabbed Zaiya's body and clutched her to his chest as the fey's face burst.

He heard her shriek, a splash behind him, and then a sound like thunder that boomed up from the water. Afterward, there was only silence.

Chapter 39

Deckard's chest constricted when Kuzunoha screamed and he turned towards her voice. He picked up his crossbow but saw Isashi helping Himiko down from her wagon. His gaze fell on her bloody ankle and he felt his power yank at him, burning through him. He gasped. He had to help her. Now. He shivered. It had never hurt to restrain himself before. This felt like he'd been kicked by a horse in the chest. He looked at Tieni.

"I'm no good with a crossbow," he told her. "I'll start healing the injured."

Tieni's eyes looked more than a little panicked, but she nodded.

"Please stay safe." She told him. He smiled at her, already running over Himiko's side. He helped Isashi navigate her down, lowering her to the ground against the wheel for extra protection. Before he bent down, Isashi tapped his head.

"Deckard, if everything goes wrong, promise me you'll run to the town with her. Carry her if you must." Isashi begged. Her eyes were wide and determined, but scared. He swallowed, remembering how much damage the fey had done in Sakre.

"I promise." He told her.

He heard someone running up behind him and saw Roe. The young man ran to Isashi and handed her a partially filled quiver.

"The rest of the shots we have, mam. Danior said they're more useful if we're not dead." The young boy turned to him. "Do you need my help again?"

Deckard shook his head. "No… wait. Yes. Go over to the side. Kuzu fell into the water. She managed to make it onto an inlet. Let us know if she's okay. If the watery tart the rest are fighting starts moving towards her, let me know."

Roe turned and blinked as he realized that Deckard was pointing past the bridge.

"She fell?" He yipped, incredulously as he ran past the wagon.

"You have to get me over there." Himiko ground out between clenched teeth as she tried to push him away. "My sister is alive and nee…"

Deckard pushed her back against the wheel hard. "We will deal with Kuzunoha in a moment. I need to see to your leg first."

"Its fine. Isashi already tore out the bolt. Kuzunoha…"

"It went all the way through." he said. He hated having to leave Kuzunoha to anyone else, but he couldn't be everywhere at the same time and Himiko needed him. "Can you still feel your toes?"

"Yes."

"Good. Can you move them as if you were going to stand on tiptoe?"

She shivered and his power dampened her pain.

"I don't know. My sister…"

"Didn't have a bolt through her leg when she fell. Can you point them or not?"

Himiko glared at him. A moment later she was muffling a scream and shaking her head no. Deckard swore.

"Stop trying and rest. It went through your tendon. I'll need to work quickly."

He reached into his kit and pulled out a small piece of softwood. He shoved it between her teeth, trying to ignore the sounds of war, coming from above him on the caravan.

"Bite on this and keep your tongue away from your teeth. This will hurt and I can't block it."

"Deckard, there's a monster with Kuzunoha," Roe yelled. "It's standing on the beach with her."

Himiko slammed forward and Deckard touched her ankle. Her scream was muffled by the wood block in her mouth as she fell back against the wagon. He didn't even glance away. Kuzunoha needed his help, but if the fey had her cornered, they would need more than him to save her. Himiko's eyes promised death and punishment, but he ignored her, cleaning the wound as much as he could.

By some miracle, the bolt hadn't severed any of her veins and had only damaged her tendon. It would hurt for weeks, even with him pushing power into her wound as subtly as he could. He stitched her closed. It wasn't done as well as he liked. If she stayed off it and he nudged power into it daily, she still wouldn't be walking without help for weeks.

He smiled grimly. Without him, she might never walk again without the aid of a cane. Deckard's power appeared again, the dragon resting on her ankle again, soothing the injured flesh and starting to mend the tendon. He tried to put the thought of people seeing out of his mind. At this point, it couldn't be helped if they had. Himiko needed more than passive healing could fix.

"Deckard, it's trying to take her," Roe shouted a moment later.

He swore inwardly and checked his work. She wouldn't be able to walk, but it would have to be enough for now. He pulled back on the power, only to find it resisting him, fighting to stay in Himiko. He frowned. She wasn't the only one that needed his help. He pushed a small bit of power into Himiko's leg and yanked the rest back to him. His power snapped like a living thing, angry and hissing at leaving her injured.

"We'll finish afterward." He hissed under his breath at it. It had never done that before, even when he'd healed Kuzunoha. Unfortunately, he didn't have time to figure it out now. "Himiko, do you…"

She cut him off, speaking around the wood in her mouth. "Take me over there."

Deckard stood and picked up Himiko, carrying her to the other side of the bridge.

When they reached Roe, he set Himiko down by the bridge with a gruff order to keep the weight off of her foot. Then he leaned over to see what was happening with Kuzunoha.

Below them, his ex was fighting the monster on the little sandbar. The creature looked like a horrific mix between human and horse, its mane looking like dying kelp. The only good thing was that it was dripping blood from a half dozen tiny slashes as well as a larger wound across its chest. The creature sidestepped one of her attacks and brought a fist down on Kuzunoha's back.

"Deckard, do something," Himiko hissed between clenched teeth.

"I can't fire a ranged weapon from here. Too much chance I'll hit Kuzunoha."

Kuzunoha stumbled to her hands and knees. Just because he couldn't kill the monster from here didn't mean he was helpless. He checked to make sure that he had his sword on him and looked at Roe.

"Get me a rope, now."

Roe ran off and Deckard watched as the creature pressed a knee into Kuzunoha's back, keeping her down. Kuzunoha started to struggle, trying to get it off her, but she couldn't move. Deckard's hands were clenched on the stone. Little bits of mortar cracked under his fists while he wished that he were already down there helping her.

"I've got one," Roe yelled from behind him. "I'll start tying it off."

Deckard's heart fell as he realized it didn't matter. They'd run out of time. The horse monster stopped, in time with one of Richard's desperate call to fire again. The creature's eyes widened and it tossed Kuzunoha into the water in one smooth motion. The creature dove in after her.

Suddenly, there was a sound of thunder in the air and the water below puffed like dust from the flurry of air. It took him a moment to realize that it was small clouds of vapor floating just above water that was suddenly shifting to clear ice.

Under the ice, he saw Kuzunoha swim up to the ice from a reddish patch of water. She hit the ice and he could see her face, panicked as her hands started pushing at the ice from below it.

"Rope," he yelled at Roe.

"I'm trying." The boy said.

His arms were filled with rope as he tried to tie the thick stuff properly to the wagon. It wasn't ready and he couldn't wait any longer. Deckard climbed onto the side of the bridge and tossed his sword to Himiko. Below, a dark form grabbed at Kuzunoha from below, dragging her away from the ice.

His breath caught in his chest. There was no more time. He wasn't going to let her die here.

"Have Roe get the others and send them down for us once the rope is ready. Toss my sword down when I get to the island."

Himiko caught his blade, her eyes thanking him through her panic. Deckard leaped from the bridge. It was only a forty-foot drop, but Deckard still had too much time to worry. With his weight, he should be able to smash through the unnatural ice and drag Kuzunoha to land. Even if the ice had thickened to a few inches, he should be able to break it without getting seriously hurt.

His feet hit the ice just moments after he heard the kompania cheer. A second later, Deckard felt the bones in his right leg shattering beneath him, almost eclipsing the pain of his left leg shattering a millisecond later. The air in his lungs escaped in a rush that couldn't even be called a scream. He lost track of everything and then his power rushed through him; coarse flames tearing their way through his body. He tried to suck in a breath, wondering if his bones were melting under the torrent. The fire stole the breath from his lungs, burning through him. Pain followed the flame and he recognized the noise on the air as his scream before he fell unconscious.

* * * * *

When he came to, Danior was crouching over him, tucking something dark around him. The man was grey. Had he always been like that?

"Deckard, are you alright?"

Richard's little creature looked over Danior from his back. She flew off him, her wings hardly holding her up. She was grey too.

"Can you tell what's wrong with him, Little One?" Danior asked.

The creature landed on his forehead. She was sweating and huffing in and out like someone who'd been exercising for hours.

"He has no air."

Deckard hadn't realized that he wasn't breathing until then. He thought about pulling in a breath and then blinked. He was cold. He was on the ice. He had come down for something. Something important… What was it? Why did everything hurt? Why was everything grey?

"He's not breathing." Deckard heard Danior yell, reminding him that he'd been trying to breathe. He tried to pull in one and shivered. It hurt too much. He could wait until it hurt less.

"Zaiya, can you give him air?"

Richard's voice asked from the reaches of the unknown. Deckard blinked. The idea that Richard's creature had made his rival invisible was terrifying. He struggled to overcome the silver fog over his mind that held every thought and movement he tried to make as though he was covered with amber.

The creature reached out to him and Deckard finally felt panic poking at the edge of his brain. She wasn't a healer, and he didn't want her touching him, using her power on him. His golden light was bad enough. At the same time, he needed air, needed to breathe, but he couldn't remember how. He had to remember. He couldn't save… who? Someone important, someone he… he had to breathe…

The creature grabbed his lips and kissed him. Cool, revitalizing air forced its way back into his lungs. Deckard nearly fell unconscious again, realizing that some of his ribs were broken. As his lung expanded, a crunch broke through the fog and his chest burned again. Fortunately, it only lasted a moment and he was able to draw in a second shaky breath. He grabbed at his chest as the first raking cough began pushing its way out of him.

With air, grey fled under an onslaught of color. The pain scorching his legs burned hotter as if he'd reached into a fire and slapped the coals onto himself. Somehow, even with the pain, he knew that the warmth was blocking him from something even worse.

"I'm okay. What did you do… how could you…" Deckard gasped, regretting his words as dizziness assaulted him. He forced himself to concentrate. Richard's weird powers weren't important. He remembered…

"Kuzu… Where's… Kuzu?"

A wave of pain shattered through him as Danlor touched his shoulder and he missed his first few words.

"… hasn't come up and we need to get you off the ice. It's been about ten minutes and the ice is starting to thin in places. Can you move?"

"Hasn't come up? She needs to breathe…"

Deckard's power could keep him alive when he couldn't breathe. He hadn't known that before. Kuzu couldn't. She needed him.

Danior's face fell and his eyes went hard.

"It might be kinder if she didn't."

The words made no sense. They had to find Kuzunoha. She'd always been there, no matter how inconvenient her presence was or how far she'd had to go out of her way to be there.

"I won't believe that." Not until he'd heard something more substantial than this shady man's opinion. Danior's eyes closed and he shook his head.

"We can't do anything about it now. We need to get you off the ice."

Deckard tried to move, his entire body protesting. He stopped when his legs spasmed and he found he couldn't breathe again. When the fire resettled in his lungs, he was able to pull in another breath.

He'd never known he could be hurt to the point where fixing other things was more important than breathing. Zaiya nodded then flew slowly away, plodding back to her master's side.

Danior stood from his crouch, shouting upward instructions up to his men. Deckard closed his eyes and tried to ignore the feeling that he had failed Kuzunoha in the only way that had ever truly mattered, while the others discussed how to get him up to the bridge.

Brandy Ackerley

Chapter 40

*H*imiko looked at the tall man standing in front of her. He was dressed in a breastplate, fancy, shiny, though she thought that the ornaments strewn across its surface were mostly for show; something to make the armor look less threatening, without making it less effective.

"Thank you for giving us your statement, Miss. I'm sorry to hear that you had any trouble traveling to our fair city."

Himiko grit her teeth. "It was more than just a little bit of trouble, Captain Horner."

She wished she could make the man sit down; having him hover over her when she couldn't stand to meet him was infuriating.

"As you say. Is there anything else you need?" The captain asked her.

"Yes. I need you to find my sister."

"Is she in town?" the man turned disinterestedly towards the city. "I can send a messenger…"

Himiko gestured towards the river. "No. My sister was kidnapped. When will you be sending someone after her?"

The man glanced at the river. His tone was condescending. "The one that drowned?"

Himiko tried to stand up and failed. Her leg hurt, burning and stinging in ways she'd never felt before and desperately hoped that she never would again. Morjiana had promised her that she would walk again, but Himiko knew that it would take weeks, maybe even months. Even with Deckard's help, if he could. She had too much to do to be lying around that long.

"She didn't drown, Captain Horner. We all saw the monster drag her away under the ice. Somebody has to get to its lair and save her."

Isashi put a hand on Himiko's shoulder, but she pushed the hand away, pushing herself up as much as she could without putting any weight on her leg. The captain's men didn't even have the decency to shift uncomfortably, like the guards in Hidan would have.

Captain Horner was worse. He looked bored.

"Miss, she's likely already dead. I won't risk my guards searching through the bones."

Himiko made a frustrated noise and Isashi gestured them away. The captain shrugged.

"I am sorry for your loss." He walked away and began talking quietly to one of his men.

"How can you do this?" Himiko said, raising her voice. The man didn't even bother responding.

If they were back in Hidan, these guards would have been crawling over each other to find Kuzunoha. She may not have been nobility, but the situation still called for more than these useless men were willing to put into it. Especially since their measured response had come too little, too late. The bandits had fled and the water wench had been defeated before they'd even started opening their gate.

"Himiko, calm down," Isashi begged her. "They've done what they can and sending people out to fight a monster isn't their job."

"They could call a hunter."

Isashi shook her head. "A hunter's job is to keep the monster population down and keep the people in their city safe. They can't save everyone, especially in a city this big."

"You mean they won't look for a girl they think is already dead," Himiko said, scathingly.

Kuzunoha had never taken the easy way in her life. Her death would be no different. She was still alive; so long as they could get to her fast enough, she would stay that way. Isashi winced but didn't argue.

"Fine. We'll go on our own. Now." Himiko told her.

Richard had been resting on the ground a few feet away, but at her words, he chuckled.

"Of course, lady, we'll get right on that."

She turned to him. He hadn't even bothered opening his eyes. He was grey with exhaustion, as was the creature who had helped him do the things he'd done. She shivered. Unnatural. Her father had always warned her of letting those tainted by inhumanity near her.

"Don't take that tone with me. If you cared-"

At that, he did open his eyes.

"Don't, Himiko. I am not going to put up with your shit right now."

She grit her teeth and Isashi stepped in front of her.

"Himiko, stop that. He cares about your sister too, but we can't go now, even if we wanted to."

Isashi sat down in a squat. It put her head lower than Himiko, and while it frustrated her to have her best friend do that, it also soothed something in her.

"There must be a way."

Isashi shook her head.

"Deckard has hardly been able to stay conscious and I don't think Richard could stand up if he tried. You can barely stand."

"You came through uninjured." Himiko started. Isashi cut her off.

"If I had the support of another hunter or anyone else that I've worked with before, I would try. I don't. Even if I did, I couldn't leave now. No supplies, no arrows, no food. It's almost dark, so no light, and I'd be wandering around an area I don't know with monsters that I haven't studied exhaustively. Even I would need to wait till morning. It's more likely something would find me than me finding her in the dark."

Himiko opened her mouth to argue, but Isashi put her hands on Himiko's legs gently, looking up into her eyes.

"I'm sorry, but there is nothing we can do right now that we won't also be able to do for her in a week," Isashi said.

"She could be dead in a week." Himiko protested.

How would their ancestors judge her if Kuzunoha didn't survive? Himiko was the matriarch, it was her job to make sure that the family thrived. She'd lost everyone else she'd ever had; grandparents she'd never known, her mother, her father… she couldn't lose her sister, too.

Kuzunoha shouldn't have been out here in the first place. She was supposed to do what all noble-born bastards did; stay too close to their home while making life difficult for their families by insisting they be treated like a true-born heir rather than the trouble they were.

"Miss…" One of the guards stepped closer. "The wagons will be here in a moment to take you into town."

Himiko closed her eyes and nodded but didn't hear the man leave. When she opened her eyes again, he was looking at her nervously and casting furtive glances at his captain.

"What is it?" Himiko straightened.

The man shrugged in on himself.

"Is your sister strong? Pretty?"

"Yes. Why?"

The man winced.

"If your sister is strong and pretty, she might live a long time… the beast has been known to take mates."

Isashi glared at him. "Don't lie to her. Monsters don't take human mates."

"It's a legend, but that doesn't mean it isn't true. One woman escaped years back and made it into town. She was pregnant and gave birth to a deformed creature with hooves. It was before my time, but all the guards know about it."

"Even if that is true, you won't go look for her, will you?" Himiko asked. The man wouldn't meet her eyes. "I thought as much. Isashi, find someone to help us get onto a wagon and collect our stuff. We'll have to find her ourselves as soon as we can."

"You shouldn't go. She might be alive, but…" The man shook his head. "It would be bad for you to go. Pretty and strong... it's what the beast looks for. Both of you... you would risk much."

Isashi stood up and stepped forward, forcing the man back. Her voice was low, filled with venom.

"I am a huntress and she is the last daughter of the Tanaka clan. We will not fall to this monster."

The man shrunk even further in on himself and ran. Himiko's heart skipped a beat. Isashi's posture and actions seemed out of place. Was she was doing it for her? Himiko reached out and grabbed Isashi's hand. Isashi jumped and the imperious huntress was gone, replaced by her friend.

"Thank you, Isashi."

Isashi didn't let her go, warming Himiko's hand with her own. Her friend let out a breath.

"Don't thank me yet. You won't be going."

"What makes you think you can make my decisions for-"

Isashi crouched again, flicking a finger against Himiko's ankle. She gasped, pain throbbing through her entire body. She glared at her friend. For the first time in her memory, Isashi didn't even blink an apology. Himiko looked away, her cheeks burning. She didn't know what she was supposed to do. Isashi had never denied her before.

Isashi's tone was soft. "You are used to having Deckard to help with injuries. He's too badly injured to do that right now. When Richard is able, we'll go. If she's alive, we'll bring her back."

"If we wait, she'll be broken…" Himiko began.

Isashi grabbed Himiko's arms hard.

"That guard is lying, Himiko. Everyone has heard a myth about a monster loving a human or using one for sex… it's all a lie. It happened to a friend of a friend who heard it from a friend's friend of theirs… Monsters don't mate with humans; they kill them."

"All the more reason to go sooner than later," Deckard said.

Himiko looked at him, but despite his words, he didn't try to move. He was lying on a wooden stretcher ten feet away, wrapped up in as many blankets as they'd been able to fit around him, and wrapped with rope. Morjiana had said that his legs had felt like they had no bones in them, only misshaped marbles. Worse, she'd said that she could hear air escaping his chest somewhere, which meant a rib puncture or worse. The old woman had suggested that he needed more care than she could provide on the caravan but hadn't said anything more than that.

Tieni was leaning over Deckard a moment later, kissing him and setting herself as close as she could to him.

"You're awake. By all that lives, don't worry me like that again," Tieni swore into his hair.

Deckard faintly tried to nuzzle her, but his words were for Himiko and Isashi. "I'll do what I can to…"

Tieni looked at him. "Deckard, don't. You couldn't have…"

His features were set in stone. "It was my fault. They were after me."

"Not just you…" she swore, before turning away.

"What do you mean they were after you, Deckard?" Himiko whispered.

Tieni swallowed but didn't answer.

Richard did.

"The bandits had been hired to attack us. We don't know who by, but they wanted Deckard, you and Kuzunoha."

Deckard glared at Tieni. "Were you ever going to tell me?"

"When we got to town."

He stiffened as Tieni reached out for him. Himiko should have let them work this out, but she needed him right now. She swallowed and reached for him.

"Deckard, we both know my sister is too stubborn to die. Can you help?"

"What do you need?" Deckard asked her.

"Can you heal Richard and me enough that we can all leave with first light?"

He paled but his lips froze into a determined line. "Come here."

Himiko took Isashi's hand and her friend helped her to stand and hobble over to him, ignoring Tieni's look of horror.

She grabbed Deckard's blankets. "You don't have to… You shouldn't…"

He pulled a hand out of his blankets with effort and grabbed Himiko's leg. His hand was warm and replaced the pain with a mild ache as if she'd overstretched a muscle, rather than had a foot of wood plunging through her leg a mere hour before. Deckard closed his eyes in concentration, and she thought she saw a dragon, nearly invisible but outlined with faint golden light, weave around her leg, caressing her through her pants.

Nausea rose, filling her mind with the taste of bile. Himiko ruthlessly suppressed the urge to throw up. She would do what it took to get Kuzunoha back, even if it meant dealing with this. A moment later, the warmth disappeared, and she saw the gold of the dragon recoil away, looking as if the magic beast was crying while they returned to their master. Deckard's body spasmed and he howled, a terrifying sound, cut short when he fell unconscious.

"Deckard? I told you, you didn't have to do this… Deckard, please, come back…" Tieni checked him crying over his still form. A moment later his chest rose in a shaky breath.

Himiko slumped against her friend. Her tone was unsteady, harsh, and rough.

"Isashi, clear out our belongings and claim Deckard's from Danior as well. If those bandits were after him, they'll think twice before coming inside the city walls. Tieni, you can come too, if you want." Himiko said. Then she looked at Isashi again. "You and Richard can leave as soon as he's well. I need that mark from her sword if nothing else."

Isashi nodded, leaving when it became clear that Tieni wasn't going to contradict her.

Chapter 41

*I*sashi had hated leaving Himiko alone in the inn with no one but Tieni to guard her, but it couldn't be helped. She wouldn't have been worrying about her at all if they hadn't had to bring in a local doctor to help with their injuries. The man was short and wide, though she never would have called him fat. His hair had been so greasy that she'd thought it was brown, not blonde, at first and, annoyingly, his beady eyes had dismissed every one of them as unimportant.

Except for Deckard.

The man may have been skilled, but she still would have rather they had simply waited for everyone to heal on their own. She sighed. Perhaps she felt that way because she had only been bruised and exhausted… nothing that wouldn't heal on its own given time.

The others hadn't fared so well. Himiko would be down for weeks without Deckard's aid. Deckard himself had shattered his legs. Kuzunoha was almost certainly dead. And Richard…

Richard didn't seem injured, but he had come away different and not just because he was greyer than her and been sleeping like one dead since they'd collapsed in the inn Himiko had rented for all of them. He'd woken only twice. Once to use the pot, and once when the doctor had tried to touch his little creature. He'd woken up and grabbed the man's hand and thrown him away from the bed, told the guy he was fine, and to help the others.

His little creature hadn't even moved from her position on his pillow when he'd done it.

She was grey-skinned, too. Isashi was worried it had something to do with the pact Richard had made with it, but he hadn't been awake enough for her to ask yet.

Isashi paused and looked around again. Nothing in this city looked familiar and the harsh stone lines irritated her. There was no individuality to the buildings. The only good point about the city was that the language they used in Hidan was also the main language they used here.

She looked at the symbol on her hand and looked closer at the symbols carved into the buildings, letting out a breath when she recognized the four symbols that covered the door for wall guards. She'd gone first to the gate she'd traveled through yesterday, but the men there had been unable to answer any of her questions. Instead, they'd told her to come here for answers.

She stepped up and lifted the huge knocker. Even the door of this building was stone. She clapped the knocker hard against the metal plate twice and waited. A moment later, an annoyed woman pushed the door open. Her hair was a dirty brown color, and she was wearing a guard's uniform, badly wrinkled.

"Why are you knocking if you don't have packages, Eleden? Even a creature as you should be able to open a door on their own."

"I'm here to ask some questions about the monsters- "

The woman didn't even let Isashi finish what she was saying.

"You should be talking to hunters then. Our guild does not get involved with them unless it's necessary for the safety and protection of Kalvettika."

That opinion still seemed wrong to Isashi. In Hidan, the wall guards hadn't been under the hunters' command, but both knew where to find the other and could answer nearly any question about the defense of Hidan, regardless of which group they were part of. The guards may not have left town to guard and clear the lands, but they still knew where all of the major creature dens nearby were. When she'd questioned the guards at the first gate, they had sworn that they couldn't answer her questions and had said that she needed to come here. Now she was being told she had to go elsewhere. She could already tell that she hated the bureaucracy in this place.

"I just need to know the location of one of the creatures." Isashi tried again.

"Talk to the hunters. We don't deal with anything outside of town."

Isashi let out a breath, wishing the men at the gates had been clearer about their denials.

"Fine. Where do I find one of the hunters?"

The woman looked at Isashi as if the question were a stupid one. "They're at the hunter's guild house, of course."

"And where is that?"

Isashi didn't know why this woman was being so rude, but she was getting tired of it.

"Oh, you're a tourist." The woman said, with distaste in her tone. She gestured Isashi inside. The room was dark, lit with a single torch. The woman walked past her and gestured to the biggest wall covering she'd ever seen. "Of course, you wouldn't know then."

It took Isashi a moment, but then she recognized the basic shape of the walls surrounding the city. Some of the buildings had been carved double or triple the height of any other and some had been marked with painted cork pins. It was the largest map she'd ever seen, carved into the wood. The woman smacked one of the taller buildings on the map.

"Five streets west and then seven blocks east from here. Don't take any of the alleys there. If you're robbed, you'll have to apply to the police about what was taken, not the guards."

She wondered why the woman had been offering the information when the woman pointed to the door. "Now if you're done, leave. Ask the hunters your questions."

Isashi realized that the woman's 'helpful' advice about avoiding the alleyways had simply been to save the woman from having to deal with her again. Isashi wished she could sink into the floor. She had received odd looks and even quite a few stares and bullying after she'd become one of the long-lived Eleden. Despite that, she'd never been treated this badly, as if she were simply goo that this woman had stepped in.

She was suddenly glad that Richard hadn't come with her. No one else should have to endure this with her. She left, her head hanging. She took a few clearing breaths that didn't work in the city's heavy stench and blinked, getting her bearings again. Then she trudged her way through the bone-dry streets of Kalvettika. The city was packed and she never saw an empty road. While she walked, some turned to stare at her and whisper. The others were worse, treating her as if she didn't even exist.

The hunter's guild was three stories tall, thick blackish stone with wooden shutters every couple of feet. The doors were wooden, too; a thick, sturdy-looking oak wood with a dark finish on it. She walked up and knocked on the door, hoping that this worked better than it had at the last two places she'd been.

Moments later, a stern-faced elderly man, spindly thin with greying hair opened the door. His back was bent with age, but Isashi was certain that he could still put any of the hunters in training on their ass.

"Young lady? Can I help you?"

Her shoulders relaxed and a breath she hadn't realized she'd been holding forced its way out of her. She showed him her badge, stating that she was a hunter. The old man looked surprised, but opened the door wide and gestured her in. The room was grey, like everything else in the city, but the walls were covered with small rugs between each window. Despite the excellent rugs, she could see they were fraying at the edges. In a few lonely spots, she could tell that it had worn down till it was thread-bare in some areas.

"You're a hunter? Pretty young thing like you? Or am I wrong in assuming you're young? I've never actually had the pleasure of speaking to one of your kind before."

"I am, sir. My name's Isashi. I'm from a small town on the coast a few weeks sail away."

"Please, call me Robyn. Isashi… That isn't a name I've ever heard before. Who are your people?"

She looked away. Her parents had been the first couple to inter-marry between the two races in Hidan. They'd thought creating her name out of the two languages would be cute. All Isashi had wanted when she was a child was for people to stop noticing her weird name. When she'd changed into an Eleden, she'd thought that she'd never need to worry about people focusing on her name again. She let out a deep breath.

"It isn't common. My mother was Sian Ku, but my father was Norin."

The man shook his head. "Some will treat you badly for that in the city, but not here. We hunters know it's more than your family ties that got you where you are. Hunters don't get by on nepotism, even on the frontier. At least, not the living ones. Were you hoping to join our clan?"

She shook her head. "I took on a job to guard Hidan's nobility on their journey here. We were on the bridge yesterday."

His demeanor changed and he showed her directly to the couch. "The nymph-thing? You were lucky you had a magi with you. From what we heard it was a pitched battle, even so. Most of our people are looking into it now. They left me here." That last fact seemed to disappoint him greatly. "Were you hoping to help with the identification and destruction of the creature?"

Isashi's breath caught in her throat. She'd seen the thing break apart into dozens of tiny little shards of ice when she'd died. How much more dead could the creature be? "I thought we had killed it."

Robyn shrugged. "The kompania said it died, but so many monsters don't die from simple wounds. According to the accounts we collected, it was killed with nothing more than regular arrows. With creatures as powerful as that one, it's unusual for them to die that easily. We need to be sure. With the amount of power that creature was throwing around, if it isn't dead, it could do serious damage. Better to see what we can learn now and kill it while it's still injured if we can."

The way he said 'kompania' told her that while he may not have minded her race, he did mind theirs. She ignored it. As for their refusing to believe the Corvidae, she couldn't fault him for that. If this had happened near Hidan, she and her fellow hunters would have been out for weeks looking into it, trying to learn everything they could. You didn't take chances when your job was to keep people alive.

"True. At any rate, that isn't what I came for. The sister of my noble patron was kidnapped by a lesser monster that you've been having trouble with; a water-horse is what your guards called it. I'm hoping to get a guide to its lair."

The man's face scrunched up, making all of his wrinkles more pronounced. It made him look even older than he appeared.

"Your friend is most likely dead now, nothing but bones if she were taken yesterday."

"We still need to try. It's important."

The man shook his head. "I can't lead you there. I'd only slow you down, especially if there's a fight. And I know none of our youngins will be willing to take you. Not for a woman dead already."

"Perhaps an apprentice nearing the end of his training?"

"We only have one boy in training right now. He's still in his first year. I wouldn't trust him as a guide outside of town, or much aid in a fight yet. He's getting better, but..."

Isashi felt nausea rise in her throat. They couldn't wait until the hunters had finished their investigation. Himiko would never allow that. Even if Richard's energy didn't return, she would push until they found Kuzunoha; or her body. They would have to leave tomorrow morning, or the next, at the latest.

"Could you give me a map and directions? And tell me about this water-horse?" She asked. "I've been a hunter nearly ten years now and one of my party, a skilled fighter, will be able to accompany me."

The old man shook his head. "The youngins have taken all the maps with them, trying to find out where the creature might be. You might be able to ask one of the cartographer's guild if they have any for sale though. If not…"

He stood and led her over to a table. Like the wall map of the city at the guard's station, this table was beautifully carved. She could see the walls of the town near the center of the map and the nearby mountains, identifying the streams and rivers easily by their faded blue paint.

"We're here. You'll want to leave by the north-northwest gate here and take this road." His fingers hovered above one of the stone paths. "If you follow it for 3 bells and turn into the trees here, you'll find the man's mustache boulders. From there, travel downriver till you get to the white beach. If you find the grizzled cat stones, you've gone too far. It'll be hours and hours over dangerous terrain, there and back, so keep an eye out. We have several smaller monsters that way. Amphibians that can come right out of the water at you. Take enough water with you. You won't want to get in the water if you don't have to. There may not be many monsters among the fish, but even some of the fish have fangs out there; sharp enough to take a fingertip from the unwary. Better to not take the risk."

She blinked trying to commit the instructions to memory. If she found a map, she would bring it back and get the old hunter's help putting the placements on it. She sighed.

"Do you mind if I try to copy this as best I can?" Isashi asked.

She was no artist, but maybe she could get the important bits down. Besides, with her luck being what it had been so far in this town, she wanted to have something to go on, even if it wasn't going to be very accurate.

She groaned. She'd have to start picking up supplies as well on her way to the next guild. Enough food for travel, more arrows, weapons for both her and Richard, and enough supplies that their companions could remain at the inn while they were gone. She shook her head. She would be running the rest of the day if she was lucky. If she wasn't, she'd have to spend tomorrow trying to find things all morning before they would be able to leave.

Chapter 42

Deckard held his hand over his chest again, glad that the healer Himiko had hired to look him over was gone. The man hadn't been useless, but pessimistic; a bad attitude to have in any healing room. Healers knew better than anyone else the body's fickleness and if someone had decided that they were going to die then more than likely they were going to. This healer had looked at Deckard, pronounced him a lost cause in a voice loud enough to wake the dead, and suggested that she purchase some pills from the apothecary to ease his passing. The man's only saving grace was that he had sounded rather sad when he said it.

"Deckard, are you well enough for company?" Tieni asked.

Her voice was soft. He sighed and looked up at her. "Of course. I'm sorry this is how things turned out."

She sat down beside him. The bed they shared in this room was smaller than he would have suggested for a patient with injuries as bad as his own, but he liked having her with him. He was still wrapped up tightly in the mismatched blankets they'd carried him up in. "No need. I'm just glad that loon of a man is gone. You're clearly not as broken as he thought you were."

"No." He told her. "The man knew his craft, even if I'd never let him within ten feet of one of my patients."

"He said that your ribs were poking holes in your lungs and that your leg bones felt more like marbles than bones," she said dryly, smoothing some of the thick blankets under her fingers.

"Both of those things are likely true."

It was hard to self-diagnose, but even more difficult to be objective and treat. It was the same reason that most healers said that they shouldn't treat their loved ones… though most still did.

A quick thought flittered into his mind before he could stop it. Kuzunoha had rarely gotten sick. When she'd been his, that had been reassuring. Now he wished that her constitution had been weaker. If it had, perhaps they'd all still be in Hidan now. Safe.

"Then why hasn't your thing fixed you yet?" Her fingers danced as though she thought his power could just make him healthy in an instant.

"It will… but with this much damage, it's slow."

Like it had been for Kuzunoha, he would be out for a few weeks at least.

Tieni's dark hair hid her face as she looked out the window. It was small, and the air coming in tasted of smoke and too many unwashed bodies. If being locked in such a small room hadn't been clearly bothering her, he would have asked her to close it.

Brandy Ackerley

She flipped her hair, beads clicking comfortably, and glanced at him.

"Since they can't do anything for you, can we leave? I can have us back with the Kompania by the end of the day. They don't have to know how badly you're hurt. Just that you need full bed rest for a while."

The last thing he wanted was to have to travel in a wagon over uneven roads with his current injuries. He would never heal properly with the constant shaking.

He shook his head. "Morjiana is better than that. She'd know."

She stood up and took the four steps to the far wall. The building was all stone. He wasn't surprised that she didn't find stone particularly relaxing, even if he had to admit that he felt even safer in this room than he had back in Hidan. She half-turned towards him.

"I'd rather we be with family while you heal."

Deckard didn't know how to respond to that. He liked the Corvidae and he liked traveling with them, but they weren't his family. Not yet. He didn't know if they ever would be. It had taken years for him to settle into Hidan and years more before he'd been accepted in return.

Himiko and Isashi weren't family, but they were more comforting to him than the folks on the wagons. Himiko had lost Kuzunoha too, and he'd known and respected Isashi as one of Hidan's hunters even before he'd gotten to know her a little better on the road here.

Of course, that meant staying with Richard, as well. Though, being honest, he didn't mind the man when he was acting rationally. Even his little flitting creature had its uses.

He wondered why they'd even brought him. He'd been miserable this whole journey. But like family, Himiko had brought him to take care of him anyway. He let out a breath and looked at Tieni.

"I'd rather stay here." She frowned and he tried to put it into words. "They aren't family… but I know them. And I don't want to leave until we find out about Kuzunoha."

Kuzunoha was probably dead… Deckard was too much of a realist not to understand that. Still, he needed to know.

Tieni frowned and they heard the door in the common area of their rooms open.

"We'll talk more about this later."

Deckard nodded. Neither of them was going to enjoy this conversation

"Isashi, you're back," Himiko called out from the other room. "I'm so glad. You were gone for hours."

"It took longer than I thought it would to go and find what I needed," Isashi told Himiko.

Deckard looked at Tieni. "Isashi, Himiko, can you come here?"

Both women stuck their heads in the room before coming in. Isashi was helping Himiko to walk, though Isashi was carrying a cane under one arm. It was a good purchase and would give Himiko more mobility than she currently had. It would help to keep her in a better mood while she healed.

While Isashi helped Himiko sit, Richard followed them in. He was still exhausted, faded. But he was up and moving under his own power, which was something. Zaiya was sitting on his shoulder hardly moving. He had been calling Richard 'grey' because of his exhaustion; the spirit actually was though. Her blue skin was the dull slate grey of the sea in late winter when even the sunlight couldn't penetrate it. Richard leaned against the wall, unwilling to sit yet.

"What did you find out?" He asked Isashi. He shivered as pain ran through every inch of his body as Tieni raised him enough that she could put a second pillow behind him. It wasn't enough to make him sit, but at least he would be able to see the room without straining his neck. As soon as the pain became manageable, he would thank her for the help.

"Well, the first thing is that the hunters aren't able to help…" She said as she stepped out. A moment later she was back in, carrying one of the thatch chairs behind her. She set it beside Richard and gestured. When his eyes narrowed, Isashi glared and pointed. They held the tableau for a moment before he nodded and sat in it.

"But they…"

Isashi shook her head over Himiko's objection. "No. I can't deny their logic. They are doing their job. In Hidan, you could ask the guards to do it as a favor. Here, you don't have the clout."

Himiko shivered, not in pain, but trying to control her anger. It had to be hard going from a big fish in a tiny pond to a tiny fish in a big pond.

"Does that mean that you won't be going?" Tieni sounded hopeful.

Isashi shook her head. "I found out where the creature's usual hunting grounds are and what I could about it. I wasn't able to get a map, but I think I have good enough directions to lead us there. With as many hunters out as there are right now, the surrounding area should be safe enough."

"So, you're just waiting for me," Richard said, querulously.

"You'll be better soon," Zaiya told him. "You did too much. More rest and we'll be better."

Himiko leaned back. "How long can we wait? Kuzunoha's life is on the line."

"Knowing Kuzunoha, she'll be fine. That girl has never known when to give up." Deckard said.

It hurt to talk about her that casually, but as a healer, if he was confident and calm about getting her back, Himiko would try to relax as well. She needed it to heal. Even now, his power stretched towards her. It wasn't even enough to be seen, and it wasn't going far enough to work on her, but he'd never seen it do that before. He clearly had to get her up and walking about before his power would relax and settle into him again.

Himiko looked annoyed, but Richard smiled at him.

"You're right, of course. Hopefully, if I rest for the day, we'll be able to go tomorrow morning."

"If not, then that will give me a little more time to see about a map and better supplies," Isashi said. "I have everything we should need, but there are a few luxuries that it would be nice to have."

"I think I can help," Deckard said. Tieni glared at him but didn't say anything.

"Don't you need all of your power, right now?" Isashi said. She looked at Himiko, but Kuzunoha's older sister didn't ask or quiet her. She wanted to see what he was offering first.

"I am too injured to fully help anyone, including myself." He told them. "However, if Richard's little creature is correct, he's suffering from exhaustion, and maybe dehydration. If that's all that's bothering you, it could take you two to three days before I'd judge you combat-ready. I think I can have you ready for tomorrow morning, without hurting myself."

Whether he did or didn't like Richard wasn't important. He did trust him to save her life, even if he wasn't sure he trusted him with her emotional well-being. Regardless, between him and Isashi, they wouldn't stop until they'd discovered the truth.

"I want her back as much as you do." He finished.

Richard nodded and Zaiya's color seemed to improve just from knowing that Richard would be better soon. He wondered if he could help Zaiya first and then she and he could work on Richard. If the two were as tied as he thought they might be, he may have to.

"Can you pick up the things we'll need tonight?" Himiko asked.

Isashi shook her head. "No. Most of the markets and stores are closed already. I'll go out first thing tomorrow and pick up what we need. We'll be ready to go by midday."

Richard looked at him, Himiko and Tieni. "Will you three be alright here on your own? We might be out for a few days."

"Well, first things first, I'll pick up extra supplies for you when I'm out tomorrow. Secondly," Isashi handed Himiko the cane, a pretty thing of dark stained wood and a red and gold painted ball to rest your hands on, "This will help give you some mobility while we're gone."

"I don't need a…"

Deckard cut off Himiko before she could finish. "As your healer, I must insist. Until you are fully healed, you need to stay off that leg as much as possible. I don't know how long it will take to heal you. I've never used my power this often or this intensely before. We'll have to see what my limits are. You'll need something in the meantime."

"Tieni should be able to help," Isashi suggested.

They all turned to Tieni. She looked away and stepped back and Deckard's eyes filled with tears. He pushed back the tears with a breath.

It hurt to know that their problems were great enough that she was considering leaving him behind like that.

Well, if she did, she wouldn't be the first. Deckard clenched his fist.

"I'll be here." She gruffly said. Yes, they needed to air everything out between them, but her admission here meant she would stay until they got back, even if the kompania left before then.

"We'll be fine," Himiko repeated. "I'm sure the innkeeper wouldn't mind bringing our meals up to us if I make it worth his while too."

Deckard nodded. Kuzunoha wasn't safe; they didn't even know if she was still alive. But they had a plan. Even if everything else in his life was messed up, knowing they had a plan to save Kuzunoha helped more than he thought it would.

He hoped she was still alive. He needed to apologize to her. He'd put off a real apology. There had always been someone else around her and enough time that he could put it off for another day. Until suddenly… if she'd died thinking he hated her; no matter how angry he'd been at her, he didn't want that.

Chapter 43

*K*uzunoha blinked, trying to force the world to come into view and closed her eyes again. Every part of her body hurt, some more than others. She shifted and pain sliced through her mind, breaking her concentration. Her shoulder… no, that area by her collarbone, it was higher than her shoulder, that spot hurt the most. Everything else hurt slightly less than that. She was cold too. Not freezing, but chilly. And she was wet. The air was thick with disgusting scents. Decaying flesh, wet fur, dead fish… old blood and sickness were hiding behind the other more obvious scents, too. She closed her nose as much as she could and took in shallow breaths, trying to taste the air as little as possible.

How did she get here? She remembered falling off the bridge. The bolt had hit her shoulder and the force had pushed her off the wagon. She remembered time seeming to slow while she fell and she remembered a monster fighting her, talking nonsense. Panic when it threw her in the water. Her chest near to bursting while she tried to break through the ice, needing to breathe. The monster coming out of nowhere and dragging her away as the ice above had shaken with something hitting it. In her struggles to stay, she'd gasped. Water had gone into her lungs, burning her lungs.

She had to be misremembering. How had she survived if she'd drowned?

She slowly reached a hand up and felt the hole in her body, shivering at the pain. The area was warm, compared to her the chill in her fingers. That couldn't be good, but even more concerning, her robe was gone.

She cracked an eye open again and thought she'd gone blind when the darkness remained. It took too long, but finally she realized that she actually was seeing shapes in the darkness above her, not just imagining them. Kuzunoha let out a breath. She wasn't blind, she was just in a room too dark to see in. It was darker than any place she'd ever seen.

Maybe the crab cave had been, though Richard had always been there with that slime of his that glowed to bring some light to it.

She brought her finger to her eyes. It looked dirty, but she didn't smell blood. That was good too. It meant that the sickness she tasted on the air wasn't hers. At least, not yet.

She shivered and felt around for a cover or a sheet. The bed was hard, covered with damp straw, not even covered with a cloth. Perhaps she was in a peasant's home? There was no cover or even a sheet. She reached off the bed, hoping that perhaps she'd pushed it off while she slept. Her hand hit cold water.

Kuzunoha sat up, panic creeping up her spine. The roof was low above the bed and she bumped her head on the ceiling above her. Dirt fell onto her. She shrieked and nearly fell into the water beside the bed. She whimpered, feeling for the low ceiling. Plants, roots, and more dirt fell on her and the bed.

Her breaths were coming in panicked gasps now. She was buried. They'd all thought she was dead and buried her in a crypt or something. Or worse, she had died and the Corvidae had it right, believing that their dead god would awaken the dead to fight for him.

She told herself that panicking wouldn't help, but she couldn't seem to convince herself. From what she could tell, she hadn't even been buried in the family's mausoleum, but in a mass grave for fish. Should she have been buried in it? Or would her sister have not allowed that? She hadn't thought that Himiko that that badly of her.

Then again, maybe she had fought off the creature and floated in here afterward. She had to find out more. She let out her breath and reached below the bed. Water met her hand, cold and clammy. She gritted her teeth and pushed further. Nearly two feet of water before her hand touched the floor, slick with some type of slime. That would make the roof somewhere around five feet high total. She would be able to stand up, but not straight. It was enough. She was getting out of here. She wouldn't stay in this grave for eternity.

She put her feet to the ground and stood, shivering as she did so. A slim scaly thing latched onto her toes and Kuzunoha yanked them back out the water, falling onto the bed with a shriek.

A growl answered her, just out of the distance she could see.

"Stop screaming."

Kuzunoha stared into the darkness while she ripped off the thing that had attached to her toes.

"Who's there?" She called out.

A match lit, casting the cave below the dirt in shadow. The brightness stopped her from seeing anything but the old lantern with reddish oil and the misshapen hand that lit it. The fish stink worsened, adding burning smoke to the mix.

The room brightened and a creature of nightmare sloughed forward.

Whatever else it was, the creature was tall. Taller than her, perhaps even taller than Deckard or Richard. The creature looked like a misshapen horse, with blackened hoof-hand that stretched into fingers. Its sickly grey mane looked like the tangled, waterlogged kelp that would wash up on shore from time to time. Its chest was vaguely human and led to a scruff of dark kelp hair below its waist that only accentuated, terribly, how male it was. Its head was that of a stallion in its prime. A thick pungent musk rose off the beast and her stomach clenched.

"Where are we?" she asked, looking around again. There was no other human around.

People said monsters were intelligent, but what they usually meant was cunning. Some of them, like the birdos near Hidan, actually created a society. They could speak to each other in the guttural barks they made, but they wouldn't respond to anyone, in any human language or their own. Every human who had tried had, to her knowledge, died.

Aside from the one that had attacked Sakre. She swallowed looking behind it, hoping that there was some human hiding in the shadows somewhere. She couldn't see anything and now that her eyes had adjusted to the light, she could see the entire cavern. There were no doors and the entire area couldn't have been larger than twenty feet from one side to the other.

"What are you?" She asked.

The creature sneered. "Think you're so powerful. You're less than a bækhest, less than the Water Woman... Less than me. Offer respect, or I eat your face."

Kuzunoha's gut clenched and she felt as if she'd just been punched and her hands twisted into claws. It would have been smarter to back down. Of course, she snarled at it.

"Why did you take me? What is it you want, Monster?"

Her false bravado nearly shattered when it brayed. It sounded more like a donkey or a mule than any horse. Still, the idea of a monster learning how to laugh unnerved her.

"You are strong. I am stronger. I will give you fish and more. When you serve, you will rule below me."

Its maleness straightened and Kuzunoha felt ill. The thought of this inhuman creature touching her made her sick. The thought of how it clearly wanted her to serve made it worse.

"I will not. My own sister couldn't make me obey; what makes you think you'll succeed?"

It stalked towards her. "I think your sister not stronger. I think you will want what I offer. Eventually. Humans kill you easier than they kill me. I can protect you. I can offer you all I have. Your best chance here."

Kuzunoha pushed herself back against the wall, swallowing hard, biting back a scream that threatened to become a war cry. If it came any closer, she would do her best to kill it, regardless of its obvious strength. It sniffed the air as if her fear had a scent it enjoyed, and it walked to a pile of fabric on the floor that made a wet nest for it a few feet further back.

"You understand. Soon."

It whined as it lay down and she realized that it was injured. It was the cause of the sickness in the air. She couldn't tell exactly how, but she knew that its blood was what was causing the place to smell like rotting fish.

She could wait until the creature slept. Once it did, she would search for the door and leave. She was a good swimmer. Maybe if she was lucky it would bleed out quickly. She reached up and tapped at the roof of the cave again. Some small crumbs of dirt fell but the rest felt like clay. She didn't think she would be able to burrow out without hurting herself or that she'd be able to do it fast enough to matter.

She wasn't dead. She could work with anything else.

"Where are my sword and clothing?"

"There." It gestured at a small pile across the room.

She was up and running to it before it finished pointing. She saw the water horse run to catch her and she took the sword, unsheathing it in a single movement.

"Sit down. This not necessary." It growled

"I am leaving." She told it.

The creature growled and moved towards her. "I have honored you. You will learn to honor me."

"Never."

It turned from her as it tried to avoid her slash. Her blade caught its rump. The creature roared as it bled. Faster than Kuzunoha could follow, its back hooves came out of the water. She was able to move fast enough to avoid getting hit in the head. She started to congratulate herself until the other hoof hit her collarbone.

The wound flashed with pain that moved through her body, a lightning bolt with no end. She fell to the water, unable to move, quivering, and limp. She heaved, and the world went black.

When she came to, she was back on the bed.

She snarled at the world and turned her head enough to see the horse monster back in its nest.

"You will learn." It told her.

Kuzunoha forced herself to sit up.

"Where is my weapon?"

Brandy Ackerley

The creature half-laughed/half-snarled.

"If you are good, I return to you. When you serve. When you whelp."

She was not going to be broodmare to this monstrous stallion.

She didn't have a sword; she had no clothing and she was injured. But all of those applied to it as well. Fine. She would clean her wound, heal and get back her strength, so the next time she attacked, she could defeat it, or escape. If nothing else, she just had to survive longer than it.

The horse snorted.

"Arrogant Fox. You will learn."

It snorted and blew the light out.

She leaned back and started to slowly clean her wounds, using the water below. It wasn't boiled like Deckard would have wanted her to use, but it was the best she was going to get for now. In the meantime, she would do what she needed to survive.

And eventually, she would escape.

Acknowledgments

My favorite phrase is that 'we' are smarter than 'I' will ever be. Right now, with the world in such a tumultuous place I feel we need to remember our community even more. Without these connections, we are alone and powerless. With our people at our back, we are bolstered and strong. Keep up with your community in any way you can. Texting, phone calls, VR, whatever it takes to get you out there. Without my community, I would be nowhere.

First and always, thanks go out to my lovely husband. Without your help, I would never get anything done. Thank you for reading my first drafts, helping me to shore up plot holes, reminding me when my blog posts need to go out, and the thousands of other details that my novels leave me no brain space for.

Next, to my family and friends. You keep me sane, listen to my troubles, and understand my more-than-occasional single-mindedness. Thank you for knowing me well enough to ask how my novel is going, rather than how I'm doing.

Finally, thanks go to my editor, Kai Kiriyama. You made editing a breeze, focused on what I needed to cut, what I needed to keep, and talked to me until I understood what you were trying to tell me. Working with you was wonderful and I'm already looking forward to doing so again.

Brandy Ackerley

About the Author

Brandy Ackerley is a creator of worlds with words. While primarily a fantasy writer of novel-length fiction, she enjoys writing in a variety of genres and lengths. She adores anime, tabletop RPG's and finding out more about mythology and culture worldwide. Brandy lives in Western Canada with her husband, both of whom are owned by their cat.

If you'd like to keep up-to-date on releases and more from Brandy Ackerley, you can follow her on Instagram, @FoxyWriter, on Facebook, at Inked Fox Press, or on her blog, Musing About the Words at www.musingaboutthewords.blogspot.com.

Brandy Ackerley

www.ingramcontent.com/pod-product-compliance
Lightning Source LLC
Chambersburg PA
CBHW020859060726
47591CB00004B/1006